WITHIN THE WALLS

Also by Fid Backhouse

By Other Means

WITHIN THE WALLS

Fid Backhouse

Hodder & Stoughton

Copyright © 1998 Scribble Ink

First published in Great Britain in 1998 by Hodder and Stoughton
A division of Hodder Headline PLC

The right of Fid Backhouse to be identified as the Author of
the Work has been asserted by him in accordance with the
Copyright, Designs and Patents Act 1988.

10 9 8 7 6 5 4 3 2 1

All rights reserved. No part of this publication may be
reproduced, stored in a retrieval system, or transmitted,
in any form or by any means without the prior written
permission of the publisher, nor be otherwise circulated
in any form of binding or cover other than that in which
it is published and without a similar condition being
imposed on the subsequent purchaser.

All characters in this publication are fictitious
and any resemblance to real persons, living
or dead, is purely coincidental.

British Library Cataloguing in Publication Data

A CIP catalogue record for this title is available
from the British Library

ISBN 0 340 70727 5

Typeset by Scribble Ink, Hopton, Suffolk
Printed and bound in Great Britain by
Mackays of Chatham PLC, Chatham, Kent

Hodder and Stoughton
A division of Hodder Headline PLC
338 Euston Road
London NW1 3BH

For an ever-tolerant mother without whom (as they say) none
of this would have been possible

PROLOGUE

Northern Ireland

CHARLES RIGBY didn't really exist, but that wouldn't stop them killing him. His cover was deep, but too many good people had died underestimating hard men who drew unemployment benefit and worked tirelessly at mauling the hand that fed them. They waged war against the British Government and took no prisoners. Rigby watched the young barman build a proper Irish Guinness. The pint of creamy stout would take several minutes to settle.

'That looks like a real black art. Give me a Bushmills while I wait. On the rocks. Make it a double.'

His accent was Boston American, the outer skin of deception. The barman lifted down a bottle from well-stocked shelves and poured a generous measure. It was the sort of West Belfast bar where you only spoke willingly to people you'd known all your life. The dour Irishman pushed the tumbler across scarred Cuban mahogany sawn and polished in the nineteenth century – an eye-blink in Ulster chronology. He crossed arms green with sectarian tattoos and finally spoke.

'No ice.'

'That's okay. I was kidding about the ice – why murder good whiskey? Bring my beer over, if it's ready in the next hour or so.'

Charles Rigby casually scanned the dimly lit room as he strolled across and set his drink on a marble-topped table. There were three other customers – elderly men in shabby clothes and cloth caps, apparently absorbed in a game of dominoes. But they were monitoring his every move. He sipped peaty whiskey, listening to the clack of domino tiles and muttered conversation. He wondered if Reilly would show. Instead, the barman arrived with his Guinness.

'This should drink like velvet. By the way, there's someone waiting to see you. Outside. Not the sort of gentleman to keep waiting.'

He set the tall glass down with exaggerated reverence. Rigby reached for an alligator-skin wallet gorged with large-denomination notes, in keeping with his brash businessman image.

'How much?'

'Sure and you can keep your Yankee dollars. On the house.'

'In which case keep the drinks.'

Expression neutral, the barman watched the American make for a door reinforced with sheet steel. Outside, two cars passed in convoy, tyres thumping over cobblestones as they headed for the Falls Road. A lone pedestrian hurried between pools of sodium light on the opposite side of the narrow street. Gerard Reilly materialized from a dark doorway, coat collar up and broad-brimmed hat tipped forward to shadow his foxy face.

'Sorry to drag you out into the night, Charlie-boy, but they're real buggers, the Brits. Biblically and electronically. Let's go somewhere we can talk safely.'

Reilly smiled an easy smile – a man to like instinctively, a politician who had done tireless good work on the city council representing downtrodden constituents.

He was also commander of the IRA's prestigious Belfast Brigade, a man known to have killed more than twenty people personally. Without counting bomb victims.

Colonel Wallace 'Wally' Richards of the Detachment – 14 Intelligence Company – scratched greying hair and looked again at page seven of that morning's *Daily*

WITHIN THE WALLS

Telegraph. The story was short and factual, containing none of the prurient speculation he might have found in the tabloids. But facts alone gave cause for grave concern.

The youngest son of tycoon Conrad Lancaster had been found dead at his weekend cottage near Bury St Edmunds. A part-time cleaner had come upon Peter Lancaster's body after it lay undiscovered in bed for several days. The newspaper reported a suspected drugs overdose, and stated that the West Suffolk coroner had been informed. The sting in the tale was a single sentence, reminding the world that Conrad had another son, James, who was estranged from his powerful father.

No more details were given, but it was enough. This couldn't have happened at a worse time. Richards was not noted for colourful language, but swore out loud. He picked up the internal telephone and asked for Captain Robin Wesley. His 2/IC was on base, and the colonel summoned him brusquely.

A moment later, the slim officer came in without knocking and sat in the visitor's chair. Formality and uniforms alike were frowned on in the Det. He wore civvies – green cord trousers, open-necked sports shirt and brown suede jacket. Wesley was twenty-nine years old, his unlined face betraying none of the dark experience which lay behind it.

'Seen this?'

Wally Richards slashed the offending story with a yellow highlighter and tossed the folded broadsheet across his desk. Wesley took a few seconds to absorb the implications before looking up, youthful countenance suddenly troubled.

'Looks bad, Wally. Do we abort?'

The colonel got up and prowled the cramped office, stopping by the window as though to stare into the misty Belfast night and divine its myriad secrets. But his Portakabin overlooked the brightly lit interior of the Shed, a vast industrial building that shrouded their secret world from prying eyes. He turned, patrician face weary.

'No. This is the culmination of a year's work. James reads the papers. We must leave risk assessment to the man on the ground. Goes with the territory. Dammit, we're so close.'

Robin Wesley tried to find relief in the prospect of action.

'Is there anything we can do? Discreet surveillance by our own Operators, or an SAS team on stand-by in case we need to lift him?'

'That's the last thing he needs. They're anything but fools, as we know to our cost. The slightest slip might compromise him further. We sweat this out, hope to hell he closes the sale before everything goes pear-shaped. If he needs help, he'll ask.'

'Right. That all?'

'Get your head down. Tomorrow could be a long day.'

The young officer was reluctant to leave, to accept that there was nothing more to be done. Except wait. His superior didn't chivvy him out. Taking a bottle of Johnny Walker Black Label and two tumblers from a drawer, Colonel Richards poured generously.

'I'm afraid he's on his own, Robin. Let's toast a brave man.'

They clinked glasses and drank, but fiery Scotch didn't make either of them feel any better.

After settling in a cracked leather-look armchair and stretching long legs, Charles Rigby glanced around the shabby sitting room.

'Nice place you've got here, Gerry.'

Gerard Reilly reached into a cabinet beneath the television set, turned and straightened. Grim-faced, he looked down at the American.

'It serves its purpose, Charlie-boy. The proud owners raised six kids in this poxy terraced house, all long gone into the wide world looking for a better life than a Catholic can find in the Six Counties. These people would no more engage in violence than the Pope himself, but they're visiting relatives up in Derry City for a couple of days, just so we can talk privately. That's what the Brits are up against. D'you know what this is?'

He held up a grey plastic box with toggle switch and speaker grille he'd taken from the video cabinet. Rigby twitched his shoulders and grinned, revealing no tension or unease.

'You got me. If this is the big test, I guess I failed.'

'State-of-the-art counter-surveillance. If a clever button on that natty overcoat of yours starts transmitting, or one of those sophisticated listening devices Army Intelligence got for Christmas is trained on the window, this screeches like a Dublin fishwife.'

He flicked the switch. In tangible silence, the two men held eye contact. Neither wavered. Reilly had no grounds for doubting the tall American. He came with impeccable references from sources close to Noraid, North America's Irish Republican fund-raising organization, and US Government agencies didn't mount covert operations in Ulster. But long-term survival meant trusting nobody, suspecting everyone and heeding the maxim that betrayal comes from unexpected quarters. The Irishman relaxed, put his smart box on the floor and perched on a sagging three-seater sofa.

'A routine precaution. Nothing personal. This war's about knowledge, and the opposition has been doing well lately. Too well. We've been losing trained volunteers and military operations have developed a nasty habit of going wrong.'

'No offence taken. My line of work isn't exactly viewed with approval by the authorities back home. I don't have a problem with security. The tighter the better. Now, can we talk cash money business?'

Charles Rigby lit a Marlboro and blew a perfect smoke ring towards the damp-blotched ceiling.

With fifteen minutes left before the *Globe*'s first edition went to bed, Dennis 'Doorstep' Wilkes wasn't satisfied. The piece was a cracker, following up a story that broke too late to get the full treatment yesterday. But something extra was needed. He stared at the big VDU which dominated his working life – the draughty stake-outs that provided his nickname having long vanished down the toilet of tabloid history.

Doorstep had become a Wapping desk man, and enjoyed every air-conditioned indoor minute. He savoured his chosen headline – *HEIRS AND DISGRACES*. He ogled the picture of larger-than-life Conrad Lancaster, raising a defensive hand against an intrusive lens – hinting at something to hide, even if it was only grief. The words he'd spun round the picture weren't bad, either – robber baron rocked by suicide of son.

The lad's death wasn't definitely self-inflicted, but Doorstep hadn't allowed disputed facts to blur a good yarn. Or been influenced by the fact that Conrad Lancaster owned a rival paper. The odious tycoon had fired young Peter from a senior position at Lancaster Trust a week since, following some imagined slight. Readers would be riveted by the rapidity of retribution. The great British public had an ambivalent attitude to the rich and famous – envying and admiring success, loving the long drop when they tumbled from lofty pedestals. Or were pushed.

Doorstep's killer instinct was legendary. He'd sensed the angle that would allow this one to run and run, and meant to get there ahead of deadly rivals on the other tabloids. He'd hunt down the missing son, James, the one who raised two fingers and walked out on his domineering parent years ago. With luck, the rebel would remain defiant, and the readership could be treated to the edifying tale of Conrad Lancaster grovelling at the feet of his sole remaining son and heir. Who would hopefully respond by shoving his silver spoon right up the old bastard's arse.

That was what tonight's story needed – a pointer to delights in store. Doorstep nervously fingered his polka-dot bow tie, then rang the picture editor – a woman of formidable competence and notorious temper.

'I know it's asking the earth, but have you made progress on that James Lancaster pic, perchance? I'm really pushed down here.'

Imogen wasn't impressed, pouring sarcasm on the ingratiating enquiry.

'Oh, I didn't realize you and everyone else has a bloody deadline around now, roughly three hundred and thirteen days a year. Of which this is one. You should've said.'

'Princess . . .'

She relented, professional satisfaction mellowing her sharp voice.

'I don't think the little bugger's ever been photographed

on his own. But I managed to come up with a group shot of his passing-out parade at Sandhurst ten years ago. We've pulled him out and aged him a little. It's only a head shot and he's in uniform, but better than a hole on the page. I have a hi-res scan waiting to be dropped into your tawdry story right now.'

Doorstep Wilkes tried to sound indignant.

'Hang on, how can you be so sure my story's tawdry?'

'Come on, darling. You may be a disaster between the sheets, but nobody doubts your literary prowess.'

He relaxed. Smiled indulgently.

'You're a miracle worker. I owe you one.'

'More like two thousand, and don't think I haven't been counting. Start paying tonight, after a candlelit supper with very expensive champagne. Oysters might help. And Dennis, you can do the cooking.'

Imogen Wilkes broke the connection. He fetched the scan and brought it up on screen. The jaunty soldier-boy portrait would sit well at the bottom of column two. Doorstep started keying a teasing caption. His wife was one in a million. A rough, tough industrial diamond.

Doubt seemed to have been banished. During a conversation punctuated by cups of coffee, the alert Irishman had probed Rigby's two cover stories – the one which would explain his presence in Belfast should the authorities enquire, and that which the IRA must never penetrate. Then Gerard Reilly had gone to the kitchen again, this time returning with beer. He started to speak openly, as though they were old rather than new comrades-in-arms.

'The Army Council's moving towards a ceasefire. There's pressure building for all-party peace talks, and we mean to have a seat at the table. Besides, we need time to regroup and rearm. We've lost a lot of weapons and ordnance lately. Frankly, the quartermaster's making my life a bloody misery.'

Charles Rigby was fascinated by this authentic glimpse into the IRA's innermost mind, but careful not to appear over-eager. He put his half-empty beer can down on worn grey carpet.

'How long d'you need?'

Reilly shrugged eloquently.

'A year, at most. We won't let a ceasefire run for more than one marching season. Then attacks on Loyalist paramilitaries and a couple of spectaculars on the mainland will push the Prods into reacting with random sectarian killings, and before the peacemakers can dive for cover it will be war as usual.'

The American laughed.

'Hey, I'm a businessman. You won't get any moral shit from me. But at the risk of cutting off my nose to spite my face, I've got to ask why you don't go for an honourable settlement, especially as your own community always suffers when the bullets fly. This sure as hell is one war you can never win by force of arms.'

He lit another Marlboro. Reilly's expression became intense, deep-set brown eyes unblinking, revealing steel behind Irish charm.

'That's the mistake the Brits always make. You must look at things the right way round, Charlie-boy. They've been fighting us for a thousand years without winning, so you don't get to retire just yet. There will always be good business for your kind in Ireland.'

Rigby nodded, allowing himself to look satisfied.

'That's what I like to hear. But I'll need time for the deal we've discussed. Stingers, laser-guided anti-tank missiles, Barrett fifty-cal sniping rifles – you don't wander into Walmart and get that shit off the shelf.'

Gerry Reilly laced his fingers, knuckles whitening.

'Which is why we came to you. We can source any amount of small arms and ammo, grenades and Semtex. Eastern Europe is awash with the stuff at knock-down prices. But the sophisticated weaponry needed to give us an edge, now that's another story. For that, we offer top dollar, so forget the slick sales pitch. We'll buy.'

'Good. Which just leaves the small matter of payment. My principals will not permit assembly of the shipment unless the necessary financial arrangements have been made. Mercenary, I know, but that's life and death for you.'

He bent down and dropped the Marlboro into his beer can, hoping the flippant comment and sudden movement would mask any inadvertent sign that the critical point had been reached. To his relief, Reilly responded without hesitation.

'No problem. Our American friends have cash waiting. We can meet tomorrow and I'll give you details. Once you've verified the funds, we finalize my shopping list. How long?'

Rigby assumed a doubtful expression.

'Providing you don't want anything especially difficult to source, expect delivery within five weeks, six max. We can go over final arrangements nearer the time. There's too much at stake to even consider the possibility of silly mistakes.'

'Six weeks and no silly mistakes sounds just fine. You'll be contacted at your hotel in the morning. Forgive me if I don't walk you back. The wife and half my street will swear on the Blarney Stone I've been at home watching TV all evening. Thank God for video machines. It would never do to be seen out and about with a dubious American businessman who's researching investment opportunities in this soon-to-be-peaceful colony of ours, now would it?'

Gerry Reilly smiled his lazy smile and reached for the overcoat and wide-brimmed hat thrown carelessly on to the sofa.

Like most foot-soldiers, Martin McDade had little grasp of overall strategy. But the streetwise nineteen-year-old from the Divis Flats knew which side he was on, and who the enemy were.

He was approaching this morning's task with customary thoroughness. For all he knew, the Movement's future might hang on the job. Or nothing at all. Either way, he'd do it right, because doing it right got you noticed and getting noticed was the way to get on. This assignment marked promotion from his role as a dicker who gave warning when security forces approached, and McDade didn't intend to remain in the sub-basement of the Command Structure for ever.

Charles Rigby's picture – snatched as he waited for a taxi at Belfast's civil airport, out at Aldergrove by Lough

Neagh – was in the side pocket of McDade's motorcycle jacket. He'd studied the photograph over a greasy-spoon breakfast, and was confident he would recognize the American's slicked-back fair hair, wide mouth and strong chin on sight.

He arrived at the phone box five minutes early. An old biddy in bulging coat and black hat was in possession, gabbing away as though she were there for life. When she finally emerged in response to impatient rapping on the glass, giving her tormentor a look which should have struck him dead, it was nearly time.

McDade inserted a coin and dialled the much-bombed Europa Hotel's switchboard as his cheap digital watch pulsed from 07.59 to 08.00. They answered immediately. He asked for Rigby by name and room number. The phone was lifted on the third ring.

'Charles Rigby.'

'Mr Rigby, go out the main entrance in fifteen minutes. You'll be met.'

'I'll be there.'

The American hung up. Martin McDade walked to a convenient bench overlooking the hotel. He'd brought a newspaper, because young men hanging around this part of town doing nothing tended to be noticed. After checking out the page-three girl and sports coverage, he turned pages and covertly watched for security activity. There were plenty of comings and goings from the Europa and rush-hour traffic was heavy, but he detected nothing unusual.

Martin McDade almost missed the story, but the boldly displayed words *HEIRS AND DISGRACES* caught his eye. He wondered what the headline meant, and a second later saw a familiar face. It was barely three inches square and the newsprint was grainy, but he'd done his homework. After surreptitiously comparing the photograph from his pocket with that in the *Globe*, there was no doubt that the likeness was striking. Soldier-boy James Lancaster and US businessman Charles Rigby could be identical twins.

The unfortunate coincidence triggered anxiety. Suppressing a desire to run first and think later, the young Irishman glanced around. Nothing had changed. No suspiciously parked vehicles. No unnaturally static pedestrians. No tiny danger signs to set sensitive antennae quivering. He looked at his Timex. Six minutes to go. He'd stick with it. Martin McDade was scared shitless, but orders were orders.

This wasn't a good morning to be alive. They'd talked aimlessly into the small hours, steadily sinking the Scotch which stunted fear. The one subject that really concerned them hadn't been mentioned. There was no more to be said. Army Intelligence thrived on action, but could do nothing. The two senior officers were the only ones privy to the sting, so they couldn't even deploy their own covert Operators to support Rigby. When they'd finally buried the bottle, Captain Robin Wesley went to his Portakabin, set the alarm for seven and fell into narcotic sleep that freed him from the waking nightmare.

Now, his temples throbbed and he could scarcely concentrate on the pile of newspapers. Two cups of black coffee had eased an arid throat and helped him through *The Times*, the *Guardian* and the *Daily Telegraph*. Not even repetition of the fact that Conrad Lancaster had an estranged son. Nothing new. Nothing dangerous. He started to relax. Middle-brow papers did nothing to raise his blood pressure, though the *Daily Mail* mentioned James Lancaster, reporting that he had opted for an army career rather than fame and filial fortune in the family business.

Wesley fetched another cup of coffee and started on the tabloids. Maybe they'd get away with it after all. When he reached page five of the *Globe*, saw the HEIRS AND DISGRACES headline and James Lancaster's picture, shock thumped his chest like a physical blow.

Rigorous professionalism kicked in – thousands of training hours and years of operational experience preparing him for this slow-motion instant. The young captain didn't consider consulting Colonel Richards. He threw down the paper and ran – headache forgotten, mind in overdrive. He burst into the headquarters ops room. The duty sergeant looked up inquiringly, catching his agitated officer's mood and putting down the newspaper he'd been reading. It was the *Globe*. As he spoke, voice controlled but urgent, Wesley registered the irony.

'Contact the RUC. Priority request for immediate action. They're to arrest a Charles Rigby, US citizen, currently staying at the Europa. Then get the hotel on the phone. Move!'

As the sergeant started talking into his headset, Robin Wesley glanced at the wall clock. The minute hand clicked forward to 08.13.

'Message acknowledged. Two HMSUs on their way. I'm dialling the hotel now. Pick up line one.'

The Royal Ulster Constabulary's élite fast-reaction Headquarters Mobile Support Units were always on stand-by, ready for any emergency.

'Get Wally Richards down here fast, Nick. Press the panic button.'

Wesley snatched up the phone and hit line one. Ringing tone. The damned hotel took an age to answer – at least five seconds.

'Hotel Europa.'

'I'd like to speak to a guest, Charles Rigby.'

'I'll try to connect you.'

A minute tiptoed by.

'I'm sorry, but there's no reply from his room. Would you like me to page Mr Rigby?'

'Yes.'

'Please hold the line.'

Never mind the line. As his hand locked on the telephone and he listened to silence, Captain Robin Wesley tried to hold on to hope.

It was a good morning to be alive. Spring sun was already well up and delicate lines of cloud streamed across blue sky like the vapour trails of vanished aircraft. Charles Rigby put on designer sunglasses and stood outside the Europa Hotel, beneath the fluttering flags of nations, a metal briefcase at his feet.

He breathed deeply. Today should mark the conclusion of a successful operation. He enjoyed the thrill of deception and living with danger, truly believing nobody could be better prepared. But however hard he tried to bury negative emotion, tension gnawed. Perhaps it was a defence mechanism, helping to ensure his guard never relaxed.

As he thought the thought, Rigby spotted a likely contact – the good-looking lad with a folded newspaper under the arm of his studded leather jacket, pausing to dodge traffic as he drifted across at an angle which would bring him to the hotel entrance. The young man came to a stop beside him and took a fat filter-tipped Major cigarette from its green-and-white packet.

'Spare a light?'

The blue eyes fastened on Rigby's face were in startling contrast to almost-black hair. Rigby produced his gold DuPont, suppressing a smile. Such elementary tradecraft would be almost comical if the business weren't so deadly serious. The contact lowered his voice to a stage whisper.

'Turn into Bruce Street, just down there on the left. You'll find a black cab waiting.'

He sucked in smoke, nodded and was gone with a loud 'Thanks, mister'. Not hurrying, but moving inexorably towards a future where he would graduate from errands and stone-throwing to bullets and bombs. Some enemy. Charles Rigby lit a Marlboro – another activity where you never admitted the worst scenario might happen to you.

Picking up his case, he started walking. The rising ululation of sirens approached. As he turned into Bruce Street and spotted his waiting taxi, the sound came to a crescendo and two unmarked police cars tore past along Great Victoria Street, each containing four uniformed RUC officers.

Somewhere, someone was in trouble.

The Royal Ulster Constabulary reacted fast, but not fast enough. When they reached the Europa, Charles Rigby had been seen leaving the hotel – destination unknown. The RUC had been stood down, to await further orders.

At the Det, Wally Richards and his second-in-command were deep in damage assessment. Their colleague was compromised. The IRA would never have penetrated Captain James Lancaster's cover unaided. With US Justice Department support, his American Charles Rigby legend was solid. But a tiny newspaper photograph meant all that counted for nothing. Without conviction, Robin Wesley tried to sound optimistic.

'Look, the op's coming to a climax. James may get what we need and be out before they wise up. It was an old photograph. His hair's longer now, done in a different style, and the face is fuller. Gerry Reilly won't exactly have introduced him around. Maybe no *Globe* readers have come across Mr Rigby yet.'

The older man shook his head.

'Possible, Robin, though not probable. Eyes everywhere.'

They shared a moment of pessimistic silence. But like policemen looking for a missing child, they had to ignore probability. Wally Richards set the damage limitation ball bouncing.

'You were right to tag him as a suspect. The last thing we need is anyone thinking he might be one of ours. So, what next?'

Robin Wesley was ahead of him.

'Turn the RUC loose with a search-and-arrest brief. We let it be known that a tip from the States has implicated Rigby in arms-running. Word'll soon reach the right ears. His credibility may even be reinforced, providing nobody makes the connection with that damn picture.'

The colonel approved.

'Good. The IRA needs this arms deal badly. Perhaps they'll hustle James out through the Republic before the penny drops. I'll have a quiet word with the senior duty officer at headquarters. Lisburn needn't know why, but if they increase the number of green army patrols that'll fit the wanted-man scenario. We'll also use our own resources. I want every Operator you can muster on the streets, looking for James. Put other assignments on hold and give this everything we've got.'

Wesley jumped up, relieved to be doing something. He had been standing next to James Lancaster in that Sandhurst passing-out photograph, but nobody was about to put a pistol to *his* head and splatter the rest of his life over the wall of some filthy barn or cowshed.

Gerard Reilly stood at the back of the darkened hall.

There were twenty snooker tables in the cavernous room. Despite the early hour, half a dozen were being used by young players allowed to practise for free when there were no paying customers. They all aspired to a professional career which would bring television exposure, fame and fortune.

The Sinn Fein city councillor in him was saddened. These dedicated cuemen might have what it took, but he doubted if any would escape from a hopeless future in West Belfast. Who understood the mysterious alchemy which selected a tiny percentage for success, in any field where rewards were great and available talent exceeded opportunity? But the lads played on, honing their skills and dreaming the universal dream.

The IRA commander watched Charles Rigby walk between lighted tables – oases of bright light, green baize and moving multicoloured balls. He was smartly dressed in tan slacks and tweed sports coat. White shirt with faint red stripes. No tie. Carrying a metal photographer's case. A good-looking man, oozing American confidence. Blessed are the strong, for they shall steal the earth. Rigby paused while a fifteen-year-old completed his flourishing shot, a red ball vanishing into the corner pocket with a satisfying thud, then arrived with a flash of even teeth.

'You sure do find some interesting places for our little chats. I been around the houses three times and haven't got a clue where we are.'

Reilly despised Americans, but needed the money donated by all those sentiment-sodden shamrock expats in Boston and New York in order to purchase the sophisticated weaponry only Yanks could provide. He looked up at the clean-cut Rigby, who topped him by four or five inches.

'Well, you can't be too careful, now can you? We won't want our little business transaction to be appearing in tomorrow's *Financial Times*. Through here.'

He opened a door and motioned Rigby through, before calling to one of the players.

'Two coffees back here, Donal. White, no sugar.'

He knew Rigby's preference from the night before. The youth abandoned his game in mid-shot, propped his cue against a pillar and headed for the deserted bar. The diminutive Gerry Reilly was a big man.

He would normally have spent the morning mooching around town, doing some shop-lifting and replaying every detail of the mission in his mind, as his adrenalin high slowly subsided. But something was bothering him. As soon as Rigby was out of sight, Martin McDade hurried up Great Victoria Street. He stopped in College Square, again comparing the photograph from his pocket with that blurred picture in his well-thumbed *Globe*. If they weren't the very same man they had to be brothers – and according to the newspaper James Lancaster no longer had a brother.

As he continued up King Street and turned left into Divis Road, McDade wondered if he should keep the discovery to himself. You were told what you needed to know, the rest you didn't talk about. His stride shortened, though the decision couldn't be long postponed. Alex Doherty was working on an old Ford Cortina in a rubbish-strewn parking area. Behind, the Divis Flats formed the rectangular, unwelcoming backdrop of home. As Martin McDade approached, Doherty's spanner slipped off a stubborn nut and he cursed, rubbing skinned knuckles. Dropping the offending tool, he wiped oily hands on stained blue overalls.

Doherty produced a crumpled gold pack of Benson & Hedges, lit two cigarettes with a Zippo and handed one to the younger man. The Cortina's suspension sagged as the mechanic parked his running-to-seed body on a rusting front wing.

'Marty. How did it go?'

'I had to turn an old biddy out of the phone box, but our friend got away right on time.'

Doherty slipped him a rolled twenty-pound note – part of the IRA's regular tax revenue from construction and other vulnerable commercial activities.

'Not bad, for a feckin little Taig bastard. Good health.'

'Thanks, Alex. There's just one thing. Probably nothing, but will you just take a look at this?'

He'd made up his mind. Martin McDade unzipped his

leather jacket and produced the *Globe*.

The storeroom had a concrete floor. Metal beer kegs were stacked against peeling brown walls and one corner was filled with a jumble of empty boxes. The two men sat on folding chairs, facing one another from opposite ends of a trestle table. They'd been through the deal from beginning to end, and Charles Rigby was about to get the reward for months of painstaking work. He finished lukewarm coffee and concluded his summary.

'The ship will be out of Halifax, Nova Scotia with a cargo of sawn timber for Dublin. She'll come round Malin Head and through the North Channel at night. The shipment will be packed in watertight containers, each with crab-pot float and radio beacon. They can be dropped anywhere along the coast. All we need from you is exact co-ordinates. All you need from us is the transmission frequency.'

Reilly was excited by the potential of his new arsenal but hadn't lost his wits, asking a shrewd question.

'And the decoy?'

'A Liberian freighter from Beirut to Belfast via Alexandria and Tripoli. Mixed cargo, including dried figs, a dozen crates of previously owned AK-47s and ten thousand rounds of ammunition. Timed to arrive the day before the real thing. Arrange for the security forces to hear a whisper. They should be so pleased with their big find that they'll forget the back passage. No extra charge. We give first-class service. Which only leaves one thing . . .'

The IRA man was enjoying the game. He pushed a folded sheet of paper along the plank table-top.

'If you don't pay the piper you never get a tune? I think you'll find this is what you want. The name of a bank in the Dutch Antilles holding an account in the corporate name you specified. The account number. A code-word which lets you check the balance of ten million clean US dollars. All you're missing is the second code-word, which allows the transfer of half our money to the destination of your choice. Once it becomes *your* money, Charlie-boy, and not before.'

It was what he wanted, all right. Rigby forced himself

to lean forward nonchalantly. Pick up the paper. Unfold it. Glance at hand-lettered contents.

'The second code-word?'

Reilly chuckled roguishly.

'Now that you get when my man has personally checked the shipment and seen it aboard in Nova Scotia, with the last five mil released on safe delivery. Trust me, Charlie-boy.'

Rigby showed perfect American teeth.

'I do, Gerry. We know where you live. You may be a serious player here, but that won't help you if the people I represent get upset. They're not forgiving men. Okay, I have your list. I don't see any difficulty, but if anything comes up I'll let you know through the usual channels. Now, I'd best get back to the hotel, grab my gear and catch the first flight out. If anyone should ask, I can honestly say I've identified some promising business opportunities.'

He closed his briefcase on priceless information. Home free. They stood up. Reilly produced a cellphone from his overcoat pocket and extended the aerial.

'I hate these new-fangled things, though we must move with the times. The enemy can listen, but I don't suppose we'll lose the war if I summon your cab.'

Before he could make the call, the instrument warbled. Reilly lifted the phone to his ear.

'Yes?'

He listened for perhaps a minute, thin face expressionless, then snapped an instruction.

'The pair of you get over here. You know where we are. Use the Transit. Side door, ten minutes.'

Reilly ended the call and put the phone away.

'Change of plan, Charlie-boy. Seems the RUC's decided you're a bad lad who should be banged up in Crumlin Road jail as of yesterday. Unless you fancy answering awkward questions, you'd best not go home via the Europa and Aldergrove.'

Charles Rigby showed a flash of anger.

'I thought you guys ran a tight-assed operation. My people will not be impressed by this sloppy performance. Make damn sure I do get home, or you whistle for your goddam shipment.'

WITHIN THE WALLS   19

Reilly raised defensive hands.

'Let's not be hasty. We'll find out what went wrong, but first we get you out. You'll go down to a safe house near Crossmaglen and over the border tonight, after dark. I hope you don't mind getting those fancy loafers muddy.'

'Hell, no. These loafers can walk on water.'

Good humour restored, Rigby put his case on the table, lit a Marlboro and sat down to wait.

Martin McDade almost hugged himself with excitement as the blue Ford Transit turned down an alley beside the snooker hall. The vehicle had been stolen down South, fitted with plates identical to those of a similar van owned by a Proddie painter from Carrickfergus, and stashed in a lock-up near the Flats to await a special job. This was the job and this was the life. They stopped. Alex Doherty spoke nervously.

'Get the back doors and watch for unwanted company.'

The overweight mechanic jumped down and rapped on the hall's aptly labelled emergency exit. McDade opened one of the van's twin rear doors. There was an old mattress on the plywood-boarded floor. He checked the alleyway. Empty. Gave Doherty a cheeky thumbs-up. The exit door sprang open and Gerry Reilly appeared, wearing his trademark black overcoat and wide-brimmed hat. Looked both ways. Beckoned urgently. Carrying his metal case, the American hurried out of the snooker hall and climbed nimbly into the Transit. He found time for a nod of recognition. McDade shut the van door and returned to the passenger seat.

Reilly and Doherty went into a huddle, whispering urgently. McDade glanced back. The fugitive had settled on the mattress, knees up and back against the van's metal skin. He was lighting a cigarette. Cool as you like under fire.

As McDade reached for his own cigarettes, Doherty got in and slammed his door. The diesel chuntered and caught. Gerry Reilly vanished through the emergency exit. The van moved off, shuddering slightly as Doherty jumped the clutch. McDade lit two cigarettes with the dashboard lighter and handed one to the driver. Cool as you like under fire.

They emerged on to the Falls Road and lost themselves in traffic. Only when they joined the M1 motorway, reached the outskirts of town and built up speed did Doherty speak, raising his voice to be sure it carried above the chugging engine and wind noise.

'There now, that's the first hurdle jumped. I'm Alex and he's Marty. We'll be looking after you for the rest of the day, then one of the boys from South Armagh will walk you over the border to Dundalk after dark. Then you'll be driven to Shannon for a New York flight. The Gardai will be snoring in their beds, so you'll be just fine.'

'I better had.'

The American's reply was laconic. Cool as you like under fire. Martin McDade wound down his window and adjusted the wing mirror, so he could watch for following vehicles and stray police cars. If Mary O'Grady could see him now, she might not switch off next time the kissing got heavy and he slid a hand beneath her best dress to touch that smooth thigh. He'd never say anything, but she'd hear her man was away up the ladder soon enough.

He'd hardly moved for thirty-six hours and was starting to wonder if he might seize up permanently. Corporal Norman 'Bilko' Pape was a Geordie with a justifiable reputation as the craftiest operator in the entire SAS. But he never shirked duty – even the hated OP turn.

Actually, Observation Post made it sound better than it was – a patch of hard ground his crammed bivvy bag did little to soften, high on a hillside. They were hidden by long grass and bracken that fringed an isolated stand of trees, half a mile from the target. Mid-morning sun seemed powerless to replace heat which had long since left his wiry body, and Bilko wanted to piss. But wriggling into a position where he could use the bottle seemed like too much effort.

The relief he really wanted wouldn't arrive for another twelve hours, tabbing in under cover of darkness. Then it was back to base for a scalding shower, sodding great supper and surfeit of sleep in a snug pit. Beside him, Trooper Jason 'Jigger' Harrison sniffed, losing patience with the drip which had been forming on the end of his nose for five minutes.

'Sorry.'

The apology, uttered within a foot of his left ear, was barely audible. A carrion crow flapped along the contour line, croaking mournfully. The bird flew over without changing course, eyesight which could differentiate between a man with a gun and a man with a walking stick at four hundred yards fooled by their camouflage. Bilko Pape waited until the crow had passed and lifted hooded 10 x 50 binoculars.

Below, there was little sign of life around the run-down farmstead – a low stone-built house with mossy slate roof, surrounded by crumbling outbuildings and abandoned farm machinery. The old man was at home. Smoke trailed down the wind from a squat chimney and his mud-spattered red Toyota pick-up truck sat in the sunlit yard, a bantam cock perched on the tailboard.

Bilko twitched the glasses, focusing on a cow byre away from the main complex. The half-collapsed building contained Armalites, handguns and pump-action shotguns. They'd put in a tech attack five nights ago, jarking the cache by concealing tiny transmitters which would betray the IRA Active Service Unit that retrieved the weapons. The job might not go down for weeks, but they'd be waiting.

Jigger Harrison touched his elbow. Bilko swung the binoculars to a point where the unmade track in the valley bottom disappeared round their hill. Jigger had hearing like a bat on speed. A blue Ford Transit drove into his magnified picture. Bilko followed the van as it bumped along to the farm, turned into the yard and stopped.

The old man – Bravo One – hurried out and opened tall barn doors. The Transit drove in. A moment later, three visitors joined him and he shut the doors. Bravo Two – under twenty, slim, curly dark hair, black leather jacket. Bravo Three – thirty-five, heavily built, receding brown hair, overalls. Bravo Four – around thirty, tall, swept-back fair hair, well dressed, metal briefcase. Pity the van's number plates had never been visible. The four men walked to the house in an untidy group. Corporal Bilko

Pape murmured an order.

'Get on the net, Jigger. Who says Christmas only comes once a year?'

There was a single Mars bar left, which he'd been saving for later. But maybe he'd scoff it right now.

Before leaving, the taciturn farmer made tea. He put a brown earthenware pot on the kitchen table, together with three mugs advertising cattle cake, a jug of milk and packet of white sugar. The two IRA men were in high spirits.

'Will you be mother, Marty?'

'I will, Alex, I will.'

The young one poured. Charles Rigby accepted a steaming mug without argument, though rarely drinking the stuff. He felt uneasy. There was something furtive about the way Alex's restless eyes roamed over him. Perhaps he was experiencing no more than a natural reaction to the unexpected setback. Rigby handed round cigarettes.

'I guess I can spare these. I'll soon be stocking up with duty-frees, right?'

Alex laughed.

'Indeed you will, Mr Rigby. You'll be fetched at midnight then it's a short country walk and away to Shannon. Sure and it will be just like the milk run. You're in for a dull day here, mind, but at least the old fella has TV and a comfortable sofa. Now I'd best take a quick look around to be on the safe side.'

The overweight Irishman went out into the yard, closing the door behind him. Charles Rigby made casual conversation.

'So, you're new to all this excitement?'

Marty looked indignant.

'I am not. We start fighting young where I grew up. I've done my share.'

'Should've guessed. Any chance of a coffee? I don't much like tea.'

The youngster rummaged in pine cupboards and came up with a jar of Maxwell House.

'This do?'

'Fine.'

Marty found another mug and spooned in freeze-dried granules. As Rigby watched him lifting a kettle that was simmering on the Rayburn, Alex came back. The big man stood in the sunny doorway, fleshy face in shadow, and pushed the door shut with a heel. His arm came up. Rigby immediately identified the pistol – nine-millimetre Sigsauer P226, a reliable automatic that rarely jammed. Too far away on the other side of the table. Rock steady. Pointing at his chest. The lilting Irish voice was suddenly harsh.

'Very still, Mr Rigby. I won't hesitate to use this.'

Charles Rigby sat very still. With his left hand, Alex produced a pair of plasticuffs from an overall pocket and held them out sideways, moving cautiously into the room.

'Cuff the bastard, Marty. Arms behind the chair. Be careful to leave me a clear shot.'

The chunky automatic never wavered. Charles Rigby should have listened to his intuition. Those furtive, tell-tale eyes were now hard and direct.

Corporal Bilko Pape could hardly keep track of the traffic. First, the Transit arriving with its three-man complement. Then the old farmer, Bravo One, departing in his Toyota pickup – getting clear before the op went down, or to keep watch where the farm track joined a metalled C-road around the hill. Just after that, Bravo Three had emerged from the house and gone to the cow byre, returning three minutes later – checking the weapons cache.

And now, a beat-up Vauxhall Cavalier bringing two more men. The driver, Bravo Five, nipping round to open the passenger door – fiftyish, tiny, bow legs, white hair, faded blue jeans. One of the ex-jockeys who form half Ireland's population. So, Bravo Six must be the boss – indeterminate age, slim, broad-brimmed hat, long dark overcoat.

Bravo Six went into the house. Bravo Five put the Vauxhall into an open-fronted cart shed, sat on a wall and opened a tabloid newspaper. Bilko bet Jigger Harrison a tenner it was the *Racing Post*. With any luck, they'd get to find out.

The honeypot had attracted an IRA Active Service Unit, which was as good as dead. Their reports would have sparked a frenzy of controlled activity. Helicopters on stand-by. A mobile relay unit moving into position to track the jarked weapons. Half a dozen four-man SAS teams making ready – checking and rechecking the tools of their lethal trade, joking around to disguise rising tension, praying to a God they didn't believe in that this wouldn't be another false alarm.

Corporal Bilko Pape rubbed the tired eyes that had made it all possible and returned to observation. Nothing had changed. But when those murdering IRA bastards finally moved out, they'd be walking into an invisible man-trap.

In the low-ceilinged kitchen, the commander of the IRA's Belfast Brigade looked down at the hooded prisoner. Alex Doherty stood by the stove, cigarette in one hand and automatic pistol in the other. Gerry Reilly spoke softly.

'Hello again, Charlie-boy. Or should that be Jimmy-boy?'

There was no reaction. Reilly waved a folded copy of the *Globe* to disperse lingering cigarette smoke, put the newspaper on the table and gestured to Martin McDade.

'Get that thing off him.'

Reilly pulled out a chair and sat down as the youngster fumbled with the hood, a green cushion cover secured at the neck with orange bailer twine. Charles Rigby blinked in the light. Incredibly, he managed to smile.

'What happened to my expenses-paid tour of the Republic?'

The Irishman felt reluctant admiration.

'My, but you're a cool one. Did you read the papers this morning?'

Reilly leaned forward and opened the tabloid. The prisoner didn't look down.

'Your man here phoned just as I was going down to breakfast, so I didn't get the chance.'

Very cool, a real pro.

'And yesterday, did you happen to see anything of

interest yesterday?'

He was rewarded with a lack of reaction – the face he was studying went still. So the gutsy so-and-so had read the news reports which might sink him and carried on regardless.

'Sorry about your brother, and I guess we can say goodbye to Charles Rigby as well. Our convincing Yankee arms dealer's references checked out fine, but he doesn't really exist, now does he? You almost got away with it, but for a bit of bad luck.'

He tapped the incriminating photograph, watching James Lancaster's eyes drop and stay down as he absorbed the implications of what they saw. Then he looked up, puzzled.

'Who is this guy? You're making a big mistake here, Gerry.'

The American accent didn't slip. Reilly shook his head sadly.

'Don't shit me, Jimmy-boy. We both know how things must end up, but I need some answers and will take no pleasure in getting them the hard way. I mean, what's this all about? I can hardly believe your people set this up just to relieve the Movement of money. I'll give you an hour, then ask again. If you don't help me out, Alex will see if he can loosen your tongue, and he's not a gentle man. Hood him, Marty.'

He watched a strong, impassive face disappear beneath green fabric, then turned to Doherty.

'Seamus is doing stag in the yard, Alex. Why don't you make him a nice cup of tea? And while you're out there you'll find a baseball bat and cordless electric drill in the boot of my car. Perhaps you'd better fetch them in, just in case.'

Reilly spoke quietly, as though discussing an everyday chore. But James Lancaster would get the message.

At last, Colonel Wally Richards had something to go on. The two SAS men on stake-out in Bandit Country were on secondment to the Det, reporting to him. Their reports left no doubt that James Lancaster had been spirited away to a safe house in South Armagh. Which didn't solve the colonel's problem.

Either the IRA had bought the deception tactic and were smuggling their American arms-dealing contact out, or James Lancaster's cover had been shattered by that treacherous press photograph. Richards had been discussing these alternatives with his 2 I/C when word of two more arrivals came through from the OP above the farmhouse. Captain Robin Wesley read the flimsy and handed it to his superior.

'They assume it's an ASU gearing up for a job, but Bravo Six must be Gerry Reilly. He doesn't get personally involved in ops any more, so James is in trouble.'

Colonel Richards looked up from the signal transcript.

'I tend to agree. But suppose we're wrong? James may not have the information we need yet. If they haven't rumbled him, he may still get it. Besides, the whole point of the tech attack on those weapons is to catch an ASU in the act, discover their target before taking them out. What if we bust in there and James is okay? We may not even get enough evidence for convictions. One of them will turn out to be a second cousin who's visiting the farmer with a few chums.'

Robin Wesley protested.

'We'll get a major weapons cache and put the farmer away, neutralize another safe house and hopefully save James's life. Surely that's the priority, even if we blow both operations?'

His superior shook his head.

'Not that simple. The PM has staked his reputation on achieving a ceasefire. Everyone knows paramilitaries will use the breathing space to regain strength, but that doesn't alter the political imperative. We have to keep the pressure on, to help drive them to the conference table. If we miss that IRA Active Service Unit, my arse is in the meat grinder.'

'I see.'

Wesley didn't bother to hide surprise, or contempt. Colonel Richards scratched his cheek, every inch an indecisive decision-maker.

'If the Rigby cover is broken James is probably dead already, in which case there's no point in taking precipitate action. It's too close to call, Robin. Tell you what. I'll toss for it. Heads we go in, tails we let things run and see how they work out.'

Intelligence wasn't known as 'green slime' for nothing. The old devil smiled and took a big pre-decimal penny from his pocket. Wesley felt a surge of relief. Wally Richards had been using that double-headed penny since his schooldays at Eton.

He didn't understand. It was normal to let an ASU move out and take them when their target was established, but this time the IRA men were being tackled *in situ*. Their OP's role was to overview the Close Quarters Battle. The sky had clouded over at dusk, and darkness was intense. Corporal Bilko Pape watched the developing scenario through his Night Viewing Aid. Better than the movies, though weird green picture quality left something to be desired. He even got to provide whispered commentary, which Jigger Harrison relayed on to the net.

Right now, they were monitoring the calm before the storm. Three four-man SAS teams were deploying below, but the NVA revealed no more than the dark shape of a guard in the yard. Throughout the day, stag duty had been shared by Bravo Two, the youngster, and Bravo Five, the ex-jockey – an hour on, an hour off. It was Bravo Five's turn.

The small man sat on his usual wall, smoking a cigarette and hardly giving the impression of someone on maximum alert. Better still, Bilko Pape had seen no sign of a hand-held radio. Behind, the soft glow of curtained windows suggested two downstairs rooms were in use – kitchen and sitting room. The farmer had not returned, so there should be four men inside.

The CQB began. For an instant, one dark shape turned into two. The guard went backwards over his wall. Then there was no more than a lonely cigarette, glowing where it had fallen. He murmured the good news and Jigger told the net.

'Bravo Five down, over.'

Bilko Pape saw shadowy movement as the assault group moved into position. The other two teams were somewhere out in the night, acting as cut-offs – to catch runners, or intercept arrivals along the farm track. He moistened dry lips and settled down to watch the fun.

Pain, blurring into the almost euphoric state which takes over when the mind finally accepts that hope has gone. A magical defence mechanism that lets living people shovel down pills or sit calmly in a car while deadly carbon monoxide bubbles through a tube beside them, because it's over.

Reilly next door watching television news. Alex and Marty kicking around Glasgow Celtic's chances of winning the Scottish League as if James Lancaster doesn't exist. His left leg feels numb and the agony of a broken right arm has subsided to a manageable ache. Soon, they'll damage him some more. Create new pain to corrode resolve. Ask questions again, and again, and again. Until then, he's free to let thoughts roam, breathing deeply to slow a pounding heartbeat, fighting the enveloping hood which sucks against his open mouth every time he gasps for air.

Poor Peter. A human being without an ounce of malice. The *Telegraph* hinted at suicide. As kids, they were close. Peter relied on him for protection. Trusted him. James feels infinite sadness, and guilt. He should never have left his brother to face the old man's overbearing arrogance alone.

Conrad Lancaster would lose both sons inside a week, ending dynastic dreams. No sadness there, or guilt. Sow the wind, reap the whirlwind. Their crude, domineering father destroyed their gentle, helpless mother. Broke her mind and body. James has never forgiven Conrad for that brutality. Never will, as if such petty considerations matter now.

Perhaps that's what they mean by a drowning man's life flashing before his eyes – a moment when everything that makes up a life coalesces into an entity that has become irrelevant, a pointless entry in the flawed ledger of humanity.

Getting light-headed. Liz Greener. Copper-red hair swirling as she tosses her head, full of life. Intent grey-green eyes watching his as she listens. Handsome face animated as she talks with that lively Australian twang. Sunlight dappling a bedroom wall. Passion in the afternoon. Togetherness. Warmth. Elusive human contact. Loving and being loved. But things aren't like that in the real world, are they?

Don't think about it. Memories might turn to hope. Breathe deeply. Steady that heartbeat. Feel the texture of smooth material against skin with the very fibre of your being. Breathe deeply. Make tiny movements, try to get comfortable despite generating shooting pain. Muster mental defences as psychological warfare resumes.

Alex and Marty are discussing imaginative new applications of baseball bat and electric drill. Young Marty less than enthusiastic, too far down the learning curve to regard such matters with indifference. But words will still translate into painful reality.

'Right, the news is nearly over. Gerry'll want another quiet word. Ready to sing yet?'

A fist thumping his shoulder. Alex's frightening Belfast voice. Keep still. Don't breathe.

'Suppose he's unconscious?'

Marty uncertain, almost hopeful. Alex not interested.

'Just hold the gun to his head while I drill the other knee. We'll soon see if the scumbag's awake or not.'

When deprived of sight, other senses compensate. Ears hear the tiny scraping of an ashtray as a cigarette is mashed, the whine of an electric drill being tested. Nose detects mixed tobacco- and wood-smoke, musty cloth and human sweat. Anticipates the smell of scorched flesh and burning bone. Then shattering, mind-numbing concussion obliterates everything.

Instinctively, James Lancaster hurls himself backwards, using his sound leg as a catapult. Still shackled to the chair, he crashes into someone, falls to the stone floor and lies still.

They'd practised until they were bullet-perfect in the killing house at Stirling Lines, but this wasn't Hereford. The SAS team leader hated going into the unknown, but a life was at stake. He'd decided on a three-man snatch.

No gas, no flashbangs – just helmets with swivel-down NVGs, light Kevlar body armour, Maglite torches, Heckler & Koch MP5SDs and Browning automatic pistols, in case one of the silenced submachine-guns jammed. Plus door charges, darkness and surprise, the most potent weapon of all.

Timing was critical. They'd checked their weapons, set torches to wide-angle beam and attached them to MP5SDs well back from the farmhouse, before taking out a sentry. The pint-sized watcher lay unconscious behind a wall, plasticuffed to an old horse-drawn roller and gagged with gaffer tape.

Each assault team member had a precisely defined task. One – initiate the power cut and simultaneously trigger door charges, before providing outside back-up. Two and Three – through the kitchen door shooting anything that moved, except the prisoner. Four – in behind the shooters to drag out the prisoner, carrying only a pistol. The leader was Two.

Silent approach completed, no sign of alarm. Muffled dialogue through the kitchen door. Unexpected sound. Electric drill? A bonus if they're occupied on some stupid task. Check the safety's off and selector set to semi-auto, for rapid-fire single shots. Ready. Torches on but shielded with steady hands.

At Two's signal, One blipped his walkie-talkie twice. Back along the track, a cut-off team member was roped to an electricity pole, open-channel radio hanging on a lanyard and bolt-cutters poised. As the double blip came, he'd snip a supply wire. When the thump of a small explosion reached him two elapsed-time seconds later, the assault team would already be inside the farmhouse.

Used to detonating door charges, the SAS team don't suffer an instant of shocked paralysis. Two and Three go in fast. Occupants disorientated by blast and sudden darkness, but recovering motive power. A hooded man falling, tied to a chair – the prisoner, first to react. Alive. Paralysed eyes in high-intensity torchlight – a kid to the right, regaining balance. Armed. Pistol starting to move. Fatboy to the left, turning away. Armed with electric drill. One player missing.

Two double-taps the kid in the head. Beside him, Three puts a couple into Fatboy's back. Ejected cartridge cases hit the stone floor before their victims. Four dragging the prisoner chair and all towards blown door, Three checking fallen bodies. Sitting-room door. Go through low. Television on. Sash window open to the night. Shirtsleeved body slumped over sill, half outside. Slotted by One, waiting in the darkness. All three players down.

The SAS team leader stood upright. They'd do the whole house room by room, just in case, but this was looking like a straightforward day at the office. The action had lasted twenty-four seconds.

Captain Robin Wesley came in on the Wessex Casevac chopper, flown by a navy crew. The landing zone was a meadow beside the farmhouse, illuminated by the helicopter's searchlight and intersecting headlamps from the assault group's Range Rovers.

He was met by two helmeted SAS men with blackened faces. One helped the paramedic lift out a folding gurney and hurried him away. After leading Wesley clear of spinning rotors, the other shouted a report, expanding an earlier radio flash.

'I'm afraid they'd already started working on your man before we went in. He's battered but repairable. Three players dead, one prisoner. We've secured the area and will hold a perimeter until the green army and RUC arrives to take over.'

'Nice work, Sergeant. We picked up the farmer, by the way. Drinking in a bar outside Newry as though he hadn't a care in the world.'

Captain Wesley went to meet the returning gurney. The injured man's face was pallid, but he managed a lopsided grin.

'Late again, Rob.'

'Sorry, mate, first things first. I was watching *Soldier, Soldier*. Great episode.'

James Lancaster replied vaguely, morphine taking hold.

'Needed a few tips, did you? I had some bad luck, that's what Reilly said. Just a little bad luck.'

'Not half as bad as his. And luck evens up. If they hadn't

chosen a safe house where we had an OP running we'd've lost you. Still, that's history. Did you get it?'

'In here. Bank details plus account number, Dutch Antilles.'

He nodded towards a metal briefcase, held against encircling chest straps by a tightly crooked left arm, the wrist adorned with plasticuff bracelet and severed cord. Robin Wesley liked what he heard.

'Brilliant. With luck they won't have time to move the cash, which would be a bonus. But either way our friends in the US Justice Department can use this information to track the money back to source and bring in indictments. The IRA's fund-raising efforts in North America are about to crash into a seriously solid brick wall.'

As they lifted Captain James Lancaster of Army Intelligence into the Wessex, he smiled a fleeting smile and drifted into unconsciousness.

West Suffolk

HIS PLASTERED right arm made dressing difficult, but he could walk with the help of elastic knee bandage and stick. An army car and driver had brought him to the low building off a country lane. The crematorium's orange-tiled roof and bulky stone chimney were set against dark pine trees which formed the distant horizon.

Mourners were leaving in ones and twos, sombre stragglers from the previous funeral. His would not begin for twenty minutes. Not *his*, though that had been close enough, but the one he was here to attend. James Lancaster thought about his brother.

The inquest had returned an open verdict on Peter, who had choked on vomit after mixing alcohol and antidepressant pills. As the coroner remarked, the dangers of such combinations were well known, but people still managed to get it hopelessly wrong. In the absence of a note, the jury would be wrong to conclude with certainty that Peter Lancaster committed suicide, despite evidence of depression and work-related problems.

A hearse drove up the curving drive and stopped beneath

the extended entrance porch. The black-and-grey Volvo's clean modern lines contrasted with its traditional burden, an oak coffin bearing one ornate wreath and a bunch of garden flowers. Neither was from him. Peter was gone and formalities meant nothing to either of them.

He didn't even want to be here, though guilt compelled him to attend. His strongest memory of that bleak interlude when he truly believed his own life to be forfeit was not pain or fear . . . but sadness and guilt at failing his little brother.

'Peter Lancaster?'

The question took James by surprise, until he realized the undertaker was referring to the deceased.

'Yes, I'm Peter's brother.'

'I understand there won't be a large family party, but his vicar will say a few words and some local friends are attending.'

The man in black raised a gloved hand, and an unctuous assistant removed the flowers to a side area reserved for the purpose. So Conrad Lancaster was too busy to say goodbye to his son, though no doubt the huge wreath was his idea of a fitting farewell.

With perfect timing, Conrad's gold Rolls-Royce turned into the carpark, challenging his assumption. But the passenger wasn't his father.

Before the chauffeur could get to her door, Elizabeth Greener stepped out of the Roller. James Lancaster limped to meet her, pale and unsmiling.

'Hello, Lizzie. Thanks for handling the arrangements.'

Cold lips brushed hers. She put a hand on his good arm, sensing distress but knowing sympathetic words wouldn't help.

'How are you, Jamie?'

'Mending. This plaster should be off tomorrow, but the knee may be a more permanent problem. We'll see. My beloved father ducked out, then.'

'A big Russian deal's reaching a critical stage, but that isn't the real reason. You know he fired Peter, some silly row over meeting him at the airport. Peter got held up in traffic and kept the old man waiting for fifteen minutes.

It's happened before and they always made up, but now Conrad's really hurting.'

A few new arrivals were making for the crematorium. She slipped an arm round his waist and they followed slowly. James was bitter.

'Feeling sorry for himself, you mean. Lost his whipping-boy, hasn't he?'

Despite the circumstances, Liz was pleased to be with him. They'd talked on the phone when he called to tell her about his accident and check if Peter's funeral arrangements were in hand, but before that they hadn't been together or spoken for three months. Until army duty took him overseas, they'd been close, despite her awareness of a secret part of his mind to which she was never admitted.

'He's too proud to ask, but badly wants to see you.'

James stopped, raising angry eyes to slate-grey sky.

'I'll bet he does, but where did he get the idea I might want to see him? No chance. I will never speak to that man or go near him again. Come on, we'd better go inside.'

Head down, he started walking again. Despite his stick and awkward gait, Liz had to hurry to catch up.

The two of them stood at the back of the airy room, with its pine-boarded ceiling and exposed structural beams. Nine people were present. Five men and one woman occupied a single pew towards the front – middle-aged country people, ill at ease in best suits which had become too tight over the years. The ninth was a young vicar, expressing meaningless but sincere sentiment from the lectern. Though an incomer who spent little time in the village, it seemed Peter Lancaster was well liked – generously supporting local causes and buying more than his share of weekend drinks at the White Horse.

When he finished the kind peroration, heavy patterned curtains glided across Peter's coffin, hiding its final passage into the flames. James hardly felt Liz Greener squeeze his arm. He was thinking about the real Peter.

The ten-year-old crying when their pet spaniel had to be put down. The boy clinging tightly when they could hear Conrad shouting at their mother downstairs. The inept garden cricketer glowing with excitement when James lobbed an easy ball he swatted through the greenhouse roof. The gregarious young man whose self-denigrating humour masked insecurity. The brother unable to follow James's example and break away from their father's manipulative influence.

Their small party shuffled out through a side door. The vicar said a few words which James Lancaster heard but didn't register. They shook hands amongst floral tributes from previous funerals. A short procession of concerned faces and awkward condolences followed. James thanked each one, genuinely touched that they'd taken the trouble to come. The woman was last. Shrewd button eyes looked into his. She studied him for a moment before addressing him in a pleasant East Anglian burr.

'You were close, even if you didn't meet up much lately. He talked about you a lot. Proud of his big brother, was Peter. I'm Angela Gallyon. I did his cleaning, four hours a week . . .'

She paused – to let him remember she had found the body, and to make up her mind about something. James replied gravely.

'He talked about you. The beautiful flowers were yours, weren't they?'

Angela Gallyon flushed, looking down at the stone-paved floor in embarrassment.

'Not from me. I just picked some cowslips and violets in his garden this morning. Nothing special.'

James smiled.

'Those are the flowers I meant. Anyone can ring up and order a flashy wreath.'

The flush deepened. She blinked rapidly. James felt her push something into his hand.

'I liked Peter. This is for both of you.'

They were interrupted by the undertaker. Before James could stop her, Angela Gallyon scurried after fellow-villagers who were waiting in the carpark.

'Will Sir wait for the last remains?'

James turned to his companion.

'Would you mind, Lizzie? Give the ashes to my old man and make sure he puts the urn on that sodding great desk of his.'

She understood his need to be alone.

'I'll see to it. Call me when you're ready.'

'I will, tomorrow.'

Liz smiled a tentative smile that illuminated her oval face. James walked away, towards the tiny Chapel of Remembrance which overlooked a windswept lawn and open fields beyond. He looked at Angela Gallyon's gift.

The twice-folded sheet had been torn from a spiral-bound notebook. His name was written on the front. He opened the note and read Peter's last three words.

I'm so lonely.

James Lancaster stood in the quiet chapel for a long time. Then he crumpled the paper and limped towards his car. There was no need for Peter to tell him. He'd known all along.

London

HE KEPT his promise, telephoning in mid-morning. They arranged to meet at her apartment in Camden Town, after work. Liz Greener didn't have time to think about what she wanted to happen, because Conrad Lancaster kept her busy all day. She was still settling into her new post as his personal assistant, which brought out the best in her. Whatever people said about Conrad, he was a charismatic, high-powered operator. Insight into his devious methodology and active participation in his decisive power plays was stimulating.

James was already inside when she arrived home. Something had changed. He seemed almost light-hearted, kissing her before she was through the front door. Chilled champagne was waiting on the kitchen table. The plaster was off his still-stiff right arm. As he awkwardly filled two glasses, she made a confession.

'I didn't have the guts to give Conrad that urn. It's in the bottom of my wardrobe.'

Liz hung her head in mock-contrition. He laughed.

'You're forgiven. Peter would much rather be looking up your dresses than under Conrad's evil eye. Let's drink to my little brother.'

Both knew banter hid pain. Liz raised her glass.

'To Peter, wherever he is.'

Alone with memories, they drank, then James cocked his head.

'So tell me about this new job of yours.'

'It helps to keep occupied.'

Safer ground – or was it? James continued thoughtfully.

'The old man must think you're special, grabbing you as his PA. Be careful, Lizzie, my father chews people up for breakfast. Ask Peter.'

Liz worked round to her real confession.

'Conrad has a soft spot for me. Well, a bit more than that. You know what they say, there's no fool like an old fool. I even wondered . . .'

She lost her nerve. James completed the sentence.

'If those lustful feelings played a part in his decision to terminate my baby brother's employment? Quite likely. You turned him down once, and he's used to getting his own way. I'd say he was perfectly capable of firing Peter to get his hands on you, metaphorically speaking.'

'It's true I wouldn't leave Peter. He trusted me and we worked well together. Perhaps I should have done the he-goes-I-go number, but I never thought. When Conrad asked again, afterwards, I said yes.'

To cover confusion Liz busied herself pouring fresh drinks. James wasn't fooled, leaning across the table and taking her hands. They shared a moment of contemplative silence before he spoke.

'Listen. We're both feeling bad about letting Peter down, but that won't bring him back. We must go on. New beginnings. You have your job. I'm leaving the forces.'

'Will you manage okay?'

'I'll get an army pension, and Peter left me everything. I'm thinking of going to the States and starting again. Something in the security line. I've got useful contacts over there. It'll be a clean break.'

'And us?'

'Wouldn't work, would it? It's been great, but we can't be together while you're working for Conrad. You'd be between the proverbial rock and hard place. You're ambitious. I can't ask you to give up a promising career for me. Even if you did, I'm not capable of offering till-death-us-do-part commitment. Deep down, you know that. Besides, my father's always dreamed of founding a dynasty, providing he doesn't have to surrender an ounce of control while there's breath in his body. If I stay, he'll never leave me alone.'

He was wrong and he was right. She would throw up the job tomorrow and follow him anywhere, but James wasn't ready for that sort of relationship. Perhaps he never would be. Feeling infinite sadness for this wounded soul, for herself, Liz Greener gently touched his cheek.

'Friends, then?'

'Always.'

They clinked glasses and drank champagne.

James Lancaster lay on his back, looking at streetlight which splashed the bedroom ceiling. His right arm was aching, and the knee damaged by the late Alex Doherty throbbed painfully. He couldn't get comfortable, yet hesitated to move for fear of disturbing Liz. Beside him, she was deeply asleep – her breathing slow and even, unruly hair tickling his cheek, a warm breast pressed against his side, a companionable arm flung across his chest.

Gently, he freed himself. Liz turned over and curled into a foetal ball, dragging the duvet with her, but didn't waken. He limped to the kitchen, lit a Marlboro and sat naked at the table, staring at the empty champagne bottle.

Half his being had desperately wanted this woman to suggest accompanying him to the States, knowing he would have accepted with gratitude and relief. But the other half knew better. She couldn't offer, because he couldn't ask. And she was right.

Their prolonged lovemaking had produced none of the frantic physical passion that characterized previous couplings. They had made love for the first time as friends, and the last. This awareness created an intense bitter-sweet intimacy he had never experienced before, and would surely never forget.

He'd miss Liz Greener, perhaps more deeply than he cared to admit. But it was time to move on, leaving the demons behind.

DAY 1 – MONDAY

Oregon

HE WAS OLDER, wiser and licensed to kill. James Lancaster eased the weapon forward, careful to make no sudden movement that might betray his presence. He would get one shot. A feather of morning breeze caressed his face, but lacked the strength to deflect his bullet by so much as an inch during its high-velocity mission.

It was a frozen tableau of life, or death, and the power was his alone. He settled more comfortably on damp earth and fractionally moved his custom-made rifle, until the telescopic sight's cross-hairs were precisely positioned for a killing shot. The bullet strike would inflict irreparable damage to heart and lungs. Death should be virtually instantaneous.

Living with violence was addictive, inducing a high that nothing else came close to emulating. James Lancaster had tried kicking the habit, without success. Though his business no longer required him to work at the sharp end, he still undertook the occasional risky assignment. In truth, he felt truly alive only when danger breathed softly on the back of his neck.

He had just returned from Mexico, a country where a canyon existed between rich and poor. As he sat at a dirty cantina table whilst an anonymous entrepreneur in check shirt and Wrangler jeans expertly examined the contents of his briefcase, a second man nonchalantly covered him with an elderly but well-oiled Colt .45 automatic. Both wore colourful bandanas pulled up over their faces, surmounted by watchful dark eyes.

The slightest hitch – perhaps no more than a distant siren as a hurrying police car pursued unconnected business – could prove fatal. But nothing went wrong. After carefully counting bundles of bills, the teller departed. The other remained, nervously snicking the Colt's safety catch on and off. Two minutes later, the boy had come in, blinking in light that must have seemed gloomy after harsh sunshine. Luis Mendez made his way over and sat down, twelve-year-old face expressing the beginnings of hope.

James Lancaster had nodded reassuringly, before fetching a drink. After taking a US dollar bill and slapping an unchilled can of Dr Pepper on the stained zinc counter, the elderly bartender resumed lazy glass-polishing. House rules precluded him from noticing pistol-waving *bandidos*. The boy drank greedily. Before he finished, the second man got up, tucked the automatic into his waistband and left as silently as the first. Tension flowed out of James like spilled *cerveza*. Weeks of delicate and dangerous negotiation had paid off. He smiled at the boy and said '*Es finito*, Luis'.

Of course it wasn't really finished. The Mendez dynasty might not miss a half-million-dollar ransom, but the youngster would never forget. And fear of another kidnapping would eat like acid at the doting parents of Luis and three younger siblings. Despite investing ten times his substantial negotiator's fee to purchase the most effective package Lancaster Security Consultants could offer – toughened vehicles, anti-hijack driving courses for two chauffeurs, advanced training for six full-time bodyguards, sophisticated electronic security at their hacienda in the hills – the family could never buy peace of mind.

Two of his best operators – ex-US Government Secret Service men – were down there now, surveying the location and making recommendations. He trusted them to do a first-class job and wasn't interested in the aftermath of his Mexican adventure. That was money-making, which didn't engage James Lancaster's passion.

Unlike this. He confirmed that the target was motionless, emptied his lungs and squeezed the rifle's sensitive double-pull trigger. One more twitch of his right index finger was all that divided life from death. He released the trigger. It had taken three hours of physical exertion and another of stealth for James Lancaster to achieve affirmation that killing was no longer for him, but the effort was worthwhile.

He worked the rifle bolt, ejecting a long brass cartridge. Even at a distance of three hundred yards, the black bear in the valley bottom caught the alien mechanical sound against the wind. The animal raised a magnificent head, sniffing clean air before resuming his slow forage along the stream-edge – a trophy male in the prime of life. James wriggled back from the skyline, got to his feet and put the rifle into its fleece-lined gun slip. Cold had soaked into his bones, cramp prickled up and down his legs and the knee ruined by IRA terrorist Alex Doherty ten years before ached. But he felt good.

The transparent tag pinned to his hunting jacket was a licence from Oregon's Department of Fish & Wildlife entitling him to take one bear in the controlled spring hunt, and he could have shot the finest specimen a hunter could hope to see. The power was still there, but he had not unleashed it.

James Lancaster set out on the lonely hike back to his Grand Cherokee Jeep, parked on a Blue Mountain wilderness trail far below.

Wiltshire

GREAT BRITAIN was no longer a global player, but – inside one hour – a single British citizen could force the world's most powerful nation to its knees. Luckily for the USA, Louise Boss had no intention of waging total cyberwar. For now, she'd settle for giving the Americans the fright of their computer-dependent lives.

Louise decided to let Henry activate Trojan Horse, based on a one-hour time limit and instructions to corrupt no more than one-fifth of nominated civilian and military target systems. She could have chosen the methodology, but Henry was smarter. He'd work everything out and cause maximum grief.

Henry was her pet mainframe computer and Trojan Horse her baby – a sleeper programme that was the most destructive software package on the planet. Unlike a conventional computer virus, which infects and destroys the unwitting host, Louise's devious mathematical mind had added a deadly dimension. Trojan Horse not only possessed the ability to worm through sophisticated firewalls that defended computer systems against intruders, but also the intelligence to reprogramme their actions. The implications were awesome. Corrupting major systems essential to the functioning of a modern economy was a recipe for disaster, but ability to redirect them at will made the destructive potential apocalyptic.

Over the previous three months, Louise Boss had invisibly implanted her lethal creation in dozens of key computer systems across the United States. Though some had thus far resisted her attempts at covert penetration, Trojan Horse was obediently waiting to disrupt everything from the tax records of US citizens to K-Mart's national delivery arrangements. It was more than enough.

After entering appropriate command instructions, Louise moved the cursor across her large colour screen to the *COMMENCE ATTACK* box. She hesitated. It was almost obscene that one person should have so much power in a fingertip – a mere woman at that. But she still clicked her mouse button.

With plenty of choice, Henry proved to be in impish mood. Using a remote fault diagnosis line, he took thirty seconds to crack authorization codes allowing engineers in Pasadena to service software controlling traffic flow on the streets of Washington, DC. Seconds later, every stop light in the capital city turned red, initiating rapid degeneration towards total gridlock.

Then it got serious, as he knocked out the FBI's Infrastructure Protection Centre, lobotomizing the brain directing the nation's defences against electronic attack. From there, infection spread like rampant cancer for which there is no treatment or possible cure. Louise Boss knew what Trojan Horse was theoretically capable of, but was still impressed by unfolding drama as Henry reported successful encounters of the terminal kind.

His attention turned to money matters, with an instruction that NatBank's automatic teller machines should add an unrecorded zero to every withdrawal request. As Henry sent Trojan Horse galloping on through linked clearing systems, the word spread and unruly queues formed. Long before the specified hour was up, every ATM in America would be empty, with ten billion in cash unaccounted for.

New York's great financial institutions fared no better. Wall Street dealers on busy trading floors were paralysed when the automated system that logged frantic buying and selling crashed. Then the impossible happened. A foolproof back-up system standing between the market and anarchy was also corrupted, with every transaction recorded over the past month erased. Within minutes, the Dow-Jones Index was in free fall, triggering automatic 'sell' instructions from fund management computers which exacerbated chaos.

Louise had to admire Henry's grasp of international finance. Cannily, he left money-dealing systems intact. As the world's most stable currency plunged in headlong pursuit of the stock market, foreign exchange dealers picked up bargain dollars at scarcely credible rates. Hungry operators in London, Frankfurt and the Far East gorged like vampires at a bloodfest. When the US Federal Reserve suspended trading twelve minutes later, it would cost the nation billions to buy back the cut-price bucks.

Telephones started malfunctioning across America, and Wall Street panic turned to national hysteria – compounded by the fact that televisions were blacking out as cable networks and commercial satellites blew in sequence. Then the lights went out. Oklahoma's electricity supply failed first, but the effect swiftly rippled outwards – reaching the Canadian border within two minutes, east and west coasts inside three, Florida in four.

Henry didn't have everything his own way, wasting two minutes in an unsuccessful attempt to sabotage the

Federal Aviation Authority's regional control centre on Long Island, which directed the Eastern Seaboard's air traffic and possessed emergency generators. Louise noted the glitch and rerouted him to pastures new, but wasn't altogether sorry. She wasn't heartless, and disliked the thought of all those frightened people hanging in the air with collisions waiting to happen and nowhere to land.

The US National Crime Information Centre was next. Henry posed as the Sheriff of Flagstaff, Arizona, and cracked in-built protection like a rotten nut. Within seconds, Trojan Horse had chewed up every criminal intelligence file in the archive and was rapaciously searching for vulnerable links to other law enforcement databases. Who knew how much crime-fighting fodder would be found and consumed before the hour was up.

From law enforcement to military matters was logical progression. Henry selected a worthy opponent in the US Navy Submarine Command Centre at Newport News, Virginia. Louise watched in fascination as megaminds traded punches. Trojan Horse was inside the system, but still encountered fail-safe defences prepared by America's cleverest computer programmers. But she was better, and it was only a matter of time before that fearsome nuclear submarine fleet fell under her spell.

A telephone tinkled, disturbing rapt concentration. Annoyed, Louise moved her cursor and clicked the *END REAL-TIME SIMULATION* box. The digital elapsed timer froze at 27 minutes and 33 seconds. A flashing message appeared on-screen as Henry proudly reported current status: *SIMULATED ATTACK ON HOLD WITH 47% OF SELECTED TARGET SYSTEMS CORRUPTED.*

Not bad. Henry's partnership with Trojan Horse was working well, though she'd have to write a patch to deal with that failure to disrupt air traffic. She answered the persistent phone with a touch of asperity.

'We're trying to work down here.'

'Louise? Where's that progress report you promised? You know we must deliver Trojan Horse in a month or face contractual penalties. Conrad Lancaster has been on the phone personally, and he's most anxious that everything should go smoothly with this project. I assured him the deadline will be met.'

It was her anxious nemesis, Gordon Holland – head honcho of Omega Dynamic Systems, who let her play all day with the most advanced hardware money could buy and paid her astronomically into the bargain. Trojan Horse was all but perfected, though Louise was happy to let him sweat.

'Sod off, Gordon. You may feel the need to say "I like your aftershave" when Lancaster breaks wind, but don't lay your insecurity on me. This job will never get done if you keep hassling me every two minutes.'

Louise Boss hung up and restarted the simulation. Perhaps she'd zap Russia for dessert. Computerized systems in the CIS were defended with rather less sophistication than America's, so it should take no more than half an hour to create meltdown in Moscow.

London

THE CITY OF LONDON had been good to him, but he hated bankers – though his Lancaster Trust Corporation had grown fat with their billion-pound support. Conrad Lancaster never found difficulty in exploiting bottomless greed that spun the commercial carousel, and the men in grey had eagerly come along for the dizzy ride over two decades of aggressive expansion. But now he was being reminded of an old but painful aphorism. Bankers rush to lend you an umbrella when the sun shines, and snatch it back at the first hint of showers.

Conrad was careful to conceal contempt. The wrinkled Swiss gnome was a ticking time bomb, threatening to blow away his empire over a paltry twenty-million loan to a small but prestigious subsidiary, Omega Dynamic Systems. Studying Conrad with laser eyes, he looked up from the folder.

'I don't wish to know technical details, Herr Lancaster, but this Trojan Horse does what is expected of it?'

The accent was as precise as the man. Before replying, Conrad lit a Monte Cristo. When the cigar was drawing to his satisfaction, he fixed the gnome with an unblinking stare.

'Couldn't tell you technical details, even if you wanted to know. Highly classified and I'm not aware of them myself. But you've seen the report from Omega's managing director. Final testing is nearly complete. Trojan Horse is a state-of-the-art electronic warfare device which will be handed over to British and US Governments within the timeframe specified under the development contract. When it is . . .'

'Yes, yes, I can read. A further tranche of fifty million dollars is made available by the Americans for final production. But this money does not come for eight more weeks, yet our loan to Omega falls due tomorrow.'

Conrad injected incredulity into his voice.

'The loan will be more than covered by the next stage payment, Werner. A little flexibility has never been a problem in the past, so why get twitchy now?'

The banker smiled a shark's smile.

'The international financial community is not so large, Herr Lancaster. People talk. Only whispers thus far, but some say your company is experiencing, how shall I put it, temporary cash-flow problems? We take pride in a reputation for absolute discretion, but my board of directors must put the bank's interests first.'

Translation – pay or we'll foreclose, pouring fuel on a rumour already flickering like an embryonic bushfire. Conrad routinely used such tactics, but now this puffed-up representative of a minor Swiss bank had the nerve to try blackmailing him. He'd be lucky.

'You personally negotiated the loan, which is currently unsecured, so I do see your neck's on the block. But twenty million's hardly worth falling out over. Here's what we do. Extend the loan for three months at the existing rate, and I'll lodge enough Omega stock with the bank to provide more than adequate collateral.'

The greedy gnome pretended to ponder the proposition, but not for long. He tried to sound as though he were conferring a big favour.

'For you, Conrad, I do it. To be safe, we require thirty million sterling in Omega stock at book valuation, plus an additional two points on the interest rate until the loan is discharged, such repayment to take place within ninety days or we are entitled to liquidate the collateral. I must take share certificates and a written agreement to this effect with me today.'

Conrad Lancaster narrowed his eyes, hiding triumph. No need for the little shit to know those Omega shares were owned by the Lancaster Trust pension fund. If things ever came to the point where rival claimants had to fight over them, he'd be beyond caring.

'Twenty-five million in stock and one percentage point and we have a deal, my dear old friend.'

He puffed his cigar back to life, savouring the smoke of battle.

Moscow

IN GOOD OLD Soviet days, Gregor Gorski had enjoyed a firm hands-on role. Sadly, he was no longer a colonel in the now-defunct KGB's Fifth Directorate, and had to be more circumspect in the maelstrom boiling beneath Russia's newly democratized surface. Much as he would have liked to detonate the car bomb personally, he could only observe.

Well-insulated from prying eyes in an astrakhan coat, sable hat and red woollen scarf wrapped around the lower half of his deeply lined face, Gorski sat on a bench overlooking Moskvoretskiy Bridge, an open copy of *War and Peace* in gloved hands. A cutting wind blew across the Moskva River, stirring the unread pages of his book. Dead leaves still uncollected from the previous autumn swirled skittishly around his feet.

There was no sign of the operatives who would carry out this morning's wet job, but they were out there, also watching for their soon-to-be-late target. Personally, Gorski had nothing against the Kremlin functionary he had marked for death – an idealist who laboured hard to bring order to his corner of the chaotic government machine. But someone had to be the first victim of a terror campaign which was about to rock Moscow, and the man's ill luck was to oversee the commission charged with agreeing a final settlement with the troublesome Republic of Chechnya.

Only yesterday, a previously unknown terrorist group called the Sons of Dudayev had publicly threatened decisive military action unless there was significant progress in stalled negotiations on Chechen independence. The now-dead freedom fighter Dzhokhar Dudayev – who rocked the then Russian Federation by declaring Chechnya a free republic from his scruffy bungalow base in Moscow's Shakespeare Street – would doubtless have approved of the subtlety with which this announcement was made, in a note delivered to the State Television Service along with an unprimed explosive device. He would also have appreciated the ruthlessness with which the war of words was about to go ballistic.

The civil servant was a creature of habit. As always, his black chauffeur-driven Mercedes E200 turned on to the bridge at five minutes before the hour, allowing its important occupant to reach his Kremlin desk by nine sharp. This morning, his waiting tea would go cold. Gorski shut *War and Peace* with a snap and stood up, anticipatory eyes on the moving car.

His men were experts. Two half-kilo packages of Semtex detonated simultaneously, one beneath each rear wheel arch, against the weaker inner skin of the toughened vehicle. The explosion was not loud, though a startled cloud of pigeons rose against the elegant backdrop of St Basil's Cathedral. The Mercedes skewed to a halt, a detached wheel bouncing into the path of an oncoming truck. Within seconds, the bridge was solid with stationary traffic.

It had begun. Ex-KGB Colonel Gregor Gorski turned and walked away without a backward glance.

London

SINCE THE COLD WAR thawed, his job had become public property. Encouraged by Agency image strategists back at Langley, Wes Remington had even discussed his work on *Breakfast with Frost*, correctly billed as the Central Intelligence Agency's London Chief of Station. They were all having to adjust to a new game plan, and his lunch companion was complaining bitterly into the thick brown concoction that passed as soup.

'You wouldn't believe what the bean counters are doing to us, Wesley. Another fifteen per cent of Five's staff have just been made redundant and you can't bend a paper clip without being asked to fill in a damage report. Bloody management consultants are the last people to tell us how to run an efficient security service. Soup all right? You've hardly touched yours.'

Angus Churchill finished scraping the glaze off his bowl. Straight-faced, Remington shook his head.

'I'm twenty pounds overweight, Gus. If I put on another ounce Helen has promised to send me to a health farm for a month. The soup looks great, but nuts and grated carrots don't appeal.'

His wife was a decisive lady, and Churchill believed him.

'Hard luck, old chap, but the lamb cutlets shouldn't hit that expanding waistline too hard. So, what's on your mind?'

The MI5 man dabbed his lips with a linen napkin. He caricatured a certain type of Englishman – tall and spare with ramrod back, sparse military moustache and drawling upper-class accent. Remington hated the way Brits clung to tradition as though it were some sort of mantra – nowhere more so than here. They were lunching at Churchill's exclusive London club, a gentlemen-only relic of the nineteenth century. When would they wise up? Still, the Brits were ruthless when it came to defending shrunken territory, so Remington trod carefully.

'My people are concerned. Langley's picked up a whisper that the Russians know about Trojan Horse. We wouldn't be happy if they got to ride that particular thoroughbred, Gus.'

Churchill removed his blade-like nose from a glass of red wine and sipped appreciatively before replying.

'This really is an exceptional claret. You should try it, or does the delightful Helen think you have a drink problem too? No need to worry about Trojan Horse. The Russians couldn't penetrate a King's Cross whore nowadays, and the security chief at Omega Dynamic Systems used to be one of ours. Took early retirement and relocated to the private sector. Excellent man, Sandy MacNaughton. One of the old school. No nonsense on his turf, believe me. Speaking of turf, you won't forget this tiny square of the world's playing field is all mine, will you?'

He jabbed a sensitive nerve. Once, the CIA thought nothing of operating in friendly countries, but times had changed. Wes Remington worked under tight guidelines, and had to think carefully before sanctioning field operations in Britain. If he got caught, the consequences didn't bear thinking about, as the smug Englishman knew. He counter-attacked.

'We've put megabucks into Trojan Horse, Gus, and don't think it didn't hurt our pride. We're supposed to be kings of cutting-edge technology, which will make Uncle Sam even more pissed if something goes wrong this end. Careers have foundered on less, and I'd sure hate to be in your hot seat if the worst happens.'

He didn't share Churchill's contempt for Russian potency. If anything, their covert activities had expanded in the climate of complacency that followed the collapse of the Evil Empire, especially in the commercial field. President Mikhail Yelkin was desperate to revive the chaotic Russian economy, and stealing a march is much easier than making one. But the MI5 man was not impressed.

'Bollocks. You're only buying Trojan Horse so your whizzkids can take it apart and devise countermeasures. I gather you've even commissioned an attack simulation on the US of A to make the job even easier. Uncle Sam's not pissed off, he's paranoid that America's long lead in information warfare might be challenged. But like it or not, Trojan Horse gives us a seat at that particular table, so we'll guard the beast as though it were the Crown Jewels. Ah, here comes the main attraction.'

Watched approvingly by Angus Churchill, a young Spanish waiter whipped off polished silver covers with a flourish and served their food. Remington looked down at shrivelled cutlets, soggy garden peas and boiled potatoes swimming for their life in thin gravy. These people were truly unbelievable.

Moscow

GREGOR GORSKI had walked briskly to the House on the Embankment, not far from the anguished sirens and frantic security activity that followed the explosive fatality on Moskvoretskiy Bridge. The distinctive edifice with twin towers and rectangular lines at Number 2 Serafimovich Street had once been the most dangerous address in Russia, housing a Party élite which Stalin went through like bubonic plague in the 1930s. But ghosts were gone, together with NKVD spyholes and a network of early bugging devices. Now, the luxury block was home to foreign businessmen and Moscow's new aristocracy – free marketeers with armed bodyguards and bundles of dollars to burn.

Number 2 also provided a Moscow base for General Sergei Sobchak, who used an apartment once occupied by Marshal Georgy Zhukov, Hero of the Soviet Union and its military saviour in the Great Patriotic War. The symbolism appealed to General Sobchak, who had an acute sense of history and anticipated a glorious part in their great country's imminent revival.

The ex-paratroop commander was Russia's best-loved politician. Sobchak's popularity had helped President Mikhail Yelkin win a second term in office, and also explained why the President and his cronies subsequently pushed their new Defence Minister into the political wilderness, almost before he'd assumed office. Starved of the oxygen of publicity, they hoped the general's appeal would burn out before the next presidential election.

But Sergei Sobchak had no intention of allowing his political career to be extinguished by self-serving opportunists. The real subject of their meeting had not been mentioned. Instead, Sobchak paced the high-ceilinged room which had become a nerve centre of resistance to the liberal virus sweeping the nation. Gregor Gorski sipped coffee at a side table, listening to the stocky former soldier pontificating on the ills afflicting Mother Russia.

True, a hard-working populace used to queue for hours to purchase the bare necessities of life. But now racketeering was rife, half the country was unemployed or unpaid and shops were awash with goods ordinary people couldn't afford. And who could deny that the Russian Bear had become toothless? The army was despised and disaffected. Vital equipment was deteriorating through lack of maintenance and spares. Strategic capability was draining away as the will supporting greatness faltered. The world once trembled when Russia whispered, but now scarcely listened when she screamed in agony.

Gregor Gorski had heard the rabble-rousing speech many times, and waited patiently. Eventually, the general came to a standstill beside him and leaned towards his co-conspirator.

'I understand some new terrorist cell has murdered a servant of the state near Red Square. A terrible outrage, but the President will not learn that these Chechens stop at nothing. We must pray no more such incidents take place.'

The general's sonorous tone was contradicted by a lupine smile. They never discussed secrets here, in case the walls still had ears – though any listeners might puzzle as to how Sobchak had learned about the recent atrocity so swiftly. Gorski replied with suitable gravity.

'We can hope, General, though instinct tells me this is only the beginning. These terrorists are set on achieving Chechnya's total independence, and President Yelkin cannot agree to that. Such a climb-down would set an unacceptable precedent for other restless satellite states. I'm afraid we must brace ourselves for further attacks.'

His face expressive, Sergei Sobchak raised bushy eyebrows.

'How soon do you suppose any such attacks might take place?'

'Regrettably, I think the answer may be *very* soon.'

Gorski rose. They shook hands. General Sobchak squeezed hard, before abruptly releasing the pressure.

'Keep me informed, Colonel. This is a serious matter with profound implications for the future of Russia. Now, if you will excuse me I have much to do. As you know, I am deeply concerned by the President's failure to secure concessions from the West regarding further NATO expansion. We must also address the equestrian situation as a matter of urgency.'

There was no mistaking the emphasis on 'equestrian'. The general's washed-out blue eyes probed his. Gorski nodded acknowledgment of the coded message and turned to leave. Home and away, his orders were confirmed.

General Sergei Sobchak intended to become the greatest President the Commonwealth of Independent States would ever have, restoring Russia's central place on the international stage. And had no intention of waiting until the next scheduled election came around.

London

WITH EFFUSIVE expressions of pleasure that the bank's valued relationship with Lancaster Trust had been maintained, the greedy gnome locked his multi-million-pound envelope of Omega stock into a leather briefcase and departed for Zurich. Or an afternoon of pleasure in the fleshpots of Soho. Conrad Lancaster didn't care either way.

As he ate a solitary luncheon in the oak-panelled private dining room at Lancaster House, Conrad gave no thought to problems solved, especially small ones. An assault course stretched ahead, and he would need to be at his best to emerge undamaged. He tinkled a small brass handbell to summon the waitress. She knew his preferences without being told, appearing with a third serving of chocolate ice cream. Food made him feel good, fuelling determination.

After coffee, he would address the sliding share price. If Lancaster Trust stock fell too far, it would invalidate loan guarantees and trigger unwelcome complications. Werner's venal behaviour would be repeated as bankers around the globe scrambled for £500 million pound's-worth of flesh, and it would soon become painfully obvious that the once-ample carcass was bare.

That couldn't be permitted. Big business was like chess, and Conrad was a grandmaster – initiating moves long before opponents discerned his strategy. In this case, he would buy in Lancaster Trust stock through offshore front companies, boosting the share price. The newly purchased stock could then be resold or pledged against further loans needed to fund the initial purchases. Checkmate in one.

Before he made the play, a pawn needed sweeping from the board. His own newspapers were not slow to trumpet their parent's virile commercial virtues, but others in the media were less compliant. Jenny Symes was a persistent pain. Her *Guardian Angel* television show attracted nine million viewers, and the bitch had been sniffing around the pension fund. Symes hadn't hit pay dirt, but now was not the moment to antagonize her.

Conrad had graciously granted the interview she'd been after for months. He would put on a good show. Flamboyant personality helped, but cameras liked him, never failing to record the patent sincerity that confirmed his probity in the minds of *hoi polloi*.

He tugged down the well-cut waistcoat that helped conceal a massive girth and shrugged on his jacket. Conrad was used to overwhelming women, who seemed to find the combination of charisma, money and power more than outweighed his ample proportions. Jenny Symes could be switched off without even realizing he was pushing her decorative buttons.

The laid-back Englishman who languidly lunched with London CIA boss Remington was not the only persona Angus Churchill possessed. To MI5 grandees occupying the pinnacle that would one day be his, he was a loyal and talented Assistant Director – a man who appreciated that it was sometimes necessary to compromise principle for the greater good. To those who worked for him, he was the hard taskmaster of K Branch – a chief who liked things done his way and didn't welcome initiative amongst the Indians.

John Tolley fell into the latter category, looking up from a surveillance report to find his superior beside him.

Churchill was glowering. Lunch had obviously gone badly, and a budget review meeting started in five minutes. Spots of vivid colour showed on high cheekbones, as a result of anger or an excess of lunch-time wine – or both, if his outburst was anything to go by.

'These bloody Yanks have got a nerve, stomping in here and telling me how to do my job. Remington thinks the Russians are after Trojan Horse and I want you to tell me he's wrong, John.'

Tolley adopted a soothing tone. It was K Branch's task to monitor the activities of foreign intelligence services. If the new cyberweapon was compromised, Churchill wouldn't climb one more rung of the career ladder, let alone capture the knighthood he coveted.

'He's wrong. We'd know if any of the regulars had made a move in that direction. None of them have been within twenty miles of Omega Dynamic Systems.'

No point in stoking the fire by adding that the Russians were perfectly capable of targeting Trojan Horse, should they have discovered – despite maximum security classification – the project's existence. If they had, and went after the cyberweapon, they wouldn't use established embassy intelligence personnel known to Five. Churchill aimed a long finger at Tolley's chest, the colour in his cheeks intensifying.

'Don't give me that "usual suspects" crap. A prize like this would more than justify a special operation. CIA says Moscow's lusting after the damn thing and I can promise you this. Your *cojones* will be in the slammer if Langley's right, so I suggest you get on the case as of yesterday.'

The thirty-one-year-old counter-intelligence officer couldn't repress a flash of frustration.

'And where am I supposed to find the resources? We're overstretched as it is.'

Bad attitude. Bad timing. Bad move. Churchill's voice became dangerously reasonable.

'You're a bright young man, John. I like to think you have a future here, so I'll pretend I didn't hear that last remark. Put a spare girlfriend on the job, deploy the lame dog, log some unpaid overtime. Use your bloody initiative if you have to, but do it.'

Lowering his smoking finger, the future head of MI5 turned on his heel and marched towards the budget meeting.

She ended the interview with a sycophantic sign-off. It was no less than Conrad Lancaster expected. While her crew packed away, she made idle conversation with the self-satisfied tycoon. Men were such fools.

To avoid suspicion, Jenny Symes had started aggressively, but soon allowed his slimy charm to ooze over her. The possibility that she might actually want suave evasions and downright lies on tape didn't seem to have occurred to Conrad. He sat back massively in his leather chair, causing waistcoat buttons to strain alarmingly.

'Mind if I smoke, Miss Symes? A good torpedo never hurt anyone.'

'Of course not. I love the smell of cigar smoke. You've been very frank. I have a job to do, so won't apologize for questioning you about the pension fund. But I'm really pleased we managed to clear everything up.'

She felt a tingle akin to sexual excitement. Conrad finished lighting the cigar and fixed her with a conspiratorial 'if I were twenty years younger' look. Jenny responded with a star-struck smile. The fat slob had no idea what was coming. She was working on a disgruntled ex-Lancaster Trust executive who might supply final jigsaw pieces. If not, someone would talk. The complete picture would make great television. Conrad Lancaster's recent performance on camera was criminally flawed. Her victim smoothed jet-black dyed hair with an unconsciously revealing gesture – shifting charm into overdrive and returning her smile with interest.

'So am I, Jenny, so am I. I can call you Jenny? It's a great satisfaction of this job, providing work for thousands of people. And as I said, we take pride in looking after employees properly, even after retirement. Lancaster Trust is one big family. Speaking of which, I'm a great family man myself. I may spend lonely weekday nights here in town, but I always get down to Gloucestershire at weekends. My wife Elizabeth and son Tom are my real source of strength in this cruel world.'

Lonely weekday nights? That was subtle. Her crew had left and Jenny Symes rose to follow, composing an expression of vacuous admiration.

'I'm only sorry to have wasted your time . . . Conrad.'

The unsuspecting robber baron got up and lumbered round his huge desk to show her out, draping an avuncular arm around her shoulders.

To intelligence professionals, trust is a worthless commodity. Wes Remington rated MI5's firm promise to protect Trojan Horse accordingly. The Brits' new military software package was simply too powerful, too destructive in the wrong hands.

When the United States was threatened, Remington didn't take chances – and to hell with constricting guidelines and the snooping Congressional Committee that policed restrictive rules. As desk jockeys at Langley were already concerned, he could always flag the situation officially. But even if clearance came through for an operation in friendly Britain, it might be too late.

One thing written nowhere in the CIA's approved-conduct manual was nevertheless understood by every Company employee. There are times when it becomes necessary to initiate independent action, preferably using reliable but deniable manpower. Should wheels come off, you duly deny. If that fails, the responsible officer is given a rogue tag and thrown to the vultures. This was such a time, and he wouldn't shirk the challenge or worry about his pension.

Remington decided to use the American freelance operator code-named Beasley, who had served him well twice before. Ironically, he was originally recommended by SIS, MI5's sister service. Little love was lost between jealous siblings, and the British foreign intelligence outfit also operated illegally on home soil, often engaging hired help to avoid the possibility of official recrimination. They'd used Beasley, been impressed and passed him on.

The man was expensive, efficient and – most important of all – discreet to the point of paranoia. The identity of his clients was safer than the Coca-Cola formula, as was the nature of any business he might undertake on their behalf. All this passed through Remington's mind as he loaded the fax in his study at home in St John's Wood, close to Lord's cricket ground. The message would be meaningless to anyone else – a series of apparently random numbers. But Beasley would know which public telephone to call, and when.

Neither was it possible to trace the ultimate destination of his call to arms. Remington knew, because he'd tried. The fax would go through a series of relays before reaching its ultimate destination, which might be anywhere in the world. He approved of that impenetrable procedure, and pressed the *SEND* key.

Moscow

FOR REASONS of security, Gregor Gorski was keeping things tighter than a sturgeon's vent. There were just five of them waiting in the flat behind McDonald's on Pushkin Square. The irony of this location appealed. These bitter, angry young men represented tens of thousands – soldiers tired of explaining to wives and families why wages were never paid, soldiers who had to grow vegetables on parade grounds and sell weapons to survive, soldiers humiliated by a country they had served well, soldiers who hated undisciplined Western values polluting Russia.

When soldier-turned-politician General Sergei Sobchak promised to place such grievances at the top of his policy agenda, the Russian Army believed him. Felt hope. Saw the tantalizing prospect of regaining status and respect, not to mention regular monthly salary payments.

Using wide-ranging contacts, Gorski had found trustworthy officers who believed actions spoke louder than indignant words, and were prepared to do anything that needed to be done. Anything. He studied five determined faces, seeing no signs of weakness. These men were fighting to regain self-respect, their very lives. He placed a buff folder on the scrubbed wooden table.

'Congratulations, gentlemen. This morning's opening skirmish went well. A communiqué from the Sons of Dudayev has claimed responsibility and threatened further reprisals should no progress be made on the independence issue. If our vacillating government is minded to make concessions, the Chechnya Commission will surely be paralysed by the sudden unavailability of its hard-working chairman.'

Their chosen leader – a thirty-six-year-old major who had lost his left eye in Afghanistan – put a hand on the folder.

'But the Sons of Dudayev are impatient?'

Gorski placed his own hands together as though in prayer.

'Thirsting for blood. You know Chechens, Valery. A violent bunch. I think you'll find they mean to rampage until their demands are met. Who knows? Their ultimate objective might be President Yelkin himself. It's all there. Names and dates, together with a detailed briefing on the habits and schedule of each target. The entire programme has been sanctioned, so you start immediately.'

Major Valery Filatov glanced around the room. His good eye roved over an assortment of boxed military hardware, while the prosthetic twin stared straight ahead. Satisfied, he returned his disconcertingly unbalanced gaze to Gregor Gorski.

'You're right, Colonel. With inside information like this at their fingertips, the Sons of Dudayev could do great damage in a short period of time. The impact of such a mindless terror campaign on an unstable government hardly bears thinking about.'

'Indeed not, Major. I shall await developments with interest. Now, if you have some glasses in this place, I suggest we drink to a better future.'

Gregor Gorski produced the bottle of unobtainable Wolfschmidt Riga vodka which had been weighing down his astrakhan coat. So much for the home front. Within one week, the President of Russia would become the final victim of the violent Sons of Dudayev, before the new terror group vanished as mysteriously as it had appeared.

Now he could think about General Sobchak's overseas objectives. No foreign government could continue to ignore Mother Russia, if she possessed the power to destroy them without firing so much as a rusty peashooter. Every one of them would soon be forced to sit up and take notice, because he, Gregor Gorski, was about to obtain the deadly Trojan Horse cyberweapon from Britain.

Gloucestershire

THE NEW HALL ESTATE encompassed over three thousand contoured Gloucestershire acres, plus a hamlet, six substantial farmhouses and a dozen pretty workers' cottages. The eponymous New Hall had been built of honey-coloured Cotswold stone in 1685, replacing an earlier manor house destroyed when melting mutton fat caught fire.

Conrad Lancaster was not a natural Lord of the Manor, though he entertained business contacts at winter pheasant shoots, and his helicopter often landed on the former croquet lawn bearing important contacts who might be impressed by graciously old-fashioned country living. Conrad moved in exalted circles, and three heads of state had visited New Hall during Liz Lancaster's reign as chatelaine.

On these occasions, she played the trophy wife to perfection – ensuring each guest's every need was met with courteous service, presiding over cordon bleu meals, dressing in a way that made husbands envious and wives spit, making intelligent conversation and no secret of the fact that she doted on Conrad. Occasionally, she was expected to repeat the trick at important London functions.

But for his interest in their nine-year-old son, Liz would hardly have seen her husband. This suited her fine, though she didn't object to parental visits. A child needs a father, and Conrad never misbehaved when he came to see Tom. Their modus vivendi was well established. They hadn't shared a bed since Tom was six months old, a banishment Conrad reluctantly accepted when Liz stated the alternative – no wife, no child, expensive divorce. After a period of outrage, insults and petty humiliations, he settled for indifference.

She understood why he countenanced an arrangement that lacerated his pride. Conrad's guiding principle was simple. If he set out to achieve something, he must always succeed. Being pragmatic, her husband added a rider. If he should fail, nobody must know. Providing she played the adoring wife when called upon to do so and dutifully nurtured his son and heir, Mrs Conrad Lancaster could write her own cheques.

As deals went, it was bearable. But Liz had become restless. It was easy to believe she liked her privileged life. To convince herself Tom benefited from growing up in this peaceful place and would one day benefit from his inheritance. To seek undemanding social contact in the easy routine of moneyed country society. Even to find uncomplicated sexual release. All true, but not the truth.

Without absorbing the contents, Liz finished reading proposed menus for a weekend house party three weeks hence, when Conrad intended to entertain a clutch of international bankers in lavish style. She was sitting by the mullioned library window, watching dappled fallow deer graze amongst oaks planted when the last Henry was on the throne.

A naïve but determined Liz Greener had abandoned Australia aged seventeen – leaving behind an outback family that didn't understand her dreams – to escape the inevitability of marrying some one-dimensional man whose horizon ended at the boundaries of an arid sheep station. Neither did she wish to bear children whose only ambition would be to plod along their forebears' deeply trodden footsteps in dusty red earth.

But she'd escaped from one prison to another. Liz thought increasingly about the past, and four Lancaster men who had shaped her adult life. Falling in love with soldier-boy James. Working as funny, self-effacing Peter's PA. The exciting career path which opened up when she transferred professionally then personally to the dynamic Conrad. Giving birth to Tom, the most amazing experience of all. Now Peter had been dead for a decade, and she was James's stepmother. She hadn't spoken to Jamie since their last, bitter-sweet night together at her London flat, soon after his gentle brother committed suicide.

Why had she surrendered so quickly to Conrad's determined amorous pursuit after James left for America?

However often she asked, Liz never came up with a satisfactory answer. The decision seemed sensible at the time – but her own resolve, Conrad's powerful mystique and her stimulating job had all failed to survive intimacy. Her husband was an insensitive, greedy man, who rightly regarded her as bought and paid for. All the easy living in the world couldn't make up for that humiliation, or painful awareness that she was hiding from the very world she once ran away to find. If it wasn't for Tom . . .

The reverie dissolved. She had resisted her husband's suggestion that the boy should be sent away to acquire a stiff upper lip, and would soon be picking him up from the local school. There was a lot of emotional capital invested in Tom. Starting over was a daunting prospect, but she had to try. That elusive truth was simple. She stayed because her husband would never let her break their bargain, and walk away with his son and heir. But now she had a greater fear – that her child would be trampled and degraded by Conrad Lancaster, like every other person he'd ever been close to.

Except James, who – even as a child – had never retreated from his domineering parent by so much as an inch.

London

UNNECESSARY WORK was the last thing he needed, but perhaps this *was* necessary. The CIA sometimes flapped needlessly, but when they spoke it mostly paid to listen. And with politicians screwing down public spending until the thread stripped, MI5 couldn't afford any image-tarnishing blunders.

John Tolley sighed and cleared a stack of pending files from his screen – there were so many he couldn't decide where to begin, anyway. He found the direct line number in his electronic notebook and picked up the phone. If nothing else, the call would be recorded and logged, so his tetchy department head could have no excuse for another gratuitous outburst. Angus Churchill's mood was unlikely to have improved during the budget meeting.

'Alexander MacNaughton.'

The voice brought back memories. The laconic Scot had been his mentor at MI5, before an enforced cost-cutting transfer to the private sector.

'Sandy, it's John.'

Omega's security director didn't miss a beat.

'Ah, young Tolley. Still cutting a swathe through the lucky lassies?'

He sounded genial, but that shrewd brain would be in overdrive. Tolley gave him a clue.

'Seen any strange characters hanging round that glass monstrosity of yours lately?'

MacNaughton snorted dismissively.

'The place is overflowing with them. You know what these computer *wunderkinder* are like. Some of them make the dearly beloved Gus Churchill of fond memory look like a raving New Age dropout. Anything I should know?'

'Not on the phone. Thought I might slip down for a chat tomorrow morning, if that's okay.'

'We don't let just anyone in, but Fort Omega might lower the drawbridge for a spook in shining armour. About ten?'

'Eleven would be better.'

A late-night session at MI5's Thames House headquarters beckoned, and Tolley wasn't the world's earliest riser. MacNaughton signed off cheerfully.

'I'll look forward to letting you bend my ancient ear over elevenses, then.'

The hell he would. MacNaughton was cunning. He'd burn midnight oil, too, rechecking every aspect of security at Omega Dynamic Systems. John Tolley replaced the phone and reached for the private address book that never left his person. So much for his eagerly anticipated dinner engagement with ice-cool Brunhilde, the bombshell blonde bond dealer from Dresdner Bank.

The penthouse apartment was a spectacular warehouse conversion overlooking the River Thames near Tower Bridge. It had been acquired by a Nassau-based company back in 1996, but the vendor's solicitors had little doubt about the true identity of the new owners. The purchase had been completed by a small man speaking with a pronounced Eastern European accent, accompanied by two large men in heavy overcoats who didn't speak at all.

He paid a million pounds in cash, producing packets of new fifty-pound notes from a suitcase. When the money was banked, the solicitors dutifully reported that yet another prime property had been sold to the Russian mafia. The fact was logged by the authorities, but the National Criminal Intelligence Service had many such records. As no UK laws had been broken and manpower was short, the information was stored in an inactive file.

Picture windows curtained, the apartment had been providing temporary refuge for four men with a mission. Two had already left, to begin operations elsewhere. Two remained, but would soon be leaving. The weather was fine, but they were not tempted to use the suntrap roof terrace. Instead, they sat before a wide-screen Sony TV set, drinking American beer and watching a pornographic video created by the entertainment branch back in Moscow. As a bemused Alsatian dog performed lewd tricks, they laughed uproariously.

Wes Remington of the CIA was not the only one who could call on able freelance assistance. Gregor Gorski also possessed good contacts, and the prospect of favours that might flow from assisting Russia's next President in his hour of need had proved irresistible to the thirty-nine-year-old leader of Moscow's most influential crime syndicate. No promises had been made by the ex-KGB man as negotiations were finalized over tea from an exquisite eighteenth-century filigree silver samovar, but none were needed. Both understood how the system worked.

When the time came to invest in an even more profitable future, the mafia boss had duly despatched four of his best men to England, to carry out Gregor Gorski's instructions. Had the incompetent British authorities managed to intercept and question them, no harm would have been done. Their mission was innocent, their story verifiable – the evidence there for all to see. They were collecting the new Fairline Squadron 65 luxury cruiser to be found in the Yacht Haven at nearby St Katharine's Dock. They'd been in the country for two weeks while the powerful boat underwent sea trials, out from Ipswich. Now they were enjoying a short break in London, before sailing her down to the South of France.

This was true, and within the hour *Lara's Song* would slip her moorings and motor down the Thames to the sea, there to set course for Monaco. If she made a small diversion on the way, who would be any the wiser?

It was turning into a good day. First, he'd zapped a gnome and averted financial catastrophe. Then he'd charmed the pants off a troublesome female TV reporter – perhaps literally. As always when things went well, Conrad Lancaster was in bullish mood. He was booming positive suggestions to the Group Financial Editor of his newspapers.

'No need to go over the top, but a small story in the dailies about Lancaster Trust shares firming up ahead of developments in the planned disposal programme might be interesting. Another hot tip straight from the horse's mouth, though I suggest you quote City rumours as the source.'

Conrad did not regard himself as a hands-off proprietor. The senior journalist stirred uncomfortably, well aware that the suggestion was an order. Without conviction, he pandered to professionalism.

'What developments?'

'When I'm ready, you'll be notified. By the way, you should run an in-depth analysis of the likely return to both investors and parent company when Lancaster Trust floats the newspapers as a separate entity. Gripping stuff. Next Sunday's business supplement would be the place for that, which gives you plenty of time to get the facts straight.'

'Based on?'

The Financial Editor was a trier. Conrad laced plump fingers across his full stomach and beamed happily.

'The new set of profit projections you can collect on the way out, Donald. Based on those figures, it looks as though the flotation will raise rather more than we first thought, say five hundred million in round figures. Make sure I see first proofs of both stories, as usual. I'd hate unfortunate errors to creep in.'

His face taut with unvoiced disapproval, the journalist took his cue. Conrad watched the stiff retreating back with amusement. Senior employees were all the same – terrified of losing over-fat salaries, executive cars and exalted status. He exploited their fear ruthlessly.

Conrad got up and poured a cognac. He held the glass to his fleshy nose and inhaled deeply. Things were looking up. All he had to do was make enough smoke to conceal the Lancaster Trust's precarious position for a few more weeks. Time for another cigar.

If powerful men have a collective Achilles' heel, it's irrational conviction that they're invulnerable. Exploiting this weakness, TV reporter Jenny Symes was stealthily stalking Conrad Lancaster, whose self-belief went off the ego scale. She finished reviewing the tape of their interview. Suitably edited, bland platitudes about a deep sense of responsibility for the Lancaster Trust corporate family would return like a razor-edged boomerang to decapitate him. Conrad was using and abusing pension fund assets to paper over widening cracks in Lancaster Trust's complex financial structure, but she still had a problem. Proof.

Her *Guardian Angel* consumer-watch programme was made by an independent production company in which she had a quarter share, but the BBC commissioning editor had final say on content. And the Corporation was cautious when it came to taking on counter-punching heavyweights with London's finest civil litigators in their corner. To that extent, the Conrads of this world were right. The Establishment *was* over-respectful of their status, to a point where they could get away with anything short of murder, or being caught in some model's bed wearing suspenders, black silk stockings and a Saracens Rugby Club jersey.

Jenny Symes walked through from the editing suite of Pandora's Box Productions and asked her secretary to get Michael Dickson on the phone. The former Company Secretary of Lancaster Trust Financial Services knew everything, and she expected him to reveal all. Though officially retiring early on health grounds, he'd actually been dismissed for daring to point out trifling legal regulations applying to unfettered use of pension fund assets. Conrad obviously assumed a generous severance provision

– paid annually over a ten-year-period – would guarantee silence.

But the forceful tycoon's judgment in these matters was sometimes flawed. She recalled a well-publicized incident when he entered a lift at Lancaster House, only to find it occupied by a young smoker. Plucking the cigarette from the boy's mouth, Conrad had ground it out on Wilton carpet and angrily announced that *he* was the only person allowed to smoke in the building. Removing a wad of notes from his trouser pocket, he thrust them into the quaking transgressor's top pocket with a terse 'You're fired'. After silently descending to the foyer, the youth departed like a ballistic missile, not even pausing to leave the visitor's pass that all delivery messengers were required to carry.

And Conrad had made another mistake in assuming that everyone subscribed to his own venal standards. Jenny Symes was confident she'd almost nudged Dickson to the point where residual conscience and resentment at being thrown on to the executive garbage heap would tip the embittered ex-insider into a passionate outpouring of devastating truth. On camera.

When that happened – and happen it would, because Jenny was very good at her job – she'd skin Conrad Lancaster alive.

Gloucestershire

WHEN PEOPLE have nothing to fear, they drop into lazy habits. Liz Lancaster had something to fear, but didn't know it yet. Her black BMW convertible swept past the farm track where their hired Mercedes panel van was unobtrusively parked in the shadow of an ancient barn. She was using the usual road at the normal time, facilitating their task. Seconds after the car vanished, a motorcycle crossed their line of vision. The two watchers exchanged glances. The biker was tasked with following the woman, reporting progress by mobile phone. If she deviated from established routine, they would intercept her wherever they could. It had to be today.

The driver climbed down and urinated against the

barn's mossy stonework. His mate was drinking coffee from a flask. If anyone saw them, it would be natural to assume they'd parked off the narrow lane for a break. He leaned against the van and studied well-manicured, empty countryside.

His name was Dmitry Travkin, but his neighbours in Hay-on-Wye had known him for a decade as antiquarian book dealer Andrew Rosson, who specialized in rare first editions of European nineteenth-century novels. He only knew his coffee-swigging companion was Viktor Kovalev because they'd been together at KGB training school for five years, learning how to blend into Britain. Viktor had become Bill Hellis, purveyor of previously abused furniture to the underclasses of London's East End. Now they were both English, and Russian *doppelgängers* were no more.

The other two team members were hired hands, part of a four-man group sent from Moscow to make up the numbers. He knew only their first names – Igor, Konstantin, Nikolai and Yegor. Rosson didn't care for these hard-faced mercenaries, disparagingly nicknaming them John, Paul, George and Ringo after famous Beatles they faintly resembled.

Apparently, they were ex-soldiers who became career criminals after leaving the forces – reliable men who would make no trouble, obey orders and do their jobs. Enough of the Slav remained in him for Rosson to mistrust the strangers, and understand that this might not be the whole story. But it hardly mattered. He wasn't here to serve Russia, but to earn a lot of money. The KGB no longer looked after former sleeper agents, and regular payments that supplemented his income as a book dealer had stopped without explanation years before.

The world had changed, and he was happy to change too – to be and remain an Englishman. But Rosson had a British wife and two small children – a family with needs. So when his former KGB controller asked for help and promised a handsome fee, he had packed a bag and told his wife he must view a nobleman's long-lost library that had surfaced in the Czech Republic.

After a complex briefing, the order he'd received from Gregor Gorski in Prague was simple. Elizabeth Lancaster and the child Thomas were to be secured and held, but not damaged. The implications had worried Rosson, but second thoughts were not an option. The only way out was to have refused the initial summons, and that wasn't a possibility either. To secure compliance, Gorski had hinted that his secret past might be made known to the authorities.

Hobson's choice, as the English would say, so Andrew Rosson intended to make the best of things. It wasn't all bad. He checked his watch. Soon, at least, he could begin to earn money that would make his family comfortable for life.

Moscow

GENNADY CHURKOV wasn't aware of the fact, but he had incurred the Sons of Dudayev's extreme displeasure. Indeed, with the death of an unfortunate Kremlin official, he had risen right to the top of their 'most wanted' list.

Nobody would be surprised that Chechen separatists hated Churkov. The ambitious politician had made many fiery speeches in the State Duma, asserting Russia's absolute right of sovereignty over Chechnya, and loudly condemned General Sergei Sobchak for brokering a premature ceasefire in the undeclared war that might eventually have subdued the rebellious southern republic.

The self-important Speaker of the Russian Parliament – with three eyes on the presidency – didn't seem to care that General Sobchak's initiative had saved thousands of army conscripts, along with greater numbers of Chechen civilians and – most important of all – Russian pride. All he could see was temporary humiliation, conveniently forgetting that superpowers never win guerrilla conflicts against freedom fighters in inhospitable terrain. That awareness passed Churkov by, though perhaps he would understand a little better when he looked down the sort of deadly gun barrel to which – from the safety of Moscow – he so casually consigned lesser mortals.

Major Valery Filatov took his responsibility as leader of

the fictional Sons of Dudayev seriously. His back to the river, he was watching the Duma – good eye fastened unblinkingly on the massive White House, now fully restored after its damaging confrontation with the Russian Army. According to the information supplied by Gregor Gorski, the target would work inside until late evening. He would then walk with two bodyguards to a Hungarian restaurant located in a basement off Kalinin prospekt. There, he would eat alone as gypsy violins played, before visiting his amply endowed mistress and eventually returning home to a frumpy wife at dawn.

Although many hours should pass before anything happened, the one-eyed observer felt no impatience. They had already decided when and where to kill Gennady Churkov, the disgusting politician who was a traitor to their cause.

Gloucestershire

WHEN LIZ LANCASTER returned the menus for Conrad's weekend house party without making changes, the housekeeper had eyed her keenly. Mrs Bernadelli was nobody's fool – a ferociously efficient Scot of Italian extraction who missed little. They were as close to real friendship as employer and employee could reasonably be. When Liz took Tom and left New Hall for the last time, she would miss Rita Bernadelli. Sensing her mood, the older woman had seemed to be on the point of saying something, but took the menus without comment.

Her husband was New Hall's chauffeur-handyman, but Liz used his services only for infrequent journeys to London. Duncan Bernadelli had been polishing the Range Rover when she collected her car from the stable block. As always, he'd offered to drive. As always, she'd refused. Liz was a fast, confident pilot, and throwing her BMW around Cotswold lanes was one of life's small but satisfying pleasures.

Today, especially, she pushed the car to its limits. By the time she reached Bourton-on-the-Water primary school, Liz was feeling more cheerful. She parked in the yard, beside the original schoolhouse – a stone building with impressive full-height front gable window and tiny cupola. The tide of home-going children flowed past her and mingled with waiting parents. Her son was always last out, reluctant to leave a world of learning he found fascinating.

Liz gave him five minutes, then embarked on a search-and-rescue mission. Over the years, the school had been extended, acquiring a sprawl of temporary classrooms that somehow became permanent. As she wondered where to start, Tom appeared, school uniform immaculate and over-full leather satchel causing his left shoulder to droop. His earnest little face brightened when he saw her.

'Mum, did you know that earthworms are hermaphrodites? That means they're boys and girls at the same time. They can have babies without . . . well, you know.'

She knew, and suspected he did too. As he scrambled into the BMW, fastening his seat belt without being told, Tom chattered enthusiastically about the day's biological discovery. Liz made a small bet with herself that his first action when they got home would be to find a garden fork and dig up some specimens for close examination.

As they drove down the steep lane from the school, something else mercifully attracted his attention, just before the conversation got awkward.

'Look, a Honda Hornet. Four in-line cylinders, sixteen-valve six-hundred-cc engine developing ninety-five brake horsepower, top speed around one-forty. They're brilliant.'

Tom indicated a motorcycle parked by the church. The range of her son's knowledge was amazing, but she hardly glanced at the leather-clad rider, who was talking on a mobile phone. Instead, she reacted like any mother.

'Don't think you're ever having one of those dangerous things, that's all.'

'Mum!'

Liz Lancaster ignored the protest. She never drove recklessly when Tom was in the car, and would never permit him to ride a motorcycle. He was the most precious thing in her life.

Andrew Rosson's plan wasn't complicated. The stunted

biker – Ringo – was shadowing Liz Lancaster, using a stolen motorcycle with false plates. When he reported their targets leaving Bourton-on-the-Water, Bill Hellis would drive the van down and wait where track met lane, Rosson beside him. The narrow country road with grass-ridged centre was infrequently used, but they couldn't risk obstructing unexpected traffic.

When her car approached, they'd turn out in front of the black BMW. The ambush site was two hundred yards further on, where high banks funnelled down to a hump-backed stone bridge over a tiny stream. Bill would pretend to stall the van as he essayed the awkward crossing, forcing her to stop. The last team member – baby-faced Paul – would come up behind in his Vauxhall Astra estate car, boxing the BMW. Behind him, Ringo would slew his Honda across the lane, stopping anyone gatecrashing. Liz Lancaster was reputed to be stubborn, but when a gun is held to a child's head the mother is inclined to co-operate.

The targets would be put into the van, thoughtfully carpeted with offcuts from Bill's shop in Roman Road. After reaching the main road via a maze of well-reconnoitred lanes, their escape route followed the fast A429 past Cirencester and Malmesbury, joining the M4 at Junction 17 – where the van could vanish into westbound traffic on the busy motorway. Paul and Ringo would tidy up – dumping the motorcycle and concealing Liz Lancaster's BMW before following in the Astra. The two Russians would travel independently to the remote final destination, after which the Mercedes van could be driven back to London and returned to the hire depot.

However often Rosson searched for flaws, the plan was solid. The mobile phone on the parcel shelf warbled. He answered, hearing Ringo's accented voice over the muted throbbing of a stationary motorcycle.

'They move. Looks like usual route.'

'Stay close behind until the Astra takes over, then drop back to protect our arses.'

He raised a gloved thumb. As Bill Hellis started the engine, Rosson retrieved a pair of sawn-off shotguns from beneath the passenger seat. They were loaded with buckshot cartridges. Maiming and killing weren't on the kidnap agenda, but it was second nature to expect the unexpected.

The drive from New Hall to Bourton-on-the-Water had taken around fifteen minutes. The more sedate return journey would last twenty. Liz Lancaster liked the school run, which provided talking time with her son – even though he bombarded her with questions to which she often had no accurate answers. Right now, she was struggling with the relative merits of Supermarine Spitfires and Focke Wulf 190s – World War II fighter aircraft weren't one of her specialities.

She resolved the problem by offering a trip to the vintage aircraft collection at Duxford Airfield, a treat Tom had asked for several times. For good measure, she promised to make a weekend of it – throwing in the RAF Museum at Hendon and Lambeth's Imperial War Museum. He was so impressed that he fell silent, until his interest was taken by a panel van lurching on to the narrow lane, fifty yards in front. Braking hard, Liz swore to herself. She might not be hurrying, but still hated the thought of being stuck behind a snail until they reached the back gates of New Hall's walled park.

'They've got a Sopwith Camel at the War Museum, Mum, and you can go in a flight simulator. That van's a Mercedes diesel. The diesel engine was invented by a man called Rudolph Diesel. He was German, too.'

Liz laughed.

'You're going to write an encyclopedia when you grow up, aren't you?'

He took the question seriously.

'I don't think so. You know I want to be a pilot and fly big jets.'

'Fine by me, but your father has other ideas.'

They ran downhill and the irritating van slowed to walking pace. There was a bridge at the bottom which Liz – having once scraped a front wing taking it too fast – knew from experience had to be treated with respect. She checked the mirror. A white estate car was right behind. She rarely encountered traffic on this stretch, but now the place was making a passable imitation of Piccadilly Circus on a Friday afternoon.

The woman reacted fast when she saw them coming – two threatening overalled figures in blue balaclava helmets carrying sawn-off shotguns. She engaged the BMW's central locking system, revved the engine and cast a desperate glance over her shoulder. Beside her, the boy watched developments with interest, as though this were a game.

There was nowhere to go. Paul had stopped the Astra within two feet of her rear bumper and was already on the move, carrying a seven-pound sledgehammer. Ahead, their van blocked the bridge. To the sides, high tree-lined banks would have defied the hardiest off-roader. Andrew Rosson took the driver's side, Bill Hellis the passenger door. Rosson raised his gun. He spoke loudly, in case the woollen balaclava muffled his order.

'Open the doors, Mrs Lancaster, or we'll smash our way in. Just be sensible and nobody will get hurt.'

She thought about it, but only for a second. Her window slid down. He admired the composure with which she accepted the inevitable. The handsome face showed no fear, merely anger, and her voice betrayed determined Australian origins.

'What do you want. Money? I haven't got any with me.'

Impressive effort, especially as she must have realized that this was no bizarre highway robbery. He gestured with the gun.

'Both of you get out of the car. Now.'

She surrendered reluctantly, opening the door and turning to her son.

'Do as he says, Tom. Don't be frightened. Everything will be okay.'

Liz Lancaster slid out, a slim red-haired figure in cream sweater and black slacks. The boy emerged from the other side, asking Bill Hellis a question. His clear voice contained genuine curiosity.

'Are you gangsters?'

Paul put down the hammer, pulled back her arms and bound the wrists with parcel tape. Liz Lancaster stared defiantly at Rosson's masked face, grey-green eyes meeting his. She really was a most attractive woman – a worthy asset for such a powerful man as Conrad Lancaster. She remained motionless as unflinching eyes were taped in turn. He took a shoulder and guided her towards the van. Similarly trussed and blindfolded, the boy was also on his way.

With a quick glance round, Andrew Rosson pulled off his balaclava and opened the rear doors. It would take no more than two minutes for Liz and Tom Lancaster to vanish from the face of the earth. Not bad for one antiquarian bookseller, a junk dealer from London's East End and two mafiosi from Moscow.

Wiltshire

OTHER PEOPLE'S RULES were for others, not Louise Boss. The twenty-nine-year-old computer programmer had discovered she was different on her first day at nursery school, when it became apparent that new classmates were incapable of simple mental arithmetic, like calculating the square root of 2,250,000.

The moment haunted her. Proud parents must have puffed her capabilities in advance. A teacher who should have known better had asked the question, turning to the board and writing up that very number. Before the last zero was completed, Louise said 'fifteen hundred' without conscious thought – an easy one, but all children like getting things right.

In awful months that followed, Louise lost count of the times she wished she'd deliberately got it wrong. Far from being impressed, the other five-year-olds made school life a misery. To compound her felony, efforts to curry favour in the playground also foundered – she had a natural eye and excelled at ball games, soon finding that nobody wanted to be outclassed in that arena either.

After a year, her parents removed Louise from school and assumed responsibility for her education. She never went back. The next milestone came at age fourteen, when she had to choose between going up to Oxford University to read applied mathematics or pursuing a career on the pro tennis circuit. Numbers won, but Louise still thought nostalgically about the alternative.

As time passed, she learned that men at work and men in love were no better than children at handling serious competition. So Louise Boss developed her own set of rules, and played by them. She worked in her own way, and her current occasional lover was a centre back from Swindon Town Football Club – an amiable giant who believed she was a secretary at Omega Dynamic Systems and treated her like Dresden china.

Louise lived in a pretty but dilapidated cottage outside Malmesbury with three pedigree British Blue cats, drove an elderly Ford Fiesta and got by with a basic wardrobe consisting of a Barbour waxed jacket, two pairs of jeans, half a dozen men's shirts and the same number of sweaters. Nobody was ever allowed to see her one small self-indulgence – a work station in the spare bedroom with sufficient computing capability to mastermind a moonshot. The white-painted room with sloping ceilings and trustworthy machines was her real home. Louise frequently worked through the night, until grey felines appeared to rub around her legs, demanding breakfast. After a shower, she'd drive to Omega and start all over again.

Tonight, she intended to deal with one of Trojan Horse's few remaining weak spots – the failure to penetrate and disrupt America's air traffic control systems during a simulated attack earlier in the day. It was strictly forbidden to take classified material home, but that rule was for other people. Louise had to go through security before leaving the Omega building, but familiarity dulled diligence. She had glued the pages and cut a tight-fitting hole for floppy disks in a slim Franz Kafka paperback. Who could be surprised that she was taking for ever to read a book like that?

This time might be different. The regular man looked embarrassed when she turned off her Walkman and switched on the usual high-voltage smile. Instead of a perfunctory rummage in her big leather shoulder bag, he asked her to turn the contents out – but he wasn't the problem. Omega's security chief stood beside him, and Alexander MacNaughton missed nothing. The spare Scot studied scattered possessions for a moment, then picked up the book. It fell open. He looked down at the snug disks and hooked them out. Louise hung her head, trying to look like a kid caught raiding the cookie jar. MacNaughton spoke sternly.

'I don't suppose for a moment that you're stealing your own secrets, Louise, but this is a serious matter. I must finish checking everyone through, so you have until morning to think up a convincing story. Nine o'clock, my office. No homework tonight – have a quiet evening by the fire with a good book. Something with all the pages intact, perhaps.'

He handed her the paperback and put the disks in his pocket. Louise scooped her things into the shoulder bag and ran. She'd been caught once before, soon after MacNaughton took over, and had promised faithfully never to take classified work out of the office again.

But there was nothing to fear. Omega Dynamic Systems couldn't afford to upset her – they needed Louise Boss more than she needed them, if regular calls from eager headhunters on both sides of the Atlantic were anything to go by.

Gloucestershire

THE COUNTRYSIDE wasn't blind. Don Sykes had noticed the distant panel van earlier, when he was inspecting traps in Roundgrove Wood, high on a rolling escarpment above Manor Barn. After checking with binoculars to make sure the buggers weren't stripping lichen-covered stone tiles off the roof, the New Hall gamekeeper had gone about his business. The day's catch was small – two rats and a weasel in tunnel traps, one magpie angrily eyeing the treacherous call bird in a Larsen cage trap – but that modest bag pleased him. His was a wild pheasant shoot, and he gave what little vermin remained on the estate no quarter.

Still, there were other kinds of vermin, and strangers on his ground bothered him. He decided to check out the barn on his way home for tea – an inadequate description for the massive fry-up and can of beer which would be waiting back at Keeper's Cottage. Nothing seemed out of place as his Land Rover bumped along the track, but when he turned on to hard standing in front of the barn he saw tall double doors standing ajar, with padlock and chain dangling uselessly.

Don Sykes went to investigate. The vaulted interior was gloomy, but there was no mistaking the parked vehicle – Mrs Lancaster's black BMW. He looked inside. Her handbag was on the front seat, the boy's school satchel lay on the floor and there was a white envelope tucked under a wiper blade, addressed to *CONRAD LANCASTER, ESQ* in bold typeset capital letters.

The car keys were in place and the engine started first time. After switching off, he took the envelope, returned to the Land Rover and picked up his walkie-talkie. Estate staff always carried them, in case he needed to summon back-up. Occasionally, a motorized gang would drive out from Bristol at night, intent on lamping pheasants by the score, and he sometimes had to confront diddicoys who appeared in battered pick-up trucks to run their long dogs after his hares. They wagered wads of grubby notes on the outcome and could turn very nasty. But this was different. He hit the button and called up chauffeur-handyman Duncan Bernadelli.

'Sykes to Bernadelli, over.'

After a moment, the reply crackled through.

'What's up, Don?'

'Listen, has Mrs Lancaster come home?'

'Went out at the usual time to fetch young Tom. Haven't seen her since. Why?'

'Either she's done a runner or we have a problem. I've just found her car inside Manor Barn. Chain's been cut. No sign of anyone, but there's a letter. I'll have a look round then come in. Can you double-check that they aren't around and let me know?'

'Will do. Out.'

The gamekeeper took his twelve-bore shotgun off the rack behind the seats and slipped in two cartridges. His lean black Labrador bitch bounded out of the cab, her keen nose analysing air for interesting scents. They wouldn't find anything, but had to look. If only he'd paid more attention to that damn Mercedes van.

London

THE CALL-BOX was on Marylebone Station's lofty concourse, an easy walk from his expensive rented home in St John's Wood. But Wes Remington took the mechanized route, switching Underground trains several times in case he'd grown a tail. If MI5 was interested in his movements, they'd be unlucky. Agent-for-hire Beasley had a series of opportunities to get in touch, and the CIA Chief of Station was too cautious to direct their attention to this particular public phone before the business was done.

His precautions were unnecessary. The fax had flown through Beasley's cut-outs and the phone rang at 6 p.m., coinciding almost to the second with the first nominated contact time. Remington didn't introduce himself or attempt to identify the caller. Who else knew?

'I have urgent work. Are you available?'

'Location?'

The American voice was muffled, precluding any possibility of an accurate voice print. Beasley was a pro. Remington liked that. Ultra-careful never hurt anyone. He pitched.

'Here in the UK. Sophisticated surveillance, so you'll need your box of electronic tricks.'

'Solo operation?'

'I would think so, but that's for you to decide when I give you the brief.'

'Duration?'

'One month max, starting now. Ten grand a week plus another twenty on satisfactory completion. Plus expenses.'

'Dollars or pounds?'

'Dollars.'

'Pounds. I can be in London by tomorrow night. I'll contact you at nine. Same place and routine as last time. Bring five grand for initial expenses in used ten-pound notes.'

Beasley broke the connection. The CIA chief rehung the dead instrument and scanned bustling station crowds, mostly commuters hurrying for trains to the salubrious Chiltern Hills and beyond. He murmured a message to Angus Churchill.

'Here's looking at you, Gus . . .'

His territorially inclined opposite number at MI5 might indeed have Trojan Horse nailed coffin tight. But Wes Remington saw no harm in peering over Churchill's shoulder. Ultra-careful never hurt anyone – especially if they weren't found out.

North Devon

Though remote, the windswept cliff-top road would be crowded with tourist cars in summer, but in late April was deserted. A steep unmade track down to the water was protected by a locked gate and *TRESPASSERS WILL BE PROSECUTED* sign, and the derelict quayside warehouse was invisible from the road above. They shouldn't be disturbed.

After a careful descent, Andrew Rosson stopped the van on uneven cobblestones. The four-storey building squatted against a sheer rock face. All the glass in square upper-floor windows was broken, with those at ground level boarded up. Rusted cast-iron gantries protruded above loading doors at regular intervals along the building, which had been constructed in the eighteenth century to grade and ship cut stone from the quarry a mile inland. When quarrying ceased between the wars, the warehouse had been abandoned.

Nowadays the only visitors – to judge from spray-painted graffiti – were bored kids. Even if they came, they would see nothing. The wide double entrance doors were sealed with metal strips bolted to weather-bleached planking, and the small Judas door providing access had a good lock. Vehicles could be hidden in an old boat shed further down the quay, leaving no visible evidence of human occupation.

Bill Hellis had fettled the place out, ferrying in the plethora of equipment needed for a week's stay – air-beds and sleeping bags, portable gas lamps, cooker and heaters, plastic garden furniture, ready-meals and bottled water, chemical toilets, battery televisions, reading matter. And automatic rifles, just in case.

Bill was beside him in the passenger seat. The woman and child – bound and sightless – were in the back. When Paul and Ringo turned up in the Astra, one of them would return the rented Mercedes van to London – laying a confusing trail if Lancaster was foolish enough to involve the authorities.

Rosson got out of the van and looked around. God knew how Gregor Gorski found the building, but it was a superb defensive position. They might be middle-aged Englishmen, but lessons learned at KGB training school were not forgotten.

Foam-flecked green water rose and fell against the seaweed-encrusted jetty, energy spent by passage through the tiny harbour's narrow entrance. Sheer rock walls towered towards low grey sky, enclosing them in a high-sided stone triangle broken at its apex by the steep access track, alongside a stream that dashed down a boulder-strewn gully. Apart from seagulls riding thermals and quarrelsome jackdaws flitting around the cliffs, there was no sign of life. He turned to Hellis.

'Get them inside. When the others arrive, Ringo drives this van to London and hires a replacement somewhere else. Take that carpeting out and put it inside. The Astra goes into the boat shed. Paul can take a walkie-talkie and watch the road. We'll each do four hours on, eight off until Ringo gets back.'

Phase One completed, on schedule. Former KGB man Gregor Gorski's objectives remained a mystery, but that was always the way. Only the head could co-ordinate the body's actions. Whatever his grand plan, Gorski expected them to move as directed, and they could not afford to fail. Andrew Rosson reached for his mobile. Time to give the man in Moscow good news.

The journey had been terrible, though she'd managed to make contact with Tom. Liz Lancaster was filled with rage that her child should be subjected to such an ordeal, but forced herself to sound cheerful. He had pushed against her, but otherwise seemed fine. She sensed it would be a mistake to talk about their shocking predicament, so they'd quietly discussed everyday things – that promised trip to the Imperial War Museum, Manchester United, the reproductive cycle of earthworms.

Her body ached from enforced immobility, but that at least must be nearly over. After a bumpy descent which had them sliding forward on the van's carpeted floor, they stopped. She heard her captors talking quietly, straining unsuccessfully to hear the conversation. Then the doors opened. Liz smelt tangy sea air and heard the plaintive mewing of seagulls. Somewhere close by, water sloshed and gurgled.

'You all right, Mum?'

For the first time, Tom sounded anxious. Another voice answered for her – the tall one with hidden face, calm voice and unblinking light brown eyes. The one who gave orders.

'If you do as you're told, you'll both be fine. We're taking you into a building.'

Hands helped her out of the van. Her legs felt weak, but held up. Someone led her slowly across an uneven surface. Old cobblestones?

'Duck your head.'

She did, and the clean sea-smell was replaced by an odour of decay. A door slammed.

'Right. I'm going to untape you. It may hurt a little.'

Parcel tape was ripped away, leaving skin around her eyes feeling unpleasantly sticky. She looked around, eyes adjusting to dim light. Beside her, Tom was doing the same. Two men flanked them, balaclavas on and sawn-off shotguns by their sides. They stood in a large open-plan ground floor, stretching away beyond the illumination provided by a hissing bottle-gas lamp. The low ceiling was supported by ornate cast-iron columns. Assorted debris littered a bare earth floor and dark stone walls ran with condensation.

Behind them, the small door through which they must have entered was set in large wooden doors that leaked daylight around the edges. Ahead, a wide flight of worn stone steps rose to a half-landing. She exchanged glances with Tom. He was so brave, giving her a little smile to show he wasn't frightened, though he must be terrified. The man she had come to think of as the leader spoke softly in his polite, middle-class voice.

'Nearly there. Please follow me.'

He led off up the stairs. Liz and Tom obediently followed. The shorter, silent one picked up the lamp and brought up the rear. At first-floor level, they turned right down a broad corridor with crumbling brown plaster walls and stopped by a stout-looking door with two new bolts. A heavy padlock hung from an open hasp. Their guide opened the door and went into darkness.

Another gas lamp popped into life, and they were pushed inside. The windowless room had a board floor. Two inflated air-beds lay in one corner, each with a sleeping bag neatly folded on top. A small television set was connected to a car battery. There was a portable toilet, two green plastic garden chairs with matching round table, four rolls of pink loo paper and two cardboard boxes. The noisy gas lamp was on the table, softly lighting the room. All the gear looked brand new. The leader stepped back.

'Hardly the Ritz, but you'll survive. Let's hope Conrad Lancaster loves you dearly, in which case your stay will be a short one. Drinks and snacks in one of those boxes. Matches, electric torch and a spare gas cylinder in the other. Don't get silly ideas about getting out. These walls are solid stone, the floor's inch-thick oak and you'll find the same above if you try the ceiling. One of us will always be next door, and we'll use these if we have to.'

He raised the mutilated shotgun before backing out. The door slammed, and Liz heard bolts being thrown. Tom hurled into her arms, and they clung together as though they were the only people left in the world.

London

THEY WERE DINING *à deux* behind the Ivy's cosmic stained-glass window, though romance was not on the menu. The Opposition front-bench spokesperson on media matters was no lady, and Conrad Lancaster didn't make the mistake of treating her like one. He liked the trendy eatery patronized by writers and the theatrical set because he, too, had a famous face. For once, the attentions of paparazzi lurking opposite the restaurant's neon-lit entrance would be welcome, and Conrad had slipped the top-hatted doorman a generous tip to ensure they weren't prevented from snapping his exit, arm in arm with another power player.

The convivial couple were sipping pre-prandial cocktails, and Conrad was unusually attentive – letting her lead the conversation and laughing appreciatively as she indiscreetly discussed fellow-politicians and their foibles. With a semi-detached husband safely occupied cultivating ten million Lincolnshire acres by day and doggedly boring his way through the county set's distaff timbers by night, she was even flirting a little.

Conrad wanted to nudge Her Majesty's Opposition into a declared commitment to relax strict regulation of excessive cross-media ownership. He already had the largest permissible slice of newspaper market, but television was the future. With new digital technology promising almost limitless channels, Conrad wanted to scoff some of that pie, too. Why should he be restricted to a few minor cable stations by outmoded legislation?

His tactics were paying off. The spokesperson was enjoying herself. Opposition benches weren't the most comfortable of parliamentary seats for ambitious politicians, so ego-stroking was always welcome. She wouldn't be in limbo for ever, and both understood the networking game. Conrad's six-figure annual contribution to her party's election war chest was not mentioned. Neither was their commitment to deregulation, which would almost certainly deliver the free media market he wanted within months of them regaining office in any event.

Their meeting wasn't about substance, but image. Lancaster Trust's expensive PR consultancy would plant an item in the press, subtly avoiding his own newspapers to provide added credibility. A couple of *TYCOON DINES WITH SHADOW MINISTER* diary pieces would do nicely. His point on media ownership would be forcefully put over by papers whose proprietors shared it, whilst her reputation as a political mover and shaker was enhanced.

Conrad chuckled at one of his companion's risqué sallies, covering and squeezing her hand with his. Providing he didn't let it show, indifference to immaculately maintained women of a certain age was immaterial – after all, her own somewhat exotic tastes in these matters hardly extended to overweight businessmen. They could still achieve genuine intimacy, because some things were more stimulating than sex.

The maître d' approached, interrupting the moment to inform Conrad that there was a telephone call. Mobiles and portables were banned at table, so he had to go out. When Conrad realized the caller's identity, he became angry – berating Rita Bernadelli for disturbing him during an important business meeting. The New Hall housekeeper kept her nerve, finally managing to explain the reason for tracking him down.

Mrs Lancaster and young Tom had gone missing. Her car had been found, but not the occupants. There was a letter, addressed to him. Everyone was out looking, so far without success, though a motorcycle had been discovered at the bottom of a deep ditch. What should she do? Conrad rightly assessed the housekeeper's dilemma. She knew his wife was becoming restless and suspected that she'd gone walkabout, but didn't dare ignore the matter in case there was a more sinister explanation. He made a decision.

'I'm sure they'll turn up safe and sound, but we can't take any chances. I'll drive down as soon as my meeting's over. Continue the search, but don't notify the authorities and don't open the letter. Understood?'

He terminated the call without waiting for an answer and returned to his dinner companion, offering effusive apologies. This was business, and Elizabeth and Tom were capable of looking after themselves for a couple of hours.

Moscow

THE PLAN was unfolding smoothly, and Gregor Gorski allowed himself a second's self-congratulation. The

Lancaster woman and her brat had been taken. After the tycoon had been allowed to sweat his fat balls off for twelve hours, he would be told the price of their safe return – the electronic warfare package known as Trojan Horse, currently being developed by his Omega Dynamic Systems company. Ownership of Omega would not be enough to grant access to the highly classified Trojan Horse project, but Conrad Lancaster was resourceful. He'd find a way. And who could doubt that such a man would do whatever was necessary to save a beloved wife, and the young heir to his gilded throne?

General Sergei Sobchak was already besotted with the sophisticated cyberweapon's potential benefit to the forceful new government of national unity he would create after replacing President Yelkin. With power like that, Russia's President would no longer be the object of international contempt, brushed aside like an irritating fly by the Americans and lapdog allies. With Trojan Horse hanging over them like a Sword of Damocles, the West could ill afford disrespect towards a nation that would become great again.

So much for foreign policy. The procrastinating diplomats really should come to him for lessons in direct action. But there was still the matter of smoothing General Sobchak's onward march to the presidency. Gregor Gorski lit one of the French cigarettes that were his only personal indulgence. He liked the classic blue package with its silhouetted black lady wreathed in swirling smoke, and savoured the taste of rich dark tobacco. But he also made a virtue of self-discipline, smoking no more than one pack a week. The excitement must be getting to him. It was only Monday, and this was the seventh cigarette.

He glanced at the electric wall clock in the modest three-room apartment where he lived alone. Soon, those fierce Sons of Dudayev would perpetrate another outrage, clearing a major obstacle from the general's path. Gennady Churkov would be a potent presidential challenger should a sudden vacancy arise. But removal of the Duma's high-profile Speaker would be no more than a promising beginning.

The best was yet to come, because Gregor Gorski intended to teach those whining democrats a thing or two about practical politics.

California

WIDE OPEN SPACES provided refuge from people who wanted something, pinned demanding hopes and expectations on him, needed him, relied on him, took advantage of his skills, tried to buy his personal attention. Yet while pressure might drive him into Oregon's wilderness, he never stayed for long. After a few days, his own society became too intense, and he would wake with a craving for action, acute as a heavy smoker's sudden desire for the next cigarette. This was such a day. The morning's intimate encounter with an unwitting black bear had cleared James Lancaster's mind, and he was returning to work.

Ahead of him lay a spinning red-tipped McCauley propeller, growling Lycoming engine and vast dome of deep blue sky. He loved flying the Cessna 182S Skylane. It was freedom – the grown-up equivalent of youthful exploits on a big old Norton ES2 single-cylinder motorcycle, flying along country roads with wind tearing at unhelmeted hair. The trim high-winged aircraft was making a steady 145 knots, and he would soon be landing in Los Angeles. Already, the vast urban sprawl's hazy outer edge was rising from the sunlit coastal panorama ahead.

He'd give the Century City office a miss. High-quality staff at Lancaster Security Consultants were quite capable of operating the business, but however successfully they did so during his frequent absences, a miasma of urgent demands always swirled around him the moment he walked into the place. Which was something he didn't need right now. Once down, he'd pick up the waiting Dodge Viper GTS and drive to his empty house on the beach.

James Lancaster smiled wryly at indifferent sky. He was the man who had everything – a profitable company with no borrowings, desirable homes in LA and the unspoiled Blue Mountain ski area, jet-set lifestyle, first-name acquaintance with top-billing stars, unlimited access to beautiful Hollywood women who rarely resisted men with everything. Yet James sometimes felt he had nothing. He was an arid example of 'grass is greener' syndrome – the almost pathological inability of humans to value the things they have, and tendency to hanker painfully after something they don't.

His intellect appreciated the irony, but understanding brought no relief. It wasn't easy to live with someone whose emotions were buried so deeply that he'd lost the ability to give of himself, a loner who seemed able only to come alive under the stimulus of physical danger. James Lancaster didn't think he was being greedy or unreasonable – he just wanted his life to mean something to someone. Starting with himself.

Reducing the Lycoming's power setting to 75 per cent, he watched the airspeed indicator tick back towards 140 knots.

Wiltshire

ALEXANDER MacNAUGHTON wasn't half as clever as he believed. The Omega security chief had been distracted by discovering those damning disks in her doctored paperback, forgetting that Rule One in the computer user's manual is 'always back up'. Louise Boss had slid a duplicate set of disks into the secret wallet pocket of her battered Barbour, concealed alongside the main zipper by the jacket's front flap.

Or perhaps he was twice as clever as she thought. Maybe there was a panic of some sort, and he wanted to be seen to be doing his job properly – all the time knowing she'd still find a way to work around the clock to the company's advantage. Trojan Horse was vital to Omega's future, as dyspeptic dictator Gordon Holland was constantly reminding her.

Luckily for them, Louise was passionate about the first professional challenge that had really stretched her. After feeding the cats and microwaving pre-packaged lasagna, she had gone upstairs, settled in her swivel chair and fired up the Cray work station. No computerized system in the world would be safe when she got this right. The breakthrough was stunning – a programme that was infinitely more than a virus. Trojan Horse possessed the intelligence to probe even the best-protected locations and force an entry, but that wasn't the real beauty. Once inside, it didn't merely disrupt the host system, but cloned with and overrode existing software, allowing the remote operator to assume control.

That offered limitless possibilities, but power didn't concern Louise. Like any good Cold War nuclear physicist, she figured that governments could do what they liked with new toys, provided they picked up the tab that let her work at the leading edge. She was only interested in ensuring that Trojan Horse was perfect, and it never occurred to her that it might be dangerous to keep such a desirable commodity in a country cottage guarded by three friendly cats.

She had long ago duplicated the main development programme and brought it home. Today's smuggled disks contained no more than a record of the simulated attack on the USA, as MacNaughton would discover in the morning. He could hardly make a fuss about a conscientious employee wanting to replay *that* on her own time.

Rerun it she did – endlessly. Buried in all those lines of code, a tiny error had prevented Trojan Horse from penetrating and disrupting a key American air traffic network. Louise couldn't find the flaw. It should work, but didn't. The US attack simulation was a requirement of Gordon Holland's precious contract, and she become increasingly frustrated as every cross-check came up negative. She didn't care about his stupid commercial concerns, but hated being beaten.

At some point during the evening, her part-time boyfriend rang. The big footballer invited Louise to attend the season's last home game on Saturday, and said they needed to talk. She agreed to meet for a drink the following evening, but turned down the match invitation. He'd forgiven her lack of interest in his career before and would forgive her again. If he didn't, too bad.

She still felt guilty, picking half-heartedly at cold lasagna as she imagined Danny Woodward's uncomprehending hurt. There wasn't an ounce of malice in the man, and he deserved better. But then Louise had an idea, and Danny was forgotten as her nimble fingers started flying over the keyboard.

Location unknown

THE OPERATOR-FOR-HIRE known as Beasley had fond memories of London and maintained an apartment in Dolphin Square, a massive residential complex on the Thames embankment once heated by hot water piped beneath the river from the now-disused Battersea power station on the opposite bank. The place – along with other boltholes in Rome, Rio de Janeiro and New York – was registered in the name of a Liechtenstein investment company, the ultimate ownership of which was impenetrable. That was how he wanted it. Trusted status and lucrative assignments from the international intelligence community depended on anonymity and a reputation for absolute discretion.

This small job for the CIA sounded undemanding, but Beasley hadn't been in England for some time and would enjoy revisiting the overcrowded, idiosyncratic island marooned off the coast of Europe. He'd worked with Wes Remington before, and respected the no-nonsense London Bureau Chief. With Remington, a deal was a deal, and no time had to be wasted unravelling some hidden agenda. If only all his employers were so straightforward.

He had recently concluded an operation for the French, who used him to investigate a senior American diplomat at the United Nations in New York – a battleground where US and French minds frequently failed to meet. Ostensibly, the assignment was designed to reveal weak spots in the diplomat which could be exploited to Gallic advantage. Beasley only understood the true rationale when he discovered that the American led a blameless personal life, but was secretly meeting France's UN ambassador. The well-meaning but indiscreet Frenchman had made a unilateral decision to improve Franco-American relationships, becoming loose-mouthed in pursuit of his objective.

Beasley said nothing, turned in surveillance reports and tapes, banked his fee and noted the French ambassador's subsequent withdrawal on grounds of ill health. That was the thing about his covert activities – they were always *interesting*. He loved knowing things governments swept under carpets, and enjoyed the fact that not one of them was aware of just how many grubby secrets had come his way over the years.

The Americans would doubtless have been dismayed to learn of his part in the abrupt departure of a valuable new source at the UN, but if he hadn't nailed their double-dealer the French would have used someone else. Then again, the Yanks wouldn't complain when he successfully completed whatever deniable dirty work Wes Remington was lining up in London. That's how his work had to be.

Now, only one task remained. He listed the sophisticated equipment that might be needed. His supplier in North London would receive the order by fax, and have everything ready for collection within twenty-four hours, in return for cash payment. Almost as an afterthought, he added a Browning automatic pistol and ammunition to the list. Beasley had bad memories of operations that had gone spectacularly wrong, and was a careful man.

Gloucestershire

CONRAD LANCASTER'S Bentley Continental whispered along the long New Hall driveway just before midnight. The uniformed chauffeur decanted his master before the house's imposing main entrance, before pulling away to garage the car in the stable block.

The April night had an edge, and Conrad thrust his hands into the deep pockets of a camel-hair car coat as he slouched towards the door. Despite the late hour, he expected Mrs Bernadelli to be waiting, and she was. The spare housekeeper stepped aside to admit him, the neutral expression he always interpreted as critical on her sharp face. Conrad stopped.

'Any sign?'

'Not yet.'

She sounded worried. He removed his coat and held out a demanding hand.

'Letter.'

Rita Bernadelli produced it from her uniform skirt pocket.

'The staff will resume their search at first light, but they've already checked the area thoroughly. Perhaps Mrs Lancaster has decided to take a trip.'

Conrad stared at her contemptuously.

'Bunch of old women, the lot of you. Bring me a turkey sandwich and large brandy.'

He took the letter, threw his coat at her and headed for the study, a small oak-panelled room off the first-floor library. He put the envelope on the leather-covered top of a large antique partners' desk and went to the ornate fireplace, briskly rubbing his hands together in the heat of a log fire that had burned down to glowing embers.

Only when Mrs Bernadelli had delivered his triple-decker sandwich and withdrawn from the room did he return to the letter. The plain white envelope bore his typeset name, with no address. He slit it open and extracted a single sheet of double-folded paper. The message, in the same anonymous typeface, was a devastating cliché: *We have your wife and child. Await instructions. Do not contact the police.*

Conrad smoothed the letter and lifted his brandy from a silver tray, absent-mindedly swirling the glass to release an aroma he didn't sample as he studied those thirteen agonizing words. Eventually, he drained the balloon glass, blinking as strong spirit burned down.

The decision was made. James might be an arrogant little swine who had rejected everything Lancaster Trust and its founder stood for, but even he would understand that some things are more important than family rivalries and injured pride.

Conrad Lancaster put down his empty glass, took out his pocket address book and reached for the mobile telephone that accompanied him everywhere.

Los Angeles

WHEN THE CESSNA had landed, James Lancaster parked the plane and walked to his waiting Dodge Viper. A pager lay on the seat, reminding him he was back. He'd switched on, and the tiny box immediately bleeped. Standing orders dictated that he should only be paged if the matter was of extreme urgency, but he hadn't rung in, figuring the real world could manage without him for a while.

Instead, he'd driven to his house, not pushing the Viper along crowded freeways, half tempted to turn around and head back to Oregon. Climate control masked tainted air, but the pollution was more pervasive than mere smog. LA hardly represented humanity at its most shining, though this self-absorbed city was a better place than most for someone who had made an art form of successful survival.

At home, he'd emptied the mailbox of junk and carried a cold Bud through to weathered cedar decking overlooking the restless Pacific Ocean. James Lancaster sat there for a long time. Only when the sun fell beneath a rose-tinted sky into darkening sea and the beach cleared of beautiful people did he return inside. The phone's message light was blinking, and he hesitated for a moment before calling the office. Thoughts of some demanding crisis were profoundly unappealing.

His Operations Director hadn't left for the night, and didn't waste time on apologies. Mr Conrad Lancaster of London's Lancaster Trust Corporation had made contact. He wished to engage the services of Lancaster Security Consultants for a major assignment, money no object, but refused to discuss quote extremely urgent family business unquote with anyone but the Chief Executive Officer. After passing the message, Carl Perazzi waited patiently. James allowed the shock that coursed through him to subside, then asked an inane question to buy more time.

'Anything special going down at the moment?'

Senior staff of Lancaster Security Consultants were well aware of deep antipathy between their CEO and his father – and of the fact the two Lancasters hadn't spoken since James left England for the States ten years before. But Perazzi also knew the boss-man retained a keen interest in his estranged parent's activities – the research department kept a comprehensive file on all Conrad's business and social activities, which James called up on screen at least once a month. The Operations Director understood, rattling on cheerfully while James collected his thoughts.

'Nothing we can't handle, maestro. We're guarding MGM's latest sci-fi epic. They have some unbelievable monster models which must be kept under wraps until their publicity campaign breaks, and big bucks are on offer for anyone who snatches pictures. We nailed a cameraman. Fired off two rolls of film with a miniature Canon while the special effects crew were on lunch break, little realizing big brother was watching on video. So I guess you could say he's now an ex-cameraman and failed snapper. Initial planning for next year's Oscar ceremony has started already, and the installation team doing the Mendez ranch flies down to Mexico tomorrow with a plane-load of mega-expensive equipment. They bought the store.'

'Great. Did my father leave a contact number?'

'Yup. Sounds like a mobile.'

James Lancaster jotted down the number on his scratch pad, thanked Carl Perazzi and hung up. The last thing he wanted to do was call his father, but his index finger had a mind of its own.

Moscow

GENNADY CHURKOV burped contentedly. He'd consumed a substantial goulash dinner, washing down spicy beef stew with a bottle of heavy red Bull's Blood and finishing up with cream cakes, slivovitz and Turkish coffee. His belt felt uncomfortably tight, so he undid it and leaned back in the comfortable armchair.

He watched Irena and Alexandra making love on the big double bed, white bodies slippery with sweat in the stuffy warmth of the centrally heated apartment. They were acting, but writhed convincingly enough. As the tempo quickened, Alexandra gasped with pleasure. Irena responded with animal noises and Gennady Churkov felt his loins stir. The girls were good. When they finished, he would be ready to join them, to take them both as they became submissive and eager to please their paymaster.

The politician stood up, let his trousers drop round thick ankles and stepped out of them, still wearing black socks supported by elastic suspenders. As he tore off a red silk tie and started unbuttoning the London-made white shirt, moving air fluttered against his bare legs. He reluctantly turned from the bed, where Alexandra was moaning convincingly as her vermilion fingernails raked Irena's moving buttocks.

Two men stood in the doorway, and they weren't his bodyguards. One – already a step into the room – wore a long black overcoat, unbuttoned to reveal a cheap grey jacket and check shirt. He was carrying a Polaroid camera, dangling by its plastic strap. His companion was shorter, with broad shoulders and barrel chest amply filling a grubby white roll-neck and quilted windcheater. He carried an ugly automatic pistol, unbalanced by a bulky sound moderator.

Roll-neck walked quietly into the room and stood by the bed. Amazingly, Alexandra and Irena were oblivious to his menacing presence, their noisy coupling coming to a frenetic climax. Gennady Churkov suddenly wondered if they really were faking, a notion that hadn't crossed his mind before.

These were serious people, who wanted something and meant to scare the shit out of an important man, to ensure he considered their proposition very seriously indeed. New Russia was a jungle, full of dangerous creatures. The Duma's Speaker and next President of Russia looked at Overcoat and raised supplicatory hands to show he understood, would oblige no matter what they asked for. Promises cost nothing, and didn't always have to be kept. These bastards could be neutralized before he was forced to deliver.

There was something odd about Overcoat. As he realised the man's scar-framed left eye never moved, the automatic's muted thump reverberated in the small room, mingling with the indescribable sound of a soft-nosed bullet tearing into tissue and bone. Alexandra screamed. Gennady looked at the bed, trying to believe this was really happening. Her pretty face contorted with terror, his bottle-blonde mistress was fighting with all her strength to push Irena's inert body away. The back of Irena's head was a mess.

Roll-neck twitched the pistol sideways and shot Alexandra in the forehead. In the silence that followed, Gennady Churkov began whimpering deep in his throat, an involuntary reaction he couldn't control. Overcoat spoke, his deep voice authoritative.

'Go and kneel beside the bed, Speaker Churkov.'

He didn't – couldn't – move, babbling words he hoped they wanted to hear.

'Anything, I'll do anything. I have friends, influence. Just tell me what you want. Please . . .'

Roll-neck was on him in two strides, seizing an arm with his free hand and dragging him to the bed. Even as he thought of hurling himself at the gun, Gennady Churkov was ignominiously forced to his knees. He smelt blood as Overcoat politely answered his question.

'We want the world to know what degenerate creatures our politicians have become. This photograph will make the point very well. Keep very still, Gennady, I'd hate to keep you waiting for a reshoot.'

The hateful voice contained a hint of amusement. A shutter clicked, followed by the mechanical hiss of an undeveloped print emerging. Gennady Churkov numbly studied the faded blue carpet, seeing every fibre. The damned thing needed a clean – though after what was about to happen they'd probably have to throw it away. He shut his eyes. His final thought was that his nagging wife would find out he hadn't really been working late all these nights.

She'd kill him.

DAY 2 – TUESDAY

North Devon

SLEEP REFUSED to rescue her. Liz Lancaster's first night in captivity was a waking nightmare. The boy, at least, had slept, curled against her like a trusting puppy. She'd hardly dared move for fear of awakening him. After hours of self-imposed immobility, her body was stiff and her mind wanted to scream.

At nine the previous night they'd been given a meal of boiled potatoes, mushy peas and tinned stew – brought on paper plates with plastic cutlery by the shorter man, his face again concealed by a blue balaclava. This provided momentary reassurance. If they were marked for death, such precautions would surely be unnecessary. As soon as he came into the room she had uselessly asked 'What do you want with us?', aware that her voice was shrill. The man had put down the food, turned and left without a word, the heavy door slamming behind him with ominous finality.

Tom had finished his supper with gusto and then – because she had no appetite – hers, washing it down with Diet Coke. They'd turned up the gas light to banish shadows, sat at the round patio table and talked. He seemed to think being kidnapped was an adventure which would end without tears, endlessly revisiting every aspect of the afternoon's events and dreaming up far-fetched ways in which their captors might collect ransom money without getting caught.

Liz had been unable to decide if he was genuinely fascinated, or manfully hiding fear. She knew she was frightened. The thought of something happening to this bright, quick youngster whose life had scarcely begun – who also happened to be her only child – was almost unbearable. But she had made a supreme effort to conceal anxiety, and ended up talking about her own childhood in outback Australia, a subject Tom never tired of. To her surprise, frequently recounted memories of a place she couldn't wait to leave were for once accompanied by feelings of nostalgia. She'd renewed her promise to take him there one day, then firmly announced it was bedtime.

They had pushed air mattresses together and zipped two sleeping bags into one, and her long night had begun. Now, the ordeal was nearly over. The luminous hands of her Rolex told her it was six o'clock, and Liz felt strength flowing through her aching body. Some time in the small hours, she had stopped thinking hopeless thoughts like *This isn't really happening* or *Please God let them take me and spare him*.

She inched out of their warm nest into musty darkness, finding the torch she'd left beside the bed. Tom stirred restlessly, but his breathing settled back into a regular sleep pattern. She used the chemical toilet, then began to explore every corner of the stone-walled room, torch beam probing for something she could turn to advantage.

Liz Lancaster had made two resolutions. She would fight for their lives using every weapon at her disposal. And if they got out in one piece, she would definitely do what she'd been building up to for many months. Even if Conrad Lancaster willingly paid the price of their freedom, the idea of facing the busy, bustling world out there without him suddenly seemed infinitely desirable.

New York

JAMES LANCASTER'S anger had simmered throughout a red-eye flight from Los Angeles to New York. Nothing had changed after all these years. No lessons learned. Not a shred of evidence that his bloody father had mellowed by so much as one iota. Conrad was still bringing pain and suffering to his nearest and allegedly dearest, and treating him like a child who was expected to jump when the whip cracked.

Though his reluctant telephone call had bounced down from the satellite in the early hours of the British morning, his father had been waiting, answering on the second ring.

'So, you called back.'

The deep, slightly nasal voice contained unmistakable triumph. Resentment had flowed through James like vitriol, but his reply was almost civil.

'Well?'

Conrad hadn't hurried to the point.

'You're good at what you do, James. The best. I've watched you build that business of yours and am proud of what you've achieved. Like it or not, you've got my genes in you. Now, I need your professional skills and I'm not too proud to ask. I'll pay whatever it takes, naturally.'

James almost broke the connection, but the sort of masochistic compulsion that causes people to probe an aching tooth drove him on.

'You really think your dirty money can buy me?'

His father had answered with confident contempt.

'Oh no, you'll help in spite of yourself. The money's just to make sure I'm not in your debt.'

Like an inexperienced fool, James walked into the trap.

'I can't think of a single thing that would make me lift a finger to help you.'

The serrated jaws snapped shut.

'Elizabeth and our boy Tom have been kidnapped. Yesterday afternoon.'

First his father reaching a dead hand from the past, now this. Lizzie, in deep trouble. Lizzie, in danger. Despite a second shock in quick succession, James stayed cool.

'You're sure? I've never understood why Liz stuck with you this long. She probably just called time on a lousy relationship, found someone who noticed she was a human being and ran like hell.'

Conrad didn't react to the taunt, forging on as though

the final sentences hadn't been uttered.

'I'm sure. No demands yet, but there's been a note. I haven't told the police and want you to handle this. I'm a proud man and you did wrong by me, but I'm asking you to set our differences aside. I've lost two sons, including you. Help me save the third. He's only a child. Please.'

Professional interest quickened. Or was it personal? Either way, James found himself being drawn towards his father's web.

'An only child, you mean – your last remaining dynastic hope. Any idea who's responsible?'

'Not a clue. I'm not without enemies, but it's probably criminals who just want money. I hope so, because that might be straightforward, providing you agree to conduct the negotiations. I'll pay, no questions asked, whatever it takes. Should be easy enough. You've handled dozens of these cases.'

James had, only two ending with a dead victim. He thought for a moment, but the manipulative old bastard was right. He *would* help. In spite of himself.

'I'll get there as fast as I can. Don't make contact with the authorities or respond to any communication from the kidnappers until I arrive. That's important. Where will you be when I get in?'

'I'll wait at the London house.'

Without a word of thanks, his father had hung up. Typical. But Conrad's boorishness had long been factored into the equation, and was not really the cause of his anger. As the 747's landing wheels thumped protestingly on to Kennedy tarmac, bringing him back to the present, James Lancaster acknowledged an unpalatable truth.

That fierce anger was directed at himself. With good reason.

Gloucestershire

EVER SINCE the rural postal service began, the first delivery of the day had always been made to New Hall. Once, this involved cycling up the mile-long drive, and a tradition had become established. The postman always received a cup of tea in exchange for the mail.

This morning was no different from any other, though the journey from imposing entrance gates to big house nowadays took Norman Webley less than two minutes in his red Royal Mail van. He drove round and parked in the rear stable courtyard. New Hall's post was beside him on the passenger seat, secured by a thick rubber band – two dozen assorted letters, mainly circulars, and one Special Delivery requiring a signature.

He was right on time – quarter to seven – and Rita Bernadelli appeared at the kitchen door. The thin housekeeper took the mail, signed the delivery slip and ushered him into her sanctuary. His mug of tea was waiting, but something was wrong. Rita seemed preoccupied, and gamekeeper Don Sykes was sitting silently at the long scrubbed-pine table.

It didn't require information technology for news to travel fast in the countryside, and the postman knew what was bothering them. One of the farm workers from New Hall drank at his local, and when Norman had dropped by for his regular swift half last evening the public bar was buzzing with speculation about the disappearance of Mrs Elizabeth Lancaster. He sipped the sweetened tea, refusing to be hurried despite an atmosphere you'd need a chainsaw to cut.

'That hits the spot, Rita, as always. What's the word on Mrs L and the boy, then?'

The Scottish housekeeper snatched the mug and poured his tea into the deep stone sink.

'You mind your wagging tongue, Norman Webley. She needed a break and they've decided to spend a few days on the master's yacht, if you must know, but keep that to yourself. Now get off. I can't stand here all day gossiping, I've got work to do.'

In the twelve years of their acquaintanceship, he'd never seen the unflappable Rita Bernadelli so agitated. The postman retreated.

'Don, Rita. See you tomorrow, then.'

A moment after the kitchen door shut behind him, urgent conversation started. Norman Webley couldn't make out words, but the tone was unmistakable. So those vanishing-lady rumours were true, and by the time his morning round was completed half the county would be sharing the secret.

Any gamekeeper worth his wages has an intelligence-gathering network, and Don Sykes earned every penny of his modest salary. The New Hall keeper had been piecing together the previous day's events, resuming his briefing when the door closed on the inquisitive postman.

'So I reckon they were taken away in the back of that Mercedes van I spotted earlier by Manor Barn. Two blokes in it and the thing was hired. They were blocked by a tractor and trailer on Mill Lane just after four o'clock and had to back up to a passing place. The driver saw a rental sticker but was too busy squeezing past to take much notice of the men. Best he could say was middle-aged and ordinary. Then there was that white estate car seen near the ditch where we found the Jap motorbike . . .'

He stopped. Rita Bernadelli wasn't listening. She'd been checking the mail, but was now staring at a white envelope with the intensity of a baby rabbit that's spotted a hunting stoat. She handed over the letter with a terse comment.

'Look familiar?'

It looked familiar – the same size and shape as the one he'd found beneath the wiper of the mistress's BMW. And Conrad Lancaster's name and the New Hall address were printed in identical bold black typeset capital letters. Special Delivery stickers. Postmarked LONDON W1. Time-stamped 10.30 a.m. yesterday. Sender J. P. Smith. You didn't need to be Sherlock Holmes to work it out. Or see that the abductors had been very sure of successfully snatching Mrs Lancaster and young Tom. He returned the unopened missive, testing his perception against the housekeeper's.

'What's happening, for God's sake?'

'You know full well, Don Sykes. The pair of them have been kidnapped and I wouldn't be surprised if this was a ransom demand. Oh, that poor lamb.'

Rita Bernadelli had no children, and adored Tom. She poured percolated coffee into a silver pot warming on the

Aga, then spilled milk as she filled the matching jug, mopping up with angry dabs of her apron. When Conrad Lancaster's breakfast tray was presentable, she propped the envelope against the coffee pot.

'He'll go mad, but there's no point in putting it off.'

Don Sykes stood up, offering hollow comfort.

'Not your fault, Rita. If our lord and master pays up they should be home before the week's out with no harm done. Everything'll work out, you'll see. I'll get on and find out if anyone noticed which way that damn van turned at the main road.'

He'd be wasting his time, because he reckoned these people were professionals. Still, any action was better than sitting around. As he clumped out and made for his Land Rover, the gamekeeper tried to convince himself that his reassuring words might be true.

Moscow

WHAT ON EARTH was happening to the nation's moral fibre? These decadent politicians were vermin – though of course that wasn't the only reason Gennady Churkov had died. The colour photographs told the world a sordid tale from the front pages of the morning's papers – the Duma's Speaker kneeling beside a bed, his expression terrified. One of President Yelkin's closest allies and possible successors lying dead on blue carpet, beside the tangled bodies of two naked prostitutes on a bloodsoaked bed.

Even television had used the pictures – repeatedly. Gregor Gorski glanced up from the pile of newspapers, checking a big Japanese colour set that was the only luxury in his spartan apartment in an unfashionable district beyond the ring road. The sound was turned down, but it wasn't hard to tell what the day's main story was. The ex-KGB colonel sipped sweet tea and watched with almost indecent satisfaction as it unfolded, precisely according to his script.

Patriotic archive footage of Katusha rockets raining down on the battered Chechen capital of Grozny was replaced by a still of the late freedom fighter Dzhokhar Dudayev, wearing a general's uniform from the time when he commanded Soviet strike bomber aircraft in Estonia. The director cut to yesterday's sequence of rescue services lifting the bomb-blasted Kremlin official responsible for stalled Chechen independence talks from a mangled Mercedes on Moskvoretskiy Bridge. Then back to those titillating Churkov pictures.

If those in authority had failed to appreciate the Sons of Dudayev's deadly agenda before, they could harbour no illusions now. The television screen filled with a tame government mouthpiece, and Gregor Gorski turned up the sound. This should be interesting.

Anton Mossberg – the plump Interior Minister – was a rising political star also talked of as a future President. He made an unconvincing attempt to play down the significance of recent atrocities. Security forces were on full alert and army units were being drafted in to assist. It was only a matter of time before these renegade Chechen separatists were captured, and made to pay the full penalty for heinous crimes.

There was, of course, absolutely no possibility of yielding to the demands of terrorists. Indeed, the government of President Yelkin was so determined to stand firm that the official commission discussing the status of Chechnya was suspended until further notice.

The obsequious interviewer let a perspiring Mossberg off lightly, but Gregor Gorski smiled as he got up and switched off the television. Security forces would get nowhere, whilst army road blocks, tanks on the streets and heavy-handed policing would further darken the mood of frightened Muscovites. Especially when the lethal Sons of Dudayev struck again. As they would.

One individual rose like a beacon above the tide of filth and violence – a strong man who could be trusted to take the firm action needed to reimpose order for the benefit of all but racketeers, corrupt officials and self-serving politicians. That person was General Sergei Sobchak, and the people of Mother Russia knew it. If by grave ill fortune anything should happen to President Mikhail Yelkin, there could be only one successor.

North Devon

ON THE ASSUMPTION that they wouldn't be allowed to starve, Liz Lancaster had planned a counter-attack. She turned up the lamp before waking Tom. He scrambled out of the sleeping bag with a broad grin. Her son's resilience was amazing, redoubling Liz's determination to be strong herself. Sensing his embarrassment, she rummaged in boxes while he used the toilet. She came up with two packets of bacon-flavoured crisps and a can of Diet Coke, setting her prizes on the round patio table with a breezy comment.

'Let's hope they come up with something a bit more substantial for breakfast. I'm starving.'

Tom entered into the spirit of things, scolding her as though he were the parent.

'Mum, I told you to eat your supper. Diet Coke won't fill you up. Artificial sweeteners just make the body hungry for the real thing.'

They crunched crisps in companionable silence, then Liz addressed their situation. It was possible that the kidnappers had bugged the place, so she spoke loudly.

'We must both be very brave, Tom. These men just want money, and when your father pays they'll let us go. Until then, we must do nothing to make them angry. Promise?'

Actions contradicted words. Tom watched wide-eyed as she put a finger to her lips, then mimed the door opening and walked two fingers across the table-top to indicate a man coming into the room. Liz stooped and lifted the spare gas cylinder, placing it on the table beside a twin which powered the hissing lamp. The foot-tall cylinder was heavy, a formidable weapon.

'I promise.'

Tom's eyes glittered with excitement as she repeated the finger-walking man, mimed a blow with the gas cylinder and let two sets of running fingers scamper across the table to safety. It wasn't much of a plan, but she had to do something. Despite earlier efforts to reassure Tom, she wasn't certain the kidnappers were common criminals. Something about the way the leader talked suggested other, more sinister possibilities. If this was connected with Conrad's business dealings, the price of their freedom might not be so easy to pay. However remote the chances of a successful escape, she had to try.

In the event, things went better than she dared hope. Liz had scarcely finished communicating her intentions to Tom when they heard sounds at the door. It swung back, and they saw the short man stooping to pick up a washing-up bowl of steaming water. He was wearing the familiar balaclava and came in with a gruff comment.

'Wash and brush-up time, folks. Breakfast in ten.'

These were the first words they'd heard him utter. His muffled voice spoke in Estuary English – the vowel-mangling urban accent that was infecting the country like verbal plague. As he stooped to set down the bowl, Liz snatched up the gas cylinder in both hands and smashed it down on his head. Luckily for him, the cylinder's weight unbalanced her, and the blow was glancing. He still went down, hands flying to his injured head. One knee landed in the bowl, which upended. Hot water cascaded over coarse black jeans. Liz dropped the cylinder and screamed 'Run'. Tom needed no encouragement – he was already moving fast.

She went through the door right behind him. Stopped dead, brief hope snuffed out almost before it flickered to life. Two yards down the dingy corridor, the taller man was holding Tom by one arm, sawn-off shotgun to her son's head. Another gas lamp flared behind them, and Tom's frantic struggles threw weird moving shadows on to blotched walls.

'Tell the boy to behave himself, Mrs Lancaster, and I suggest you do the same. I'd hate to shoot either of you, but will do whatever's necessary.'

The middle-class voice was soft, but projected authority. Her son stopped fighting. The man gave him a shove, and Tom threw himself into her arms, burying his face in her chest. He burst into tears. Liz hugged him tightly, staring at their tormentor with hatred. He wasn't wearing his balaclava – a pleasant-looking, ordinary man aged about forty-five with regular features, dimpled chin and short dark hair greying at the temples. He was dressed like an off-duty bank manager – polished black shoes, grey slacks, Aran sweater over open-necked white shirt. Stony brown eyes stared her down. When her defiant gaze dropped, he gestured with the gun.

'Back inside.'

She helped Tom through the door. Her victim was on his feet, one hand clutching the side of his head where her blow had landed. None too steadily, he walked past her and out of the hateful room. The door shut, and Liz Lancaster heard bolts slide and the padlock click. She felt a stab of fear, and guilt at the possible consequences of her impulsive action.

They'd both seen his face.

Location unknown

THE MAN KNOWN as Beasley hadn't left for London. He had no packing to do, because he was always ready to move at the shortest of notice, travelling light. There was ample time to catch the flight that would carry him into Heathrow Airport and his scheduled meeting with Wes Remington of the CIA. But first he would make a telephone call.

Beasley was renowned for absolute discretion amongst intelligence agencies that used his services, deploying him on covert operations where official action was impossible. Sharing secrets that came his way would have been enough to render him unemployable or even – should he betray a more touchy paymaster – accidentally dead with no one to mourn his passing. But Beasley's loyalty to his employer of the moment was accepted without question. There were never any comebacks, and none had ever received so much as a hint that one of the dirty little games he played on their behalf had been compromised. This enviable reputation ensured a steady supply of stimulating, well-rewarded assignments.

If he'd had a conscience, Beasley would have almost felt guilty for taking money under false pretences. Acquiring classified information might not be easy, but the real difficulty lies in making use of such sensitive material without revealing the existence of an inside source, whose identity can usually be established by analysing the nature of the leak.

Beasley survived because his unofficial controller was a strategic thinker who never felt compulsion to act on information received from his roving agent. Sometimes, just knowing was enough. When it wasn't, he still did nothing, even if the consequences might seriously damage his cause. Beasley was too valuable to lose, because he provided unique insight into some of the more questionable activities of rival intelligence organizations around the world. Year after year.

The deal was simple. No money ever changed hands. When Beasley had something to say he talked, and his controller listened. Picking up a cellphone that looked like any other, but contained an encryption chip that made interception of his digitalized voice impossible, the freelance agent keyed the number of a dedicated mobile that rang only when he called, or some clumsy idiot misdialled. His controller answered immediately, and it was good to hear that familiar voice – one certain thing in an uncertain world.

'Yes?'

'I'm heading for London on CIA business. It's a UK-based operation. I'll be in touch.'

'Be lucky. And be careful.'

'Aren't I always? On both counts.'

Beasley replaced the secure phone in his slim executive briefcase and spun the brass dials of twin combination locks. Time to leave for work.

Gloucestershire

CONRAD LANCASTER had been almost civil when the housekeeper found him in his study, waving her away when she pointed out the letter propped against the silver coffee pot. He didn't need an explanation – a child could have worked out what the letter was. Face pinched with anxiety, Mrs Bernadelli had scuttled out, visibly relieved at escaping the rough side of his tongue.

People were oh-so predictable, and Conrad never saw reason to treat them with respect they didn't deserve. But other things were on his mind. He hadn't slept, grappling instead with an unfamiliar enemy. Fear. Lancaster Trust was his life, and his life was threatened. Much of the night had been spent on the telephone, issuing orders to Monica Cogswell, his personal assistant back at head office in London.

In fact, he had three mature female PAs who each worked eight-hour shifts, allowing him to do business around the clock. Because he had to trust them, he bought total loyalty with massive salaries. And he never became angry, even when they slipped up, always deploying interested-in-*them* charm which could work wonders with women. Indeed, Conrad was convinced that all three were half – or completely – in love with him.

Monica had been tasked with initiating the covert buy-in designed to prop up the falling Lancaster Trust share price, and would doubtless carry out his detailed instructions to the letter. As his anonymously owned offshore companies mopped up Lancaster Trust stock, the price should stabilize or even – with luck – start climbing.

You don't build a business empire without taking chances, and Conrad had undertaken illegal manipulations of many kinds. Why not? The regulators were weak. But this time was different, because he'd staked the store. He'd already pledged everything from vast personal stockholdings to pension fund assets as collateral against massive loans, and there was nothing left. Should the share support operation fail, the only predator he feared would show no mercy.

Fair-weather lenders would come after money when Lancaster Trust stock fell below the price that guaranteed their loans. He might have brushed Werner Anschütz aside, but one Swiss banker was nothing. The collective clamour of twenty would prove terminal. And the offshore companies had to resell Lancaster Trust at a good price within seven days to fund the original purchases, or at least secure new loans using that stock as collateral. If they couldn't, the share price would plummet and the markets would eat him alive.

Conrad Lancaster picked up the white envelope and tapped it on the leather desktop, taking comfort from a small triumph. At least his bolshie son had fallen into line. James might be proud and stubborn, but he too was predictable. Conrad poured a cup of coffee and slit the envelope with an onyx-handled opener. The typeset ransom demand was explicit.

Do not contact the authorities if you want to see your wife and child again. They will be returned unharmed if you deliver a full working copy of the classified Trojan Horse software programme produced by your Omega Dynamic Systems company within three days. Await further instructions.

After a moment, Conrad Lancaster picked up the phone. First things first. The market would start trading in an hour, and there might be early indications of the impact all those buy orders was having on the opening price of Lancaster Trust stock. No need to agonize over the other thing. James was coming, and Conrad was certain his wayward son could be persuaded to do whatever was necessary to resolve the kidnapping.

North Devon

AFTER THE FIASCO of their failed escape attempt, they had clung together for several minutes. Even as she had comforted her shaken son, one hand pulling him close and the other stroking silky fair hair, Liz Lancaster silently cursed herself. She'd achieved nothing, and now their captors would be doubly vigilant. Worse, they'd both seen the tall man without his balaclava. Eventually, Tom broke away. Though her son's elfin face was tear-streaked, the expression was determined and his clear voice firm.

'We can't give up, Mum.'

'Of course not, but we mustn't do anything silly. These men could hurt us, really hurt us.'

She was a fine one to talk, but Liz was relieved that Tom had started to take this seriously, and hoped his defiant mood would hold up. They watched the morning television news, which didn't mention them. She said this was good, suggesting Daddy hadn't called the police and was already discussing their release with the kidnappers. Then they had their first row. Tom wanted to keep the portable television on, but she switched it off. They had no way of knowing how long the car battery would last and she decided to confine viewing to news bulletins.

They were still arguing when the door opened. This time, no chances were taken. Hot water in an enamel bucket was brought in by someone new – slimmer than the stocky man she'd felled. Younger, too, judging by the athletic way he walked. Blue jeans, plain white cotton sweatshirt and standard-issue balaclava. Without taking his eyes off them, he carefully set the bucket on the floor, picked up the bowl emptied earlier and backed out.

The leader watched from the doorway, sawn-off shotgun ready. Liz was relieved to see that he, too, was now wearing a balaclava. Perhaps he hoped she wouldn't remember his face from those confused moments in the ill-lit corridor. Some hope. Those bland bank-manager features would be with her until the day she died. Liz felt an involuntary tightening of her stomach. That might not require a particularly long memory. He spoke softly.

'You've disappointed me, Mrs Lancaster. I was led to believe that you're an intelligent woman and treated you accordingly. But this morning's behaviour suggests you are both foolish and impetuous. These precautionary measures are for your own good. Please get up and raise your arms.'

He jerked the gun to emphasize the order. Tom started off his chair, but she stopped him with a restraining hand. As Liz stood up, the younger man returned, carrying bolt cutters and a coil of shiny new lightweight metal chain. He stopped in front of her and put down the cutters. She smelt his sweat. Or was it hers?

She lifted her arms, staring down as the chain was wrapped twice around the cream sweater at her waist. Tightly. The board floor still bore the dark stain of spilled water, and the man was wearing new Nike trainers. He slipped the hasp of a small but solid brass padlock through two links and snapped it shut, before paying off a length of chain which he secured to an old iron ring set into the wall, using an identical padlock. Finally, he fetched the bolt cutters and snipped off spare chain.

'You can reach everything, apart from the door. May be a little awkward, but you'll know who to blame for that, won't you? No breakfast this morning, either. You've been a naughty girl.'

Sending a knife through her heart, Tom shouted 'My dad will get you for this' at the closing door, his voice high with childish indignation. Just as their captors intended, Liz Lancaster felt humiliated, powerless, afraid. She was totally dependent on Conrad to end this awful ordeal – and save her son.

Wiltshire

ANOTHER DAY, another red alert. Alexander 'Sandy' MacNaughton yawned and rubbed exhausted eyes. He'd been due to address the local gardening club's Monday evening gathering, finally revealing one or two interesting techniques that had contributed to his wizardry with prize-winning chrysanthemums. Amazing how the humble corn marigold could arouse such horticultural passion. They'd been after his secrets since he moved to the area three years ago, and weren't pleased when he cancelled. But the telephone call from erstwhile protégé John Tolley couldn't be ignored.

If MI5 was sniffing around Omega, question marks might be raised against his operation. He'd know more when young Tolley appeared, but for now he'd done all he could. MacNaughton had spent the night studying the logs of alarm systems. Calling in and questioning uniformed guards to confirm that they hadn't noticed anything unusual, however small or apparently insignificant. Checking and rechecking everyone who had visited the facility over the previous six months, to make sure no vipers had slithered through his defences.

Alarms had been functioning perfectly. Nothing unusual had been noticed. Every visitor checked out. Which left the awkward matter of Louise Boss, who'd just arrived in his office.

Knowing Louise, she hadn't had much more sleep than him. But the company's star property showed no signs of fatigue. True, she looked as though she'd come to work backwards via hedge and ditch. Curly black hair was exploding in all directions and her casual clothes were crumpled. But that was usual, and Louise's startling blue eyes were alert and a half-smile played around her full lips as she waited for the lecture to begin.

He normally turned a Nelsonian eye when she smuggled out classified material and worked at home – partly because she was clever enough to outwit his best efforts anyway, but mostly because Omega was the beneficiary. When he'd informed Gordon Holland, after catching Louise for the first time, the ambitious MD had been delighted and said so, enthusiastically welcoming the thought of his most productive employee doing long hours of unpaid overtime. MacNaughton sighed. This time things were more complicated. If MI5 had discovered that Omega was leaking, and she was the crack, they'd all be in bad trouble.

'Listen carefully, Louise, and stop smiling. A bright young spark from my old outfit is coming in this morning, which means we may have a problem. As you know, Trojan Horse has maximum security classification. If MI5 decides the project's compromised, they could close us down tomorrow and ship the whole bang-shoot to the States for topping and tailing. If that happens the Yanks won't pay and this company will be finished. There are seventy jobs on the line here, not to mention my hitherto-unblemished professional reputation.'

Louise frowned, sounding genuinely horrified.

'Hold on. You don't think I'd sell out my baby?'

He didn't – and to her credit she obviously hadn't considered the fact that if Trojan Horse went, only sixty-nine jobs were on the line. Her unique skills would have to go with the project.

'Of course not, but what about the stuff you keep taking home? Is it possible someone's getting at Trojan Horse while you're here at work?'

She smiled, and the sun came from behind a cloud.

'If that's all you're worried about, relax. This may come as a shock, but I'm not a complete idiot. Everything on the machine at Beggar's Roost is secure. Very secure. I'd know if someone had been tampering with my computer, which they haven't, but even if they managed to crack the access codes and open Trojan Horse material they wouldn't get anywhere. Those files would self-destruct before anyone could blink, much less read the contents. Same thing would happen if they copied files or even carted off the whole work station and tried to extract the information at their evil leisure. Can't be done. Trust me, Sandy, I'm a computer programmer.'

MacNaughton couldn't help smiling.

'Who'd ever think of looking for the nation's most secret weapon in a ramshackle country cottage that's rather less secure than a wet cardboard box? It's brilliant, Louise, you'll go far. All right, back to work. I'll let you know if anything comes out of my meeting with Five. Let's hope this turns out to be a lot of fuss about nothing.'

Louise stood up, stooping to pick up her old Barbour jacket from the floor – the one with the hidden pocket she thought he didn't know about. She smiled innocently.

'They've probably discovered Gordon Holland's been fiddling his expenses. You really ought to look into that.'

Sandy MacNaughton could have sworn her hips acquired an extra-provocative wiggle as she swung out of his office. Try as he might, he could never stay angry with Louise for long.

Whilst policemen might still seem older to Louise Boss, computer programmers were definitely getting younger. At twenty-nine, she was a veteran – her six-person project team boasted a combined age of 133 going on seventeen. None was allowed full overview, but despite youthful indiscipline and high spirits their flair was essential to the Trojan Horse development. Her long night's work had produced interesting possibilities, and Louise couldn't wait to set them going.

It wasn't to be. She was nailed by her nemesis, Gordon Holland, who accosted her as she looked for the swipe card giving access to her programming suite. The MD hopped from foot to foot, face sagging with the weight of responsibility. He wasn't a pretty sight. There were dark pouches beneath his eyes, he'd cut a fleshy jowl shaving and dandruff spattered the shoulders of his dark grey suit. His voice aspired to gravitas, but never dropped below plaintive.

'Ah, Louise, I was hoping to run into you. How's everything going along? Well, I trust.'

'Badly.'

The wretched man had undoubtedly been lurking with the express intention of bothering her, and she couldn't resist the low blow. Holland's head jolted up, a hunted look chasing across his face. With a supreme effort that fooled neither of them, he clamped on an expression of polite enquiry.

'Badly?'

'Yes Gordon, badly. Half a dozen of the world's finest mathematical minds are sitting on the other side of this door, eager fingers poised over Gameboys, keyboards and mice, waiting for me to aim them and pull the trigger. Yet here I stand, already half an hour late after confessing to Sandy MacNaughton that I exchanged Trojan Horse for a number fifty-three and bowl of prawn crackers at the Chinese takeaway. Better still, I'm being held up by someone who should be able to think of much better things for me to do with precious time he's paying a lot of money for.'

She found her card buried among assorted debris in a Barbour pocket, flourishing the thing as though she'd been ready to use it two minutes ago. He twitched, but plodded gamely on.

'That's as may be, but you should know that Conrad Lancaster is visiting this building today. In person. He's bound to ask for confirmation that Trojan Horse will be delivered on schedule and can be a very impatient man. Which is putting it mildly. What on earth am I supposed to tell him?'

Louise swiped the card, keyed her PIN and addressed the voice-recognition microphone.

'My name is Louise and I'm not an alcoholic. Yet.'

The door slid open. She swept through with a final dig at the can-carrying executive.

'Conrad Lancaster – who he?'

The polished steel door closed automatically, giving her the last word. Fortunately, the pain-in-the-arse managing director of Omega Dynamic Systems didn't have security clearance to enter her inner sanctum.

Moscow

THE OPERATION might yet malfunction, like any other precision instrument vulnerable to the failure of one component amongst hundreds. But his plan was ticking along like a Swiss watch, and Gregor Gorski was feeling optimistic. Conrad Lancaster should have received his morning mail by now, and if anyone could penetrate the tight security surrounding Trojan Horse it was the forceful tycoon. Once the cyberweapon was secured, Russia's status as a heavy hitter would be guaranteed. But that lay in the future.

First, there was the more pressing matter of General Sergei Sobchak's presidential ambitions. If adherence to the principles of method acting was the only criterion, the chunky ex-soldier could have made it big in Hollywood. Gorski was sitting unobtrusively at the back of a darkened television studio, watching an overhead monitor that showed the nation's most popular-by-far politician being interviewed at length.

Recent events had ensured that compliant media could no longer pander to the government's self-serving agenda, which called for Sergei Sobchak to receive minimal exposure. President Yelkin and his cronies were frightened of him, with good reason. His siren message resonated for an electorate exhausted by belt-tightening whilst the few grew fat. The Russian people yearned for order and stability, *poryadok*, and only one man could be trusted to deliver.

He was a performer, all right. No ranting and raving, no histrionics – just intense sincerity and patent honesty as he spoke sadly of Russia's ills, predicting anarchy and chaos as a weak Government failed to act decisively to stem endemic corruption, economic collapse and terrorist violence on the streets. The recorded interview would reverberate across the CIS, further enhancing Sergei Sobchak's reputation as his predictions proved to be disturbingly accurate.

In truth, it isn't so difficult to be prescient when you possess advance information, but as with all brilliant conjuring tricks the effect is spectacular. Now, Sergei Sobchak was moving on, talking about the good old days like a favourite uncle weaving a spellbinding tale beside the log fire on a long winter's evening. Of course, those days weren't really as he described them, but nostalgia had a habit of sweeping logic aside.

Gregor Gorski stood up, satisfied that the general was playing his part to perfection. It was time to slip away and initiate the next move. As he left the studio, the ex-KGB colonel nodded in self-appreciation. Small wonder Russians were the world's finest chess players.

Wiltshire

BULLYING HIRED HELP was one of life's rewarding pleasures, and Conrad Lancaster was an artist. He'd been in the executive offices for two minutes, and already Omega's MD was panic stricken, scrubbing his sweating brow with a damp handkerchief. How easy – and satisfying – it was to intimidate people. Conrad smiled a humourless smile.

'So, I have your personal guarantee that Trojan Horse will come in on schedule? I hardly need tell you how important successful delivery is for the future of this company and everyone who works here . . .'

Especially *you*, he didn't need to add. Gordon Holland gabbled self-justification, words tripping over each other in their eagerness to please.

'No problem, Mr Lancaster, no problem at all. I spoke with the leader of the project team just before you arrived. They're well into fine tuning and final testing. We still have four weeks and will make it with time to spare,

I can promise you that. Of course these creative types can be temperamental, even difficult, so I have to keep on top of them, but . . .'

'Security, Gordon, what about security? I know this place is better protected than Fort Knox, because I've examined the arrangements myself. But how can we be sure that someone on the inside isn't leaking information?'

Conrad crashed in, stopping Holland dead. As intended, the change of direction threw the agitated executive. He swallowed hard, uncertain what was wanted. The answer was defensive.

'That's Alexander MacNaughton's responsibility. First-class man who came highly recommended. Ex-MI5. Does an excellent job. I have every confidence that we more than meet our statutory obligations with regard to the contract's demanding security clauses.'

'With respect, Gordon, I'm afraid that particular buck stops here. Absolute secrecy is critical on government contracts, especially this one, and I hear a murmur that our paymasters are concerned. If they find the slightest evidence security's slipping all hell will break loose, with severe consequences for everyone concerned. That said, suppose I ask you to give me a full working copy of Trojan Horse, so the Americans can satisfy themselves that everything really is going as well as you say?'

This was exquisite. Conrad savoured Holland's expression, which would have put a cornered rat to shame. The man desperately wanted to roll over, but couldn't.

'Well . . .'

'Well what, Gordon?'

'Well actually, Mr Lancaster, that's extremely awkward. If it was up to me, I'd be happy to oblige, but even I'm not privy to the operating details of Trojan Horse. No one is, except the development team, and even most of them aren't allowed to have the complete picture. Access to the project is governed by extremely strict rules . . .'

The voice trailed away helplessly. Conrad stood up and rested his hands on the MD's desk, knowing the intimidating effect of his bulk. He smiled reassuringly.

'Good to know security really is as tight as it should be. Even so, we can't take chances now we're so close to paydirt. I've got a suggestion. My boy James runs one of the most successful security consultancies in America. Does a lot of sensitive work for the US Government. He's pricey, but suppose we ask him in to run an eye over your arrangements, just to be on the safe side? He's flying in from the States today, actually.'

Gordon Holland's countenance brightened, relief washing away anxiety and gushing into his reply.

'Excellent idea, Mr Lancaster, absolutely excellent. That should certainly lay any official worries to rest. Oh yes, yes indeed.'

'That's settled, then. Expect him when you see him. Full access to everything. In the meantime, I suggest you turn your mind to obtaining that copy of Trojan Horse. It may not fall within the letter of the law, but you have my personal assurance that the project's integrity will not be compromised. After all, we're only talking about a sneak preview by the authorized end user who has footed most of the bill. Have it ready in your safe no later than noon tomorrow, but keep this between ourselves. Security remains paramount.'

Holland twitched, the hunted look galloping back.

'But . . .'

'No buts, Gordon. You know my motto – don't upset me with problems, give me solutions. This will please the Americans, ensure that payment is expedited. And when it is, there will be the usual substantial bonus for those responsible for Omega's latest success. Right, I'll leave that with you. I must be off to town. You're doing a fine job here.'

Conrad well understood that after thrashing a dog to show who is master, the subsequent pat of forgiveness and promise of reward is an even more potent motivator.

Omega's low-rise building occupied a double plot on a new science park outside Swindon. The glass-and-concrete structure was set back from the road, behind tall brick walls designed to block the view of any curious observer. The spacious grounds were not landscaped with shrubs and trees. Instead, the place was surrounded by an expanse of closely mown grass, broken only by metal floodlight pylons at regular intervals. These also carried cameras and motion sensors, to detect intruders if CCTV went down.

The only access was via a single entrance, manned by uniformed guards who sat in reinforced booths, one on either side of an electronically operated gate. There were separate in and out lanes, implanted with the sort of flip-up spikes used to prevent motorists leaving carparks without paying. These were lowered only when the guards had thoroughly checked vehicles and occupants.

Everything had looked solid on paper when John Tolley studied the Omega file back at Thames House, and was working efficiently in practice. He'd arrived an hour early for his meeting with Sandy MacNaughton, parked well back up the road and watched. Confirmation that corners weren't cut had come – and gone – in the long shape of Conrad Lancaster's peacock-blue Bentley Continental, identifiable by its personalized number plate. The vehicle was stopped and searched both ways, suggesting that mere mortals had no chance of escaping the net.

Still, it wouldn't hurt to rattle the back door. John Tolley took a tennis ball from the glove compartment, locked his Mondeo and strolled past the entrance gate. He turned on to a footpath that ran alongside adjacent warehouse units. Omega's red-brick perimeter wall was too high for him to scale unaided, but he found a wheeled rubbish bin belonging to one of the warehouses. After confirming that he was unobserved, Tolley pushed the bin against the wall and scrambled up. The plastic lid sagged, but took his weight. He tossed the ball over, then pulled himself up with one fluid movement. A second later, John Tolley was straddling the wall.

Two blue-uniformed security guards were waiting, one accompanied by a massive brindled Alsatian dog which watched alertly – head cocked, tennis ball clamped in a vice-like jaw. The effect was marred only slightly by the fact that all three were panting. A voice boomed from the building, metallic amplification failing to disguise a Scottish accent. Or the note of satisfaction. Sandy MacNaughton, stealing his line.

'I suppose you want your ball back, John. Come on

down, we've been expecting you. I'll put the kettle on.'

Tolley dropped to the turf. Smoothing rumpled clothing, he made firm eye contact with the dog and reached for his wallet. Slowly. The goons were bound to demand some identification, just to prove they weren't half asleep.

London

WES REMINGTON had passed on breakfast, despite Helen's thin-lipped disapproval – it was supposed to be quality time he spent with the kids, and his wife rightly suspected that a stomach empty of healthy muesli would later be consoled with lethal hamburger and fries.

What the hell. The kids always appeared late, grabbed a half-cup of coffee and ran for the bus. Muesli stuck in his throat. Hamburger and fries was America's greatest contribution to world cuisine. Helen was too uptight about everything. And he was the CIA's finest. So he'd reached the embassy on Grosvenor Square at 8 a.m., cleared his desk and aimed his mind at the day's main business.

Riding unofficial herd on Trojan Horse would consume a good chunk of his contingency budget. If the money was to be well spent, Beasley required a proper briefing. Cash wasn't a problem – he merely had to open his safe, remove banded bundles of used ten-pound notes and put them in a Jiffy bag. Providing he entered the requisite amount in the audit book and blandly wrote *Payment to informant* it was a done deal.

But putting together the necessary briefing wouldn't be so easy. Since the Aldrich Ames fiasco, the Company had beefed up internal security, reckoning that allowing employees continuing freedom to remove suitcases full of classified material might be seen as a tad lax. Actually, they'd gotten pretty tough. Every time he accessed a file on his desktop computer, the fact was recorded. When hard copy was printed off, he had to account for it, which meant producing the original for monthly audit or shredding in front of a witness. Each photocopy taken in his section had to be identified and logged by a duty operator.

There were ways around these checks, but if the Beasley

operation was to retain deniability, no incriminating traces could be left. Obliterating tracks might take time. While he was still thinking through the options, his direct line rang. Remington checked that the scrambler light was on and picked up.

'Yeah, Remington,'

'Wesley, it's Angus Churchill. Look here, old man, I think I may have come on a bit strong over lunch yesterday. Wouldn't want you to think we don't take your worries seriously. If Trojan Horse falls into the wrong hands it will make World War Three look like a storm in a teacup, so I just thought I'd set your mind at rest. I've put one of my best chaps on the case and I'll keep you posted. In the unlikely event that he comes up with anything, you'll know two minutes after me.'

Churchill oozed bonhomie. So, the canny MI5 man was already in butt-shielding mode. Wes Remington replied casually, as though other, weightier matters had already claimed his attention.

'That's great, Gus, but to tell you the truth I never gave it another thought. If you say everything's okay that's good enough for me. I'm happy to leave the matter in your capable hands. Like you said, your turf.'

'Your confidence is much appreciated, Wesley. Must be away – duty calls. Another wretched cost-cutting committee. I sometimes wonder if they really want us to catch the many and varied insects trying to bore their way into the national fabric. Good day.'

Remington replaced the telephone gently. Saying 'to tell you the truth' might have been a mistake. For all his laid-back Englishness, Angus Churchill didn't miss much. What the hell. They were all on the same side in the end, and the stout timbers of the Special Relationship were strong enough to withstand a few deathwatch beetle holes.

Wiltshire

ALL IN ALL, the morning had been satisfactory. The control room had spotted John Tolley on an external surveillance camera five minutes after he parked the supposedly unobtrusive maroon Ford Mondeo. Sandy MacNaughton knew how the MI5 man's mind worked. When Tolley had started prowling the perimeter, the Omega security chief guessed he'd try an unauthorized entry and deployed his forces accordingly. The end result had been gratifying.

Better still, the visit wasn't down to suspicion on Five's part that Omega's security was flawed. Instead, his former colleague had warned him of vague rumours originating from the CIA that nameless outsiders might be after Trojan Horse. As that particular assumption was the basis of MacNaughton's entire professional existence, the revelation didn't bother him. All intelligence services were paranoid, none more so than those staffed by Americans.

The security chief's homework had not been wasted. They'd spent over an hour going through his meticulous paperwork, which recorded no unusual activity that might indicate an attempt to steal Omega's secrets. Then he'd taken Tolley on the tour so he could evaluate state-of-the-art physical defences for himself.

There was one more thing. MacNaughton studied the self-possessed agent. He'd been John Tolley's superior at Five, helping him develop from bolshie Cambridge graduate who knew nothing into bolshie counter-intelligence officer who, despite or because of a frictional tendency to resent authority, was the best in the business. A man who was both efficient and trustworthy. Reading his thoughts, Tolley raised black eyebrows and smiled the smile that could charm birds into his hand.

'Remind me to take a few quid off you at poker some time. Come on, Sandy, you've got that shall-I-shan't-I-tell-him look on your face, and you're lousy at keeping secrets. Spit it out.'

Ruefully, MacNaughton returned the smile.

'This is strictly off the record, but you should know. It's Louise Boss, who heads up the Trojan Horse development team. She's been taking stuff out of the building, working at home. The project's on a tight schedule and the future of this company more or less depends on successful completion. She's Grade One security cleared and assures me the material can't be accessed by anyone else. Even so, the risk element worries me. Suppose someone busts in there and forces the access codes out of her?'

Tolley looked shocked.

'If that happened we'd both be in deep ordure, Sandy. Churchill would fire me and have you out of that comfortable chair faster than he could say "It's not Gus's fault". As it is we're ankle deep. You're not seriously expecting me to leave this out of my report?'

MacNaughton said nothing. Tolley held the horrified expression until he realized his bluff had been called, then grinned.

'Maybe you're not such a bad poker player after all. Okay, but I must have a quiet word with her. Good-looker, is she?'

'Don't be led astray by those turbocharged hormones, John. Louise is an attractive young woman, but she lives for her work. Sure, there's a man, but she isn't really into sex. I could explain why, but'll spare you the psychobabble. My advice is simple. Cling to that old maxim about not mixing business and pleasure as though your soul depended on it.'

Tolley laughed, obviously thinking his old mentor was behaving like a neurotic mother hen. Sandy MacNaughton shook his head sadly and reached for the phone. The *boychik* had no idea what was about to hit him.

London

THE THRUSTFUL young investment banker intended to lure her into bed, and Jenny Symes was playing the sort of admiring innocent who would surely let him have his wicked way. She gazed adoringly at his animated face as he waxed lyrical about his latest penis extension.

'Yuh, I agonized for weeks before deciding on the convertible. It was ten grand extra, but I made the right decision. Just the job as a summer runaround. I had her up to one-forty on the M11 going to my country place, and the wind in your hair at that speed is something else. A turn-on, or what? You really must try it some time.

Next weekend sound good?'

Jenny managed a girlish giggle.

'I'd love to, but I'm sort of tied up with this story I'm working on at the moment. Conrad Lancaster. I actually interviewed him yesterday. Rather charming, I thought.'

The banker's eyes narrowed. He'd already run through his annual bonus, Docklands apartment, moated Essex farmhouse, three expensive sports cars, vintage Bentley, powerboat, flying lessons with a view to purchasing a modest twin-engined aircraft, and recent holidays in some of the world's most exotic locations. Small talk was running out, and he detected a hint that his prospective trophy might be snatched away by an even stronger competitor. He sipped his glass of ninety-pound-a-bottle claret before speaking gravely, like a wise parent to straying daughter.

'Don't be fooled, Jennifer. Everything in that particular garden isn't quite as rosy as it seems. I could tell you a thing or two about that fat slug, believe me.'

'Really?'

She allowed subtly plucked eyebrows to go into orbit. The banker looked at her and entirely failed to notice an incisive investigative journalist. Instead, he saw an attractive blonde TV presenter with big tits, whose conquest would be the talk of City dealing rooms for weeks. He glanced around the dimly lit basement wine bar and leaned towards his victim.

'Rumour has it that Werner Anschütz was seen coming out of Lancaster House yesterday . . .'

He paused, knowing she didn't understand the significance of this damning snippet. For once, he was right. Jenny assumed the disappointed expression of someone expecting a juicy revelation who has heard nothing.

'So?'

The banker smiled and tapped the side of his nose with a well-manicured forefinger, preparing to overwhelm her with inside knowledge.

'So Werner Anschütz is a senior director of a second-rate Swiss bank which is carrying a relatively modest loan to a Lancaster Trust subsidiary company. The sort of thing subordinates deal with in ten minutes on the telephone. But those dogs in Zurich have noses like bloodhounds.

Take it from me, if Werner wants his poxy few quid back and makes a special visit to London to get it, there's big trouble brewing for Mr Conrad-smug-bastard-Lancaster's business empire.'

Jenny looked hurt.

'But he told me things have never been better.'

She looked at her tiny Cartier watch. Two minutes to go. Her suitor grinned foxily.

'He would, wouldn't he. But there's been some strange activity in the market this morning – heavy demand for Lancaster Trust stock from offshore buyers. Put the two things together and it's obvious. The cunning old huckster's buying in his own shares to artificially inflate the price. But we've seen it all before. I unloaded my Lancaster Trust before breakfast and the rest soon got the message. Despite all those buy orders it's down thirty points and falling. We'll take him for every pound he throws at us, then watch him sink like a stone. Before the rot really set in, I even sold ten million's worth of shares I haven't got. I'll be able to buy in the same packet for seven before I have to deliver. Three mil for the bank and a nice earner for me. Not many people have what it takes to trouser three hundred grand for a day's work, sweetheart.'

Face flushed, he finished his wine and poured another glass, enjoying the prospect of profiting from the tycoon's troubles ... and the stimulating thought of Jenny Symes on his satin-sheeted water bed wearing no more than a black velvet ribbon around her neck. She injected indignation into her voice.

'Conrad *lied* to me!'

The banker placed a sympathetic but proprietorial hand on hers.

'You weren't the first and won't be the last, my dear. Better minds than yours have been taken in by Conrad Lancaster. He's an operator, I'll give him that. Now ...'

Right on cue, her mobile burbled. She freed her hand and rummaged, finally producing the patient phone from her bulging Gucci shoulder bag. As expected, it was her secretary.

'The rain in Spain stays mainly on the plain, Little Miss Muffet is sitting on her tuffet and the rubber plant in reception badly needs watering.'

'I see. Yes, of course. I'll come at once.'

She smiled sweetly at the bemused banker.

'Must fly, Hugo. Crisis at the office. It's been *really* interesting. We must do this again some time.'

Jenny Symes – presenter of TV's top-rating *Guardian Angel* consumer show and quarter owner of Pandora's Box Productions – swept up her coat and bag, pecked bonking banker Hugo Savage on the cheek and fled. She knew to the penny what he'd earned last year, because he'd told her three times. It was peanuts.

North Devon

TOM LANCASTER'S body was cold, but the chill inside was worse, He wasn't so much afraid for himself, though this no longer seemed like an adventure, but for his mother. Since the fizzle of morning excitement when freedom briefly beckoned, they'd hardly spoken. After the men chained her and left them alone, she'd withdrawn into herself, lying on the air-bed and curling up tightly. Though she tried to hide the fact, she'd been silently crying.

But they shouldn't, wouldn't, *couldn't* give in. He was kneeling on the floor examining his discovery with the torch. A hand-forged nail, five inches long and dark with old rust, was wedged in the wide crack between ancient floorboards. With luck and a suitable tool, he might be able to prise it loose.

There were sounds outside the door. He darted to his mother, sitting cross-legged beside her as though he had not moved for an hour. When the two masked men came in, he eyed them stonily. The first was the tall one who did all the talking; the second looked like the one clouted with the gas cylinder. He was carrying a video camera and battery pack. The in-built flood filled the room with bright light, and Tom was afraid they'd notice his nail. But their minds were on other things.

'Get up, Mrs Lancaster, sit at the table. Tom, put the TV set on the table facing this way. It's time to send your doting dad proof you're alive and well.'

He did as he was told, but not until his mother had scrambled up, chain rattling as she eased into the patio chair. Her face was pale. He squeezed her hand before lifting the small television on to the table.

'Switch on, then sit down. BBC One. The news should just be starting.'

Tom pushed a button and the set came to life. Though the picture was snowy, sound quality was perfect – the newsreader was beginning a story about trouble in Russia, where politicians were being murdered by terrorists.

'Good. That'll do nicely. Say cheese.'

The tall one came over and smoothed down his mother's red hair, which was a mess. It was an insulting reminder of their helplessness, but she didn't react until he stepped back, when she shook her head violently to undo his remedial work. Tom felt like hitting the man, but settled for clenching his fists. He looked into dazzling light as the short one raised the camera and started shooting.

Moscow

HOW DID the world of espionage function before digital mobile phones were invented? They made life – and plotting – so simple. When Gregor Gorski had been a young KGB field operative, half his energies went on devising secure contact mechanisms with agents – covert radio sets, dead-letter boxes with telltale marks chalked on lamppost or tree, couriers adept at exchanging one folded newspaper for another, microdot full points buried in books, mail containing coded instructions posted from neutral countries, cryptic messages on Moscow Radio. The permutations were endless.

Now you pulled out your Motorola, hit the right buttons and waited for the connection. Interception was difficult though technically possible, but with millions of calls simultaneously bouncing round the ether, the chances were remote. Even if he'd been targeted and scanners were locked on, he wouldn't be giving much away.

'Hello.'

The well-remembered voice was bellclear. Dmitry

Travkin might have been in the next street, rather than five thousand kilometres away. Gregor Gorski switched to English, which he spoke well, reminding himself that he was not talking to a former star pupil of the KGB Academy but Andrew Rosson, antiquarian bookseller.

'Can you talk?'

'Yes. I'm in the warehouse. We've prepared the invoice and I'll despatch it personally. I don't anticipate problems with payment. Collection should take place on Thursday.'

Gregor Gorski kept the conversation businesslike – if interested ears were listening, they would hear no more than a thoroughly modern Russian entrepreneur wheeling another deal.

'Shipment arrangements are as agreed. Don't release the goods until I confirm safe receipt of payment, and don't forget they must be kept in perfect condition.'

'Of course.'

The instantaneous answer told a tale, which Gregor Gorski read. Rosson had been softened by years of comfortable Western living, and was only undertaking this mission for money. Or fear of the consequences of declining. The man was relieved he wouldn't be required to engage in any violent action. Gregor Gorski broke the connection and redialled. When it came to violence, he had a much better option.

The technology really was marvellous. How else could you travel from Moscow to Devonshire and on via a nautical relay to a luxury motor cruiser somewhere in the English Channel, all inside a couple of minutes, briefing two sets of agents along the way? When the radio telephone on the flying bridge of *Lara's Song* was answered, Gregor Gorski kept his instruction short, but sweet.

'It's on for Thursday, as arranged.'

This was too easy for words.

Wiltshire

SHE WASN'T PLEASED by the urgent call to Sandy MacNaughton's office, which had come in the middle of a shouting match with one of her team – a bright kid afflicted with a head full of Roman candles. So Louise Boss had ignored the peremptory summons, left her phone off the hook and concentrated on refocusing the young programmer's explosive energy. Not even Omega's head of security could get at her inside the programming suite.

Eventually, after keeping MacNaughton waiting for an hour, she relented, breezing into his office with a cheery 'Something came up'. Louise stopped. Sandy had a visitor, and she was surprised by the tingle that ran through her circuits. Early thirties, longish straight black hair, well-made face, tanned complexion, athletic shape, casually bouncing an old tennis ball and catching it without taking intent grey eyes off her face. But she had all that just a phone call away, right down to the ball skills. It was something else – an unexpected frisson that shouted 'danger'. Louise flopped into the spare visitor's chair.

'I'm knackered. Must be all these late nights. So, who's your friend, Sandy?'

Unlike the intriguing stranger, MacNaughton had risen courteously, and made formal introductions.

'Louise Boss, our superstar programmer, John Tolley. John's down from London to run the slide rule over our security arrangements. Everyone's getting a bit nervous about Trojan Horse. We're doing all right thus far, mind. My lads caught him *in flagrante* climbing over the side wall.'

She laughed.

'I'm not surprised. Anyone who still uses a slide rule deserves to be arrested.'

The man smiled, and Louise felt another lurch.

'Just testing. This miserable bastard used to be my boss, and I've been trying to put one over on him for years. One of these days . . .'

The light, amused voice trailed away and he shrugged deprecatingly. She crossed her arms.

'A spy-catcher! I guess you're going to thrash me to within an inch of my life for indulging in unnatural after-hours security practices.'

'Sorry to disappoint you. I could arrest you under the Official Secrets Act and make sure you're put out of harm's way for the next thirty years, but you'll have to settle for a slapped wrist this time. Sandy tells me you're a law unto yourself. They're all shit scared you'll down tools and screw up the precious project. But I will read you the Riot Act.'

There was a warning beneath the banter. Louise stood up.

'Buy me lunch. The staff restaurant does a mean toad-in-the-hole with spotted dick to follow.'

He followed her up, looked down from his superior height and flashed that damned smile again.

'I think I'm man enough for that. Lead on, Boss.'

Louise had to restrain a ridiculous impulse to slip a companionable hand beneath Tolley's arm, aware that Sandy MacNaughton was watching with a sardonic expression on his craggy Scottish face.

London

HOPEFULLY, articles planted on the business pages of his newspapers might yet bear fruit – a faint hope, but better than nothing. Conrad Lancaster was experiencing the stomach-tightening thrill of a roulette player staking everything on one last play. The wheel was spinning, the ball circulating . . . but where would it fall?

The omens weren't good. Despite rapacious demand for Lancaster Trust stock from his own offshore trusts, the share price had tumbled all morning. Conrad had spent £40 million he didn't have on the support operation, but would continue for as long as his buy orders were accepted. There was less than nothing to lose by carrying on until the bastards finally cut him down, or he burst through enemy lines and emerged triumphant.

He leaned back in his leather chair, interlaced plump fingers and squeezed until the knuckles whitened. Defeat was not an option. He was meaner, tougher and more determined than the lot of them put together. The City of London might be a formidable foe, but possessed one critical weakness – herd instinct.

Right now, hard-nosed traders were stampeding to sell

Lancaster Trust. The sharper ones, seeing the trend, were selling stock they hadn't got – expecting to pick up contracted shares at lower cost before settlement day. But sudden fear of getting caught short could cause the stampede to falter. Slow to a walk. Stop. Then the herd would gallop back in the opposite direction, to pick up the Lancaster Trust stock they needed before a rising share price turned their positions negative. All he had to do was frighten them.

He felt good – only those capable of gambling with their very lives could know *how* good – and Conrad Lancaster was a winner. Panic was a weak, despicable vice. He relaxed, took a cigar from the humidor on his large desk and accorded it full ceremony – chopping the end with a silver cutter, stripping the band, squeezing hand-rolled Cuban leaves, striking a match and allowing the sulphur to burn off before lighting up. Only when the Monte Cristo was burning evenly did Conrad get up and go to the wall safe, tastefully concealed behind a large framed colour photograph of himself, arm in arm with Russia's President, Mikhail Yelkin.

Conrad removed a small notebook from his safe, returned to his desk and flipped through to the right entry. After jotting some numbers on to a pad with his thick-nibbed Mont Blanc, he picked up the phone. All calls had been held, but the duty PA didn't make the mistake of bothering him with a list of frustrated callers.

'Yes, Mr Lancaster?'

'Arrange the immediate transfer of two hundred thousand pounds sterling from my personal account in Geneva to a numbered account at the Kreditbank of Zurich. Come in and I'll give you the details. When you've done that, get me Peregrine Greenfield-Wright. Then tell the dining room to serve a late lunch in twenty minutes.'

Doreen Scott appeared almost before he put the phone down, immaculate in charcoal pin-stripe suit and white blouse. He ripped the top sheet off his pad. As she took it and retreated without a word, Conrad wondered when she last experienced real excitement – if she ever had. He savoured the cigar. Some moments in a man's life were too exquisite for words, and this might be one of them.

The telephone buzzed.

'Mr Greenfield-Wright for you.'

'Put him through. Perry, how goes it?'

'Not well, as far as you're concerned. I see Lancaster Trust is down thirty-two and in free fall.'

The upper-class voice expressed no more than casual interest. As one of the country's most respected financial journalists, lobbying calls from commerceocrats were routine. Conrad exhaled a plume of aromatic smoke before continuing.

'Oh, I don't know. You saw those few bits in my rags this morning about the planned disposal programme. Well, the market obviously dismissed them as typical hot air, but you might consider snapping up a few Lancaster Trust for your private portfolio. As you know, Microsoft is set on becoming the major internet player. I've just come off the phone with Bill, and he's agreed to pay two hundred million dollars for my NetAxS operation in the States. In cash . . .'

Both men knew Conrad Lancaster had never even spoken to Bill Gates, and that NetAxS was optimistically valued at fifty million, less substantial over-borrowings. They also knew that Peregrine Greenfield-Wright's column in an authoritative broadsheet newspaper not owned by Lancaster Trust was the first thing most City players turned to over early morning tea and toast. His integrity, regular delivery of solid inside information and almost supernaturally accurate predictions were legendary. The guru's plummy voice remained neutral.

'Microsoft swallows NetAxS for megabucks? Great story, even if Gates denies it. Perhaps there's a confidentiality clause which means the deal's off if some enterprising journalist breaks the story. But that won't become apparent for a few days, will it? You're right. Lancaster Trust might be a good short-term buy, if I ever dealt in shares affected by anything I write. I'll just make an overseas phone call to check everything is in order, then start rewriting tomorrow's piece.'

'Everything's apple-pie, Perry, believe me. With cream.'

'I do hope so. Give my best regards to your lovely wife.'

'Of course. And mine to your handsome companion of

the moment.'

Conrad Lancaster gently laid the telephone to rest. Insurance could be a life-saver, especially when you didn't have to pay the premium until a claim was necessary. This one-off arrangement had been negotiated months ago, for just such a crisis. Conrad had little doubt that Greenfield-Wright's representatives would be gobbling up Lancaster Trust stock options at low, low prices, just before the market closed.

And when Bill Gates failed to deliver, well, even the best of financial journalists could be excused an occasional honest mistake.

Somerset

ANDREW ROSSON could have sent one of the others to post the videotape, but it was good to get away from the claustrophobic quayside building. His fee was earmarked for the kids' school fees, among other things, but he was beginning to appreciate how gravely the only life he had left was threatened.

The woman and child had seen his face. The woman and child were not to be harmed. The woman and child would be released if ransom was paid. What then? There was nowhere to run to. He was no longer Russian patriot Dmitry Travkin, who had been erased from all but most secret records. He was no longer a KGB sleeper, awaiting his country's call – the organization that once nurtured and placed him was defunct and chaotic new Russia had forgotten he existed.

He was British citizen Andrew Rosson, with an English wife and two children. The authorities would leave no stone unturned in pursuit of kidnappers who dared to snatch a woman and child associated with a citizen as prominent as Conrad Lancaster. Even if the tycoon kept quiet until his nearest and dearest were returned, the subsequent manhunt would be relentless. Kidnapping was not tolerated in Britain.

The Astra estate car droned along the picturesque A39 coast road, carrying him towards Bristol at a steady 60 mph. But his mind went full circle. The woman and child had seen his face. The woman and child were not to be harmed. The woman and child would be released if the ransom was paid. What then? They would talk. There would be descriptions. E-fit pictures in all the newspapers. Television appeals. Tabloid hysteria. A neighbour in Hay-on-Wye who remarked on the uncanny likeness, or an alert customer who noticed resemblance between kidnapper and antiquarian book dealer. Then the first, tentative telephone call to the police, after which it would only be a matter of time.

Not enough of emotionless, KGB-trained Dmitry Travkin remained in him, after all. He respected the Lancaster woman, who had spirit, and the boy, who had courage. He knew exactly what action Dmitry would take if these innocents threatened his very being. But there had to be another way, because such ruthless behaviour was not for Englishman Andrew Rosson.

Mid-Atlantic

THANKS TO adverse time zones, 220 scheduled minutes of flying time would allow the clock to advance by almost nine hours before James Lancaster landed at London Heathrow, after departing JFK in New York at 08.45. Without investment of over five thousand dollars in the supersonic assistance of Concorde, arrival time would have been even later.

He was trying to rest as the sharp-nosed plane arrowed through rarefied air, but sleep was an elusive haven. It was always that way on a job. Adrenalin cut in, blocking his body's demand for downtime.

His mind struggled with unwanted memories and unbidden thoughts – images that flashed and danced like random frames from a surreal silent film. A man cheating death in a run-down Irish farmhouse. A wild bear granted life in an Oregon valley bottom. An empty house on the ocean in LA. Money that didn't buy freedom. The expression on the face of a small Mexican boy as hope rekindled. His own mother's careworn face, his brother's trusting face, his father's treacherous face. Simple garden flowers beside a showy wreath on an oak coffin. A woman loved and lost. Betrayal.

He wondered how Liz had changed in the lifetime since last they talked, laughed at nothing, made love, parted. Now she had a son, a husband, perhaps virile lovers who satisfied her without realizing how lucky they were. The air pressure in Concorde's narrow cabin hadn't changed, but James Lancaster swallowed hard. His father couldn't have found a more cruel – or subtle – way of punishing him for breaking away.

Predictable from Conrad, but James had never stopped being angry at Liz for co-operating so willingly, so soon. Yet anger was hollow, filled with corrosive self-contempt. The fault wasn't hers. If only he had been able to summon the courage to ask, Liz would have come with him. But that sort of commitment meant he had to open himself to the possibility of hurt, so he chose to run away. Alone. And it hurt anyway.

Now the woman and her child were lost. Though it meant doing his father's bidding, bending to his father's will, playing his father's mind games, James Lancaster had no choice. He would put everything he had into finding the missing ones. Not for Conrad, or even for Liz and Tom. But for himself.

Wiltshire

HE LEFT the Omega building and walked to his car, parked up the road outside. No point in hanging around – he'd found nothing that might justify CIA fears that Trojan Horse was vulnerable. Hadn't expected to, because Sandy MacNaughton ran a tight ship. But John Tolley didn't drive away.

After reassuring the Scottish security chief that all was well, he'd given the man a damned good talking-to. Describing Louise Boss as 'an attractive young woman' was a knee-capping offence under the Trade Descriptions Act. The programmer was drop-dead gorgeous. Over a light lunch in Omega's futuristic staff restaurant, they'd taken guard like Olympic fencers, probing mutual defences with lightning-fast repartee and enjoying every moment of the contest. That was a stand-off, though what followed wasn't.

Louise had picked up his tennis ball from the table, told him there was an indoor court in the basement health club and asked if he played. He said, 'A bit, but I'm not that good'. Lie. He played for two hours every Sunday and – though he said it himself – wielded a mean racket. But for her he was willing to suspend ferocious will to win and go easy. She'd replied, 'Same here.' Lie.

She found him some kit and – after a brisk knock-up that suggested going easy wasn't an option – had thrashed him 6-0 in nineteen minutes. As she shook his hand over the net, barely out of breath and smiling demurely, John Tolley had gulped down his pride and decided he was impressed.

They'd showered and gone their separate ways, but she must have seen something in him, too. MacNaughton later revealed that Louise Boss spending two consecutive hours away from her work station was less usual than the Queen getting down on her knees and scrubbing the front steps of Buckingham Palace.

With a resigned twist of the key, John Tolley started the Mondeo. He probably wouldn't be coming back – this trip said more about Gus Churchill's overdeveloped sense of self-preservation than any real threat to Trojan Horse. The boss of K Branch was famously defensive when it came to his rear end, and doubtless felt it prudent to go through straining motions after receiving the CIA's warning. And now, if something did go wrong, on whose head would the steaming pile land?

Sod it. He switched off the engine and reached for his mobile, keying #M1 for an automatic connection to Churchill's office. The great man was unavailable, so Tolley left a message on voicemail. He gave the general gist, careful to say nothing that might cause alarm – all quiet on the Western front, but sensible to stay down here for a couple of days and sniff around Omega some more. Just in case the CIA have got something right for once. Expect me when you see me.

London

NO SECURITY SYSTEM can be omnipotent, and Wes Remington had decided on a crude but effective solution to his little problem with the Beasley briefing documents. As CIA Chief of Station, he was not expected to undergo the indignity of being frisked by US Marines every time he left the embassy. So he simply jammed the wad of printout in his briefcase and walked out into Grosvenor Square, jauntily whistling 'The Star-Spangled Banner'. He strolled to a self-service bureau off Regent Street and photocopied the lot. There were also a number of photographs, which he put through the Canon colour copier in batches.

While he worked, Remington considered how fully he could enlighten his freelance agent. Beasley was discreet, but should be told no more than he needed to know to do his job – a task that hardly required the release of any state secrets.

The brief was simple. CIA feared an imminent attempt to steal sensitive military software from Omega Dynamic Systems. Omega's security was rock solid. Therefore, any penetration was likely to involve suborning person or persons with the necessary inside track. Observe and report back. No active intervention. Knowledge would be enough, and Beasley was the best information-gatherer money could buy.

Remington felt no need to impart the nature or name of Trojan Horse, but a question remained, circling Conrad Lancaster like a persistent albatross. CIA analysts were suspicious of the man, whose proximity to such a sensitive project was the cause of present unease. Omega had developed the technology, so there was no choice, but that didn't mean they liked the situation.

Nothing had ever been proved, but the tycoon had Russian links going back to Nikita Khrushchev's day. He'd been doing business there for decades, operating smoothly where other Western companies stumbled over countless obstacles. He was doing business there still, which indicated new and dubious alliances. If the Russians knew about Trojan Horse, how did they find out? And if they coveted it, who better to turn to for help than Omega's dynamic proprietor?

Yes, he'd better tell Beasley to put a microscope on Conrad Lancaster, who was less trustworthy than a starving gorilla on a banana boat. Decision made, he sealed the copies into a large brown envelope, settled the bill in cash and took a taxi to the embassy. Safely back in the office, he put the Beasley papers in his safe and called his secretary. The crisp collegian was there in a flash, eager to please a boss whose reports would determine his future in the Agency. Remington gestured casually at the original print-out, innocently sitting in the middle of his desk.

'Cal, there's concern about a major software project we've funded here in Britain, code-name Trojan Horse. Possible security leak. I've gone through the files to get up to speed and want you to sign them off before I shred. Then draft a signal. Tell Langley I've spoken with Gus Churchill of MI5, who assures me they're busting their busy asses on this one. I'm not one hundred per cent happy, but there ain't a whole lot more I can do.'

'Yes, sir!'

As the youngster bent a crew-cut head over the files and started checking off reference numbers on the record sheet, Wes Remington placed his hands behind his head and leant back in his chair. They also served who only sat around, apparently doing absolutely nothing the goddam rule book prohibited.

Wiltshire

HE WASN'T really playing truant. MacNaughton was right – leaving one of the nation's most sensitive secrets lying around a country cottage was a serious security risk, whatever electronic protection Louise Boss had installed. As the counter-espionage professional tasked with protecting Trojan Horse, checking out Beggar's Roost was John Tolley's bounden duty.

The fact he was doing so without shackling himself in official paper chains didn't bother him. MI5 had always bugged and burgled as necessary. Certain members of the government had taken exception to being spied on in their formative years, and the introduction of tough new regulations on phone tapping and covert entry was a predictable if ineffective knee-jerk which changed nothing. Besides, a formal request would involve explanations that would drop his mentor and friend Sandy MacNaughton right in it.

None of which had anything to do with the reason he was studying the pretty but run-down cottage with miniature field glasses. Ancient roof tiles were lichen-covered, and stone walls were almost obscured by unitidy flora – virginia creeper, honeysuckle and clematis – which had been allowed to run riot, almost concealing tiny windows and boldly scaling the roof. No sign of life or – equally significantly – burglar alarm.

John Tolley was spying on Beggar's Roost because Louise lived there. He wanted to know more about her, and was good at finding things out. He drifted through the overgrown rear garden and tried the ledge-and-brace back door. Secured with a Chubb dead-lock, quite possibly bolted on the inside. Leaded diamond-pane ground-floor windows had solid-looking locks, too, but forcing entry would be easy. There was no sign of an alarm, so he didn't anticipate difficulty in getting inside without leaving traces.

He went round to the front. No houses overlooked the secluded cottage, and nothing had used the lane while he'd been watching. Green paint was peeling from the solid front door, sheltering beneath a tiled porch with oak uprights smothered in chocolate-box climbing roses that had started to bud. He picked the deadlock inside a minute and loided the Yale with a rectangle of stiff plastic from his junior locksmith's kit, stepping onto a large *WELCOME* mat in a cool, dark hallway with low ceiling and uneven floor of honey-coloured tiles.

Tolley paused, listening to silence as he assessed the layout. Passage through to rear kitchen. One main room to the left, another to the right. Somewhere, a staircase. Upstairs, maybe two bedrooms and a bathroom. Kitchen first – untidily lived-in. White-painted, in need of refresher coat. Unwashed mugs, cutlery and plates in china Belfast sink. Mud-spattered black rubber boots by the back door, which was indeed bolted. Unopened junk mail scattered on a small pine table, turned legs scarred by feline claws. Three licked-clean food bowls on rush-matted floor. Two ladder-back country chairs. Fridge-freezer, microwave, electric cooker, with washing machine and tumble-drier beneath tiled worktop – all looking as though they could do with a wipe-over. Cobwebs in corners of the beamed ceiling. A flap clattered and a grey cat appeared, padding expectantly to the empty bowls. Tolley rubbed its head, and was rewarded with loud purring.

Austere dining room next – little used, dust filming polished mahogany table and matching Victorian chairs, apricot carpet, framed watercolour seascapes on William Morris walls. Tidy living room – boarded floor scattered with bright rugs, inglenook with piled logs and heaped wood ash on blackened brick base, overfull built-in bookshelves each side of the fireplace, comfortable-looking sofa and two matching armchairs. Television and video. No sound system. Answerphone with blinking light.

He listened to the message. Some man confirming a date for that night. Deep voice. Slight West Country accent. Just a hint of diffidence that John Tolley read like a book – however much he wanted to, this guy couldn't quite get his legs far enough under Louise Boss's table.

After rewinding the message, he used the narrow door hiding a dog-leg staircase. Upstairs, John Tolley glanced through the open door of Louise's bedroom, which had sloping ceilings, dormer window and brass bedstead with floral duvet cover. But personal curiosity was overcome by professional instinct, and he turned to the double-locked door across the tiny landing. Her computer room.

If the policemen hadn't been so stupid, they might have caught him. He'd just slid a pick into the first lock when he heard a distant siren, and kept the tiny tool in his hand as he raced downstairs. Resecuring the front door took for ever, and when the lock finally clicked, two-tone noise was rising to a menacing crescendo. He fled round the cottage, catching a flash of blue strobe light through the thick yew hedge. Car doors slammed as he made his escape via the back garden, devoutly hoping they hadn't brought a dog with them. He'd had enough of slavering Alsatians for one day.

A bloody silent alarm. He'd looked, but hadn't spotted anything. Smart little lady. As he recovered his breath and slowed to a walk, safely on a public footpath, John Tolley realized he was starting to enjoy himself. With the tennis fiasco, that made the score 2-0 to Louise Boss – but the match was just beginning.

Moscow

VOYEURISM might be a weakness, but Gregor Gorski couldn't kick his addiction. Once, the KGB had provided him with the opportunity to indulge himself personally, but now he had to settle for watching. And to be fair, he hadn't attended the execution of Gennady Churkov, instead making do with those disgusting photographs which caused such a stir in the media.

The National Hotel, across the road from Red Square, was one of Moscow's most prestigious hotels. Built to I. A. Ivanov's grand design in 1903, and home to Lenin in 1918, the National had just enjoyed a major facelift ahead of its hundredth birthday. The lobby was busy – foreign businessmen of every colour coming and going, elegant women trawling for hard currency, home-grown entrepreneurs heading for the restaurant surrounded by men with bulges beneath the arms of expensive suits. And a crowd of media hyenas jostling outside the barber's shop. Only the beautifully dressed women spared Gregor Gorski a glance, experienced eyes quickly deciding that he not only lacked the necessary dollars, but was best avoided. He licked dry lips.

Those unruly journalists were awaiting the appearance of Interior Minister Anton Mossberg – a vain man who had thinning hair primped here every Tuesday, no matter what crises were swirling around the government. The plump politician had obviously recovered his composure since the flustered interview Gregor Gorski had watched on television that morning – striding grandly out of the barber's surrounded by bodyguards. Everyone who was anyone in Moscow needed bodyguards, but they would not save Mossberg from the Sons of Dudayev.

Their next target was the former hardliner whose Red grandfather had fled from Berlin to Moscow back in 1933. Without so much as a hint of regret, Anton Mossberg had abandoned the ideology of five generations and become an ardent free marketeer. Gregor Gorski felt nothing but contempt for opportunism, and shuddered to think that such a man was within striking distance of the top. If anything happened to President Mikhail Yelkin, he might even be the government clique's preferred candidate. Which couldn't be allowed to happen.

Despite the agitation of his minders, Mossberg intended to take full advantage of this opportunity for publicity, raising both arms in immodest salute as he prepared to spout meaningless platitudes. The media surged forward, microphones jutting and cameras flashing. Even Gregor Gorski didn't know where the silenced shot came from or – for a moment – that it had come at all. Then one of Russia's most senior politicians staggered slightly and fell against one of the bodyguards, who tried to hold him upright. The others drew Makarov pistols and pointed them uselessly at the mêlée of journalists, which scattered in all directions. Women screamed. Pandemonium engulfed the lobby.

As Gregor Gorski shut his battered copy of *War and Peace* and faded out of a side door, the braver television crews were already training their cameras on the body of Anton Mossberg, which by now lay face down in a spreading pool of blood.

Wiltshire

AT FIRST, the call from Sandy MacNaughton had been another irritation in a disrupted day. When the security chief told her the alarm at Beggar's Roost had gone off, Louise Boss hardly seemed to have settled after crossing rackets with the man from London. No sign of forced entry, so it was probably a system malfunction. But the police would wait until she got home, in case an intruder had failed to escape and was lurking inside the cottage.

Upon reflection, the enforced break was no bad thing. That electric encounter with John Tolley had been disconcerting, undermining her usual ability to focus totally on the programming problem of the moment. And she had a date with Danny Woodward. If she'd got locked into catching up on undone work, the amiable footballer would doubtless have been stood up – again. He deserved better.

She turned through her side gate and parked the Fiesta. A police sergeant came to meet her, repeating the story she already knew. Louise thanked him and walked round to the front, where a constable was waiting. After unlocking the green door, she told the policemen to wait and stepped over the *WELCOME* mat. Lifting it gently, she looked at telltale evidence beneath – two ill-defined but obvious footprints in flour sprinkled beneath the mat.

'Looks like someone's been and gone, Sergeant, but you're welcome to take a look.'

They did, following her as she checked that nothing was missing. The tape in a hidden fibre-optic videocam that automatically started recording if the computer room door opened was blank, so the intruder hadn't got that far. But the skilled entry – and relocking of the front door – hardly suggested a common thief disturbed in the act. Assuring the concerned sergeant that she'd be fine, Louise walked the two policemen out and saw them on their way. When the police car had vanished down the lane, she went back in to make two telephone calls.

The first was to Sandy MacNaughton, telling him what had happened. The second was to Danny Woodward's four-bedroomed executive house on an exclusive estate just outside Swindon. He shared it with six perfectly trained English springer spaniels and several photographs of his ex-wife, who had followed the Robins' star goal-poacher when he got a big-money transfer to Tottenham Hotspur.

Danny sounded pleased to hear her voice, and surprised when she said 'We are on for tonight, aren't we?', as though the assignation had never been in doubt as far as she was concerned. In fact, he sounded pathetically grateful that she would be there, and Louise felt a rush of affection for her uncomplicated, gentle giant.

West Suffolk

DARKNESS was falling as James Lancaster turned off the A14 just short of Bury St Edmunds, negotiated a roundabout and took the road for Fornham All Saints. He'd pushed the hired Volkswagen Golf GTi hard, ignored speed cameras and been lucky – for once, traffic on the infamous M25 circling London flowed freely, and the journey from Heathrow had taken less than two hours.

He turned left on to a minor road. The last time he passed this way, long ago, he had been in an army car *en route* to Peter's funeral, just after that last near-fatal mission in Northern Ireland. As if to remind him of an ordeal he tried to forget, his still-troublesome left knee started throbbing, though this probably had more to do with chill evening air flooding through the open car window than unhappy memories.

Death respected civilized working hours. The crematorium was closed, but the green cross-barred gates were open, and he drove up to the empty carpark. As he limped towards the brightly lit Chapel of Remembrance, James Lancaster relived a miserable day. He thought time had blurred the edges, but now everything snapped back into focus. Conrad noticeable by his absence. A man of God speaking kindly about someone he hadn't known. The tiny gathering of mourners who witnessed his brother's final departure from a world he'd never learned to live in. Liz Greener before she became someone James no longer knew. The sad face of a middle-aged cleaner called Angela Gallyon, handing him a note to guard a reputation. James had inherited the Suffolk cottage, which was let to Angela's nephew for a nominal rent. Peter would have approved.

James stopped beside the tiny chapel, standing in half-light with his back to neatly tended flower-beds. Ahead, fields of winter wheat rippled in evening breeze, rolling away to dark woodland that defined the horizon. Three words. That was all it had taken to sum up his brother's life, and a pointless death that still weighed heavily on his conscience. *I'm so lonely.*

James Lancaster knew the feeling. But there was no easy way out for him. He hadn't been there for Peter, but he was here. The journey down memory lane had been necessary. Now it was done, he was ready to face his father, and deal with whatever Conrad threw at him.

Wiltshire

WHEN DANNY'S Land Rover Discovery pulled up in the lane, she was waiting outside her front gate. He leaned over to open the passenger door. Louise jumped in and grabbed his outstretched hand. She kissed him hard, putting the captive hand on her breast and finding his tongue with hers. After a frantic moment, he disengaged himself with a smile.

'Sorry. No sex in match weeks. The boss says it saps our moral fibre.'

'And which boss is going to have your ear tonight?'

She pouted, and he laughed.

'If it's only my ear you're interested in, forget it.'

There was something different about him. As they drove off, Louise wondered what it was, but couldn't define the change. Danny was relaxed, the slight air of anxiety that accompanied him everywhere except on to a football pitch noticeably absent. Perhaps it was just that another soccer season was ending – one in which small-town club Swindon had done far better than anyone expected. Or was there suppressed excitement in the air?

People who live in the country notice the unusual. Even though she was thinking about her lover, Louise half saw a maroon car in the gloom, parked off the lane on a track leading up to woods behind her house. Wondered briefly what a vehicle was doing there. Pigeon shooter? Dog-walker? Courting couple? Forgot it.

Hostelries were few and far between in the empty countryside east of Malmesbury, so they settled for the nearest, the Three Crowns at Brinkworth. Louise sat beside the log fire, at a table fashioned from a polished blacksmith's bellows. Danny fetched drinks – half of lager for himself, a pint of best bitter for her. He sat down, his expression a strange mixture of hunger and sadness. There was something wrong.

'Danny . . .'

He stopped her with a shake of his leonine head.

'Louise, I've got something important to say. Hear me out. Liverpool want me. Came as a complete surprise. Thirty next birthday and the boss called me in yesterday to tell me a top team's after me. I'm out of contract at the end of next season and the club have agreed to sell, so it's up to me. I guess they're cashing in while they can. I've played over three hundred games for them and always thought I'd end my career with the Robins, but now there's a three-year contract worth ten grand a week on the table, maybe even an outside chance of playing for England if I cut it on the pitch and stay injury-free.'

'Danny, that's wonderful news . . .'

As she said it, Louise knew her uncertain tone was contradicting the words. This was all so sudden, so unexpected, with implications she instinctively didn't like. He reached both hands across the bellows table and put them on her shoulders, leaning close. His eyes held hers and his voice was soft.

'I would've stayed if there was any future for us, but you're like a wild bird who can't be caged. Oh, I know you think I think you're just a secretary. I may not have a clue what you do at that hush-hush place, but it sure as hell isn't taking dictation and fetching coffee. I'd've settled for whatever you gave me if this move hadn't come up, but it has. It's been the hardest decision of my life, but I'm not going to hang around here and live in hope. I want commitment, kids, a relationship I can count on. Don't worry, I'm not going to make the mistake of asking you to come with me. But if the medical's okay, I'm signing for Liverpool.'

Louise put a small hand on his big arm and dropped her head. There was sudden tightness in her chest, and she felt treacherous tears blurring her eyes.

'Danny . . .'

'Don't say anything, Louise. We've had good times. Let's remember it that way.'

He tilted up her head, stroked her rebellious hair and kissed her softly on the lips.

He was always parking somewhere, close enough to see, but far enough away not to be noticed. This time, the Mondeo was in a lay-by, positioned for a quick U-turn beside an old Gilbert Scott red telephone box. It shouldn't be necessary. John Tolley was sure they'd drive back this way. All those wasted hours, sitting in a car waiting for something to happen. He'd never found a satisfactory way of combating boredom, and as someone who would rather spend thirty minutes driving round unknown side roads than ten stuck in a traffic jam, John Tolley detested observation duty.

This was particularly bad. Sure, he could tell himself it was legitimate work. Louise Boss was the key to Trojan Horse, and MI5 had to ensure the cyberweapon's secrets remained firmly locked. But that was bullshit. He was here for one reason and one reason only – he was painfully attracted to the woman, and the pain must be jealousy. She was inside the pub with the diffident man on the answerphone, and John Tolley didn't like what that awareness was doing to him.

It was everything he disciplined himself never to be – emotional, irrational, out of control, compulsive. Now he was in a fever of impatience. Would they go on to the man's place? Return to hers? Was it possible he might drop her off and leave after a nightcap, or would they spend the night together? John Tolley had to know, but didn't want to find out.

Eventually, common sense prevailed. This was ridiculous. He was behaving like a besotted adolescent and should know better. But John Tolley still hadn't quite managed to start up and drive away when he saw them emerge from the pub in his wing mirror – arm in arm as they strolled across the well-lit front carpark. He sank into his seat.

A moment later, the Land Rover Discovery came past. Common sense forgotten, he reached for the ignition key.

Fifty yards ahead, brake lights blazed. The big off-roader stopped. Reversing lamps snapped on accusingly, headed back his way. No time to drive off, nowhere to go anyway.

The Discovery swerved across the road and stopped beside him, passenger door flying open. Louise stepped down and marched two paces towards him. Tolley buttoned down his window and looked up at her, hoping his greeting was pleasantly neutral.

'Fancy meeting you here.'

Her eyes shone dangerously in the glow thrown by the Discovery's lights. Behind Louise, the man was watching, but not interfering. Big guy, looked as if he could handle himself. The chill factor in Louise's voice was arctic.

'I thought I saw this car parked near my place earlier. What do you security freaks say – once is coincidence, twice is careless? I suppose it was you creeping around my home this afternoon. Well, I hope you enjoyed rummaging through my knickers, and now I'll do you another favour. If you must know where I'll be for the next eight hours, save yourself a journey. I'll be spending the night with a man I can trust.'

Shoulders back, she turned and jumped into her seat. If the thing hadn't been so solidly built, the way she closed the door would have broken every scrap of the Discovery's glass.

London

THE CHANCE of finding a particular telephone box unoccupied at a busy London railway terminus was minimal, but Beasley didn't take chances. They'd made contact at King's Cross before, and Wes Remington knew the routine. He walked to a pair of kiosks outside the Pancras Road entrance, and saw the rendezvous was on. One bore an official-looking *OUT OF ORDER* sticker which prevented the door from opening.

Remington was sure he hadn't been followed, but looked around anyway. The station surrounds were busy, and if there were watchers he'd never spot them. He certainly didn't see any aimless perambulators or static sentinels who might be Beasley, though doubtless the man of mystery was close by, lurking with his mobile in some black hole where the galaxy of city lights didn't reach.

He slit the sticker with a thumbnail and entered the kiosk, opening his briefcase to remove two well-filled envelopes. Seconds later, the phone rang. A muffled American voice asked an impatient question.

'Got the briefing and my expenses?'

'Right here, including a contact number where you can reach me to report back or request additional information. It's a recorder, but I'll touch base regularly. If I need to update you or amend the assignment I'll fax word through the usual channels, okay?'

'I'll check in twice a day. Anything else?'

'You'll find all you need in the briefing, but I suggest you pay particular attention to Conrad Lancaster, the big businessman. Nothing specific, but my gut feel says he's worth a close look. Lives right across the street from my office and has a country place in Gloucestershire, west of London. Do you want any special equipment?'

'No, everything's arranged. I'll get what I need from my supplier straight away and make a start. You'll hear from me when I'm ready. Now go, and don't turn around.'

The line went dead. The CIA man hung up and walked into the station, leaving the two envelopes on the parcel shelf. Behind him, he imagined swift movement as Beasley appeared from nowhere and slipped into the kiosk. But he didn't look back. This guy was the best, and if childish games were part of the deal, that was fine. Providing he delivered.

Naturally, his father's town house had to be situated in the most prestigious area of central London. Which meant Mayfair and a tall double-fronted brick house on Upper Brook Street, once owned by one of the nation's oldest and most distinguished aristocratic families. That gave deep satisfaction to Conrad Lancaster, the self-made billionaire born in a Whitechapel tenement who dreamed of founding a thousand-year dynasty of his own.

James Lancaster had long decided he wanted no part of that particular nightmare, but at least felt able to banish rage and face his father. If he managed to revive Conrad's dynastic hopes by recovering Liz and the half-brother he'd never met, so be it.

He dumped the Golf on a double yellow line right outside the house, marched through an open gate in decorative iron railings and up one stone step to the front door, set within an imposing portico. Security looked good. Side steps led down to a tradesman's entrance, but both basement and ground-floor windows were well protected – the former with fixed iron bars on the outside, the latter with latticed steel grilles inside.

A middle-aged butler answered the door. James didn't know him from the old days, but wasn't surprised. His father used servants badly, and loyal retainers had always been thin on the ground. The man stood aside to reveal an opulent entrance hall – lushly carpeted in yellow going on gold, fabric wallpaper, sweeping staircase that divided halfway up, marble busts on tall plinths, ancestral oil paintings whose subjects most certainly hadn't contributed a single gene to the Lancaster pool. He stepped through the door.

'Is the old bastard in, by any chance?'

The butler's face remained impassive.

'Mr James? I'm Aitken. You're expected. Mr Conrad is waiting in the blue drawing room. I'm instructed to show you to him immediately, unless you wish to freshen up first. If you care to leave your keys with me, I can arrange for your car to be driven round and parked in the garage.'

James Lancaster handed over his leather coat.

'If I decide to stay, I'll do that myself. All right, take me to your leader.'

After reverently laying the scruffy garment across a convenient gilded Regency chair, Aitken turned and glided upstairs. James followed – uncomfortably aware that despite earlier resolve he felt like a naughty schoolboy summoned to the headmaster, or an apprehensive child when the dentist coos 'This won't hurt a bit'.

When he heard the distant doorbell, Conrad Lancaster posed carefully at one end of a long blue velvet sofa, producing a three-page report from his briefcase and immersing himself deeply in data. In fact, the contents were already burned into his brain, right down to the last pound sign – it was the list of his anonymously controlled offshore companies and the substantial amounts each had recently invested in Lancaster Trust stock. Should his attempt to support the share price fail, the numbers would sink his business deeper than RMS *Titanic*, and he'd go down with the ship.

No point in worrying – at least until the markets opened in the morning. That venal Perry Greenfield-Wright's authoritative article coupled with City greed for surplus Microsoft millions should do the trick. If not, he'd think of something else. In the meantime, there were other matters to worry about. Tom had been taken, and Conrad was feeling nervous – not an emotion that frequently afflicted him. But James was stubborn and he needed the little sod's help. Badly.

When Aitken tap-tapped and entered with a sonorous 'Mr James Lancaster', Conrad didn't look up, turning a page to emphasize the point. The door closed softly.

'Cut the crap. You asked me to come and here I am. If you want to play games feel free, but I'm gone.'

He hadn't heard it for nearly a decade, but the voice was the same. So was the hard character edge remembered from countless confrontations. Conrad lowered the papers and swivelled his head.

'You took your bloody time.'

The boy had kept in shape. He was lean and muscular, at an age when Conrad himself had started bulking out. His face was starting to wear, with cynical lines crinkling out from the eyes, but the expression was as self-contained as ever, giving no hint of what he might be thinking. The fair hair was longer, curling over the collar of a tweed sports jacket – last time he'd seen him James had sported a soldier's crop. As he appraised his flesh and blood, James stared right back, making his own assessment. He walked over and sat at the opposite end of the sofa, as far as possible from Conrad. There were other places to sit, but he chose one where his face couldn't be watched.

'I had a sentimental call to make along the way.

Remember Peter? I do.'

'Your brother was weak.'

'And you're strong? I'm not here because the master called, but because Liz needs help.'

'Of course, you two used to be close friends.'

He threw in just enough emphasis on the penultimate word to remind James that certain privileges accompanied leadership of the pack.

'Don't bother with that macho stuff. You're wasting your breath. I'm here to negotiate the release of Liz and Tom, period. It's what I do. Nothing else will change. Have the kidnappers made contact?'

Conrad heaved himself to his feet and lumbered to the drinks cabinet, pouring a stiff brandy before replying. He turned and faced his son.

'They have, and it's about as bad as it could be. They don't want money, but something else. See for yourself – that envelope on top of my briefcase.'

James reached over, extracted the note and quickly scanned the contents. When he looked up, something told Conrad he was no longer dealing with an estranged son with a chipped shoulder, but a consummate professional.

'Trojan Horse?'

'Secret defence project being developed by one of my companies on a joint British–US Government contract. They tell me these electronic weapons will eventually make bombs and bullets redundant. I can probably get hold of the thing, but if we hand it over the repercussions are frightening. Even under these circumstances, I could lose the business, maybe go to prison.'

If James noted the 'we', an easy assumption that he was willing to become a co-conspirator, he gave no sign. Instead, he made a brisk recommendation.

'Then we contact the authorities immediately. That way you're off the hook. Besides, official involvement is logical, because they have the resources to look for Liz and Tom.'

Conrad's hand tightened on his glass.

'No! These aren't penny-ante criminals. They're probably not criminals at all, though God knows Trojan Horse would be an attractive proposition for any major crime syndicate. This operation has almost certainly been mounted by a foreign government – Russia, China, Iraq, Libya, Israel, could be any of them. They mean business. What are the chances of finding Elizabeth and Tom alive, even if every policeman in the bloody country's looking for them?'

James looked tired, massaging temples as he considered his reply. When he looked up, his face was bleak.

'Probably not good, but a hell of a lot better than doing nothing and hoping. I'm sorry. I told you to sit tight until I got here, assuming the kidnappers were after money. If I'd been around when this note arrived we could have got things moving straight away, but as it is we've already lost valuable time.'

His pride didn't want to throw itself on James's none-too-tender mercy, so Conrad took a steadying belt of brandy before making his pitch.

'You think I'm a heartless bastard and may be right, but you're wrong about one thing. I think about Peter all the time and blame myself for his death. I'd do anything to stop the same thing happening to Elizabeth and Tom. If these animals want Trojan Horse, I'll give it to them and to hell with the personal downside. James, I'm asking, *begging* you to help me get my family back . . .'

He hadn't lost his touch. The boy was thinking this through, and wouldn't be able to resist the opportunity to prove himself – once and for all – to the father he'd rejected yet couldn't help admiring. Conrad relaxed. It might have been a close-run thing, but James would strain every fibre of his being to recover Tom and Elizabeth, though not necessarily in that order.

North Devon

THE TINY NOISE might have been made by active rodents in the night, but wasn't. She lay on the twin air-beds, wrapped in blue quilted sleeping bags, listening to Tom at work. Her son really was something – refusing to let the situation get him down and radiating breezy optimism that Liz Lancaster suspected was assumed entirely for her benefit.

WITHIN THE WALLS

Tom had found a sturdy old nail, wedged between two floorboards, which he'd painstakingly retrieved with the handle of a plastic knife supplied with supper – glowing with pride as he finally showed his trophy, as though it were a magic talisman to solve all their problems. Now he was sharpening the nail, rubbing its blunt point against the stone wall.

They'd watched *News at Ten* on television – still no mention of their kidnapping – before turning the lamp right down to conserve gas. The weak globule of light barely provided any illumination, but took the edge off total darkness that was too depressing to contemplate. She moved awkwardly. The tight chain around her waist and constraining pull of the tether made it difficult to get comfortable. The monotonous scraping stopped.

'You all right, Mum?'

Tom's shadowy figure materialized. She tried to make her reply sound cheerful.

'You bet. How are you getting on?'

'Great. Look . . . another couple of hours and this will be ready.'

The electric torch snapped on and he knelt beside her, showing off his tool. Or was it a weapon? The rusty nail was long, with rectangular head and thick square shaft. Tom's intentions were obvious. The final inch was bright metal, where he'd been filing the tip to a needle point far sharper than the Victorian blacksmith ever intended. Liz inspected the nail before handing it back.

'Looks good, but you'd better get some sleep. You need to build up your strength. Come on – bed.'

Whilst she manoeuvred to make room, Tom hid the nail in one of the provision boxes, which also contained another secret weapon – the boiled potatoes that came with supper. He'd insisted on saving them in an empty crisp packet, but refused to tell her what they were for. She had played along, making silly suggestions like 'You're going to starve us until we're thin enough to wriggle under the door'. He'd dismissed each feeble effort with a vigorous but silent shake of the head, but by the end they were both laughing and feeling a lot better. Then he'd started on that nail.

Tom took off his shoes and climbed in beside her. He turned his back and moulded against her. She laid a protective arm over him.

'Sleep tight.'

'You too, Mum.'

Within a minute, his breathing said he was asleep. The kid must have pushed himself to exhaustion. Liz Lancaster lay awake in the semi-darkness, strength returning. They could humiliate her all they liked, but wouldn't break her spirit, couldn't steal her soul. She and Tom had each other, and would face whatever was coming. Together.

London

UNLIKE AMERICAN equivalents, British intruder alarms are often regarded as devices to deter burglars from entering empty houses. Trusting Brits often leave them off at night, particularly if the premises are bolted and barred. This lazy attitude might save them the hassle of switching off every time they pad down to raid the fridge, but is God's gift to the uninvited. The sophisticated alarm that guarded the house in Upper Brook Street had not been activated – Conrad Lancaster liked small-hours snacking, considered his house to be impregnable, or both.

But Beasley was an expert. He had already attended to the Bentley, which slept below a chauffeur in the mews behind the house – taping a tiny radio microphone from the consignment picked up earlier in North London beneath the passenger seat and clamping a special voice-activated transmitter/recorder to the underside of the chassis, contained in a waterproof plastic box. He could follow and listen in. Or the first two hours of any conversation in the car would be captured for subsequent remote collection at the touch of a button.

His prime target was Conrad Lancaster's mobile phone. Nobody discussed sensitive matters over land-lines, because they were too easy to tap. Wes Remington had pointed a suspicious finger at the tycoon. If Conrad was playing both ends against the middle, his mobile might talk. Beasley found the instrument in a calfskin briefcase, on a massive blue velvet sofa in an opulently furnished first-floor living room with four tall windows facing the street. The heavy curtains were drawn, and he had lit up a Tiffany lamp that adorned a mahogany side table beside the sofa.

Inserting a tiny microphone was the work of a moment. Only a specialist would recognize the extra component, which looked like in-built circuitry. He tipped back the sofa, slit the hessian underside with a scalpel and pushed a transmitter/receiver deep into horsehair intestines. It was identical to the one hidden in the Bentley, and its triplet had already been concealed in Conrad's book-lined, leather-look study one floor up. Beasley could eavesdrop from the street outside, or subsequently play and rewind the tape at any time if absent on other business.

He righted the sofa, carefully rearranged cushions and sat down to study his prize – the kidnap letter which had also been in Conrad's briefcase. He took a tiny Olympus digital camera from a deep pocket and photographed the typeset note, together with its envelope. Later, when he could get back to the flat in Dolphin Square, he would feed the images into his computer and run off copies.

The CIA's man in London would be impressed by such rapid progress, and interested to learn that he was right and wrong. Right to suspect that Conrad Lancaster represented a threat to his precious cyberweapon, wrong to assume the duplicitous bastard was willingly selling out. Still, those to whom Beasley reported would have only one objective – stopping Trojan Horse falling into hostile hands. And they were ruthless when it came to protecting their interests.

He turned off the Tiffany lamp and left the room. Standing on the darkened landing, Beasley heard no more than the ticking of cooling radiators. The house was fast asleep.

DAY 3 – WEDNESDAY

London

THE CUPBOARD was bare, but Conrad Lancaster managed a full English breakfast with extra sausages and bacon. He munched a slice of marmalade-laden toast, shedding crumbs over the three-page list lying on the polished table beside breakfast debris. Every last pound of assets and credit his offshore companies could muster had been invested in Lancaster Trust stock. If his buying spree didn't cause the share price to rise, the business he'd built over forty-two years would vanish like summer mist when the sun gets up.

But that wouldn't happen. Conrad licked sticky fingers, put the list in his briefcase and picked up an open newspaper. Peregrine Greenfield-Wright's private pension fund deserved its sudden boost. The obliging journalist had delivered. Microsoft's munificent cash bid for Lancaster Trust's NetAxS company was the respected column's lead item, and the Seattle software giant's flat denial would only convince the City of the story's veracity. Everyone knew Bill Gates wanted to dominate the internet, even if it meant paying much too much money for little-leaguers like NetAxS. By the time it emerged that Microsoft's disinterest was nothing but the plain truth, Conrad would have saved his empire.

He poured another cup of coffee and spooned in sugar.

Life was sweet indeed. Prickly, defiant James was back – burdened by guilt over his dead brother, hating himself for losing Elizabeth to a better man, unable to escape the past however hard he tried. Conrad had only been half lying when they talked the previous evening. True – he did think about his deceased son frequently. False – he blamed himself for Peter's suicide. Lacking the steel of a true Lancaster, Peter had spurned an opportunity some would kill for. Following his emotionally fragile mother into an early grave was the bravest thing he'd ever done.

James was different, always had been. Conrad sipped coffee, feeling reluctant respect. He'd never been able to dominate his first-born – a fact he found hard to accept, despite incontrovertible supporting evidence. As independent business success proved, James would have made the ideal successor, but stubbornly refused to touch the golden chalice, let alone drink. Still, young Tom could be moulded into a worthy substitute, and the irony appealed – if anyone could end the boy's kidnap ordeal and bring him home, it was his rebellious elder son.

Conrad dabbed his lips with a linen napkin. He never forgave, he never forgot, he never gave up. It might be impossible to impose his will on James by direct methods. But that didn't mean he couldn't use other, more subtle means.

He might serve many masters, but the man called Beasley was not without honour. The CIA's Wes Remington was picking up the tab, and could expect an honest return for his covert investment of US tax dollars. Which is what he would get, though not quite as expected. Beasley keyed the contact number Remington had supplied. The machine picked up on the third ring, emitting a single beep to confirm that the tape was turning. Deepening his voice, he spoke into a crumpled tissue that covered the folding mouthpiece of his mobile phone.

'As you suggested, I started with Conrad Lancaster. He's brought son James over from the States. Look him up. You'll find he's a high-powered security consultant, so something may be going down. No idea what, but I'm smothering the Lancasters with electronic surveillance.

I've already covered mobile phones, London house and a couple of vehicles in the mews garage. I'll do the country place as soon as possible. I think your hunch is right. Those two know something. They talk, I'll be listening.'

The agent-for-hire terminated the call. He appreciated the intricacies of the duplicitous world in which he operated. He was doing Remington a favour. If the senior CIA man's fears concerning Trojan Horse were confirmed, he would be forced to act. Yet to be credible, such action would involve revealing a career-risking foray into the internal security affairs of America's staunchest ally. For Wes Remington, ignorance was bliss in disguise.

Beasley rekeyed. It was early. His controller was probably in bed, or showering, but picked up the call after thirty seconds.

'Yes?'

'I'm in London. Someone's after a powerful software weapon code-named Trojan Horse, being developed by a Lancaster Trust company called Omega Dynamic Systems. They've kidnapped Conrad Lancaster's wife and child. I've got a copy of the note, and no prizes for guessing what the ransom is. I haven't told Remington everything, so there shouldn't be interference from that quarter.'

'I know about Trojan Horse. Stay with it. I'd dearly like to know who's behind this, but the weapon must be protected. Five are on the case, though that hardly fills me with confidence. Can Conrad deliver?'

'I'm not certain if he can get hold of Trojan Horse. I'll find out soon enough, especially if you can keep Five out of the picture. The last thing I need is that lot crawling over Omega. Any chance?'

His controller thought for a moment before replying.

'Tricky, but I'll take advice and see what we can manage. You realize the responsibility this places on you? The security of Trojan Horse must not be risked under any circumstances.'

'It's your call. How badly do you want the full picture? Must go, busy day ahead. I'll keep in touch.'

'Make sure you do. Be lucky. And be careful.'

'Aren't I always? On both counts.'

The ritual sign-off was somehow reassuring. However

isolated he might feel, Beasley knew he was never truly alone.

Gloucestershire

A MAILMAN'S LIFE was never dull. As Norman Webley turned through the permanently open wrought-iron entrance gates of New Hall's extensive park at 6.43 a.m., he was whistling the opening bars of 'Postman Pat', over and over like a short loop tape. The irritating tune had popped unbidden into his head, and refused to go away.

Norman didn't mind. He was feeling chirpy, anticipating the buzz that would surround his little red van on the day's delivery round. There was kudos in being the very first to communicate shocking news, and the benefits didn't end there. Played cannily, this should be worth at least five pints from interested regulars at his local in Stow-on-the-Wold.

People assume that a mere postman must be a mindless machine, but Norman Webley had a gift. He could read mail without opening a single letter or package. Monday – rumours that Mrs Lancaster and her boy had gone missing. Tuesday – a Special Delivery from London, more than likely one folded sheet in the DL envelope with typeset label, signed for by a patently agitated housekeeper. Wednesday – a Special Delivery from Bristol with identical label, almost certainly containing a video cassette. The latter lay on the seat beside him, and he patted the Mail Lite envelope with satisfaction.

No doubt about it – the woman and child had been kidnapped. Ransom note yesterday. Video proving the victims were still alive today. Perhaps – if he got really lucky – a further letter with delivery instructions for the ransom tomorrow. True, some might see this dramatic scenario as far-fetched, but few of Norman's regular listeners would express doubt. He had a gift.

If further evidence were needed, Rita Bernadelli soon provided it. When he turned into the stable yard and parked in his usual spot, the thin housekeeper was waiting outside the back door – an unprecedented occurrence.

Mentally rehearsing a couple of subtle questions, Norman walked over with his usual sunny smile. She didn't respond – signing the proffered delivery sheet, snatching the bundle of mail and vanishing into the house like a bolting rabbit before he could utter a word. The back door slammed on her pinched expression.

No tea, for the first time ever! The postman was outraged – a reaction that soon evolved into grim satisfaction. Everyone knew the old battle-axe doted on young Tom. As he drove back up the mile-long drive, Norman Webley was already weaving the housekeeper's extraordinary behaviour into a story that got better and better.

North Devon

HER SPIRIT was broken. Andrew Rosson took in hot washing water himself, just to be sure. The woman was a picture of dejection in feeble lamplight, huddled in a plastic chair staring at her feet. The tether chain snaked away to its iron ring in the stone wall, symbolizing helplessness. Pale face partly concealed by an unkempt mass of copper-red hair, Liz Lancaster didn't look up when he set down the steaming enamel bucket.

The boy wouldn't acknowledge him, either. He sat cross-legged on the floor, watching a noisy breakfast show on television. But his face remained impassive as cartoon characters slugged it out on screen, and something about the set of his body suggested Tom remained defiant. But what could he do? He was a child.

Rosson backed out and relocked the door. There was much to be done, and the last thing he needed was defiant captives who required constant monitoring. He returned to the large room that served as living quarters, just along the well-lit first-floor passageway that ran the length of the old quayside building. After yesterday's escape attempt, he'd rigged a line of forty-watt bulbs from a small Honda generator that now murmured monotonously at the top of the stone staircase.

Bill Hellis was making breakfast on a portable gas cooker. The smell of frying bacon mingled with the building's sour odour, and Rosson felt a sharp hunger pang. But it was more than that. He thought of his own wife and children, getting ready for another routine day in the comfortable Georgian house on the outskirts of Hay-on-Wye. Perhaps one of the postcards he'd left to be posted in Prague would arrive this morning, promising his girls he'd soon be home, with a carload of rare first editions and presents for everyone.

But that was antiquarian book dealer Andrew Rosson's world, and he had to be his former self for a few more days. So KGB-trained Dmitry Travkin sat at a patio table identical to that used by their captives and wiped the vision of normality from his mind. The stocky Londoner who had once been his classmate thumped down two laden plates of bacon, eggs and baked beans, fetched mugs of coffee and sat down. They ate in silence.

When the food was finished, Bill Hellis glanced at the bunk bed where the man nicknamed Ringo was sleeping after standing an uneventful eight-hour night watch, before handing over to fellow mafioso Paul. The Russians needed to know no more than they needed to know. Hellis spoke softly, his husky voice urgent.

'We could go down for this. Why don't we house-clean? Won't make any difference to the operation, and I for one can do without fifteen years in some stinking cell at Wormwood Scrubs.'

Rosson cupped his warm coffee mug with cold hands.

'Kill them, you mean? Out of the question. We've been instructed not to damage them.'

'To hell with that. Makes sense to me.'

'We need them. Suppose the pick-up goes wrong, or Lancaster needs more time? We may have to turn the screw. Besides, if they've got any sense they'll insist on getting the child back as part of the exchange, or at least demand proof the pair of them are still alive. We stick to the plan.'

Andrew Rosson finished his coffee and stood up. He had no intention of killing anyone, and brusquely ended the conversation before it got out of control.

'Right. I'm off to set up the handover. Do their food. They won't make trouble, but go carefully. No silly accidents,

Bill. I don't want to be the one who has to tell Colonel Gorski that we have disobeyed explicit orders and lost Trojan Horse.'

'Okay. You're the boss.'

Hellis scratched his broken-veined nose, but nodded reluctant acquiescence.

Moscow

BECAUSE TIME seemed to be accelerating, Gregor Gorski needed every moment of each remaining day. But he couldn't resist wasting his first waking hour. The newspapers had been delivered by General Sergei Sobchak's personal driver before dawn, and the ex-KGB colonel felt entitled to leisurely appreciation of press reaction, along with frequent cups of tea and French cigarettes. The stylish blue packet containing his weekly ration was nearly empty, though Wednesday had scarcely begun.

If yesterday's media reaction to the violence rocking Moscow had been explosive, today's was thermonuclear. The brazen murder of Interior Minister Anton Mossberg at the National Hotel dominated every front page and television news bulletin. Unlike the earlier demise of venal Duma Speaker Gennady Churkov, the latest atrocity had no prurient sexual dimension, but represented a frontal attack on President Yelkin's government by renegade Chechen terrorists.

By one of the delightful twists that made Gorski's work so rewarding, ravening media had turned on the bloodied victim – savaging the government itself for failing to deal with the murderous Sons of Dudayev. For allowing anarchy to reign on the streets. For impotent inability to impose the order and stability people craved. For simply being in charge as wheels flew off. All that anger . . . even before today's unspeakable outrage burst upon a nation about to be shocked to its very core. The people had to understand that they, too, were not immune.

Gregor Gorski had read and seen enough. Domestic events couldn't be going better, but the Trojan Horse cyberweapon was not yet secured. Time to leave for the day's first appointment. He carefully rinsed and dried his teacup, turned off the television and pulled the power plug, though the wide-screen set was not a combustion-prone Russian model but Japan's finest, recently manufactured in South Korea.

He put on his astrakhan coat and set the sable hat at a rakish angle. Before leaving his unpretentious apartment, Gregor Gorski picked up next week's packet of Gitanes and stripped the slippery cellophane covering with almost sensual pleasure, before thrusting the cigarettes into a deep coat pocket. All things considered, modest reward was no more than his due.

London

HIS FATHER was surrounded by the debris of a breakfast large enough to sustain a Third World family for a week. James Lancaster paused on entering the imposing ground-floor dining room, pushing down his instinctive animosity. People he cared about were depending on him, whether they knew it or not, and personal feelings couldn't be allowed to blunt professional sharpness. Conrad looked up from a newspaper, fleshy face wobbling in a parody of a sincere smile.

'A good-news day. One or two little bits that should have a rather positive effect on the Lancaster Trust share price. Slept off your jet-lag? You've lost enough valuable time as it is.'

'I thought you might be rather more interested in Liz and Tom than your precious business affairs.'

James walked over and poured a cup of black coffee. He didn't sit down. Characteristically, the old man ignored that which he didn't want to hear, continuing relentlessly in the slightly nasal voice that aspired to upper-class Englishness but never quite escaped East End origins.

'Of course I am. I've just had the New Hall housekeeper on the phone. There's been another communication. Royal Mail Special Delivery posted in Bristol. I could have it driven up here, or you can take my helicopter and call at New Hall *en route* to Omega.'

Conrad had explained his plan the previous evening. Though in reality there to collect the master copy of Trojan Horse demanded by the kidnappers, James was ostensibly visiting Omega as a security consultant – a ploy appealing mightily to his father's warped sense of humour.

'I need to see that message as soon as possible. I'll fly down. Expect proof they're still alive, a Polaroid or video, perhaps with instructions for an exchange. Just pray I don't find your child's ear or Liz's wedding finger, complete with expensive rings. I suppose they were expensive?'

'Seventy grand the pair. Nothing but the best for my darling girl.'

The man really was outrageous. James was aware that his temper was flickering, defying his resolution to remain cool.

'So how come you're taking all this so casually?'

Conrad shrugged, switching on a sly grin calculated to pour petrol on flames.

'Just because I don't wear my heart on my sleeve like a lovelorn adolescent, it doesn't mean I don't care. Of course I'm frightened, but I never lose sleep over something that's beyond my control. I've done everything I can. Trojan Horse should be waiting, even though it could cost me my reputation and my business, and now I'm trusting you to do a proper job. You're supposed to be the best, too, remember? Sort this mess, James, get my family back. How does that old saying go – don't employ a dog and piss on lampposts yourself?'

His father raised thick eyebrows, daring him to explode. For a nitro-second, James felt a blaze of pure hatred sear his mind. But he didn't allow his face or voice to betray momentary weakness.

'And if I can't get Trojan Horse?'

Conrad's reptile-black eyes glittered in pouchy sockets. He knew he'd got through.

'You're the bloody expert, so stop asking these stupid questions and get on with it. My man Holland should have the damn thing gift-wrapped for you. Just ask. If not, we have a problem, but let's not anticipate the worst.

My helicopter's yours for as long as you want. Ask for the security chief once you've got Trojan Horse – MacNaughton. Go through consultancy motions, or he'll get suspicious. Don't let me down. Despite your poor opinion of my priorities, I badly want Elizabeth and Tom back where they belong.'

The bear-like tycoon picked up his briefcase and grunted to his feet, delivering a final swipe as he lumbered towards the door.

'You ran off with your tail between your legs and let Elizabeth down once before, sonny boy. Try not to screw up this time, because you won't get a third chance to ease your conscience. And don't expect me to hold your hand. I've got a business to run, which happens to be their future. Keep me informed.'

James counted to ten, slowly, before following him out. You had to hand it to the old bastard. However despicable the buttons he pushed, the man was a master motivator.

Wiltshire

GORDON'S CHOICE was simple – do, or don't. But not simple at all, because either route was fraught. On one road – Conrad Lancaster, who would demand the impossible and exact swift retribution if denied. On the other – nameless guardians of national security not noted for a forgiving attitude if their precious state secrets were compromised, and more than capable of blighting his entire life if he broke the rules.

After a restless night and an early arrival at the office, Gordon Holland was standing in reception, pretending his painful choice rested with the fickle finger of fate. If Omega's Data Manager appeared first, Conrad would triumph. Should the first arrival be Security Director Alexander MacNaughton, duty would perforce prevail.

But the outcome would owe nothing to chance. The bluff Yorkshireman who looked after the secure basement data storage facility containing Omega's digital diamonds was an early starter. Sandy MacNaughton had worked into the night and left word with the desk that he would not be back in until ten o'clock. This had spawned an idea. Perhaps there *was* a safe way, after all. As he waited, Holland turned the proposition over in his mind, probing for flaws. There were plenty, but it just might work. When Peter Clough walked through the automatic doors at 8.30 precisely, he was ready.

'Ah, Peter, I've been waiting for you. Come with me, please.'

The owlish Data Manager looked startled, but obediently followed to the second-floor office – the man was an able employee, but no rebel. Holland settled him in a visitor's chair and started the coffee percolator, studying the older man as he did so. Clough was in his mid-fifties, a few years from retirement. He wore metal-framed glasses with wire arms hooked over prominent ears that jugged out beneath wings of white hair. The otherwise-bald head gleamed as though polished. Holland didn't hurry the coffee, ratcheting tension. Every so often, magnified eyes strayed in his direction and anxiety flitted across the old boy's ruddy-cheeked face. Excellent. Finally, Holland set two cups of coffee on the desk.

'I know you prefer tea, Peter, but until my secretary gets in this is the best I can do. Milk, sugar?'

Clough shook his head. With lessons from the great intimidator fresh in mind, Holland went round behind the desk and planted his hands, staring down at his subordinate. He could even remember some of Conrad Lancaster's better lines.

'Sorry to drag you up here, but I'm afraid I've got a mini-crisis on my hands. You know how important the successful delivery of Trojan Horse is to the financial wellbeing of this company? Well, the Americans have decided they need to make an immediate evaluation of progress, what might be described as a preview by the authorized end user who paid most of the development cost. I know it's a damn nuisance, but I need a copy of the master file up here ten minutes ago.'

The Data Manager's apprehension dissolved.

'No problem. If you just prepare the official release and get Mr MacNaughton's countersignature, I'll get on to it straight away.'

Holland sighed.

'There's a slight problem. Sandy MacNaughton won't be in until mid-morning, but the Americans are sending a security van to collect at nine-thirty. If that disk isn't waiting there will be hell to pay, believe me. Just do it. You have my personal assurance the proper paperwork will follow, and that the project's integrity won't be compromised in any way.'

Peter Clough's anxiety returned.

'But surely they'd wait? This is most irregular.'

Time to put the boot in.

'Apparently the material's much too sensitive to be sent Stateside by electronic transfer, and they've booked the disk on a scheduled military flight that waits for no man.'

Holland walked back round the desk and parked his buttocks on the front edge, leaning towards the hapless Data Manager before continuing softly.

'Must I spell out the consequences if our American paymasters get annoyed? If we give them the slightest excuse they'll jump at the chance to pull the project and complete it over there, in which case the future of this company and everyone who works here starts to look rather bleak rather quickly. And I'll know where to start. Do you really fancy job-hunting at your time of life? I know I don't, so I'm making this a direct order.'

Garbage, of course – but threatening with it. He folded his arms and stared down implacably. Clough was frightened by the spectre of the scrapheap, and bespectacled eyes dropped. Gordon Holland was enjoying himself. It was gratifying to see someone else impaled on the horns of a dilemma he himself was about to sidestep so neatly. To his master's complete satisfaction, and with no risk of damaging comeback from the powers that be.

London

FOR A MAN with $500 million in his briefcase, the merchant banker looked remarkably relaxed as he strolled into Conrad Lancaster's large office. But then Ralph-pronounced-Rafe Powell-pronounced-Pole was the sort of upper-class Englishman who had been brought up to believe that the world owed him – and his well-networked peer group – a handsome living. Conrad hated every one of the smug bastards, but at least they were predictable. He rose from his black chair, arms flung wide in greeting.

'Sit down, old man, sit down. Done your homework, I trust?'

The sleek thirty-five-year-old Powell parked a pigskin case and clicked the catches before unbuttoning his double-breasted suit jacket and sitting down. A smile ghosted across his aristocratic face.

'Not personally, no, but my people have done their sums.'

He produced the hundred-page draft agreement that entitled Lancaster Trust to buy one-eighth of the soon-to-be-privatized Russian state telecommunications company and set the spiral-bound document on the desk.

'Every line of the English version's been checked against the original Russian. I've noticed that past translations have tended to shade certain points in your favour, but this one's spot on. The terms are very generous. One might even go as far as describing them as a steal. Have you any idea how *much* this stake will be worth in five years' time?'

The banker's expression said it all. Conrad felt euphoric, like a condemned man in the electric chair who hears the phone ring at one minute to the appointed hour. He shot up bushy eyebrows and injected incredulity into his reply.

'You don't mean I'm actually going to be left with a half-decent profit when you City bloodsuckers have gulped down your fill?'

Powell had the decency to laugh.

'A few pounds, perhaps. Seriously, you do seem to be getting an awful lot of potential for our money. Half the world's communications companies are after the lump of Russia Telecom on offer to overseas buyers. So where's the catch?'

A done deal. Conrad rammed home his advantage.

'No catch. We've done business together for a long time,

Rafe, and my Moscow contacts have served us both well over the years. When everyone makes money, everyone's happy, including Russian friends in high places. Just don't enquire what *their* cut is.'

The merchant banker placed a hand over his eyes. See no evil, hear no evil, speak no evil . . . providing the bank got its share. But with the risk element in mind, he felt a need to probe.

'Of course there's the worrying business of your share price, which is a bit off. Leaves you a tad exposed, I'd say, unless these rumours of a big cash windfall from a sale to Microsoft are true.'

Conrad didn't make the mistake of repeating the lie to his lead banker, but neither did he manage to give the wrong impression.

'You know I never comment on press speculation, even by respected oracle Perry Greenfield-Wright. But I have a feeling you'll see a sharp rise in the Lancaster Trust share price in the next few days, so worry you not. And that's *before* good news from the Russian front. Sky's the limit when that becomes public in ten days or so.'

Ralph Powell produced a single sheet from his open briefcase and pushed it across the desktop.

'Then we're all set. Here's the loan memorandum. We've taken the lion's share, but spread the action – Germany, Japan, the States. You can draw the money down when the deal's officially announced in Moscow and we've received our certified copy of the sale agreement.'

Leaving the $500-million piece of paper where it lay, Conrad moved on, spinning his chair to one side and hitting the key that brought up the Financial Times 100 Share Index on his Reuters screen. He scrolled down to L and looked at Ralph-cum-Rafe Powell-cum-Pole the bloodsucker, unable to keep a note of triumphalism from his voice.

'Lancaster Trust is already up three points from last night's low. You really should buy a few for yourself, Rafe, before they go into orbit.'

Knowing what he did, the banker was prohibited from profiting from market-sensitive information. But illegal insider dealing was endemic, and those who couldn't hack a safe path through the rules really shouldn't be stalking the City jungle in the first place.

Wiltshire

SHE STOOD at the side gate of Beggar's Roost and watched her lover depart for the last time. Danny gave her a crooked smile, climbed into his Discovery and drove away without a backward glance, heading for a future that no longer included Louise Boss. It was her choice, and she could make no other. They had promised to keep in touch, but wouldn't.

Taking her by surprise, the pain of imminent loss had expressed itself in lovemaking of almost wild intensity, unlike anything she had known before. Crudely put, she had not only experienced the first orgasm of her life, but also the second and third. In the cold light of morning, Louise found such passion disconcerting. Sex had never been a problem – a satisfying experience that took its place alongside other snatched physical pleasures in her life, like an occasional good meal or tough game of tennis. So why had she behaved in such a wanton fashion, and why was she feeling so miserable?

As she lingered over untouched cornflakes in her cluttered kitchen, Louise tried to rationalize the negative emotion. Danny Woodward had the opportunity to make a great career move that would take him to the other end of the country. He wanted a wife, she needed an undemanding lover. Their relationship could never have lasted. But still Louise felt a rush of guilt. When the big footballer had told her he was moving on – and why – she had felt an instinctive flash of relief. His feelings were becoming too intense, and if he hadn't jumped she would eventually have pushed. She knew, because her two previous long-term sexual relationships had ended that way.

She understood emotional caution. That first, shattering day at school and the humiliations that followed had caused her to retreat from people's casual, effortless power to hurt her. It was so much easier to gain risk-free self-esteem from intellectual application, where success and ego-boosting praise were attainable, quantifiable and entirely within her control. The choice was conscious, the result inevitable.

Without warning, her mind switched to John Tolley. The man was a despicable snooper, a professional charmer who'd invaded her home and raped her privacy. He wasn't worth another thought. But she could picture the exact way a wayward lock of black hair fell across his forehead. Those intense grey eyes. That heart-tugging smile. And remember their easy repartee of the previous afternoon almost word for word.

Louise had always admitted the possibility that defences might crumble. Perhaps even hoped deep down they would. But she had never really expected it to happen, or happen so suddenly. The feeling was at once exhilarating, confusing, frightening and real.

For the first time in as long as she could remember, she didn't want to go to work. But at least her computer room at Omega was familiar, secure territory. So Louise Boss fed insistent cats and dragged herself out of the door.

Have your cake and eat it was Gordon Holland's tasty motto for the day. Everything was working out, and that angst-ridden night was a fading memory, overwhelmed by more recent affirmation of his own brilliance. The cowed Clough had delivered up Trojan Horse with no more than a whimper – trying to protect himself with a formal protest which, unfortunately for him, was merely verbal. The Data Manager was weak, and weaklings never prospered.

Holland looked at the 1.2 gigabyte optical disk that lay on his desk. Truly amazing that such awesome power could be contained within this tiny, vulnerable package. Vulnerable because, as generations of software pirates had proved, it mattered not how complex software might be. With access to an original, making a copy is simplicity itself. Which was precisely what he'd done, using office computer, optical drive and spare disk. A complex code sequence was required to unlock the master disk. But as Managing Director, he knew the codes. True, the three-minute data transfer in his locked office had been frightening, with the progress bar moving across his screen like a paralysed snail. But he hadn't been disturbed.

And now it was done, apart from an alibi. He delicately buttoned the intercom and asked his secretary to locate Alexander MacNaughton. The security chief's immediate presence was required on a matter of extreme urgency.

While he waited, Holland locked the life-saving duplicate disk into his safe, just as Conrad Lancaster had ordered. They were two of a kind – ruthless achievers who ignored problems, found solutions and despised losers. When the spare Scot marched into his office without so much as a token tap on the open door, he was ready – indicating a chair even as he went and closed the door, to stress the gravity of what he had to say.

'Sit down. As you know, Conrad Lancaster mentioned security during yesterday's visit. I reassured him that you run a very tight operation, but he's still sending in his son to double-check. As the boy's some sort of expert, we must be totally fireproof. So I conducted a little experiment this morning, and I'm afraid your systems aren't quite as good as you think . . .'

MacNaughton's eyes fastened on the damning disk as though he couldn't believe what he was seeing, and didn't want to hear what he was about to hear. His response was defensive.

'What exactly are you getting at, Gordon?'

'A chain is only as strong as its weakest link. Take two guards down to Data Storage and escort Peter Clough from the premises. He's fired. While you're at it, replace this copy of Trojan Horse in the secure facility. I fed Clough a spurious story and ordered him to bring a master copy of Trojan Horse to this office. I admit I browbeat him, but was *praying* he'd insist on following proper security procedures. Sadly, he didn't, and the proof's right here on my desk. This reflects badly on you, Sandy, and I must have your firm assurance that nothing like this will ever happen again. Read every member of staff the rules, and make sure they listen this time.'

The security chief looked shattered.

'I see.'

Of course he didn't, but Gordon Holland wouldn't worry

about that. He could even afford a dash of magnanimity.

'I'm glad you do. Our linen must be whiter than white when this James Lancaster starts rummaging. I respect your professionalism, Sandy, always have. No harm done, and one mistake shouldn't be allowed to spoil an otherwise impressive record, so I won't mention this to him or anyone else. As far as I'm concerned, the matter will be closed the moment Clough's out of this place, so get moving. Close the door as you go.'

Without another word, MacNaughton picked up the disk and went, clearly shaken. Omega's MD had to stop himself laughing out loud. The world was divided into winners and losers. He'd glimpsed the latter chasm, and didn't like what he saw. But when push came to shove, Gordon Holland had what it took.

London

ANGUS CHURCHILL sometimes wondered why he came to work every day. He didn't need the money, and could certainly do without the relentless pressure. Assorted secret-stealers, big-league criminals, damaging drug runners, whistle-blowers, sheep-shaggers and anti-social riff-raff who provided the security service's official opposition didn't bother him. He liked nothing better than a dirty fight with the scum of the earth.

The real problem was the enemy within. Scalpel-sharp forensic accountants hell-bent on gutting MI5. Ungrateful masters who expected more for less. Rivals battling for the reduced ration of power, prestige and resources that remained available to Britain's peace-dividend intelligence services. Fellow-professionals playing their devious one-upmanship games. The Secret Intelligence Service invading his jurisdiction. So-called friendly foreign services trespassing on his turf. Even the police force was trying to get in on the act with their new national task force. The hate-list of ambitious, interfering miscreants was endless.

And now this . . . this insult.

Churchill stood at his office window, looking down at a traffic jam below. Mindless lemmings. What did they know about the ceaseless battle that allowed them to sleep soundly in their suburban beds, insulated from evil-doers who sought to undermine Britain and with it their placid lives?

In truth, the MI5 Assistant Director in charge of K Branch loved every aspect of his working life, especially playing the politics of influence. He was intimately familiar with complex corridors of power, and canny manoeuvring therein would one day be rewarded with the Directorship of MI5 and accompanying knighthood. Sir Angus Churchill sounded so right, and he took anything that threatened acquisition of the short but significant prefix very seriously indeed.

This was just such a threat. He had returned from a budget meeting the previous afternoon in buoyant mood, having staved off another threatened cut in his department's staffing level, to find John Tolley's reassuring message on voicemail. No problems at Omega. Security tight. Trojan Horse secure. Despite an attitude problem bordering on insubordination, Tolley was a good operative – his best. Wes Remington had been chasing shadows all along.

So Churchill had dictated a memo for the record, stating that the matter had been investigated at the CIA's request and Langley's fears concerning a threat to Trojan Horse found to be groundless. He had then gone on to a dinner engagement with a senior Home Office civil servant, talked some interesting shop, swapped insider gossip and not given the wretched cyberweapon another thought. Until now.

The terse communication from the Joint Intelligence Committee had come as a bombshell. The JIC co-ordinated activity amongst the nation's competing intelligence organizations, forcing left and right hands to move in unison and policing rivalries that might otherwise become damaging. The committee's word was law, its power absolute. And they'd just issued a security alert on Trojan Horse, as a result of unspecified information received from Military Intelligence. Military Intelligence, for God's sake! What did belligerent soldier-boys know about anything that mattered?

It got worse. Five, the agency responsible for looking after Trojan Horse, had been specifically instructed to back off until the situation was reviewed at the next scheduled JIC meeting in one week, by which time any problem should be neutralized. The damage this bland statement would inflict on MI5's reputation – his own reputation – was incalculable. He could almost hear the laughter of hyenas who'd been waiting for him to stumble – including two who would be serious rivals when the top job at Five fell vacant.

Angus Churchill's chest was tight and he was aware of a pounding heartbeat. He took a deep breath, massaged his neat moustache with thin fingers and returned to his desk. If they thought he'd roll over, they were gravely mistaken. He buzzed his secretary.

'Get John Tolley on the phone. He's swanning around somewhere in Wiltshire, and his mobile better be switched on.'

She came back twenty seconds later.

'He's at his desk, actually. Shall I put him through?'

'No. Tell him to get in here. Now.'

Despite his intention to remain calm under even the most extreme provocation, the last word came out with the gentle inflexion of a whip crack.

What a God-awful mess. John Tolley had crept back to London after his humiliating encounter with Louise Boss and her well-built lover. Sleep wouldn't come, so he'd spent the night soaking up bottled Belgian beer, watching *film noir* classics on video and feeling sorry for himself. Not because he'd transgressed basic tradecraft, messed up a simple surveillance and been spotted by the subject, but because *she'd* caught him. Though he liked women a lot, they rarely had this sort of impact. The experience was uncomfortable, especially as he'd managed to look such an idiot.

And now Gus Churchill was running amok. He knew, because the department head's secretary had a soft spot for him, and issued a storm warning along with a summons to attend the great man in his office. Now.

Should Louise Boss have complained, the imminent

encounter would be painful. But even if she had, he wouldn't betray her after-hours security lapses. When he walked in and sat down opposite the large modern desk without being asked, Churchill was standing at the window, back ruler straight as he gazed at dirty sky that squatted on the South Bank skyline. He asked a curt question without turning.

'Trojan Horse?'

'Didn't you get my message? Everything solid. I'm just finishing my report now, but couldn't pick holes in Sandy MacNaughton's security operation.'

Churchill spun round and marched to the desk. He didn't sit down. The nostrils of his blade-like nose were flared and he glared down at his subordinate with malignant intensity. Clearly one very unhappy department head. Tolley met the fierce stare, briefly wondering what his severance package might be worth. Churchill cocked his head like a watchful hawk.

'You also said you were staying down in Wiltshire to check a few things out. So why are you sitting here in my office, John?'

Trick question? He'd soon find out. Tolley assumed a puzzled expression.

'I thought I'd hang around Omega for a few hours, see if anything went down after the staff left. You were the one who suggested I might put in some unpaid overtime, remember? But nothing happened and I decided to call it a day. Like I said, everything seems fine.'

Churchill's hand slapped the desktop with explosive force, the sudden noise reverberating round the room like a rifle shot. A loose pencil jumped into the air.

'If everything's fine, John, how come JIC has just issued a security alert on Trojan Horse? Based on information received from Military Intelligence, to add insult to injury. And Five's officially off the case. I can't believe it.'

He sat down abruptly, shoulders slumping as anger sputtered and died. Tolley exhaled gently. So he was – almost – in the clear. Time to offer his shaken leader some support. Aspiring to high office could be a morale-sapping obstacle course.

'I'm sorry. But the green slime do have some good

sources. The threat could be IRA, Loyalist paramilitaries, anything Irish. Perhaps we've been pulled because they've got an op running. You'll eventually find out what's going down and it's hardly Judgment Day. This sort of thing has happened before and will happen again.'

Churchill looked up, sharp features taut.

'Not to me, it doesn't. As of now you're on leave of absence. Sign over your case-load and be out of the building in ten minutes . . .'

Shocked, John Tolley opened his mouth to protest. No way was he going to take the rap for this one, despite yesterday's irregular activities. Before he could find the right words, Churchill continued, his voice dangerously even.

'Get back down there and see if you can find out what the hell's going on. Unofficially, of course. Low profile will do nicely, invisible would be better. Report to me verbally. No voicemail, no messages, nothing on paper. Use my mobile number after office hours. Should be just the assignment for a rebel like you. And if you manage to get caught, I'll deny everything and that leave of absence will become permanent.'

Tolley recovered fast, grinning foolishly.

'Don't tempt me. Okay, but I may need access to the computer.'

'Out of the question. If you need anything, information or resources, let me know. No promises, but I'll do what I can. You're on your own, John. Eight minutes left, and counting.'

The interview was over.

'Right. I'd best be off, then.'

John Tolley got up and stormed out past Churchill's startled secretary, slamming the door behind him. If he was to be cast as bad guy, the command performance might as well get off to a resounding start.

Gloucestershire

FROM HIS vantage point beside the pilot, James Lancaster watched with mixed feelings as New Hall grew from Gloucestershire countryside. His father had owned the fine old house and sweeping home park for over thirty years, and the place held memories good and bad. Mostly bad.

When their mother was alive, endless rows in the night they weren't supposed to hear. After she died, endless rows in the day they couldn't avoid. But happy times, too, mostly during Conrad's prolonged absences. The two brothers, together. Cricket in the garden. Peter's delight when he smacked a ball through the conservatory roof. Huge teas in the kitchen with Mrs Bernadelli. Banana sandwiches. Fresh scones with clotted cream and strawberry jam. As much moist fruit cake as they could eat. The smell of baking bread. Him and Peter, alone together.

And now New Hall was Liz's home. Only Liz wasn't there.

The gold-and-black-liveried Bell JetRanger helicopter landed neatly on immaculate turf close to the house. Duncan Bernadelli was waiting. James was glad the dependable Scottish couple had survived in his father's employ. They'd almost been surrogate parents for long periods of his adolescence, and never let him down. The chauffeur-handyman's seamed face lit up with quiet pleasure as he relieved James of his heavy briefcase. A strong Glaswegian accent hadn't mellowed, despite decades amongst the Sassenachs.

'Mr James. It's been a long time. I hear you've done well for yourself in America.'

'Duncan. How are you both?'

'Mustn't complain, but of course we do. Rita's in a rare old state. She's fond of Master Tom and this kidnap business has hit her hard, but she can't wait to see you.'

'What's the boy like? I've never met him.'

'A fine lad, Mr James, a fine lad. A clever one, too, always asking questions and working things out.'

'And Mrs Lancaster?'

'Aye, well enough.'

But something in the Scot's dry tone contradicted his bland assurance. They walked round the house in silence, into the stable yard and through the kitchen door. Rita Bernadelli was waiting. She came forward and put her hands on James's shoulders, looking up at him with a critical expression.

'I see you've no been eating properly all these years. There's a game pie in the oven, and we have some of your favourite raspberry ice cream in the fridge. You will get them back, won't you?'

Her eyes were moist. James kissed a lined cheek and gently freed himself.

'Good to see you, Mrs B. I'll do my best, but can't make promises. For reasons best known to himself my father refuses to go to the police, so we've got a job on our hands. I'd better look at that package.'

As the housekeeper fetched it from the built-in pine dresser that occupied one wall, James pulled on a pair of thin surgeon's gloves, in case things ever got as far as forensic examination. He was not surprised when the Mail Lite envelope yielded a video cassette. James carefully extracted the tape and held it up.

'This is almost certainly proof that Liz and Tom are still alive. Why don't I take it up to the library and have a look? Perhaps you would bring me some coffee, and I could murder one of your special Welsh rarebits.'

The last thing he wanted was cheese on toast, but Rita Bernadelli would feel a whole lot better with something useful to do.

Wiltshire

UNFORTUNATELY, her tardy arrival at Omega Dynamic Systems didn't go unnoticed. When Louise Boss came into the building, she was stopped at reception and told to report to the Managing Director. Immediately. The moment she walked into Gordon Holland's spacious office, she knew he was in masterful mode. The portly executive leapt up, placed his hands flat on the desk and leaned towards her with an aggressive expression.

'Sit!'

She took off her Barbour, threw the ancient waxed coat across one ultra-modern visitor's chair and sat in the other. Despite appearances, it was surprisingly comfortable. Holland pointed a stubby finger at her nose.

'Mr Lancaster asked about security yesterday, and I told him there was absolutely nothing to worry about. But that's not quite true, is it? It's come to my attention that you've been flouting the rules by smuggling classified material out of this facility. Don't ask me why, but I saved your pretty backside this time. If I'd mentioned this reckless behaviour you would have been in *deep* trouble, young lady. . . .'

Conveniently forgetting he'd known for months and been all in favour of the unofficial arrangement, Holland the bully paused dramatically. Louise said nothing. She was more familiar with Holland the fortysomething senior executive who lived in constant fear of being fired. Conrad Lancaster's tolerance was legendary. If the perspiring manager had admitted to security lapses that breached the Trojan Horse development contract, the poor sod would probably have been forced to surrender the keys of his Mercedes and walk home, whistling vainly along the way for a pay-off that would deaden the pain.

Conrad Lancaster had kicked the dog, so now the dog was chasing the cat. Satisfied he'd imposed the full authority of his personality on a less-than-perfect employee, Holland sat down. He produced a crumpled handkerchief and wiped his forehead before continuing zealously, a true convert to the cause of increased security.

'I've decided to bring in a security expert to check our procedures – Mr Lancaster's son, James. An excellent man whose company does similar work for the US Government. We're lucky to get his personal services. I suggest you don't mention your irregular activities to him, for your own sake. In the meantime, I've issued instructions that you're to be subjected to a rigorous search every time you leave the building to prevent any repetition.'

Louise already had everything she needed to work on Trojan Horse at home. If she could be bothered, after this pathetic display. The lowest form of wit seemed ideal for Holland.

'Perhaps you'd like to conduct a few body searches yourself? I've always fancied being examined by a really masterful man. Maybe I'll be so overcome that I'll quit on the spot.'

His face reddened.

'There's no call for that kind of language. Besides, you can't resign. You're under contract.'

'Who said anything about resigning? I may fail to make progress on tidying up Trojan Horse's loose ends, though.'

She picked up her coat and left the irritating little man to sweat it out.

London

THE SOPHISTICATED message centre occupied a locked cherry-wood cabinet in Wes Remington's office. But he was late arriving at the embassy, not getting Beasley's short report until mid-morning.

His wife was pissed that he'd skipped breakfast the previous day and didn't get home until late, after making contact with the freelance operative at King's Cross rail station. Helen hadn't betrayed her feelings by word or deed, but he knew. After years of the disrupted family life that went with marrying a CIA field agent, she kind of hoped promotion to Chief of Station and the plum London posting would mean they got to spend time together in a great city. Things hadn't worked out that way, but Remington cared for his wife, despite a martyred aura that enveloped her nowadays and her disconcerting habit of producing unexpected remarks like 'Do you still love me?' or 'Talk to me'.

So this morning he'd manfully masticated muesli and sat over coffee for an hour talking about their offspring – one of her favourite subjects. They'd – *she'd* – raised good kids, insofar as the adjective could ever apply to teenagers. He was confident Dan and Julia would work out just fine, but Helen probed every nuance of adolescent behaviour for evidence to the contrary. He'd listened patiently and made supportive noises.

If he'd known Beasley would blast off the blocks so fast, he might have postponed domestic fence-mending until the morrow. After listening to the agent's brief message twice, he dialled up Angus Churchill, the fingers of his left hand beating an impatient rhythm on his knee as he waited for the MI5 man's direct line to be answered. Eventually it was, in a snappy tone that suggested life was too short to be squandered on frivolous telephone calls.

'Angus Churchill.'

'Gus, it's Wes Remington. Listen, I've been thinking about this Trojan Horse business . . .'

'Wesley, I can't keep my best man tied up indefinitely on the somewhat unsatisfactory basis that the CIA has heard whispers in the shadows, now can I?'

Ouch! Earlier diagnosis confirmed – a bad morning over at Thames House. Remington poured snake-oil on to troubled waters.

'You're absolutely right, Gus, you need to know more. I've spoken with Langley and fleshed out the story. You know Conrad Lancaster owns Omega? Well, apparently he's in the running to buy a big slice of Russia Telecom when it's sold off into the private sector. That's a big prize he wants pretty bad. The Russians aren't stupid. Maybe they've found out about Trojan Horse through him. Hell, maybe Lancaster even told them – he's been doing business over there for a long time. Getting my drift?'

Churchill remained frosty.

'Military secrets for commercial advantage? Perhaps, but then again maybe one of the President's big campaign contributors is after the same slice of Russian cake. The President murmurs in Langley's ear. Langley has a quiet word with you. And good ol' Wesley persuades MI5 to jump on one of our biggest businessmen, screwing a deal that could be worth billions in foreign earnings to this country over time. No, it's not on. As of now Five's off the case, and that's official.'

Did he detect a note of bitterness in the Englishman's terse statement, or perhaps a subtly coded message? Remington's antennae quivered, but he kept his reply light.

'Like I said, you're point man on this. If you're happy everything's okay, there ain't a whole lot more I can say, right?'

'Right.'

Rudely, MI5's Deputy Director in charge of the disruption and suppression of espionage activity in Great Britain hung up. Very deliberately, Wes Remington replaced his mute handset. Something was going down, all right. But what?

Cars didn't excite him. As long as the engine started first time and they punched him back in his seat when he hit the gas, John Tolley regarded them as tools to be used and abused. Normally, the tools were official issue, but this time he was driving his own car – a dark blue Jaguar XJS with battered bodywork and 110,000 miles on the clock. As he shoved through slow-moving traffic on the Cromwell Road, impatiently changing lanes with sudden bursts of acceleration, he reflected that enforced leave of absence from MI5 was an oblique compliment.

It was easy to mock Angus Churchill's passionate self-interest, but John Tolley had discerned something else in his recent outburst. The swirl of unexplained activity around the top-secret Trojan Horse cyberweapon, and Five's humiliating exclusion from the equation, was causing his superior grave concern – for right as well as wrong reasons. Churchill might be overly ambitious, but he was also a dedicated individual who cared deeply about his country's interests.

And in all modesty, John Tolley couldn't think of another Five operative Churchill would have trusted to watchdog Trojan Horse unofficially – or one who would so willingly have accepted an assignment that might abruptly end his career. Tolley felt sudden empathy with his boss. Both were driven professionals with a secondary agenda. Tolley had no desire to climb the organizational ladder, but had found an equally strong personal motivation.

Louise Boss. He couldn't stop thinking about the enigmatic programmer, or the summary manner in which she'd dealt with his juvenile behaviour the previous evening. Tolley liked women, most women seemed to like him. That didn't mean he was never rebuffed, and such rejections had never bothered him before. But Louise's was different.

The Jag was progressing along the Great West Road at a speed that would have shamed a crawling infant. He gunned the motor, feeling trapped. As the Hogarth roundabout loomed, an Audi in the outside lane hesitated, the lone occupant distracted from the dogfight by a pressing need to light a calming cigarette. Tolley accepted the opening gratefully, grazing the Hun's bumper as it belatedly lurched forward. He blasted out into the roundabout and cut back across a big Iveco truck. The driver had to choose between hitting the Jag or his air brakes, and bottled it.

As a cacophony of horns erupted, Tolley started feeling better. Not far to the M4, where he could pedal the metal. He'd decide tactics on the motorway, but one thing was certain. He'd soon be seeing her again. As fast as the Jag could get him to Omega. Once there, he might get a second chance with Louise Boss, but that wasn't the point. He was good at what he did, and was relishing the challenge that lay ahead – especially the opportunity to do things his way, liberated from the irritating constraints under which he usually operated.

Ramming an old Led Zeppelin tape into the player, John Tolley sang along tunelessly, loudly, wildly. If someone wanted to steal Trojan Horse, they'd have to steamroller him first.

Moscow

SOME CONVERSATIONS are best handled face to face, and this was one of them. Gregor Gorski travelled by Metro – partly for reasons of anonymity, but also because on this day of all days riding the clattering, crowded trains gave him a frisson of predatory excitement. What must be will be. And later today *would* be.

He emerged from the Universitet Station on to prospekt Vernadskovo – an unremarkable middle-aged man in an old-fashioned coat and fur hat who stopped, causing the chattering wave of students in fashionably casual Western clothes to part and flow past him as they surged towards morning classes. Gregor Gorski stared up at Moscow University. The massive neo-Gothic edifice towering above Sparrow Hills was one brash legacy of the Soviet vision of grandeur that was unlikely to be swept away in a hurry. But there was nothing wrong with the world-class intellectual and technical expertise contained within its ugly walls.

His meeting in fifteen minutes would be with an eminent electronics professor, a man reputed to have the finest grasp of advanced computer science in the whole of Russia. Which made him a genius. Equally significantly, he supported the cause. Gregor Gorski had known the scientist long before he was reduced to his current academic status. With rather more than fond nostalgia, both remembered how much more satisfactory things used to be.

Once, that brilliant mind had served the state, in return for generous access to scarce resources – an entire Military Scientific Institute occupying prestigious premises in Leningrad, truck-loads of smuggled American hardware, the best young programming talent, a brand-new Swedish automobile, GUM privileges, a dacha outside Moscow and holiday home on the Black Sea. Plus the ability to ask the KGB to steal relevant research data from Germany, America or Japan. Which was how Gregor Gorski came to know Professor Otto Shebarshin in the first place.

Now, the embittered scientist was expected to survive on a salary that barely kept his family in beetroot and potatoes. To operate with outdated equipment that wasn't replaced when it died of overwork. To teach students only interested in computer science as an intelligent alternative to armed robbery. To live with chronic loss of recognition, standing and prestige. All of which was as nothing beside the frustration of talent capable of Nobel-prizewinning achievements.

Hardly surprising that he had welcomed the opportunity to assess a new Western software weapon, quietly and discreetly. Gregor Gorski might regard the acquisition of Trojan Horse as vital for the future of Russia as a reborn world power, and be certain the threat to Conrad Lancaster's wife and child would achieve that very result. But he had no intention of shouting about his coup until the potent weapon was in the palm of his hand.

Gregor Gorski looked at his watch. Time to move. Professor Shebarshin was eagerly awaiting the opportunity to analyse the British world-beater, and probe the pedigree of Trojan Horse. He'd be delighted to hear that delivery was expected within thirty-six hours.

Gloucestershire

LIZ AND TOM had not spoken during a two-minute sequence, taped during the BBC television news. A portable colour set sat between them on a round plastic table – picture fuzzy but sound clear – reporting an outbreak of terrorist violence in Moscow. James Lancaster looked at *The Times*, which sat alongside the *Financial Times*, *Wall Street Journal* and his father's own tabloid rag on the library table – a daily service provided in case Conrad happened to be passing.

The TV news didn't mention the afternoon murder of a Russian government minister at the National Hotel; the newspaper did. So the tape had been made no later than lunch-time yesterday. James was encouraged. If victims weren't killed immediately there was every chance of a successful exchange, though in this case he wouldn't be dealing with professional kidnappers with a vested interest in unwritten rules that safeguarded future business.

He studied a single sheet that came with the tape. The paper featured a typeset mobile telephone number and nothing else. To avoid revealing any numbers the kidnappers might have called, it would be a dedicated instrument held in a false name, used for nothing but forthcoming discussions. Their negotiator was probably well away from Liz and Tom, to guard against an official trace that could identify the transmission cell where the phone was being used, pinpointing the location to within a mile or so. Cool, competent methodology.

James had no intention of making contact until he knew whether he could pay their price, and to find out if Trojan Horse was available he had to visit Omega Dynamic Systems. But first he watched the tape again, before freeze-framing and studying the flickering image.

He forced himself to look at Liz, who was wearing a cream sweater and black slacks. Had she changed? Hard to tell. Her head was down, and a mass of auburn hair fell forward, half obscuring her face. He'd back the Liz he'd known to withstand the ordeal, but ten years of marriage could have worn her down. Then again, a near-decade of survival as Conrad's wife might have made Liz tougher still. She looked slimmer, and the cut of her hair had altered, but otherwise she seemed unchanged from the woman he remembered. But she must be different, a stranger reshaped by experiences about which he knew nothing.

James switched his attention to the boy – a slight school-uniformed figure sitting beside his mother, swinging feet that didn't quite reach the floor. His narrow face was determined beneath an unruly thatch of straw-coloured hair, and restless eyes dominated the sharp face – flicking from the invisible cameraman to the table and back. The object of his attention seemed to be a cheap salt cellar – and at one point towards the end of the tape his hand even strayed across and touched the salt.

Gutsy. The lad was trying to say something, though precisely what remained a mystery. As a whole, the tape offered few clues. The room seemed to have no natural light, and a rough plank floor and barely distinguishable stone wall behind Liz and Tom suggested an old building. The furniture was a green patio set of two chairs and round table, widely available from garden centres and DIY superstores. He could see what looked like the corner of a red-and-blue air-bed. The chain securing Liz looked new, as did the brass padlock locking it around her slim waist. Otherwise, nothing helpful.

But they were alive yesterday, and instinct told him they were still. These well-organized people had targeted Trojan Horse, a major military asset. Liz and Tom were no more than the means to that end, and disposing of them before the cyberweapon was acquired made no sense. Afterwards was another matter, but afterwards was down the road. James recovered the tape, put it in his briefcase and walked through to the study. He picked up the phone and called Conrad's mobile. His father's throaty voice answered immediately.

'Lancaster.'

'Same here. It's a video. Everything was fine yesterday and I'm prepared to bet it still is. Listen, it's not too late to consider an official course of action . . .'

James was non-specific, because phones could be treacherous. His father's response was instantaneous and massively indiscreet.

'No! We've been through that. I've spoken to Holland and he'll deliver. So get your arse over there and get on with it. I'll be tied up in town all day, but keep me abreast of developments. Don't let some misplaced sense of duty screw this up. What did this country ever do for you, apart from getting your knee rearranged by a Paddy with an electric drill? Give these people what they want, retrieve Tom and Elizabeth and let me worry about the consequences of delivering up Trojan Horse to God knows who. I want my family back.'

The connection was broken without warning. James sighed, experiencing grudging admiration for his father's driving determination. And awareness that – for once – he would bend to the old man's will. Because Conrad was right. Patriotic considerations aside, co-operation *did* offer the best chance of getting Liz and Tom back alive.

London

HOLIER-THAN-THOU, strong-willed James would do as he was told for the first time in a lot of years. Conrad Lancaster had to believe that one son would rescue the other, because any other outcome was unthinkable. Add the $500-million loan pledge in his safe, and Conrad could start to relax. Contemplate a return to business as usual. Wonder what the fuss had been about. Feel a wonderful sense of omnipotent well-being. When the going got tough, nobody got going like him.

Conrad had to admit his adroit manipulations were brilliant. The share price was rising steadily on the back of Peregrine Greenfield-Wright's bought-and-paid-for

Microsoft story, as more prudent bears hurried to market with 'buy' orders. The first few might cover their positions and make a profit, but the price had already bounced back from yesterday's sharp fall. The vast majority who'd sold Lancaster Trust short would be badly burned, because the stock they needed wouldn't be available at any price.

The determined raid by his offshore companies had mopped up every floating share – and Conrad had decided not to resell a single one. Yet. The desperate share support operation was turning into a major money generator. When the sensational Russia Telecom deal was announced in Moscow, Lancaster Trust stock would shoot up like a champagne cork. Not only would he have an extra forty-million worth to cash in, but it played well in the short term. Continuing lack of in-demand shares would drive the price up, until the Russian big bang drove them into orbit.

Which only left one small problem – paying the original purchase costs. He smiled a fat-cat smile and reached for his mobile. There was usually someone for whom a problem represented an opportunity – someone who might offer expensive bridging finance secured against the new offshore stockholdings. A person with an eye for a quick buck and flexible attitude to regulation, who knew something the rest of the City didn't – that Lancaster Trust was sitting on a soon-to-be-revealed gold mine.

In short, his old friend Ralph-pronounced-Rafe Powell-pronounced-Pole.

Was life a gourmet feast, or merely good enough to eat? At the smoked-glass Docklands offices of Pandora's Box Productions, Jenny Symes had finished briefing her crew on the day's assignment, which should provide the evidence needed to stage Conrad Lancaster's public trial and execution. Former Lancaster Trust employee Michael Dickson had finally allowed bile – or delayed-action conscience – to get the better of material considerations, agreeing to talk off the record about pension fund shenanigans.

They'd drive out to his Hertfordshire house after lunch,

and she was confident the embittered executive could be persuaded to abandon discretion, reveal the location of buried bodies, open cupboards where skeletons dwelt, bare his very soul. On camera, naturally. Jenny could afford to ignore the diktats of feminism. The fact that men tended to go weak in the head when she fluttered long eyelashes wasn't unsisterly exploitation, but unemotional professionalism.

Meanwhile, events elsewhere were also moving her way. Unexpectedly, Lancaster Trust shares had soared as a result of favourable morning press coverage – not in newspapers Conrad controlled, which would leave City pundits unimpressed, but in Peregrine Greenfield-Wright's famously independent financial column. It looked as though her large but nimble target had rolled out from under the falling guillotine, which suited Jenny. When Conrad's head finally rolled, she wanted only one hand on the lever. Hers.

She wondered about Hugo Savage. For every substantial winner – in this case the temporarily reprieved Conrad Lancaster – there had to be corresponding losers. One of them might be the testosterone-charged merchant banker whose hot tip had pointed her towards Conrad's financial troubles. With Lancaster Trust shares at their present level, Hugo would have to find £13 million to buy in stock needed to fulfil the option he'd sold for £10 million in anticipation of a continuing slump. Unless he'd baled out in time.

Being of sound but enquiring mind, curiosity won the day. She decided to ask. Her PA tried to reach the banker, without success. Apparently the thrustful trader was viewing a penthouse at Chelsea Harbour and hadn't yet appeared on the dealing floor. Oh dear. Jenny raised her eyes to the heavens before reaching for her gold Dunhill and writing a short note on faintly perfumed personal notepaper.

Hugo. Anyone who can trouser a three-million-pound hit without his eyes watering is a man after my own heart. Or will it be four million by the time you're reading this? Love and kisses, Jenny.

To be sure he got the message, she'd have it biked to the bonking banker with a dozen red roses.

North Devon

THE IRON WALL RING that anchored the constraining chain was immovably set in the joint between two stones. Her son's plan had become clear. He was working away with his sharpened nail, boring into old lime mortar that was yielding under pointed attack. Tom had placed an empty cardboard box to catch the falling debris. He regularly mixed accumulating spoil with boiled potatoes so mysteriously hoarded from the previous night's supper, making a stiff paste that could be used to conceal the excavation.

Every so often, he glanced over his shoulder – eyes bright in the lamplight, excitement illuminating his elfin face. Liz Lancaster marvelled again at his courage, the stubborn refusal to give in without a fight. It was impossible that any harm could come to such an innocent, engaging human being with so much spirit . . . and so much living still to do.

She thought about Conrad, her mind wandering through the wreckage of their marriage, before repeatedly returning to an inescapable irony. She disliked her husband. And despite the armed truce that had long kept him out of her bed, she had come to hate his possession of her life, the wounded pride that trapped her like a trophy in a locked cabinet. Yet now – at the very moment when both knew she was finding the courage to break away – Liz found herself in another kind of cage. And Conrad was the only one who could set her free.

If only she'd escaped sooner. If only she'd curbed youthful arrogance that blindly led her to accept Conrad's marriage proposal, in the mistaken belief she could run the relationship on her terms. If only James had been able to admit the possibility of love. If only, if only, if only. Used together, they were two of the saddest, most pathetic words in the English language.

Liz wiped her eyes with the back of her hand and shook

her head, swirling heavy hair in an effort to banish depression. This was not the moment for self-pity. She got up from the patio chair and went across to Tom, chain chinking in her wake. She knelt beside her son.

'Come here.'

He was in her arms in an instant. She hugged him tight, then held him at arm's length. Her smile required no effort.

'That's a great job you're doing, Tom. Are you really going to work that thing loose?'

He nodded, his little face deadly serious.

'Honestly, Mum, you don't really think I'm going to let them keep you chained up? Never let the bastards grind you down.'

It was one of Conrad's catch-phrases. Under normal circumstances she would have scolded him for using such language, but this time she squeezed his shoulders.

'You'd better get on with it, then.'

By the time she got back to the chair, he was hard at work. Deep down, Liz didn't believe his brave effort would make the slightest difference. But she felt angry, defiant. Never let the bastards grind you down. Never. Despite their differences, Conrad was right about that.

Herefordshire

FEELING LIKE A CRIMINAL, he was spying on his own house. The collar of his overcoat was turned up, a cloth cap pulled well down. If his wife appeared, she must not recognize him. But he wanted to see her, and kids he adored. Even from afar. It was reckless self-indulgence that threatened them as surely as him, yet Andrew Rosson couldn't keep away.

Self-defence was supposed to be second nature. After confirming that the Lancaster woman and her child were resigned to captivity, he'd climbed into the white Astra estate car and driven up the steep track to the cliff top, though he didn't really believe they'd try to trace the area where his cellphone was operating. That would mean official involvement, and Conrad Lancaster had good reasons for keeping the authorities in ignorance.

When the contact call came, he meant to be well away from the quayside warehouse. Anywhere would do. As he'd reached the main coast road and turned towards Bristol, Andrew Rosson had known where the journey would end, though pretending that any destination would do. However unlikely the possibility of a phone trace, he was contemplating an unnecessary risk. The last thing he needed was any pointer to his real life, if that life was to continue undisturbed.

As he drove, he'd wrestled with unwelcome truth. This messy business was turning into a disaster, because he *did* want his life to continue undisturbed. Badly. The patriotic fervour of being a member of the KGB's chosen élite which led to a deep-cover assignment in Britain twenty years ago was long gone, overwhelmed by the insidious attractions of existence in the West, a reality far from the promised decadence.

He had a wife and two children. A pleasant home in a quiet country town where decent people went quietly about their business without harming others. A job that barely paid enough but interested him. A future for his family. All he lacked was freedom to enjoy these things as of right, because Colonel Gorski's siren summons from the past threatened everything he had come to hold dear.

The mental progression had been predictable. At first – shock at being activated, long after deciding he would never be called upon. Then self-deluding rationalization as he considered the undeniable attraction of a large fee. Followed by irrational excitement – reawakening as middle age approached of stimulating covert skills he had never used in anger. And finally, awareness that the whole thing was destructive madness from which there could be no escape. If he betrayed Colonel Gorski, retribution would surely follow. But if he went through with the plan, the end would almost certainly be bitter.

After joining the M5, he had swung towards South Wales, crossed the Severn road bridge and immediately left the motorway at Junction 22, turning north on a circuitous route that would bring him home to Hay-on-Wye. Andrew Rosson wanted to behave cautiously like his Russian alter ego, Dmitry Travkin, but the vehicle had a will of its own.

So now he sat here in the parked Astra, with BBC Radio 5 Live playing quietly on the car radio, just in case a sensational kidnap story broke. Not two hundred yards from his rambling, flat-fronted Georgian house. Hoping for a glimpse of his wife and the girls. Thinking about a central heating boiler overdue for servicing and a cracked pane of glass in the greenhouse which needed replacing. And waiting for the silent mobile telephone on the seat beside him to come alive, precipitating him back into intrigue and violence he desperately wanted to escape. But couldn't.

Wiltshire

OMEGA'S lawned grounds provided ample room for a helicopter to set down. The pilot had been before, and knew the routine – radioing ahead to announce their imminent arrival after a short hop from New Hall. When the gold-and-black JetRanger badged with the flamboyant Lancaster Trust shield touched down, a reception committee of one was waiting – a tall man in green tweed jacket, brown cord trousers and brogues who stood motionless, white hair blowing wildly in the draught from decelerating rotor blades.

As James Lancaster exited the chopper, he guessed he was about to be welcomed – or not – by Omega's security chief. His father had urged caution, warning that Sandy MacNaughton was cut-throat sharp, despite his innocuous appearance. In the event, James would have worked that out for himself. First impressions rarely let him down, and he saw straight through the weatherbeaten face with its bland expression. The faded blue eyes were the giveaway, watching his approach with focused intensity. This was someone to reckon with. They shook hands – a brisk formality that neither man used to reveal anything of himself. The Scot's greeting retained the lilt of his native Highlands.

'MacNaughton, the old fool who's been labouring under

the misapprehension that he looked after security here.'

'James Lancaster. Sorry. This wasn't my idea, but you know my father.'

The security chief nodded, neither friendly nor hostile.

'Aye, well, we all have our crosses to bear. I'm to take you up to the Managing Director, Gordon Holland, then place myself at your disposal for the rest of the day. That should provide more than enough time to allay your esteemed parent's fears. This way.'

They walked round to the entrance. A large reception area tasted of filtered air, and expensive-looking tan leather sofas were scattered about the polished marble floor, surrounded by impressive potted greenery. MacNaughton made his first serious point, ushering James into a side room where a uniformed security officer captured him for posterity. The fixed camera produced four passport-sized colour photographs inside a minute, one of which was used to produce an encapsulated security pass. The security chief handed it over with a lopsided smile.

'Wear this while you're in the building. I hope you've nothing to hide. One spare picture goes to the front gate so they can identify you on future visits, one's for my records and the last will be wired to MI5 in London. They think we should be extremely careful who we let into this place. Right, follow me.'

The lift was card-operated. When they reached the top floor, MacNaughton steered him across an open-plan area with half-height panels segregating busy beavers bent over computers. The Managing Director's enclosed office occupied a corner, and they were expected. An attractive young secretary had been watching their approach from an impressive work station, and pointed a crimson-tipped finger at her boss's door.

'You're expected. Go straight in.'

MacNaughton led on, pausing inside the spacious office to introduce James.

'James Lancaster, Gordon Holland, our MD.'

Holland exuded bonhomie, beaming a sycophantic greeting as he waddled round the big desk – a short, overweight fortysomething wearing an off-the-peg suit and overloud floral tie.

'Mr Lancaster, so pleased you agreed to place your expertise at our disposal. Whilst Sandy here does an excellent job, your father and I both agreed that it would do no harm for someone like yourself to take a second look. No harm at all.'

He pulled a Space Age chair back two inches like a fawning head waiter, continuing eagerly as James put his briefcase down on deep yellow carpet and settled.

'Thank you, Sandy, that will be all. Mr Lancaster and I have confidential matters relating to the effectiveness of security at this facility to discuss . . .'

Holland dared the older man to challenge him. Though the curt dismissal suggested his own competence might be on the agenda, MacNaughton didn't react, looking from Holland to James before leaving wordlessly, expression unreadable. He quietly closed the door. If first impressions of the Scotsman were positive, the reverse was true of the plump MD.

James watched as he scuttled over to a large framed colour photograph of Conrad Lancaster, mover and handshaker, clasping Prime Minister Thatcher's fingers in one of those stagy poses beloved of the mighty, which are held without a muscle twitching or smile wavering until the last camera flash dies. The picture was hinged. Holland swung Conrad and Maggie away from the wall, revealing a compact safe. He spun the dial, clicked a lever and opened the thick door, watching James conspiratorially over a dandruffed shoulder.

'Your father telephoned earlier. I understand you'll be taking this.'

He produced a boxed optical disk with a flourish, like a conjurer at the climax of a particularly impressive stunt – which, in a way, it was. After all, he was offering up a top-secret software package which had not only cost the British and American Governments millions to develop, but was also protected by rigorous security procedures. Yet this self-important little man had not only obtained Trojan Horse, but was also offering the goodies like a 1950s adolescent trying to impress his first date with expensive chocolates. James held out his hand.

'Give.'

Holland gave, before returning to his executive swivel chair. As James stashed the precious disk in his briefcase, Omega's MD showed the first tiny sign of anxiety.

'That will be going directly to the Americans, yes? Your father explained, and I see no harm in the authorized end user having a preview. But I take my responsibilities very seriously. It goes without saying that Trojan Horse falling into the wrong hands would be a disaster.'

James smiled reassuringly.

'It may go without saying, Gordon, but I'm still glad you mentioned it. Security is my business, and we professionals can never be too careful. Rest assured. This briefcase won't leave my sight while I'm here, and then I'll fly straight to Mildenhall in the company helicopter to hand this to our American friends.'

'Excellent. As soon as they confirm safe receipt I'll provide the access codes so they can open our box of tricks and marvel. They'll be most impressed, though I don't mind telling you the Yanks are fed up that it took good old British know-how to develop Trojan Horse. They're livid, actually. Damaged pride, and all that.'

If the pompous idiot hadn't been so dangerous, his gushing self-satisfaction would have been laughable. James stood up, betraying no hint of contempt.

'I'd better see MacNaughton. He doesn't need to know I've got more important things to do this afternoon. I'll also tell my father how helpful you've been. Is there somewhere private I can make a telephone call?'

'Of course. My secretary will show you through to the conference room, then take you down to Sandy's office. We aim to please.'

Gordon Holland sprang to his feet and rushed to open the door. The parting quip actually said a whole lot more. James followed. He was no longer amazed by how easily the most sophisticated security systems in the world could unglue if personal weakness was exposed, explored and exploited. But what the hell. The flawed side of human nature paid his wages.

The rapid journey had vented aggression. He'd pushed the XJS hard, slicing past perambulating traffic to left and right at speeds of up to 130 mph. By the time he reached the science park on the outskirts of Swindon, John Tolley was calm. Focused. In control. Dealing with the disconcerting impact of Louise Boss would have to wait, because he was what he was, which happened to be the world's greatest counter-intelligence operative. Well, one of them.

This assignment was too intriguing to ignore. The Joint Intelligence Committee's intervention was puzzling, and Tolley hated unsolved mysteries. If JIC wanted MI5 off the case, something he didn't know about was happening at Omega Dynamic Systems. Protecting Trojan Horse was Five's business. He was damned if a bunch of Whitehall schemers would change that, though he'd also be damned if they discovered he was giving them the proverbial stiff-finger salute.

For now, that insubordinate act was a secret shared with Gus Churchill, so he had an innocent excuse prepared for Omega's gateman – important papers left in Alexander MacNaughton's office after yesterday's visit. Thin, but better than nothing if the JIC mandarins should find out he'd arrived at Omega within hours of Five being ordered to stay away. The guard made a call, then slid back his booth window and held out the phone.

'The boss would like a word.'

Not Louise, presumably. Tolley scrambled out of the low Jaguar and took the instrument.

'Sandy, I thought you promised to discuss that Fort Knox complex with your analyst? Getting through this gate is a real pain. I'll come over the wall next time.'

MacNaughton didn't respond in kind. The Scottish voice managed to sound simultaneously suspicious and sour.

'Why have you come back, John? This isn't a good time.'

Tolley had noticed the helicopter squatting alongside the building, boldly proclaiming the presence of a senior Lancaster Trust executive – perhaps the great Conrad himself. The plot thickened.

'Not fooled by my brilliant lost document cover story, then? We must talk, Sandy. I wouldn't be here unless it was important.'

His old mentor's acceptance was immediate and ungrudging, dry humour returning.

'Okay. Hand me back to Godzilla and I'll tell him you're here to ask for Gordon Holland's autograph. Wait for me in reception. This better be good, or I'll personally set the bloody dogs on you.'

'Come off it, Sandy. Your bark's far worse than their bite.'

He surrendered the phone and eased back into the Jag. A first-class man to have on your side, was Sandy MacNaughton. He'd understand. And if he didn't, no problem. Tolley adored Alsatians, especially big ones with sharp teeth.

Herefordshire

RISK had been rewarded. Eventually, Andrew Rosson's vigil produced the glimpse of normality he craved, however fleeting. The old red Volvo appeared from his driveway and stopped. For an instant, he saw his wife's face as she glanced his way, seeing only the traffic-free road she was looking for. Then the big estate car moved off in the opposite direction, towards the centre of town. Perhaps the girls were strapped into their child seats, but the distance was too great for him to be sure.

The sighting didn't have the desired effect. Far from cheering him up, the brief non-encounter left Rosson profoundly depressed, and for a crazy moment he seriously considered driving to the house. Letting himself in. Making a cup of strong instant coffee. Catching up with the post. And waiting for his family to return. But of course he did none of those things, instead turning the Astra round and heading for Abergavenny and the A40.

Five miles along a minor road that skirted the Black Mountains, his phone rang – the virgin mobile exclusively reserved for negotiations. Rosson didn't answer until he found a passing place to stop the car, but they didn't give up. He left it for another thirty seconds to escalate tension, then hit the button. Silence, then a voice. Not Conrad Lancaster's, familiar from television. Younger. Firm and assured.

'Do I have the right number?'

'You're interested in horse-trading?'

'I am.'

'This is the right number. You are?'

'James Lancaster. I have experience in these matters, and my father has delegated the responsibility for reaching a satisfactory agreement. You talk to me and me alone.'

Rosson had no objection, but let him sweat for a moment before agreeing.

'Very well. You have the merchandise?'

'By five this afternoon, guaranteed.'

'Together with necessary access codes?'

'Yes.'

'We have the means to check. It wouldn't be wise to attempt deception.'

'There will be no deception. No faulty goods. No police. No effort made to apprehend you once the exchange is effected. My father insists nothing should be done to jeopardise the safety of his wife and child. But it will be an exchange. You choose time and place, I'll be there with the material. Alone. However, unless Elizabeth and Tom Lancaster are there, forget the whole thing. Both must be released before I will hand over the disk. Is that clear?'

Very, but hopelessly optimistic. Rosson laughed.

'Perfectly, but unacceptable. Instant verification of the goods will not be possible, and there's no question of releasing anyone until we're satisfied. This is done on our terms or not at all.'

Lancaster didn't fold.

'I'll settle for one of them, and that's final. You'll still have the other to protect you against any double-cross. Take it or leave it.'

Tough words, and Rosson sensed they weren't empty. Lancaster wouldn't budge. He lowered the phone and looked at the digital display, which showed the caller's number.

'I'll take advice. You're using a mobile phone?'

'Yes. Want the number?'

'Thanks to the wonders of modern telecommunications, it's before my very eyes. Don't switch off the phone or let your battery go flat. Okay, you know what they say. Don't call us, we'll call you. Soon after five, to confirm that you can pay the price. A word of warning. One flashing blue light means end of dialogue and your relatives messily dead, Mr Lancaster. Shotgun loaded with BBs. One barrel each, in the head, the mother first.'

The crude threat was for effect only. Now the endgame was beginning, he was feeling a surge of confidence. Conrad Lancaster would surely insist that Trojan Horse was safely delivered. Then it was over. Dmitry Travkin could be buried for ever, and Andrew Rosson reborn.

London

GREED had triumphed. At a usurious short-term interest rate, blue-blooded Ralph-cum-Rafe Powell-cum-Pole had shovelled over another forty million of his blue-chip bank's pounds, secured against rapidly rising Lancaster Trust stock held by offshore companies. Electronic paperwork would be completed within an hour, and with it an emergency rescue operation that had magically turned into another massive earner.

Conrad Lancaster felt no surprise, or relief. As a child, he'd worked for an uncle and two cousins who made rich pickings from West End theatre-goers, setting up the three-card trick on an orange box in the maze of streets behind Shaftesbury Avenue. Conrad acted as lookout, warning the team if a policeman approached, but saw enough of the action to learn a lesson for life. Punters knew the Queen of Spades was there. The frenetic atmosphere and promise of easy money overrode prudence, fostering flawed belief that the elusive Black Lady would soon be fingered. Wallets empty, they wondered how they could possibly have been so foolish – yet Conrad had seen the same mugs return, convinced they were victims of unlucky aberration.

On such insights were mighty business empires built. Conrad Lancaster heaved himself to his feet. He deserved a treat, and the dining room beckoned seductively. His mobile warbled. Annoyed, he dragged the phone from a jacket pocket and hit the button. Hard.

'Lancaster.'

'Snap. I'm at Omega.'

James. Conrad sat down again.

'And?'

'I've taken delivery and opened negotiations, but there's a snag. Your man rolled over like an over-anxious puppy, but nobody gets into the master disk without access codes. Holland bought your story, but assumes the Americans will confirm safe receipt, allowing him to release the codes through official channels. The man's a jumped-up idiot, but even he's not dumb enough to hand over the keys of the castle on your say-so.'

Conrad pretended to ponder, but not for long.

'The master copy's kosher?'

'I'd bet on it. Holland was full of himself.'

'That's something. At least we can give the kidnappers what they want and get Elizabeth and Tom in exchange. But they know about the access codes and won't do business without them?'

'Correct. This project is supposed to have maximum security classification, but they seem remarkably well informed. Any ideas on getting those codes?'

Conrad pondered for real. The boy was tiresome, but had a point.

'You'd better twist Holland's arm. It'll break. So what's the deal?'

'I have to consider things you might not want to hear about, and don't want you muddying the waters by questioning my judgment. I'll get back to you when something concrete emerges.'

James sounded snappy. A conciliatory response was in order.

'Fine. I'll rely on your expertise. Tom and Elizabeth would, too, if they knew. Do whatever's necessary, money no object.'

'Including telling the authorities what's going on?'

'Except that. We just can't risk their lives, and at least there's a chance if we play ball. Try to get them back for me. Please.'

'What the hell d'you think I've been doing all day?'

Same old James – so quick to take offence, so easy to rile. And, in this particular situation, motivate. He almost chuckled, but instead spoke humbly into the phone.

'Let's not waste any more of your valuable time, then.'

Conrad Lancaster ended the call. He had a heavy afternoon booked with the Group Finance Director, and there was no question of discussing complex money manipulation and slick three-card share transfers on an empty stomach.

Wiltshire

HE RARELY misjudged people – but was he willing to stake two lives on instant evaluation of a middle-aged Celt who was harder to read than *Finnegans Wake*? James Lancaster was still turning the question over when Holland's secretary left him at Sandy MacNaughton's door. She'd waited outside the conference room while he used his mobile, welcoming the break from regular routine. He was sympathetic, exchanging small talk as they walked. Working for the self-important MD must be the job from hell.

MacNaughton had a visitor – male, thirtyish, thick dark hair combed back off the face, good-looking enough to arouse instant antipathy, wearing faded blue jeans and a soft brown leather jacket. James looked enquiringly at the security chief, aware that the stranger was returning his assessment with interest.

'John Tolley, James Lancaster. John's an old colleague from MI5, recently acting as my official watchdog. But you won't need to fight over my shortcomings, this is a social call. He's on leave of absence as of today. Take a pew.'

As James put down the briefcase and arranged his chair so he could see both men, MacNaughton turned to the matinée idol.

'Mr Lancaster's an expert from the States, imported at great expense by our security-conscious proprietor, who happens to be his father. Seems you're not alone in thinking I couldn't protect the virtue of an elderly nun in a closed convent.'

There was no bitterness in the comment. The Five man laughed, an easy riposte suggesting that the pair were long-time buddies.

'It's true. What does a tight-arsed Calvinist like you know about religious ecstacy? Well, if you two are going to compare ravished nuns, I'd better make myself scarce.'

James made a decision. This was more than a pretty face who was cocky with it. He liked the way Tolley's eyes met his, the quirk at the corner of the man's mouth. Trusting first impressions would land him in trouble one day, probably when dealing with pros who concealed true personae automatically. Just like these two. He bought a little second-thoughts time with a casual question to the spook.

'Leave of absence?'

Tolley smiled – an electric smile beaming 'trust me' so brightly that it should have set off every alarm bell within miles, but didn't. Answered in a pleasant tenor voice that contained self-deprecating confidence.

'Suspended on full pay. A disagreement with the management, with whom I don't always see eye to eye, being prone to temporary blindness on occasion. We loners suffer for our sins.'

An uncannily encouraging reply. Either Tolley was telepathic, or those goddam first impressions were right on the bunny. Academic. There was no choice. He couldn't do this alone. If MI5 piled in like the Seventh Cavalry, that would be too bad. James nodded judiciously.

'Sounds a bit like me and my dear old dad. Stay a while, John. You might find this interesting.'

He'd made mistakes. Done – or not done – many things remembered with regret. But James Lancaster had never betrayed his country and never could.

Sins of the father shouldn't automatically be vested in the son, though Sandy MacNaughton had been more than willing to resent the intruder. But it was hard to remain unimpressed by James Lancaster. Like a powerful animal that harboured no aggressive intentions yet was capable of attacking savagely if threatened, he had a dangerous quality that compelled attention and inspired wary respect. His stern face somehow suggested it had seen the worst the world had to offer and survived, stronger for the experience.

MacNaughton had watched, fascinated, as the two young lions sized one another up. He wasn't one for snap judgments, but couldn't help feeling they'd reached some sort of unspoken understanding in a short space of time. Or that James had been testing the ground ahead of a significant announcement. After a considered pause, he was ready to begin, his measured voice containing no hint of the accent so many transatlantic expatriates acquire.

'I have an outfit on the West Coast that does sensitive work for the US Government from time to time. I personally have top-level security clearance over there. You may feel the need to confirm that, but for now take it on trust. Although the Americans have a vital interest in Trojan Horse, I'm not here on their behalf, but my father's. He also has a lot riding on the successful completion of the contract. You've been told I'm here to double-check security?'

The question was addressed to him. MacNaughton responded cautiously, unsure where this was leading.

'Gordon Holland may have mentioned the fact, on about twenty separate occasions.'

'But you both feel there's nothing to worry about, and that my involvement is likely to be a complete waste of effort?'

This time, the question included them both, and MacNaughton let John Tolley reply.

'I was down here yesterday, going through everything with Sandy. Looked fine. Access to Trojan Horse development files and operating software is tightly controlled and rigorously enforced. I gather that only this morning a senior member of staff was dismissed for failing to follow approved procedure to the letter, even though his actions didn't compromise the project.'

Young Lancaster was a master of the loaded question, issuing a sardonic challenge.

'Is that a fact? Your suspension on full pay is of recent

origin, then. And Omega's firing staff for lax security. Did anyone bother to think there might be a connection?'

The man was a quick lateral thinker. They hadn't. But then John Tolley had barely finished explaining his covert mission when this disconcerting player appeared. MacNaughton took the wickedly spinning ball and played it back to the bowler with a dead bat.

'Meaning what, exactly?'

He was rewarded with another surprise delivery. James Lancaster smiled, transforming the stern face.

'I'm a great one for trusting first impressions. Naïve, perhaps, but it often works for me. I hope I've made a good impression on you guys, because I'm about to put my life in your hands. Not literally mine, but someone's. As proof of good faith, I'll also return my personal copy of Trojan Horse, if that's what you want when you've listened to an interesting story.'

This James Lancaster was some operator. He sat back in his chair, totally relaxed, and awaited their response.

As show-stoppers went, it wasn't bad. The two hardened security men were temporarily rendered speechless. James Lancaster followed up relentlessly, reaching down for his briefcase. The catches snapped loudly in the silence of MacNaughton's office. He put the optical disk box on the desk and continued cheerfully.

'There, one slick computer programme, allegedly HM Government's most hush-hush weapon, though the secret seems to be out of the bag. But I don't have access codes, if that's any consolation.'

It wasn't. Shock subsided, and John Tolley cleared his throat. Before the MI5 man could get his question out, James answered, advantage complete.

'Handed to me not half an hour ago by Golden Bollocks, straight-as-a-die MD of Omega Dynamic Systems. No idea how he short-circuited your vaunted security procedures, but for what it's worth Holland believes your American paymasters have demanded evidence of progress and thinks this little firecracker is destined for the proper authorities in America.'

Sandy MacNaughton chipped in bitterly.

'I think Peter Clough's chances of winning a wrongful dismissal claim at any industrial tribunal in the land just went platinum.'

'Peter Clough?'

James looked at him interrogatively. Still angry, the Scotsman explained.

'The Data Manager dismissed this morning. Gordon Holland ordered the poor sod to deliver up a master of Trojan Horse, then claimed it was a ploy to test security ahead of your visit. Fired him for failing to follow proper procedures. The crafty swine must have copied the data, before telling me about Clough's lapse and making him the scapegoat.'

'I wondered how Holland did it. My old man must have put the fear of God in him. But in fairness to Conrad, this isn't straightforward theft of Trojan Horse for profit . . .'

He paused for effect, but there was no need. He had their full attention.

'My father's wife and young son have been kidnapped and he'll do anything to get them back. I'll show you ransom notes and a video later, but the price of their safe return is Trojan Horse and I'm supposed to negotiate the exchange. Another speciality of the house. Now, true to type Conrad's playing this cool, but underneath he must be desperate, because he'll give these people what they want to get Liz and Tom back, even if he loses his business and finishes up in jail for a gross breach of the Official Secrets Act.'

'But you're not? Willing to give them Trojan Horse, I mean. Hence this conversation and the dutiful surrender of the material your father bullied so hard to procure. Though perhaps that isn't the end of the interesting story you promised us?'

John Tolley's first contribution. In contrast to MacNaughton, the Five man had watched and listened intently, never blinking. The security chief had looked here, there and everywhere in disbelief, but mostly at the disk containing the data he was supposed to be protecting. James made his pitch.

'Gentlemen, I'm asking for forty-eight hours. If you report this now, you may be signing the death warrants of an innocent woman and child. We have no way of knowing what information sources these people have, and if they find out Trojan Horse is lost to them . . .'

'Who *are* these mysterious people?'

John Tolley's second contribution. Ahead of the punch line. Businesslike. Unsentimental. James rubbed a hand across his chin before replying – honestly, but with guile.

'No idea, and I don't really care, so long as I can try for the exchange. Catching enemies of the realm is more your department, John, and wouldn't you just like to know?'

Tolley might have been tempted, but he didn't deviate or give ground.

'If you're genuinely concerned about protecting Trojan Horse, you could easily have put the disk somewhere safe and carried on with the exchange, using a dummy. Presumably you're hoping to get at least one of the hostages and track back to the other from the handover. Not exactly brilliant, but about the best you can do without actually giving them what they want. So why bother with this touching confession which could screw even that lousy plan?'

Oh, but he was good. James decided it was time to close the sale. Or not.

'Because I want you to lend me Trojan Horse and provide the necessary access codes. If the damn thing can be totally disabled whilst still looking the part at first glance. I've talked to the kidnappers. They know about the access codes and claim to be able to make an authenticity test on the data. If I was willing to give the thing up I'd've screwed the codes out of Holland, and you wouldn't have seen my helicopter for dust. At least this way you know what's happening, so how about it?'

He watched Tolley and MacNaughton exchange glances. Nothing was said, but a message passed. John Tolley communicated the result.

'We need ten minutes. No phone calls, no reference to third parties, just talk. We'll let you know our decision before taking any action.'

'Make it five minutes. The clock's running and two lives depend on doing this right.'

James picked up the disk, then put it down again.

Whatever else might happen, Trojan Horse wasn't going anywhere. And if that trusted ability to make accurate first impressions should choose today to let him down, neither was he.

Moscow

TRUE GENIUS was not averse to the occasional short cut. In anticipation of peering into the minds of the West's most innovative programmers, the eager Professor Shebarshin had secured one uninterrupted day at his department's most powerful work station, for preliminary assessment of the Trojan Horse cyberweapon. The prospect was so stimulating that – after confirming the simple method by which these digital riches would be sucked into his system – Russia's most brilliant computer scientist had smackingly kissed their provider on both cheeks.

Though Gregor Gorski regarded such emotional displays with distaste, he had given no hint of the fact. Or of his own growing excitement, which must be rigidly held in check until the co-operative academic confirmed Trojan Horse's authenticity. The implications of such a prize were almost beyond calculation, but the ex-KGB colonel had no intention of crowing prematurely. Long experience suggested such intelligence coups could never be taken for granted, however meticulous the planning or promising the omens.

As he strolled away from Moscow University's brutal sky tower, Gregor Gorski considered the way in which technology was not only facilitating intelligence work, but also altering the world's strategic landscape. Extracting stolen secrets from a foreign country used to be a logistical nightmare. And not so long ago, enough rockets and nuclear warheads to destroy the world thrice over were essential for membership of the exclusive superpower club. But perceptions changed, and such hardware was becoming yesterday's arsenal – which was fortunate, considering that Russia's once-formidable array of SS2 ICBMs was little more than a pile of inoperable junk. The future was electronic, with weapons not only capable of destroying the complex command systems needed to direct both nuclear and conventional attack, but also of inflicting almost limitless economic disruption. Possession of such awesome capability would transform Russia's tarnished international status at a stroke.

But that would be a bonus, of no value unless his master was confirmed in power, the unchallenged President of the Commonwealth of Independent States. Trojan Horse would be Gorski's gift to the only man capable of successfully leading Russia into a brave new millennium. He increased his pace. Not long now. One more headline-grabbing atrocity, and then on to the *pièce de résistance* – a daring attack by the despicable Sons of Dudayev on President Mikhail Yelkin. That aspect of the battle was entirely within his control, whether or not the cyberweapon was captured.

The day was going well. He was heading for a meeting with General Sergei Sobchak, to review progress and reassure the popular politician that his time was nigh. Already, a rash of eye-catching red posters featuring the general's uncompromising square face above the single word *PORYADOK!* had erupted, pasted overnight on every convenient surface from shop windows to lamp posts. City employees were attacking the pervasive propaganda, but it was a hopeless task – they were few and the siren posters were many. The frightened citizens of Moscow would warm to the message. What could be more attractive in these troubled times than the promise of strong leadership, coupled with restoration of the order and stability so many craved? Especially after this afternoon's terrible outrage.

Gregor Gorski's mobile rang, interrupting the satisfying reverie. He was on Leninskiy prospekt, opposite a Radio Shack store that symbolized the rapid foreign commercial invasion of the nation's capital. He glanced around before answering the call, but mobile telephones were no longer a novelty in Moscow. None of the self-absorbed pedestrians showed interest as they hurried about their business. He pushed the button.

'*Da?*'

'Gregor?'

Rosson. He switched to English.

'Yes.'

'The sellers have made contact. They have acquired the merchandise, but have asked for payment in full with delivery. Negotiations are being handled by the principal's oldest son, who is taking a tough line.'

Gorski spoke judiciously.

'I know of him. He has considerable expertise in this field. This is no more than a ploy. Full payment is out of the question. Offer half on exchange, and no more. The smaller half. They'll settle for that. Understood?'

'The smaller half? Yes, I understand. And the onward transmission of the merchandise?'

For someone born as Dmitry Travkin in the Ukraine, who had never set foot outside the Soviet Union until until he was twenty-three years old, Rosson's English accent was remarkable. But then these things were always done properly in the old days.

'The arrangement is unchanged. Our friend in Bristol will be awaiting your visit. Do not forget that he believes this material is nothing but innocent academic research. Notify me immediately when the data transfer has been completed.'

Oh, the wonders of modern science. Gregor Gorski ended the call and resumed his leisurely stroll towards Gorkiy Park and his momentous meeting with General Sobchak, the stocky ex-paratroop commander who would be the next President of Russia.

London

HIS HAND HADN'T strayed very far from the special telephone all day, as though willing the mobile to come alive. When it finally did, Beasley's controller pounced, strangling shrill sound in mid-warble.

'Yes?'

'Did you get Five off the case?'

'For a while. Wasn't easy. Their man Gus Churchill's screaming foul, and the Joint Intelligence Committee has only given us two days. Then we have to put the other agencies in the picture, after which they'll all want their piece of pie.'

'Churchill may be doing more than complaining. There's a Five operative at Omega now. Any money you like says Churchill sent him in unofficially. He may get together with that crafty James Lancaster, who has boldly suggested running with the exchange in an attempt to retrieve the kidnap victims. Conrad Lancaster managed to browbeat Omega's MD into supplying a master copy of Trojan Horse on disk, but honest James owned up, so there's no question of the weapon being compromised.'

'I'd hope not. Two questions. Are you happy to try and find out who's behind the attempt on Trojan Horse, and do you want me to initiate some discreet enquiries into the kidnap?'

'If things get out of hand I'll call for back-up, but for the moment I'll run with it. One problem. What do I tell Wes Remington, if anything?'

'Beasley's too valuable to lose, so you must try to retain credibility. Tell him what's happening, but make it clear we're on the job and there's no threat to Trojan Horse. The last thing we need is the CIA crashing around like a loose cannon, and it won't hurt to remind him that we're not totally incompetent on matters of national security. Just keep him sweet.'

'Will do. Anything else?'

'No, but I'll put a team on stand-by in case you need rapid support. Be lucky. And be careful.'

'Aren't I always? On both counts.'

For once, Beasley's habitual sign-off sounded almost cheerful. The controller put down the dead phone. Sighed theatrically. He'd take a lot of stick when this operation was over, but in the final analysis his jealous rivals would – however reluctantly – be forced to accept the logic of his strategy. Because he was the clever bastard with an agent in place.

He needed a wasted afternoon like a third serving of his wife's muesli, but Wes Remington had been unable to duck a luxurious lunch gathering being thrown by the ambassador, who had boldly hijacked a visiting arms procurement mission from Indonesia. Officially, the select gathering was no more than a polite exchange of courtesies. But the international arms business was ultra-competitive, and it would be downright unpatriotic to let the Brits have a free run at this one.

After the feast, the military attaché would be showing a video featuring state-of-the-art American crowd-control equipment, as the Indonesians were particularly interested in the imaginative application of science alongside more traditional brute force. Likewise, the most modern covert surveillance technology was on their shopping list, so the CIA's London Head of Station was expected to add a dash of undercover flavour to the occasion.

But, in the unavoidable absence of its master, the recording machine in his office cherry-wood cabinet remained on watch, automatically picking up an incoming call on the third ring. An American voice spoke quickly to the tape. The muffled, staccato words were clearly audible, and the needle on a green-lit sound level monitor flickered rapidly.

'The Lancaster surveillance has paid off. Listening devices are telling us all we need to know. Conrad Lancaster's wife and son have been kidnapped. I'll send you a copy of the note. Haven't identified the kidnappers, who're proposing an urgent exchange. Their price is something called Trojan Horse, developed by Omega Dynamic Systems. I guess that's the military software package covered in your briefing. I mentioned the other son in my last report. James. I've been following him, listening. He's been brought in to handle negotiations. The old man's crazy about his wife and kid and hasn't notified the authorities. Terrified he'll lose his family if the heavy hand of the law starts stirring the pot. But British Intelligence are aware of the situation. MI5 are at Omega, so the stable door's almost certainly shut on Trojan Horse. More later.'

The recorder shut down one second after Beasley's call ended. When Wes Remington eventually returned from his sales conference, fuming at the enforced waste of three valuable hours, the agent-for-hire's reassuring message would be waiting.

Wiltshire

TO TRUST or not to trust, that was the question. Or rather one of many that had extended the promised few minutes into half an hour, as John Tolley and Sandy MacNaughton wrestled with slippery options. There wasn't a satisfactory solution.

They kept coming back to the ban on MI5 involvement with Trojan Horse, which could only mean one thing – another agency was running an operation that might be compromised if the security service crashed in. Tolley remembered Angus Churchill's parting words. If they officially notified him of worrying developments, the irascible chief of K Branch would be in an awkward position. Churchill had been warned off, and wouldn't want to explain why one of his agents had surfaced at Omega.

Then there was James Lancaster, and that heartfelt plea on behalf of his kidnapped relatives. He'd made a good impression, and handed back the stolen Trojan Horse disk when he didn't need to. But he might be pursuing a hidden agenda. Both men knew enough about Lancaster charm to appreciate that what you saw wasn't always what you got. Tolley couldn't even run a background check, so it all came down to a judgment call. Having reached that point – twice – they were talked out. In lengthening silence, John Tolley looked at MacNaughton. They'd done enough professional analysis for one day.

'Okay, Sandy, here's what I suggest. We go with young Lancaster, on the understanding that I push the panic button and to hell with consequences if the developing situation warrants urgent intervention. In the meantime, I won't say anything to Churchill. He *expects* me to do my own thing. Five can't be seen to be involved in this, and if I get caught and Churchill disowns me, my file won't exactly contradict the suggestion that I'm capable of unorthodox independent action. Trojan Horse isn't threatened, so what can we lose?'

There were plenty of negative answers, but the canny Scot actually smiled.

'It hasn't escaped my notice that your mind's made up. Has been from the beginning, if I'm not mistaken. This is the sort of crazy escapade you never could resist, John, never. Which is, as you so rightly say, why Gus Churchill turned you loose in the first place.'

As usual, Sandy didn't miss much. Tolley nodded.

'So the mind-reader of the month award is yours, yet again. But we had to think this through, and you must admit it's a not unreasonable course of action under the circumstances.'

MacNaughton's dry voice acquired a steely timbre.

'Aye, but let's make one thing clear. We cannot proceed if there's one chance in a million that Trojan Horse will be at risk.'

'How do we guarantee that?'

As he asked the apparently innocent question, Tolley almost hugged himself. This was working out perfectly.

'We must bring Louise Boss in. Unless she can substitute worthless files that look the part, our Mr Lancaster hasn't got a deal. If she can, there's nothing to lose and something to gain. If you ferret out the people behind this kidnap, Gus Churchill might even welcome you back with open arms and grant security of tenure.'

'Will she play this our way?'

The Scot's reply was tart.

'Loves a challenge, does our Louise, and knows a bit about information-gathering. She'll be a real asset.'

'Deal. Don't tell her I'm here, or she'll probably refuse to show her face.'

MacNaughton gave him a scalding look.

'I hope this is about more than rogue hormones. I warned you not to mess with that one. Out of your league.'

Tolley hammed, placing a hand on his heart.

'And I should've listened. Father knew best. No harm done, and it will be strictly business from here on in. That's a promise.'

'What makes me think various portions of your anatomy are crossed? All right, I'll call her. Wheel our persuasive friend back in and we'll break the good news. I hope neither of us lives to regret this.'

'Even if we do, we'll have fun along the way.'

'That's what worries me.'

The Omega security chief went all puritanical again,

but did reach for the phone as Tolley jumped up and headed for the door.

A bad day at the office was recovering. Seeing John Tolley in Sandy MacNaughton's office had been unexpected, and she'd assumed he was seeking revenge for the previous evening's cutting put-down. A report to MI5 on the after-hours security breaches of Louise Boss would be awkward, resulting in time-consuming hassle. This negative assumption had been reinforced by the presence of a third man – older than Tolley, with an attractive but careworn face that commanded attention. Tolley's superior, here to put in the boot?

Anger had surged through Louise, compounded by awareness that Tolley was having a physical effect on her. Before she could go on to the attack, the stranger had introduced himself as James Lancaster – yes, his son – asked that she treat what he was about to say in strict confidence and talked for five minutes. His story of kidnap and intrigue was bizarre, but told with clarity and conviction. Trojan Horse was being attacked, and they needed her help.

Tolley had watched her throughout the recitation, but hadn't unleashed that unsettling smile. When he took over from James Lancaster, his voice contained none of the mocking humour characterizing their first meeting. Was it only yesterday?

'We can't do anything unless you are able to provide a convincing dummy disk, Louise. The whole plan hinges on that. Can you put something together that will hold up for long enough to give us a reasonable shot at tracing the kidnappers?'

She met clear grey eyes, and saw only a determined security professional. The atmosphere in MacNaughton's cramped office was charged, and Louise felt extraneous emotion fall away. Her team had written the patch that corrected Trojan Horse's failure to disrupt US air traffic, and she should be running another simulation to confirm its efficacy. But this was real, and different – a challenge offering some serious stimulation. Besides, her baby had been threatened, and that was unacceptable. Seamlessly, she integrated with the new dynamic, focusing totally on defined objectives.

'No problem with the disk, but I want to stay with this to the end. I may be able to help with the tracking. Can you fix time off with Holland?'

MacNaughton answered grimly.

'Leave Gordon to me. He doesn't know it yet, but our irritating MD has a nasty shock coming. He's been a bad lad, and when we've dealt with this business I'll make sure he pays the price.'

Louise laughed.

'Couldn't happen to a nicer person. So, where do we go from here?'

James Lancaster replied, easily assuming command – an assumption the other two seemed to accept without resentment.

'The kidnappers should ring at around five. When we have heard their terms and have details of the proposed exchange, we plan our campaign. Is it possible to rig a recorder and speaker?'

MacNaughton took the cellphone that James Lancaster produced from his briefcase.

'I'll put this on my speaker cradle. We'll all be able to hear and the call can be taped.'

Louise butted in.

'If he's using a mobile the location can be plotted. Now, these people will know that and make sure contact calls don't reveal their base. But not everyone knows that a live mobile phone sends a regular orientation signal, whether or not it's used. That signal can also be tracked. If you can persuade them to leave their phone on stand-by, we just might nail them.'

Nobody queried her expertise. James Lancaster nodded.

'He'll be on a mobile.'

They looked at each other, enjoying a moment of shared anticipation, the taut cameraderie of combatants on the brink of battle. MacNaughton reached for his phone.

'They say an army marches on its stomach, so I'd better order sandwiches and coffee.'

Louise let her eyes wander away from James Lancaster,

slide sideways towards John Tolley. He was waiting for her, and smiled that bloody smile.

Herefordshire

FOLLOWING THE UNSETTLING glimpse of his wife and subsequent contact with tough-talking James Lancaster, he'd driven aimlessly, allowing the Astra to wander along country roads. Somewhere near Hereford, Andrew Rosson had pulled into a pub carpark and telephoned his master in Moscow, careful not to use the mobile exclusively reserved for negotiations with the Lancasters. With thoughts of his own children occupying his mind, Gregor Gorski's instruction to exchange the boy had made him feel better.

Until he made the call to Conrad Lancaster's representative, the other son, it was impossible to return to the quayside warehouse in North Devon. With time to kill, he'd tried to sleep in the car – turning awkwardly in the front seat in search of a comfortable position, managing no more that a series of unsatisfactory naps. Rosson kept starting awake with his head full of some all-pervasive nightmare that vanished with full consciousness, before he could grasp its enormity. And still the hands of the dashboard clock had hardly seemed to move.

When the pub opened at five o'clock, he went in for a cup of reviving coffee, making casual conversation with the elderly landlord in an empty lounge bar. His car had been noticed, and Rosson claimed to be an overworked publishing company rep, catching up on lost sleep after a two-day trip. They shared a typically English moan about the ever-increasing demands of commercial life. When the landlord paused for breath, Rosson cut into a diatribe on the iniquities of modern pub tenancy agreements by picking up his phone from the bar. With a quick 'Sorry, duty calls', he scooped up loose change, leaving a pound coin by way of apology. He retreated to the far side of the room and keyed the number. The phone was answered immediately.

'James Lancaster.'

The voice was as before, measured and untroubled. Rosson glanced up, but the landlord had huffily retreated to the public bar. He still spoke softly.

'Mr Lancaster. We can meet you halfway. Your package in return for the boy. We keep the mother until authenticity is confirmed. That's non-negotiable. Agreed?'

'What arrangements do you propose for the exchange?'

'Drive the package to Bristol, tomorrow morning. Alone. Park in the Templemeads Station approach. Be there at noon. Wear a bright red anorak or jacket for identification purposes. I'll ring with further instructions, and you'll have ten minutes to reach the rendezvous. If you're one minute late the deal's off, with no second chance.'

Snappy. Authoritative. To the point. Lancaster wasn't ruffled.

'And if tomorrow morning's too soon?'

'Don't do this. You're an expert, Mr Lancaster, and conventional wisdom requires you to prolong the negotiations. But you must play this our way. Just be there, and remember to include access codes in your package. I must also say you don't get the boy free and clear. He'll have four ounces of Semtex and a remote radio detonator strapped to his body. If there's any sign of police activity during or immediately after the exchange, I don't need to spell out the consequences. We have no desire to harm him, and you'll be able to remove this device quite safely inside two or three minutes, by which time our people will be safely away.'

There was no reaction to the threat, just a calm question.

'Mrs Lancaster?'

'Released when the authenticity of the material is confirmed. You'll have to trust me on that one, though in the event of a double-cross her fate will be particularly unpleasant. Just be straight and things will work out fine for everyone.'

'Very well, I'll do as you ask. In return, do something for me. Please make sure I can make contact on this number at any time between now and tomorrow morning. The security service is active. They're not aware I have the material, but I'll need to be sure they're not following me. If anything threatens a smooth handover, I must be able to notify you.'

Rosson considered the request. It was reasonable, and hopefully they both wanted the exchange to go without a hitch.

'Not a clumsy attempt to trace me to my lair, I hope? As you no doubt surmise, I'm nowhere near your benighted relatives and won't accept a call if I am. Should it be essential, use this number. Hang up after three rings and I'll call back within one hour. One can't be too careful in this hostile world, Mr Lancaster. Let's hope such a call proves unnecessary. I can assure you we'll deliver on our end, but should unforeseen complications arise I must remind you that both Mrs Lancaster and young Thomas are . . . vulnerable. Do you want me to repeat the contact arrangements?'

'This has been taped.'

'I expected nothing less. Until tomorrow, then.'

Rosson ended the call, left the phone on stand-by and slipped it into his jacket pocket. Returning to the bar, he slapped a shiny button-topped brass bell to summon some service. A small Scotch for the road was in order. And one for the long-suffering landlord.

Moscow

BEING A STAUNCH traditionalist, General Sergei Sobchak used an elderly Zil limousine, custom built in the 1970s for the Soviet Union's first citizen, the then Chairman of the Communist Party. Not for Sobchak the German machinery beloved by new Russians who wished to make a sleek statement of arrival. The Zil was built like a T-52 tank, though with slightly thicker armour plating, and the general approved of the way the eyes of older Muscovites followed the black monstrosity's stately progress with a mixture of nostalgia and respect.

Once, this car would have glided unobstructed through priority traffic lanes, needing brakes only at journey's end. Such privilege was a thing of the past, but something remained unchanged. Everyone noticed the Zil, and many knew it belonged to Russia's most popular politician.

Therefore, it would be logical to assume that the general himself was sitting behind darkened glass as the distinctive vehicle set out from the House on the Embankment for an aimless – and frequently obstructed – perambulation through the traffic-choked streets of central Moscow. Which was, of course, the intention.

But General Sobchak was elsewhere. Muffled in fur hat and woollen scarf, with the collar of his old military greatcoat turned up, he was anonymously walking in the park, unaccompanied by bodyguards. Gregor Gorski, his back to City Clinical Hospital No. 1, had been watching the general's stocky figure stamping up and down a path beside the L-shaped lake. The late April afternoon was lead grey, with a harsh east wind that fired periodic bursts of stinging raindrops across the city. There were few pleasure-seekers in Gorkiy Park, and the ex-KGB colonel finally approached, satisfied that Sobchak was unobserved. They fell into step, walking for fifty paces before Sergei Sobchak pulled down his scarf and made a gruff statement.

'Your dogs of war have made an impression, Colonel. It would seem President Yelkin's government has no answer to this unexpected wave of violence. And you were right. The newspapers and television suddenly want to hear my message, relay my words of hope to the people of Russia. What do your contacts within the security apparatus tell you?'

'They are like chickens without heads, General. As intended, none doubt that the Sons of Dudayev are Chechen terrorists, but it will come as no surprise when I tell you they have no leads whatsoever. No idea how to find these elusive killers. No rational policy for containment. No coherent guidance from the politicians, just angry but impossible demands for successful countermeasures. A truly vicious circle.'

The two men strolled on in silence, and Gorski sensed that the general was nerving himself to say something difficult. When Sobchak spoke, the assessment was confirmed. Uncharacteristically, the soldier-politician's decisive voice contained a plaintive note, a craven hint of appeasement.

'We have done so well, Gregor. No, *you* have done so well on my behalf. Perhaps we should consider the possibility of calling a halt. This week's events have given my campaign for the presidency a tremendous boost, there can be no doubt of that. With such momentum behind me, I can go on to win the next election by a landslide. Why take any more risks?'

Gorski had expected backsliding, was ready. Wars were not won by the faint-hearted.

'With respect, General, the election is not scheduled for two years. Much can happen in that time. The Sons of Dudayev cannot continue to operate indefinitely. Our whole strategy is built on the imposition of a short, sharp shock that includes destruction of the President. As you know to your cost, Yelkin and his cronies in the media are more than capable of stifling your message, or even stealing it for themselves. We must be decisive, pursue our plan to its inevitable conclusion.'

Sobchak placed a hand on Gorski's arm and leaned close, watery eyes blinking anxiously.

'I accept that President Yelkin must be removed from the equation as a matter of urgency. But is this afternoon's action absolutely necessary? I must confess this aspect causes me grave concern.'

They resumed their measured walk, the wind biting their backs. Gregor Gorski pretended to consider the question, though he wasn't in the business of soothing troubled consciences. His answer was uncompromising.

'We have discussed this before, and my views are unchanged. It is not enough merely to cull politicians. That removes political rivals for the presidency, but these functionaries are despised, reviled. The public must be made to see how violence and disorder directly threaten *them*. As a soldier, you surely understand that it is sometimes necessary to make sacrifices for the ultimate good of the greater number. Russia needs you, General, and you can do great things for Russia. If you give me a direct order I will abort this afternoon's operation, against my better judgment. But I cannot believe the man who holds the people's destiny in his hand will shirk this painful duty. Do you wish to give me such an order?'

Again, the general stopped, but this time did not turn to face his companion, instead staring north towards the distant Kremlin. A burst of chill rain lashed across them, and both men huddled into their heavy coats.

'You are right. Russia is depending on me.'

The voice had regained strength, and arrogant self-belief. Gregor Gorski already knew, but could leave no room for misunderstanding.

'We proceed as planned with this afternoon's attack?'

'Yes.'

'And the assassination of President Yelkin?'

'Yes.'

'You are a true visionary, General Sobchak. A man of courage who is prepared to do what must be done to secure the future of our great country. I salute you, and will be proud to serve under President Sobchak when the time comes, as soon it will.'

Gregor Gorski came loosely to attention. Equanimity restored, the general turned to him and smiled.

'Thank you, Colonel. Leadership can be a lonely tribulation, but those of us lucky enough to be chosen must not fight our destinies. Go to the Sons of Dudayev, and let them play their part in fulfilling mine.'

The former paratroop commander straightened, squared broad shoulders and marched defiantly into wind and rain, every inch a soldier. He didn't look back. Gregor Gorski watched him out of sight, then reached into his coat pocket and turned off the small recorder that had captured the conversation. Insurance never hurt anyone. Especially in Russia.

North Devon

PERSISTENCE had been painfully rewarded. There were blisters on Tom's palms, but he brushed aside maternal protests. His excavation was progressing well. Using the sharpened nail, he'd dug at the joint between two stones all day, stopping only when food was due – plugging the deepening hole with patent potato filler. Liz Lancaster had decided they should project an image of cowed resignation to lull suspicion. When the short man had brought their midday meal, mother and son were on the air-beds, watching a fuzzy television picture. They barely acknowledged his arrival. He put two plates of stew on the patio table and removed the remains of breakfast. For all their darting, watchful eyes behind the balaclava noticed nothing.

She wasn't hungry. After token argument, Tom emptied both plates, then returned to his self-appointed task with a conspiratorial grin and perky thumbs-up. Liz turned off the television and watched him instead, glad to be spared the effort of creating conversation. Captivity was taking its toll, the fight against creeping despair becoming harder. There was nothing new to say, and she could only make so many confident pronouncements about Conrad's commitment, advancing negotiations and the probability of imminent release. And clinging to certainty that such words weren't worthless required mental effort, as did suppression of darker thoughts. Even when her husband paid up, release wasn't guaranteed, whilst the alternative to freedom didn't bear thinking about.

Thank God for her son's optimism. Eventually, he called her over with an urgent whisper, and proudly demonstrated that the old iron wall ring was loose. Together, they worked cold metal from side to side, moving the ring a little further each time. When Tom was satisfied, they retreated a couple of paces, braced themselves and heaved backwards on the padlocked chain. For a long moment, nothing happened. Then something gave. The ring flew out of the wall, complete with anchoring T-piece, dislodging a shower of mortar dust into the cardboard box. They tumbled backwards. Ring, chain and two bodies hit the floor with a jangling thump that shook the room.

They lay still in the absolute silence that followed, ears straining for the sound of bolts being hastily shot, an opening door and humiliating discovery. Nothing. Tom sat up, eyes bright in subdued lamplight.

'Told you. Now I'll put the ring back and fix it so they won't know. If we get a chance just pull and you'll be free. Be careful not to move when they're in here. It'll come out easily.'

'Did anyone ever tell you you're brilliant?'

Liz gave her son's grimy forehead a kiss. As they picked themselves up, he repeated Conrad's aphorism.

'Never let the bastards grind you down, Mum.'

His treble voice was at odds with adult sentiment. Another true Lancaster, though Liz hoped and believed he'd escaped the emotional frigidity that seemed to accompany the family's legendary single-mindedness. Tom was so *nice*. When they were up and dusted down, he produced the wickedly pointed nail from his trouser pocket.

'I'll sharpen the end again, then you must take it. Not as good as a proper dagger, but you could kill someone with this if you stabbed them in the right place.'

'Tom!'

She looked at him in horror, but his little face was deadly serious.

Wiltshire

SANDY MacNAUGHTON's office was their command centre, with the Omega security chief acting the genial father figure. For the moment, he'd suspended inborn Scottish caution in the face of youthful enthusiasm. The three young experts seemed to have no doubt that they were up to the challenge, and being around as they methodically analysed the options was stimulating, reminding him of his own best years – a time when risk-taking was part of life, and fear of wider consequences a minor consideration.

Mostly, he'd just listened. MacNaughton was honest enough to admit that prolonged study in the school of life could not only instil wisdom, but also conservatism. Yet it was impossible not to be impressed by the way in which ice-calm security consultant, brash MI5 operative and brilliant programmer had meshed. If he had to nominate a leader, James Lancaster would get the nod, but the three of them were working together like Grand Prix mechanics during a pit stop.

The plan that emerged was of necessity both simple

and flexible. MacNaughton volunteered to take notes and prepare a written summary. His secretary had left at five, and he'd use her word-processor. James nodded to Louise, who began the final reprise. They'd taken her ability to provide a convincing fake disk as read, and now she explained how.

'We provide genuine access codes, which get them into the disk. They'll then be faced with over one hundred named files together making up the complete Trojan Horse programme, each of which has a unique code without which it cannot be opened. These codes will not be supplied. Their experts will copy the closed files, which is so easy that even lame-brain Gordon Holland managed it. They start experimenting, and that's when disaster strikes. Remember what I told you about that naughty stuff I keep at home, Sandy?'

She looked at him mischievously. The security chief responded ruefully.

'Aye. So I take it data supplied on this dummy disk will self-destruct when each file's opened?'

Louise Boss pretended to be insulted, tossing her dark curls contemptuously.

'You're not suggesting I'm that soft a touch, surely? No, when you attempt to open a file, you're asked to key in a code. If you get it wrong, that file automatically erases. The code consists of six different numbers between zero and ninety-nine in a specific sequence, though they have no way of knowing that. It's impossible to crack, not least because you have to load a new copy of the file each time you get it wrong. Even if they did manage to get one file open, the data itself is encrypted and cannot be accessed without a different six-figure sequence. Enter anything but the right code and the data's wiped, putting you back to square one.'

John Tolley chimed in, quick mind appreciating the beauty of her scheme.

'It won't be genuine Trojan Horse material, but there's no way they can be sure of that, right? If anything, the fact the files have such ferocious in-built security will convince them they've got the real thing, just waiting to be cracked. So they will take another copy and try to neutralize the self-destruct facility. Should the protection be as good as you say, they could be busy for quite a while.'

Louise Boss smiled modestly.

'Given a very powerful computer directed by a genius working round the clock, they just might manage to open one file in a thousand years, though I wouldn't bet on it. Shouldn't take me more than four hours to stitch the disk together, then I'm free for other things. I'll use the genuine Trojan Horse file names with garbage inside. I've got all I need at home and will work from there to avoid any comeback on Sandy and Omega.'

James Lancaster nodded.

'Good idea. If it's okay with everyone, I suggest we use my father's place in Gloucestershire as our base, for the same reason.'

Nobody argued. MacNaughton decided to make one of his occasional contributions.

'When these people get stuck, they'll come back and demand the second set of codes, with the woman's head on the block if we don't oblige. Or they might even go after you, Louise.'

John Tolley jumped in – rather too quickly, and only picking up half his point.

'I'll personally look after our star programmer, Sandy, just in case.'

So he *did* fancy Louise. James Lancaster dealt with the other half.

'The disk should keep them occupied for long enough to give us a good run at tracing Liz's whereabouts, and the very fact they may need her as a bargaining counter should keep her alive. Okay, what about bugging the disk?'

MacNaughton's contribution. He was ready.

'Like I said, we use largish boxes for transporting important disks, to protect them against exposure to X-rays or magnetism. I'm sure we can doctor one to take your tracking device.'

'Good. Do that. I'll also talk to my operations manager in LA. We've developed a briefcase that doubles as a satellite transmitter and have a contract with Sat-Nav for just such eventualities. I can get one flown in overnight, for use during the handover. Worth a try, though box and case will probably be ditched. Let's not forget that our priority for tomorrow is getting young Tom back. Nothing must compromise that, so I follow their instructions to the letter. We play the follow-up by ear, but I still want you watching from the helicopter, Sandy, in case you can pick them up after the exchange. Keep your distance until then.'

Tolley laughed.

'If Five wants a surveillance chopper we fill in ten sets of forms and hope we can scrounge one from somewhere. You tell your pilot to take off and Sandy's airborne two minutes later. Looks like the private sector has a lot to recommend it.'

James Lancaster shrugged eloquently.

'My pushy father's pilot, actually, but you're not wrong. He'll do fine. Ex-navy flyer, and those boys are always game for a bit of action. The chopper's a long shot, so we'll rely heavily on that phone trace, Louise. Let's hope our mystery man leaves his mobile on stand-by. We don't make a decision on a rescue operation until we have a location, but that's probably the moment to summon official help. The same goes for John's pay-off. Identifying the people behind this attempt on Trojan Horse does not become a priority until the hostages are safe. Agreed?'

John Tolley nodded. Louise reached for notebook and pen.

'Give me his mobile number and I'll start rummaging the networks as soon as I've finished disk compilation. I'll put Trojan Horse through its paces for real. Hope the damn thing works, or this has been a lot of fuss about nothing.'

The self-appointed operations director resumed his briefing, now completely in command.

'Okay, as soon as we're through here Louise and John head for her place and get started on the disk. I'll hop over to New Hall, order the equipment we need from LA and get some rest. I've hardly slept for three days and need to be in good shape for tomorrow. After dropping me off the chopper goes back to London. The pilot will collect my bits and pieces when they arrive from the States. You three rendezvous back here at eight in the morning. He'll pick you up as soon as possible and lift you across to New Hall. Don't forget the disk.'

MacNaughton's innate caution had evaporated. In spite of himself, he was being swept along by irrational excitement. He squared away his end.

'Holland will be gone by now, but I'll leave word on his voicemail that Louise has called in sick, and inform him none too politely that I've been summoned to an urgent security conference in London.'

Louise giggled infectiously.

'I had a run-in with the little creep earlier and threatened to down tools, so my absence won't altogether surprise him, though he'll certainly sweat at the thought of his precious contract going pear-shaped before the cash is in the bank.'

John Tolley reached over and put a hand on her arm.

'You're a dangerous woman to know. I'd better sleep on the couch tonight.'

She removed the hand.

'Have my bed. I won't be using it, but it's still the nearest you'll ever come to heaven.'

The coolness that divided them had dissipated in the heat of battle. Their light-hearted exchange broke the tension. James Lancaster stood up and dismissed class.

'Let's get going. One final thing. My father believes I'm playing this his way and I have no intention of telling him anything different. He'll go mad if he finds out we're trying to sucker the kidnappers, but like the man said to me only yesterday, why employ a dog and piss on lampposts yourself? We can do this. Okay, we have contact phone numbers in case anything unexpected comes up, but otherwise we meet up at New Hall in the morning as planned. If you come with me to the chopper, Sandy, I'll give you that tracker for the disk box.'

As the security chief followed their leader out of the room, he heard John Tolley address Louise Boss, voice dripping with stagy innuendo.

'Your car or mine, madame?'

Sandy MacNaughton sighed. The boy never listened to

a word he said, and runaway sexual attraction was hardly a sound reason for risking an entire career. Which didn't go one inch towards explaining why he himself was behaving like a crazy maverick. But then he already knew the answer to that one. He'd never forgiven the powers that be for throwing him out of MI5 when he still had so much to give. And give it he would.

London

SO FAR, so very good. As expected, James was dealing competently with the kidnap. He'd reported in from the company JetRanger, *en route* from Omega to New Hall. Information was shouted over background engine noise, and the call was brief – but Conrad Lancaster got the message he wanted to hear. Trojan Horse would be exchanged for Tom tomorrow. James was playing hardball – no Tom, no handover. Unsurprisingly, the kidnappers were refusing to release Elizabeth until the cyberweapon checked out. But then his wife would have eager-beaver ex-lover James on her side, raddled with guilt for once abandoning her and moving heaven and earth to atone.

Conrad Lancaster had no doubt the exchange would go smoothly. James might be cantankerous, but he understood the way these things worked. He sipped Colombian coffee from an antique Worcester porcelain cup, then dabbed his lips with a snowy linen napkin. He'd just finished an extended supper in the private dining room, and was looking forward to a leisurely Monte Cristo over the finest Napoleon brandy money could buy. With everything going smoothly, relaxation had been earned. When this was over, he might take Tom down to the yacht. Get to know the boy properly. Mould his mind. Help him forget his dreadful ordeal during a leisurely Mediterranean cruise. Let him steer the damned boat, or play with a jet-ski. The young were resilient, healed quickly.

Lancaster Trust stock had risen steadily all day, closing thirty-nine points above yesterday's low. He was several million pounds ahead as a result of his inspired share-support operation, with some financial help from Ralph-pronounced-Rafe Powell-pronounced-Pole. The banker wouldn't be disappointed. When the Russia Telecom deal went public, a few million would look like small change.

The world was a massive oyster, and Conrad Lancaster saw no need for restraint when it came to slurping down more – much more – than his fair share of succulent flesh. And whilst many tried to curb his appetite, none succeeded. He was insatiable.

So far, so very good. Disgruntled ex-Lancaster Trust executive Michael Dickson had cracked like a rotten egg, and there was nothing his former employer could do to dissipate the stink of corruption. Conrad Lancaster was about to become big news, then a guest of Her Majesty at salubrious Ford open prison. All thanks to next week's sensational edition of *Guardian Angel*, which should rocket the ratings into earth orbit.

When the Pandora's Box Productions Renault Espace had turned into the gravelled driveway of an expensive new house in Ayot St Lawrence, just down the road from George Bernard Shaw's former country pile, Jenny Symes wasn't over-optimistic. The tiny Hertfordshire village was surprisingly remote for commuter-land, tucked away at the end of a single-track road, but in the end their effort proved worthwhile.

Jenny knew a man who couldn't wait to unburden his soul – or get revenge for a real or imagined slight – when she saw one. Dickson had been waiting at the open front door. Even before her camera crew could set up in a big living room overlooking woods and fields, he was spilling assorted papers from an old suitcase on to dusky pink fitted carpet. Dickson might have played hard to get, but now his mind was made up he was hers – wooed, won, talking . . . and talking.

When she'd steadied him down, they had filmed for two hours, capturing the whole sordid story. Conrad Lancaster hadn't just dipped daintily into the pension fund, he'd gobbled its entire contents twice over – transferring assets to private offshore companies and pledging those same assets against massive loans to the publicly quoted Lancaster Trust. Jenny Symes was used to trawling the sludgy depths of human frailty, but even she was shocked. This wasn't just about massive malpractice. When the mess was exposed, liquidators would be asking careless banks some extremely awkward questions, and legal eagles wouldn't be far behind – claws sharp and hooked beaks open.

At first, journalistic scepticism had led her to doubt the voluble informant's story. Dismiss wild accusations as the ranting of an embittered loser. Start fearing Conrad would sidestep her attack yet again. But Michael Dickson had produced documentary evidence – reams of it – to back his allegations. A team of financial experts was sifting his packed suitcase now, but even a casual rummage suggested the material would check out. In spades.

They'd left him on his doorstep at six o'clock, arm wrapped tightly around a plump, grey-haired wife. Dickson's haggard face had worn an expression of relief, a burden shed, and Jenny Symes had decided the man was genuinely acting out of conscience. He had, after all, just said goodbye to large annual redundancy payments that were supposed to buy silence. And then she'd noticed the wife's serene expression, and wondered just whose conscience had resulted in the scoop of the decade.

The motive mattered not. Jenny Symes had enough dynamite to blow three Conrad Lancasters out of the water, corpulent though he was. She'd spend the night in an editing suite as the results of her long investigation were cut together into an explosive edition of *Guardian Angel*, which even the BBC's Establishment-friendly lawyers would be unable to fault.

Jenny contemplated the communiqué that had been waiting on her desk when she returned from Hertfordshire. It was hard not to be amused by twelve white roses and a bottle of vintage champagne, accompanied by a handwritten note on heavy card bearing the words *FROM HUGO SAVAGE* in gold-embossed lettering.

Jenny. Anyone who can't trouser a three-million-pound hit without his eyes watering doesn't deserve you. And no, it wasn't four mil. Not quite! My country place this weekend, so you can lick my wounds? Love and kisses, Hugo.

She had to admit the bonking banker had balls, but she had bigger sweetbread to fry. Jenny Symes couldn't wait to confront Conrad Lancaster with the final tape. Tell him what it contained. Watch his face as he realized that this time he'd finally lost.

Moscow

OKHOTNY RYAD Metro station, close by the Kremlin, had been chosen to make a point – that nobody was safe from the Sons of Dudayev, and nothing could be done to contain their violent predations. Especially not by the bankrupt administration of President Mikhail Yelkin, who skulked close by in his gilded palace on Red Square, beyond the Tomb of the Unknown Warrior and Alexander Gardens. If the place had been chosen to make a statement, the time had been selected to make that statement so forcibly that the whole of Russia – and the world – would have to take notice.

The train was packed with home-going workers. Foreign tourists returning to hotels after a day's sightseeing. Young Muscovites in Western clothes heading for bright lights, flirting and laughing. Foetid old men in worn overcoats belted with string, who rode the Metro all day because crowded carriages provided a warm haven from cold streets above. Right beside him, a pretty young mother stood with two young children, arms shielding them from the press of humanity.

This was not something Major Valery Filatov wanted to do. The one-eyed soldier understood the consequences of explosions in confined space. He'd seen the evidence often enough in Afghanistan, during the war that couldn't be won. Picked through the remnants of villages and villagers disintegrated by the fearsome firepower of Mil MI-26 Halo helicopter gunships. Looked inside personnel carriers hit by armour-piercing missiles smuggled by mujahedin fighters over the mountains from Pakistan. Heard haunting screams from the maimed, and the whimpering of those who were about to die. Gagged at the sight of swimming blood and splattered tissue, detached limbs and decimated torsos, unrecognizable lumps of meat and the sickly sweet smell of roasted human flesh. Gathered fragmented body parts for burial in graves that would never carry an individual name.

When such experiences became almost routine, a man had to harden his soul to survive. But that was war in a faraway place. And this was terrorism at the heart of the Motherland. Humanity. Living human beings. A throng of travellers with minds full of everyday minutiae and no inkling this journey would be their last. Potential victims of another kind of war – the war for Russia's future, which must be fought to the death. And won.

Yet still the serving soldier hesitated. The train was entering the station, decelerating past a blur of faces, the masks of nameless people jostling for position as they waited to push into packed compartments. It would be so easy to reach down and unlock the chain securing the briefcase to a metal upright, pick up the case and walk. Or leave the thing unarmed to await discovery, a potent warning of what might have been. Decadent politicians were scum who had betrayed Russia and deserved everything that came to them. This was something else.

The train stopped, doors opened and the moment passed. Major Filatov was a soldier, and hardened his soul. The briefcase contained five kilos of Czech-made plastic explosive, plus a three-minute electronic detonator he could activate by pushing the button on a small black box in his pocket. Should the abandoned case be noticed in the crush, seized upon by some thief or curious passenger, it could neither be opened nor removed from the train in the time that remained. He stepped on to the platform, pressed the button and joined the lucky ones making for the exit.

Still panting from his upward dash, the executioner hurried from the station into Manezhnaya Square and found the taxi that waited, with one of his men behind the wheel. As Valery Filatov scrambled into the Lada, he wondered where Gregor Gorski was lurking, like an impotent but manipulative voyeur who observes others performing the sexual act through a one-way mirror. When his orders were implemented, the relentless ex-

KGB colonel was never far away.

The taxi lurched forward, cut rudely into heavy traffic. As his mental count reached 170, Major Valery Filatov knew the bomb would go off within ten seconds. If the train remained at the platform, the explosion would be catastrophic. Were it already in motion, lurching and rattling though a bomb-case tunnel, the effect would be infinitely worse.

North Devon

THE LANCASTERS appeared to be co-operating. But Andrew Rosson felt uneasy. Things were going too smoothly. Perhaps tomorrow's exchange would turn into a trap, or the transmission of Trojan Horse to Moscow might hit trouble. Like the kidnap itself, both exercises had been planned down to the last detail, but that didn't mean they'd work out.

Away to his left, a blood-orange sun had sunk into the sea, leaving a ruddy afterglow in darkening sky. Red sky at night, kidnapper's delight. He wearily opened the gate, drove through and stopped. As he relocked it, Ringo materialized from tangled undergrowth, walkie-talkie in hand and Uzi machine-pistol hanging muzzle down from a shoulder strap. The squat Russian's menacing appearance was undermined by twigs and leaf fragments clinging to greasy brown hair. He gave Rosson a cheerless nod and pushed back into cover. All well, then.

He pointed the Astra estate car downwards, engaging second gear and keeping a foot poised above the brake pedal. Dipped headlamps slashed the dusk, illuminating patches of gorse and rock as he followed the steep track's twists and turns. A rabbit fled, scut bobbing white in the lights. When he hit bottom, Rosson drove along uneven cobbles and parked in the boat shed. Two more days and they'd be out of this dank place, obligations discharged and fat fees earned.

As he walked back to the warehouse, he looked at the narrow harbour entrance. Conditions were calm, but still the sea surged powerfully back and forth between unyielding granite walls. The boat was out there somewhere, not far away, but wouldn't creep in to berth alongside the stone quay until full darkness fell. Rosson was met at the Judas door by baby-faced Paul.

'Problems?'

The Russian looked surprised.

'No problems. The others come in boat, yes?'

'Soon.'

Paul went outside to have a look around. Rosson left the door ajar and clumped up dimly lit stairs, past the putt-putt-puttering generator and on into their living quarters. A portable radio chattered away softly. Bill Hellis glanced up from a classic car magazine. Rosson repeated his question.

'Problems?'

'Nothing about us on the airwaves, and they've been good as gold down the corridor. Not a murmur. Everything go all right your end, did it? You look done in. I'll make a nice cuppa.'

He got up, filled the kettle from a five-gallon plastic water container and lit a gas burner. Rosson crashed on to an MFI bunk bed, exhaustion washing over him. The day must have been more stressful than he had realized.

'Thanks, Bill. All arranged. We'll put the kid on the boat after midnight. They'll hate being parted, even if it does mean he's going free. Be careful while I'm gone. She might not be prepared to wait quietly for her turn, and we've already seen what a spitfire she can be.'

Bill Hellis counted round bags into a large aluminium teapot.

'Nobody'll go in there alone while you're in Bristol. Just do the business and get back in one piece. Think you'll face a reception committee tomorrow?'

'Doubt it, but you can never be sure. This deal should go like clockwork, but there's always the risk some clever dick will go and jam a sodding great spanner in the works.'

Normally, such mangled imagery would never have passed his lips. But he was tired, and it was Bill's kind of language. As Rosson waited for his mug of tea, he stopped thinking about the dangerous job in hand, abandoning endless – and pointless – consideration of a thousand-and-one things that might go wrong. Instead, his mind went home. His wife, reading the girls a story. Kissing them goodnight – once for her, once for Daddy, who'd soon be home. Going downstairs with a contented smile on her face. Poking embers to life and putting another seasoned oak log on the open fire. Thinking about him. She was a good woman, and he missed her.

Gloucestershire

HE'D BEEN WELCOMED like a long-lost son – which he was, though not theirs. The temptation to linger with Duncan and Rita Bernadelli in the warm New Hall kitchen had been almost irresistible, but instead James Lancaster settled for a quick coffee at the scrubbed-pine table. Without raising undue hope, he'd told the Scottish couple that Tom might be home tomorrow, asked Rita to prepare a hot meal and gone upstairs to his father's study. He pulled out his mobile and got a maximum four-bar signal. Duncan had told him a story about that.

When mobile phone companies first started operating, the Gloucestershire countryside wasn't top of their coverage list. So Conrad Lancaster built a mast at his own expense, tucked away in a hilltop wood, and bullied a network into providing immediate service. Now, with the proliferation of radio communication and tightening of planning regulations, such masts were valuable assets. Conrad's served a dozen operators and earned over £150,000 a year in rental. It was typical. Everything the man touched turned platinum.

James hit the button and his tiny contribution to Conrad's income flew away via the lucrative mast, heading back through time zones to LA. It would be late morning on the Pacific coast, with the best part of a working day still ahead.

'Lancaster Security Consultants. How may I help you?'

He recognized the receptionist's lilting Southern voice. Saw her handsome face in his mind. Felt momentary nostalgia for the familiar life he'd made in America, free of responsibility to anyone but himself.

'Sally Ann, it's James. Carl there?'

'Sure is, Mr Lancaster.'

The connection was made almost before she finished speaking.

'Perazzi.'

'Nice surprise, Carl. You're usually on coffee break when I try to catch you at your desk.'

'Speaking of desks, we gave yours the elbow last year, seeing as how you and it never even got acquainted. Hi there, Jimmy. Yeah, well, you got me. I'm here because the doc diagnosed caffeine poisoning and prescribed a coupla hours at the rock face, but don't you worry. I ain't going to make a habit of it. How's the family?'

The wisecracking New Yorker never worked anything less than a straight twelve-hour shift, often more. James offered a throwaway answer, knowing his Director of Operations wouldn't ask time-wasting questions once they got down to business.

'Mostly kidnapped. Is the Gulfstream available?'

Lancaster Security Consultants operated a brand-new $30-million private jet for the convenience of Hollywood players who didn't quite run to their own high-flying status symbol, but were eager to pay $20,000 a day to pretend they did.

'On the tarmac right now, scheduled for a bus-stop run to Aspen via Palm Springs tomorrow morning. Want me to cancel out?'

'No, hire a replacement. Ours flies here overnight. I want one of those special briefcases on my side of the pond no later than zero seven hundred hours GMT. Also a full night combat pack and a red ski jacket. My size, and don't ask. Some people read too much pulp fiction. Stash everything in the special compartment. Choose an airfield within fifty miles of London where Customs aren't too hot, and I'll have a chopper waiting to lift the equipment. Call me the minute you have flight details.'

'I feel an ulcer coming on, but what's one more among many? Guess we can make that. You gonna be using this special briefcase, or is it just for show?'

'Organize an up-link with Sat-Nav from eleven hundred

hours GMT. Monitor the trace from there. Programme a large-scale UK map into your machine. I'll need an open phone link to pick up information as you receive it. This is a long shot, Carl, but let's do it anyway.'

'You're picking up the tab. That the lot?'

'That's all.'

'Okay, I'll get right on it. Have a nice day, but don't kill anyone unless you have to. I hear those tight-assed Brits are tough on shit like that.'

Always partial to the last word, Carl Perazzi disconnected. But what Carl said he'd do got done. James Lancaster laced hands behind his head, tilted back his father's comfortable black leather chair and closed his eyes. He was temple-throbbing tired and a long night beckoned, but James wouldn't allow himself to catnap. Something about this whole set-up bothered him, and he couldn't rest until he knew what was wrong.

Things didn't quite work out like that. Instead, he found himself thinking about Liz Lancaster within constraining walls. Knowing nothing of what was happening outside. Frightened for her son, herself. Hoping, yet hardly daring to hope when the boy was taken away. Praying to a God she'd never believed in. Waiting. Trusting James Lancaster without even knowing he was here. Did she ever think about him?

Perhaps her chances would have been better if he'd done things Conrad's way and turned over Trojan Horse. Then his mind played one of those clever tricks that always surprise, addressing with startling clarity the question he'd put on the back burner. It wasn't in Conrad's nature to forgive and forget, much less delegate meaningful action to lesser lights, at least without constant interference. That's what didn't make sense. James sat upright. What the hell was he *doing* here?

Wiltshire

COMPULSIVE COMPUTING was a way of life, but this had added dimensions. The break in routine and stimulus of a new challenge were energizing. The sudden appearance of two rather attractive men in her life wasn't upsetting, either. Nor was the fact she'd surprised herself by instinctively responding to their magnetism. One had already left her – James Lancaster, the dangerous one with a deceptively calm air.

But the other was downstairs, ingratiating himself with the cats and preparing to rustle up a cheese omelette when she gave the word. This time, John Tolley was a guest rather than snooping spy. His presence within jealously guarded private walls – those in her mind as well as the stone variety holding up the roof of Beggar's Roost – caused a tingle whenever Louise Boss visualized his compelling face and heart-tugging smile. Which she did with unexpected regularity.

Despite the distraction, she was making good progress. The simulated Trojan Horse files were finished, and she spared a thought for the unfortunate fellow-professional who would be given the impossible task of trying to break through impregnable defences, little appreciating – at first – that the only logical outcome was a lingering nervous breakdown. Louise keyed the instruction that would load fake data on to a dummy disk, and decided she'd take a break. The transfer would take a few minutes, so this was the time for John Tolley to whip up that omelette and open a dusty bottle of wine from the back of the kitchen cupboard.

Then the fun could really start. Louise was already planning her invasion of mobile phone company records. There were four networks to rummage, but with Trojan Horse it should be a breeze. She'd soon find the kidnapper's service provider from his allocated telephone number. Thereafter, it was a matter of sifting through records to identify the base station responsible for relaying each of his outgoing calls over the last month. And, if she got lucky, the one that was currently picking up his phone's orientation signals. Once she'd squeezed that information source dry, she had one or two imaginative ideas for following up – tantalizing possibilities she hadn't actually mentioned to the others, but was itching to try. With some help from her clever baby.

After confirming that data was flowing smoothly from

hard disk to portable optical, she went downstairs. Her protector was asleep on the sofa, arms flung wide, legs outstretched. A lock of dark hair had strayed across John Tolley's face, moving slightly with each even breath. One grey cat was curled up on his lap, another snuggled against his flank. But they were anyone's. Louise glanced at her watch, and was surprised to see it was after eleven.

She watched the sleeping man for a moment, then walked through to the kitchen. Thick yellow omelette mix was ready in a china bowl on the draining board, beside a ready-oiled frying pan. He'd even borrowed a torch and explored the overgrown garden. Her beech-wood chopping board was decorated with diced chervil. It looked as though John Tolley was making himself at home. Louise turned on the cooker and went to rummage for that bottle of wine.

He wasn't wrong. She was special, and no amount of psychological health warnings from Sandy MacNaughton could change that. Even the name rolled seductively round his mind. Louise Boss. Louise Boss. Louise Boss. Yes, he could happily live with a name like that, given the slightest encouragement. Which he was either getting, or not.

She'd woken him gently, chased the cats away and told him supper was ready. After apologizing for falling asleep on duty, he followed her to the untidy kitchen. Two full glasses of red wine were waiting. Louise cut a smoking omelette in half, sprinkled chopped chervil on top and served two charred portions on unmatched, unwarmed plates. She told him the dummy disk was ready, then they ate in companionable silence. Afterwards, as she spooned instant coffee into mugs decorated with cartoon cats and waited for the electric kettle to boil, he felt a strange compulsion to mend fences.

'Louise, about last night . . .'

She stopped him with an impatient shake of her springy curls and crossed bare arms beneath her breasts, determined to avoid an inquest.

'Last night's forever ago. Things have changed. Danny's gone. He was a good man, but I couldn't give him what he needed. Nothing to do with you. There's something wrong with me, because it's always like that. Anyway, you have responsibilities, a job to do. I'm pretty single-minded that way myself, so I understand. Honestly. And now we both have a job to do.'

John Tolley looked at her, and realized that he wanted to talk – *really* talk – with this self-contained person. Communicate. Establish a rapport.

'Why did you get involved in this? It's not your fight.'

She seemed to share the mood of the moment, speaking frankly.

'Think lioness, Tolley, and think of Trojan Horse as my threatened cub. Besides, I took to James Lancaster. Rather an impressive man, who made me want to help without stopping to ask why. That poor woman, and the child. I can contribute something no one else can. It's good to be needed. You? Seems to me you're breaking just about every rule in the book.'

He considered his answer, replied truthfully.

'There are reasons why this can't be done by the book, which I won't bore you with. Let's just say that made the decision easier, but the truth is I've never been much of a team player. I get a real buzz from counter-intelligence work, but MI5 tends to cramp a man's style. This is a challenge.'

'More demanding than breaking into my house and following me round the countryside, you mean?'

Louise looked at him reprovingly, reversing her earlier decision not to hold an inquest. It was the opportunity he'd been waiting for.

'Last night wasn't about work, Boss. Getting in here and creeping about wasn't either. Silly, really, but I did it because I hoped to find out more about you. You fascinate me, if that's not too forward, and I'm not used to women having that effect.'

She put two cups of coffee on the table and sat down, studying him intently.

'I see. Do you often bunk off work to chase strange girls, or should I be flattered?'

He laughed.

'Flattered to be chased by a cynical old intelligence pro? I don't think so. My turn. Do you make a habit of luring strange men on to tennis courts, beating the shit out of them and destroying their egos with that bloody double-handed cross-court passing shot?'

Louise gave the question serious consideration, and her answer was disconcertingly simple.

'No. I don't.'

They looked at one another for what seemed a long time, but was probably no more than a few seconds. He touched the back of her hand.

'Then I'm the one who should be flattered. So what's the plan, Boss?'

She took a deep breath and stood up, a teasing smile illuminating her perfect oval face.

'My bedroom's on the left at the top of the stairs, but you already know that, don't you? I meant what I said. The bed's yours. Me and my machine have things to do, so I'll see you bright and early in the morning. Don't bother with the washing up. I never do. But you may as well feed the cats, as they've obviously fallen for your charms in a big way.'

As he watched her walk away with the easy grace of a natural athlete, John Tolley felt that some sort of understanding had been reached. But this wasn't the moment to establish what it was, or where it might lead.

London

THE DAY had sprinted away, with the evening chasing behind. At the afternoon extravaganza, Wes Remington got snarled up with an Indonesian general who had a disconcerting squint, spoke plummier English than MI5's Gus Churchill and wanted to know all about stun guns and the use of red-light lasers to temporarily blind rampaging troublemakers. Dissident-bashing wasn't Remington's field, but every time he'd tried to edge away the ambassador had caught his eye and frowned. The CIA's London Head of Station hadn't got back to Beasley's message until gone six.

At a quick evaluation, it wasn't all bad. The agent-for-hire was earning his corn, getting right inside the problem in no time flat. So Langley was right – Trojan Horse had been targeted by hostiles. And half right about Conrad Lancaster – the man was a threat, but acting under duress. Still, the Brits knew what was going down and seemed to be ahead of the game. One brownie point for good old Gus Churchill.

Maybe things weren't quite that simple, because they never were. But he hadn't been able to take time out for a long, slow think. He was due at a PTA meeting over at the school, and Helen would take the kids and leave him if he struck out on that one. Assuming she could find them.

He'd made the meeting and sat through two hours of well-meaning verbal diarrhoea with an expression of polite interest frozen on his face. Milled around the school hall afterwards, exchanging platitudes on the non-existent standards of youth today with other disinterested parents. Driven Helen home when she lost patience with his foot-shuffling. Real life was a pain in the derrière. They'd eaten a calorie-free salad supper, during which the atmosphere slowly eased. When she laughed at his barbed comment about the ambassador's impressive new hairpiece, Wes Remington had judged the moment safe. He'd informed his wife he needed air, kissed the top of her immaculate blonde head and slid out of the house. He left Helen watching *Newsnight* and waiting for the kids to return from wherever they'd been.

In case she looked out to check the car, he took a cab to the embassy. The man called Beasley was lucky to be unencumbered by domestic responsibilities. When Remington unlocked his cherry-wood cupboard, the recorder's red message light was blinking. He rewound and played the tape. As ever, the delivery was muffled, and his informant sounded like he was in a hurry.

'Trojan Horse is secure. James Lancaster and an MI5 guy called John Tolley have made contact with the kidnappers. They're planning to exchange fake material for Conrad's son, then they'll try to track down the wife before the penny drops. My guess is that Five have given clearance for the operation, in the hope of identifying the bad guys, better yet who they're working for. I don't know what back-up the security services are providing, if any, but I'm on the case.'

Wes Remington listened to the message a second time, then Beasley's earlier offering. The man had never let him down before, but something wasn't right. Hard to put a finger on just what, but it was like listening to a melody played perfectly on an ever so slightly-out-of-tune piano. Superficially brilliant, but flawed. He locked both tapes into his office safe, reloaded the recorder and headed for Grosvenor Square, hoping he'd find a cruising taxi instantly. *Newsnight* was long over, and the damned kids probably weren't home yet.

What the hell. He'd have plenty of time to ponder the imponderable over smuggled chocolate-chip cookies and hot rum-laced milk in the kitchen. And tomorrow wouldn't have to work too hard to be a better day.

DAY 4 – THURSDAY

North Devon

THE MILLION-POUND motor yacht crept into the tiny harbour just after midnight, the throb of powerful MAN marine diesel engines bouncing back from encircling rock faces, seeming to come from many directions at once. The night was luminous, and the big cruiser was clearly illuminated by an auroral moon that burned a cold hole in hazy cloud. Andrew Rosson watched from the quayside as *Lara's Song* manoeuvred towards stone steps, engines slowing to idle.

An incandescent glimmer where her sharp bow cut calm water faded as she lost way and drifted towards the quay, expertly handled by Nikolai, the one Rosson called George – a tall, pencil-thin former marine special forces officer recruited from the Russian Navy. Moscow's underworld offered lucrative employment for state employees with specialist skills whose country no longer needed – or could afford – them. The engines stopped, returning the night to the sound of sea and pounding surf.

The second crew member was Igor, nicknamed John – a bespectacled ex-policeman from St Petersburg who'd transferred to the opposition. He jumped nimbly on to slippery steps and ran up with a mooring rope, which he secured to a pitted iron bollard before turning to Rosson. All four mafia hired guns spoke reasonable English, an ability that doubtless influenced their selection for this assignment.

'I get other rope and throw for tying back of boat.'

None of them knew Rosson or Hellis spoke Russian like the natives they once were, and he had no intention of telling them. John returned to *Lara's Song* and tossed up a second mooring rope. When the boat was resting snugly against her fenders, George and John joined him.

'We leave no later than four, to be into Bristol at good time, yes?'

George's English was marginally better. Rosson took his arm in a comradely gesture.

'Come inside and have a hot drink. We'll put the boy aboard later. Can you keep him secure?'

'Front cabin has hatch and no window. Shut him there. Make no trouble.'

They walked into the warehouse and went upstairs. Bill Hellis had the kettle simmering. It wasn't a full reunion, because baby-faced Paul was on watch at the top of the track, but Ringo rolled out of his bunk bed and greeted the newcomers boisterously. Soon, Rosson would need to go through the plan again, to ensure there would be no mistakes during the exchange. But first he let the three chatter in Russian as they drank coffee, careful to give no hint that he understood.

The voyage had gone without a hitch. *Lara's Song* was a dream, and one day George meant to have just such a boat for himself. Ringo – Yegor to the Russians – had more immediate ambitions. He wanted a woman, and the two mariners taunted him with chapter and verse on two uninhibited teenagers rented before leaving London, on a share-and-share-alike basis. They were impatient to finish this job in a faraway land and return home – eagerly anticipating increased status within their criminal family after completing such a demanding task for the patriarch. George had a mobile phone to maintain contact with 'the man in Moscow', who was in regular touch – though whether the string-puller was Gregor Gorski or the mafia boss was unclear.

Interesting. Even allowing for George's desire to inflate his importance, it was obvious that Gorski's assertion that Rosson had absolute command of the operation was not entirely truthful.

Moscow

ICY EXTREMITIES were starting to thaw. Communal central heating in his poorly constructed 1970s apartment block went off at midnight, and Gregor Gorski had stripped off outdoor clothing and switched on an electric fan heater. Now, as sensation painfully returned to chilled feet and hands, he thought about the chaos so recently witnessed on Manezhnaya Square, reflecting the charnel house below.

From his vantage point outside the Central Exhibition Hall, he'd observed Major Filatov hurry from the Okhotny Ryad Metro station and jump into his waiting Lada. Seconds after the one-eyed soldier departed, the very bowels of the earth grumbled. The ground beneath Gorski's feet trembled, and a thunderclap of noise burst from the station entrance, hurling a storm of debris into the square. He'd been ready, with cotton wool in his ears and a steadying arm wrapped around a lamppost. But others were not. As the explosion's majestic voice had rolled away into city twilight, it was replaced by other sounds, blending into confused cacophony – a crashing chain-reaction glass fall, the rending thump of vehicle hitting vehicle, shrieks and cries from shocked or injured street vendors and passers-by, the frantic yelping of stray dogs. Then unnatural silence, broken only by the wail of a jammed car horn.

Already in a state of high alert, emergency services had reacted rapidly. Within minutes, dozens of fire tenders and ambulances were arriving, and militia had cordoned the square, pushing back people who appeared from all sides, propelled by universal human *schadenfreude*. There but for the grace of God, went they – which was, of course, precisely why he'd sanctioned such drastic action. Gregor Gorski despised these ghoulish spectators. His own interest was strictly professional, and they were obstructing his view.

He had forced himself to remain at the back of the crowd as drama unfolded, one figure amongst hundreds who pressed forward against newly erected barriers, exchanging disbelieving questions and ill-informed speculation. Or simply watching in stunned silence. Activity had intensified, and eventually an order was given to clear the square. Reinforced by baton-wielding colleagues in riot gear, the militia eventually prevailed, pushing back the crowd until it broke and scattered, freeing convoys of rescue vehicles backed up in choked streets.

Only then did he abandon his vigil and return home – a journey that took some time, because he had to walk several blocks before finding a taxi willing to take him out to Slobodka. The garrulous driver had been full of the latest atrocity. Gorski said nothing, but was satisfied by round condemnation of President Yelkin's government, and its inability to prevent outrageous terrorist activity on – and now below – the streets of Moscow.

Back home, it had taken his hands five minutes to reach operating temperature, but now he was able to rub them together in brisk satisfaction, rather than to restore circulation. Gregor Gorski lit a Gitane, sucking smoke deep into his lungs and holding it there until the nicotine rush hit his brain. He was well into next week's packet, but who was counting?

Confused television reports were saying a bomb went off just after a Metro train left the platform at Okhotny Ryad, close to the Kremlin – planted by Chechen terror group the Sons of Dudayev, who had telephoned a useless warning to Moscow Television, one minute before the blast. Some forty corpses from the rear of the train had been brought out, together with over two hundred injured passengers. But this was thought to be no more than the tip of an awful iceberg. Damage was so great that rescuers had barely started penetrating the mangled mass of metal and masonry blocking the underground tunnel.

He went to the kitchen and heated lentil soup. After the simple meal, Gregor Gorski intended to sleep for a few hours. Awake refreshed to the day when the final headline mission would take place – the assassination of President Mikhail Yelkin himself. But when that historic moment arrived, Gregor Gorski would not be watching. He'd be at the heart of the action, savouring the fruition of careful pre-planning and dedicated endeavour.

Wiltshire

RIDING TROJAN HORSE into battle made victory a formality. Computerized telephone company records barely had level-one commercial protection, and Louise Boss charged through the first mobile network's firewalls in minutes. Once within, she explored at will, soon discovering the number James Lancaster had given her wasn't listed. She moved to the next supplier, penetrating defences with equal facility. Success. Not only did she find the number, but also details of the deal that took the kidnapper's fancy.

He'd opted for a pay-in-advance line rental package, with an hour's worth of free calls per month, purchased for cash at a retail outlet in London's Tottenham Court Road three weeks earlier – no doubt a busy store where customers would not be remembered. The name on the airtime agreement was Alan Tilney. He'd supplied a bank direct debit for billing purposes, along with an address in Roman Road, East London. She'd follow that up, but first checked outgoing calls. One only, confirming that this phone was used specifically for kidnap negotiations. Yesterday's date. Timed at 17.14. Duration 193 seconds. Routed to James Lancaster's mobile.

Louise was more interested in the relay station that handled the call. The network coverage map showed hundreds of overlapping cells, but a single keystroke brought up the relevant one – an area of some twenty square miles near Hereford. It might be possible to find a more precise location by checking signal reception in adjacent cells, but that would take time, and no kidnapper would have been careless enough to call from home base.

Of more interest was the orientation signal automatically sent by mobiles – a procedure not widely publicized. If their quarry was unaware of this, and had left his phone on stand-by for emergency contact purposes, there was every chance of tracking him to his lair. He wasn't, he had, she would. Louise watched in fascination as a jigsaw fitted together on screen, in response to sequential information requests.

Tilney's phone had moved off from Hereford shortly after the call. From there, his progress was inexorably logged. It was like a motoring organization journey map – Cheltenham, Bristol, Bridgwater, Minehead, Barnstaple . . . and finally nowhere in particular, where he'd stopped and remained ever since. Nowhere in particular was a lightly populated area around Hartland Point on the North Devon coast, serviced by a relay station near the picture-postcard fishing village of Clovelly, a popular tourist attraction.

She'd pinned him down within a few square miles, and could travel no further along that particular route, though a cross-check against signal reception in adjoining cells suggested he was somewhere towards the north-west corner of the primary cell. Louise noted co-ordinates and decided to study the terrain. She could have consulted the tattered road atlas from her car, but instead paid a flying visit to the Ordnance Survey master database. Much more informative.

While she waited for Trojan Horse to effect unauthorized entry to the nation's topographical treasure-house, Louise went downstairs to get a glass of chilled Perrier water, planning ahead as she went. First, a six-inches-to-the-mile print-out of the target area. Then a glance at Mr Alan Tilney's banking arrangements. And finally a transatlantic foray to enlist some unofficial assistance from the US military. All in all, she was a rather good swivel-chair detective.

On the way back to her work station, she peeked into the bedroom. John Tolley was sleeping in the big double bed. His clothes were neatly piled on the floor – a full set as far as she could see, which probably meant he was naked. She listened to steady breathing. People were so vulnerable in sleep – though super-agent Tolley of MI5 would probably bounce upright, gun in hand, if she took one step towards him.

The room was illuminated by landing light spilling

through the open door, but he'd pulled the duvet up and buried himself. She studied what little there was to be seen – a swaddled shape and the top of a dark head on the white pillow. With a mixture of shame and pleasure, Louise Boss recalled what she and Danny had done in that self-same bed for most of the previous night. She decided it was a funny old world, and shut the door.

North Devon

WHEN THEY CAME for her son, she was dozing fitfully, but muttered voices outside brought her fully awake. After she was chained, they'd separated the sleeping bags. Liz Lancaster crawled out of comforting warmth into chill air, careful not to pull on that awkward chain and dislodge the anchor ring. The room was in darkness. One cylinder for the gas lamp had been used, the spare started. Heat and light were too precious to waste while they slept. She found the torch.

By the time conversation ceased, bolts disengaged and the door swung open, she had wrapped herself in a blanket and was seated in a chair. A powerful beam followed by dark shapes came in. Liz watched through slitted eyes, understanding the panic and paralysis of deer transfixed in car headlamps. The beam swung to her sleeping son, back again. Exhausted by his labours, Tom didn't stir. She could feel the sharpened nail he'd given her, hard against her right thigh, and moved her hand towards the pocket of her slacks. She would go down fighting.

'Mrs Lancaster, I bring good news. Your husband has something we want. His son is handling negotiations, and insists on receiving young Tom here in exchange. We're happy to oblige. Your boy should be home by teatime.'

The leader's sane, reasonable middle-class voice. Liz struggled to accept, believe. Jamie close by, involved? Confusion must have reached her face. The reassuring voice misunderstood.

'Please believe me. Tom's being released. I'm afraid you can't go with him, but your turn will come. Very soon. Right now, I need your help. He's a plucky kid, and won't want to leave without you. If you can persuade him, it'll make life much easier for everyone. Will you do that? We'd hate to use force, which would be so unnecessary.'

He gave her time to think, stepping forward and lighting the gas lamp with a cigarette lighter. He was wearing a balaclava, as were the two men by the door, but she remembered his face. A harmless, decent English face. Panic squeezed Liz's chest. Every instinct urged her to fling herself at Tom, hold tight, never let go. But if she did that they'd wrench him from her arms, tear them apart, terrify him, drag her son away kicking and shouting. And she'd be powerless to prevent it. She responded calmly, surprising herself.

'You're really letting him go?'

'Yes, Mrs Lancaster, we are. This is business.'

It was insane, but she believed him. Or wanted to so badly it seemed that way. The persuasive voice continued reassuringly.

'You have ten minutes to get him ready to travel. He will come to no harm.'

Transient belief was consumed by doubt and fear. The men left, relocking the door. Liz knelt beside her son. Stroked soft hair. Felt tears start. Blinked rapidly, angrily. Wiped weakness away with an impatient hand. She had to be strong, for both their sakes. Tom's eyes opened. He stared up at her, momentarily disorientated.

'Mum. Is everything all right?'

'Everything's fine, little man. You're going home.'

Liz Lancaster smiled. Leaned down and kissed a forehead furrowed with incomprehension. Hoped with all her being those last three words were true. That Jamie would *make* them come true.

Gloucestershire

THE GULFSTREAM V with its covert payload was three hours down-range from LA. Until the incoming aircraft arrived there wasn't much more James Lancaster could do. The company jet would land at London Gatwick for Customs clearance, then hop to Cambridge. There, sensitive equipment could be transferred away from official scrutiny. When James phoned his father's pilot, the ex-navy chopper jock had taken a while to answer. He must have been asleep, but repeated instructions back accurately and promised to make the pick-up before flying down to Omega.

Battery-charging wasn't such a bad idea. James was dog tired, despite an ex-soldier's ability to function with no more than occasional catnaps wherever he stood. So he'd come up here to sleep. Or try to. The small room was on the top floor of New Hall, in now-disused servants' quarters under the sloping roof, and was just as he remembered. So was Peter's, next door. He'd looked, while Rita Bernadelli was putting freshly ironed sheets on his narrow bed. The housekeeper had explained that Conrad never said anything, so she left everything as it always was. Pausing outside the door, she'd looked at him shrewdly.

'In all those years, the only person who's been up here apart from myself is Mrs Lancaster. She used to come often. Not that there's much to see, mind.'

Rita had reached up and lightly pinched his cheek, a childhood bedtime routine he found oddly comforting. Alone again, James had put his mobile on the bedside table, alongside a hideous tassel-shaded lamp – evidence of early moves towards independence. The lamp base was a raffia-covered Chianti bottle stolen from the debris of a long-forgotten business banquet, and the table was an old double-compartment orange box rescued from the kitchen.

In those days, rejecting his father's attempts to buy affection and respect with *things* had been one way of trying to hit back. But none of those pathetic efforts ever generated more than paternal anger. And indifference. He still couldn't fathom Conrad's current agenda, but perhaps it was no more than determination to impose his will on a son who had defied him, because Conrad Lancaster was a pathological winner. And maybe childish defiance extended into adulthood had not left his father as untouched as James supposed.

He'd sat on the bed and looked at his mother, smiling

from a silver photograph frame on the dressing table. She was so young then. Beautiful. Happy. In love. Not yet getting detached from unfolding reality she couldn't cope with. Or dying, to leave him and Peter in Conrad's loveless care. His mother's image was the only thing in the room that mattered. Adolescent possessions only brought back bad memories. So why was he here, instead of in one of the many lavishly appointed guest bedrooms? And why had he come running when Conrad called?

Sombre introspection was an old enemy. That was the sort of question James had spent a lifetime asking himself, without finding satisfactory answers. For a while, he'd drifted in and out of sleep, his mind filled with disconnected images that might have been conscious thoughts or unbidden dreams. But now he was fully awake, staring at the ceiling. Soon, it would be time to go downstairs. Have a reviving cup of black coffee. Joke with Rita and Duncan Bernadelli to try to raise their spirits. And start the operation to rescue Liz and Tom.

When all was said and done, this began and would end with Liz Lancaster. He'd give it everything. He owed her that. But she was Conrad's wife, and there could be no going back.

Wiltshire

AS ALL-NIGHT sessions went, this one had gone like a dream. Louise Boss had prepared the dummy disk that would buy time to track the kidnappers, and acquired a great deal of useful information to support that pursuit. The men of action would be pleased – and if her final foray into cyberspace paid off, they might even be impressed. But Trojan Horse was handling that, and results wouldn't be in for a while. Until then, she'd keep quiet about her most ambitious hacking session yet.

She was sitting in the kitchen, drinking coffee and throwing a catnip mouse for her moggies, who fought for the privilege of killing it. John Tolley's alarm clock would not go off for an hour, so all she had to kill was time. Without knowing how or why she got there, Louise found herself thinking about a childhood incident. Aged about nine, she'd been walking in the countryside with her father. It was summer, and he'd ordered a break from intensive theoretical mathematics. So they'd talked about tennis, her other love. The All-England Championships at Wimbledon were in progress, and Louise was prattling about becoming the first British woman to win the ladies' singles final for almost as long as anyone could remember.

One day, she'd have to choose between God-given talents – mathematician or tennis player? But her father was clever. He never took sides, or sought to encourage her one way or the other. The choice must be hers. To this day, Louise didn't know his favoured option, and he took that secret to his grave. Instead, he taught her to achieve.

They reached a stream. Perhaps twelve feet across, it meandered through water meadows. The path followed the bank, before crossing a railway-sleeper bridge further down. She decided to jump the stream. Louise knew it was too wide but had to try – she wanted to get to the other side, and the bridge was too easy. When he realized her intention, her father said nothing – just watched. She hurtled into the jump of her life. Hit water with a tremendous splash and toppled backwards. As she scrambled up the far bank, soaked to the skin and covered in black mud, Louise had looked back. Her father was nodding approval.

Father's first theorem of excellence was simple, and she'd learned well. You never know how far it's possible to go without straining mind, nerve and sinew to jump further than you'd ever jumped before. Again, and again, and again. But as life went by Louise also learned something else. However far she jumped, peace of mind was – like the other side of that long-ago stream – theoretically attainable, but beyond her reach. At least for now.

Abandoning the catnip mouse to its fate, Louise finished her coffee and went up to the bathroom. She undressed and showered, shampooing her hair under water as hot as she could bear, before spinning the dial to cold. After two icy minutes, she stepped out of the shower and dried off, rubbing her skin with coarse towelling until it glowed.

Without hesitating, she walked across the landing, opened the door and padded into the bedroom. She pulled up the duvet and climbed into her bed, grateful for warmth radiating from the sleeping Tolley. She'd been right, he was naked. He stirred, adjusted his position. Louise crept closer, wondering if he'd be aroused by her presence. In more ways than one.

John Tolley had been woken by the sound of running water. He'd lain still, thinking about her. Seeing her face. Imagining her under the shower. He loved everything about women. Was at ease in their company. Went well with them. Enjoyed having uncomplicated sex with them, taking and giving uninhibited sensual pleasure. Usually managed to part on the best of terms, often remaining friends with former lovers.

But the intensity of his reaction to Louise was different. Unsettling. Almost frightening, because he didn't understand the implications. If it wasn't for her, he wouldn't be here. Tautology, yet indicative of one thing he was certain about. Something fundamental was happening, and his life was going to change. Louise might be a catalyst, but he wasn't throwing himself into this unsanctioned kidnap rescue merely because she was involved, let alone with the intention of delivering the bad guys' identity to his masters in return for a pat on the head.

Anything but the most superficial personal life was consumed by the job, and suddenly superficial wasn't enough. If he'd been a woman, the patronizing explanation would have been 'body clock ticking'. But perhaps he'd just had enough of counter-intelligence, of donning a mask for all but colleagues, and sometimes them too. Total commitment to undeclared war that could never be won was frustrating, and hidebound superiors more concerned with appearances and budgets than spy-catching didn't help. Or was he simply pissed off because devious old Gus Churchill was using and abusing him?

When the bedroom door opened, Tolley feigned sleep. Louise Boss slipped in beside him, bringing a flutter of cold air. His back was turned. Just as well. She gently pushed against him, her skin cool and slightly damp. He felt the press of yielding breasts against his back. Hair tickled his neck and a light arm rested on his. She murmured a greeting.

'Hello, Tolley.'

He considered and rejected assumed unconsciousness. This had to be faced, and postponement would only add complications. Besides, playing possum would probably be rewarded with an elbow in the ribs.

'Boss. This is an unexpected surprise. I haven't slept with my landlady since I was at college.'

'We're a demanding breed. Anyone for tennis?'

He laughed. Rolled over. Propped himself on an elbow and looked down at her in faint night light from the uncurtained dormer window.

'We tried that, remember? Never again. Now, turn over.'

After a moment, she did as bid, arranging herself in a comfortable foetal position. Tolley lay down and moulded himself to her body. Kissed the back of her neck. She shivered against him, and he had never felt more alive. He stroked springy hair. Spoke quietly, wanting her to understand she wasn't like all the others. That something important was happening.

'I don't believe I'm saying this, but I want to sleep with you, *really* sleep with you, before, well . . .'

'The alarm goes off in half an hour? Yes, I'd like that, Tolley.'

She reached back and found an arm. Guided his hand between her breasts. And was asleep in seconds, breathing silently with no more than the regular rise and fall of her chest to indicate that she, too, was alive. John Tolley lay awake in the darkness, holding Louise and thinking about a future that just might be anything they wanted to make it.

London

UPPER BROOK STREET was awake, and the sound of early morning traffic on the narrow street was invading the master bedroom of Conrad Lancaster's tall house. It didn't bother him. He always rose early, and liked the hustle and bustle of city life. Double-knotting the cord of a voluminous silk dressing gown to avoid the possibility of fall-open, he emerged from the *en suite* bathroom. He wasn't ashamed of his gross body, but hated exposing himself to ridicule. Not that his women ever hinted at such feelings, because they always wanted something,

Conrad was past the age when sex ranked as a primary drive, up there alongside knocking hell out of the world and making lots of money. But still it mattered, because ability to attract beautiful young women to his bed was affirmation of power he'd earned and loved exercising. But he despised the willingness with which they fulfilled his most depraved demands, and the transparency of their venal motivation.

Last night's was typical. He couldn't even remember her name. Conrad's first target had been Jenny Symes, the television journalist. After that excellent interview, Jenny had given every indication of being willing, but was out on assignment when he called the previous afternoon. Her turn would come. The substitute had been adequate – a Titian-topped bimbo who worked in telesales on his tabloid. He stood by the vast bed and looked down. She was a sorry sight in the light of twin bedside lamps. Lacquered hair had collapsed on to the white satin pillow, her make-up was a mess and she was snuffling as she slept.

He'd picked her as a possible weeks ago, stopping and exchanging a word on one of his grand tours of Lancaster House. Noted her reaction and entered her now-forgotten name in his pocket diary for future reference. Recognized signs he'd seen a thousand times before. When his PA had phoned down to invite her to a late supper with the chairman, Charlotte hadn't hesitated. No, Charmaine – that was it.

The Bentley had fetched the girl from some grotty flat in Clapham, where she'd rushed after work to pour herself into an overflowing black cocktail dress. They'd dined expensively at La Gavroche, across the road. He'd eaten steadily and listened with attentive interest, she'd nibbled and talked non-stop. Charmaine dreamed of graduating from telesales to page three, and Conrad said he couldn't understand why such a sensational person hadn't already made the leap. An unspoken bargain was struck, and she hadn't declined the offer of a nightcap.

She'd delivered, and so would he. When the bruises faded from her heavy breasts, she could expose them to four million slack-mouthed readers with his blessing. And if that led to better things, good luck to her. Everyone was entitled to make the most of any cards they held – but as far as he was concerned Charmaine had played her only trumps, and was history.

Conrad marched through to his dressing room, feeling buoyant, invincible, immortal. Rough sex always put him in the right frame of mind for a big day, and today would be one of the biggest. He'd clinch the Russia Telecom deal. Tom would come home. And that sanctimonious little prick James was not only going to do all the hard work, but also pick up the tab.

While others slept, she'd worked through the night at Pandora's Box Productions, building a torpedo that would sink Lancaster Trust's over-confident chairman, and a leaking business empire that was rotten from stem to stern. With the taping of a few continuity shots and a hard-hitting introduction, Jenny Symes would be ready. Her best-ever *Guardian Angel* programme was pointedly titled: *CONRAD LANCASTER – A QUESTION OF TRUST*.

She sent the weary-eyed videotape editor home. He emerged from the editing suite and blinked in harsh daylight, tired but happy with his contribution to the sort of great television that did no harm at all to annual profit-sharing bonuses. Before leaving to snatch a few hours' rest herself, in order to be at her immaculate best for studio cameras later in the day, Jenny left voicemail instructions for her secretary.

Task One – get in touch with Conrad Lancaster's office, and request a reaction to *Guardian Angel*'s contention that pension fund assets had been looted. Jenny wasn't over-interested in journalistic balance, though a prim 'Lancaster Trust was invited to comment on these serious allegations, but declined' might add a little something.

No, these powerful men were so predictable, and the litigious fat boy would seek an immediate injunction. The bewigged judge would doubtless want to oblige, but would be unable to do so in the face of her rock-solid evidence. And the sort of massive publicity money couldn't buy would be guaranteed.

Task Two – arrange a viewing with the BBC producer responsible for *Guardian Angel*, whose approval was required before the show could go on air. The man not only suffered from hyper-caution, but compounded the felony by making periodic passes, conveniently forgetting the wife and three children left behind in Dorset during his four-day working weeks in London. He, too, would be unable to argue with proven facts. And if Conrad Lancaster went for that gagging injunction, the BBC would have to make a stand against such a brazen attempt to bully the Corporation into silence, picking up the legal costs in the process.

Task Three – contact Wendy Lang's PA and have him reschedule pre-noon meetings, because the boss and majority shareholder of Pandora's Box Productions would be otherwise engaged.

Duty done, Jenny Symes tucked a copy of the explosive videocassette into her Gucci shoulder bag. She couldn't wait to share this latest triumph. Her mind raced ahead to the flat-fronted Georgian riverside house in Narrow Street, Limehouse, a few moments away by car. She'd climb into bed, wake her lover and they'd watch the tape together on their flat wall screen – a far better turn-on than pornography could ever be. Then she would have passionate sex with Wendy Lang, her partner in business and partner for life.

Gloucestershire

ONE ADVANTAGE of a large country estate was an ability to rustle up a small private army. While he waited for the helicopter to arrive from Omega, James Lancaster assembled a home guard made up of estate workers – chauffeur, gamekeeper, woodsman and three farm workers. If Tom was brought back to New Hall later, he would be protected. However unlikely the possibility of retaliation when the operation to rescue Liz got under way, James couldn't risk Tom's safety. The kidnap had taken place within a mile of the house, so the enemy knew the terrain.

Duncan Bernadelli was co-ordinating a round-the-clock guard inside the house, with armed men always on watch. Weaponry arrived by appropriately named Land Rover Defender with Don Sykes, who'd emptied the gun cabinet at Keeper's Cottage. He provided two deerstalking rifles, an old bolt-action .243 used for fox control, and assorted shotguns. As the men clustered round Rita Bernadelli's big kitchen table drinking tea and examining their chosen weapons, Duncan handed out walkie-talkies and ammunition, before starting his briefing. James watched and listened, but decided he could retreat to the library with a cup of coffee. The Scottish chauffeur – who'd done National Service fighting Mau Mau guerrillas in Kenya – was deploying troops with crisp efficiency.

James sat in a comfortable club chair and thought about the day's activities with quickening anticipation. His restless night was forgotten. Action was the antidote to introspection, and instinct said the first phase would go smoothly. Extensive experience as a kidnap negotiator provided a nose for deals likely to work out. If he'd done his job properly, the kidnappers believed they could not acquire Trojan Horse unless Tom went free. They'd keep Liz as insurance, so there was no percentage in holding on to the boy. But he could be wrong.

Either way, James was determined the half-brother he'd never met would be released. Then the endgame could begin. Providing Louise Boss delivered on her casual but impressive promise, ingenious in-built protection would ensure the Trojan Horse disk couldn't be exposed as a fake. The kidnappers would have to return, threatening to kill Liz if the right codes weren't supplied. He'd counter by proposing a straight swap. They'd refuse. He'd offer half the codes as a gesture of good faith, with Liz exchanged for the balance once the first batch was authenticated. This delicate dance marathon would buy time – and dramatically increase the chances of tracing her hiding place.

These were the battles he relished. Was good at fighting. Generally won. Gambling with people's lives required ability to make testing calls and back them with iron will, unclouded by sentimentality. The balance was gossamer light. For professional kidnappers, victims were a means to an end, and damaging them was bad for business. That was the logic, but criminals did not always behave rationally.

On two occasions the scales had tilted against him, for reasons that never became apparent. In one case, the result had been the body of a fifteen-year-old petrochemical heir – minus an ear sent earlier to encourage speedy and discreet settlement in defiance of Italian anti-kidnap law – tossed from a speeding car on the Autostrada del Sole. In the other, the twenty-two-year-old daughter of a newspaper tycoon had simply vanished, presumed fed to the carnivorous Florida Everglades. Money had been paid in good faith, but despite unwritten rules things had gone terminally wrong.

This was more complex. These kidnappers were not career criminals. Their operation was a one-off, probably initiated and controlled by a foreign espionage service – Russia, Iran, Iraq, Israel, China. There was no shortage of candidates who would kill for such a powerful cyber-weapon. But therein lay weakness and strength for both parties. They had no interest in facilitating future kidnapping activity, and might intend to eliminate Liz and Tom as a security precaution. But they also wanted Trojan Horse and believed he could deliver. So James had refused to part with the disk without securing Tom's release. He'd stand by his considered decision. On balance, their need should be greater than his.

If the affair ended badly, James Lancaster would have to live with responsibility that was his alone. It went with the job, and having someone to blame comforted those left grieving at the graveside. He'd visited that lonely place before – but never when the losers were a woman he once loved and her only child. Leaving no one to blame but himself.

Moscow

THE TINY APARTMENT behind McDonald's on Pushkin Square had become claustrophobic, a prison whose walls were closing in. It didn't matter. The five of them would soon escape from this place, never to return. When today's assignment was completed, they could end the extended 'compassionate leave' arranged by Gregor Gorski's friends in the military hierarchy. Rejoin units scattered throughout Russia and the shrunken empire, taking the secret that must never be told with them. Become proper soldiers again. Await rebirth following the painful but necessary convulsion that was about to shake Mother Russia to her senses.

Despite raucous late diners fighting for hamburgers in the American restaurant below, and a night filled with the sirens and racing engines of agitated security forces, his men had slept, slept still. He could not, and envied them. But they hadn't planted the bomb at Okhotny Ryad Metro station, which was bad work for a soldier. Major Valery Filatov had switched on neither television nor radio, having no wish to establish *how* bad.

Instead, he'd sat in an upright chair at the scarred dining table, drinking steadily. Vodka didn't bring oblivion. Every time he closed his good eye, Valery Filatov saw the mother with two young children who had stood beside him on the train, attempting to shield infants from the press of humanity. But she hadn't been able to protect them – or herself – from forces far beyond her control. From the deadly briefcase left at her feet. From him. Though at least she could have known no sense of failure. The end would have been mercifully quick.

At the moment of truth, as the soldier Filatov fled like the cowardly assassin he was, Gregor Gorski was somewhere close by – observing the unfolding of his plan with all the emotion of a granite rock. He would spare no regret for the human cost. Filatov had met many ruthless men in his time, but none so bloodless, or whose eyes were so dead. Yet, somewhere inside the desiccated ex-KGB colonel, something burned at white heat. Why else would he always be there in person, watching and waiting like some ghoulish harbinger of death?

Such thoughts made endless circles. Valery Filatov had been slumped for a long time, elbows on the table and face in his hands. He sat upright and poured a final vodka, staring into the peppered spirit as though some elemental truth might be hidden in its depths. But there was nothing. The major drained his glass and stood up, stretching cramped limbs. He'd awaken the others, and they would prepare to do what must be done, for the sake of a great nation seeking a brave new future.

Bristol Channel

EVERYTHING had happened too quickly, from the moment his mother shook him awake and told him he was going home. Tom didn't want to leave without her, but she made him promise to do as the men said, and be brave. Almost before he could argue, he'd been blindfolded and carried away, slung over the right shoulder of a tall man they hadn't seen before, with no more than the memory of her last, desperate hug and whispered 'See you soon' to take with him.

He'd registered jolting progress – along the passage where their escape attempt failed, down stone stairs, through a narrow door where the man stooped and Tom's elbow banged the frame, into salty air and the sound of the sea, down more stairs, on to a rocking boat. Moments later, he'd been dumped on a bunk. His masked captor had stripped off the blindfold and climbed out through a round roof hatch, leaving him in a tiny cabin lit by a bulkhead lamp, provisioned with shrinkwrapped sandwiches and Thermos flask.

As he sat on the narrow bunk, blinking in harsh light, despair had rolled over him. Alone in confined space, Tom Lancaster finally surrendered. He'd tried so hard to be brave, but with no one but himself to impress the effort proved too great. He curled up and cried like a child – great tearing sobs that racked his body, leaving him mentally and physically spent.

Engines had started, making his portholeless prison

vibrate. Tom had sat up, distracted from misery by this development. The boat soon got under way, gently at first, so it had been impossible to be sure they were moving at all. Then there was no doubt. As speed increased, the boat had risen and fallen alarmingly, crashing into riven water with rhythmic slaps that sounded loud against tapering walls. From their shape, Tom assumed he was at the bow, with not much more than one thickness of fibreglass between himself and angry sea. He'd started wondering how fast they were moving, how long the voyage would take and where it might end.

He had no answers, but asking had taken his mind off other things. He could only guess at the speed, but big powerboats cruised comfortably at 20 knots. Tom knew a knot was a nautical measure, slower than land speed, so if a car travelled at 20 knots it would actually be doing 23 mph. He liked calculations like that. Time was harder to estimate, but he'd tried, adding one hour to the journey each time another hour couldn't possibly not have passed. So far, he'd got to four hours, and would soon make it five. As to their destination, there was no way of even guessing.

But wherever it was, they might be getting close. The engines were throttling back and the boat settled into a more even motion, no longer fighting the waves and wind outside. Tom started to get excited. The sooner the kidnappers released him, the sooner he'd be able to keep a promise whispered to his mother just before they dragged him away – that he and Dad would rescue her, whatever it took. His father was sometimes frightening, but always strong.

London

CHARMAINE had arrived stylishly by chauffeur-driven limo, but the girl he had loved and was happy to lose would creep home by black cab. Conrad Lancaster needed the Bentley to transport him to the office, and left a fifty-pound note with Aitken. The imperturbable butler would summon a taxi when the slightly soiled lady surfaced. In fact, Conrad was certain she'd been awake when he left the bedroom – remembering the night, hoping her face wasn't marked and wondering if her best card had won the trick. But Charmaine didn't dare ask – would he deliver on that page-three promise, or had she been had twice?

Of course he'd deliver. What was the point of such diversions if nobody got to know about them? He called the tabloid's Picture Editor on the car phone as the Continental whispered past the US embassy and on through Grosvenor Square. Passed on Charmaine's name. Suggested she merited some serious exposure. The word would race round Lancaster House – the old dog was still getting first pick of the young bitches, reminding everyone who led the pack.

He punched the number of James's mobile. Conrad needed to know how the kidnap was being handled.

'James Lancaster.'

The moment the phone was answered, Conrad took control.

'Where are you?'

'Library at New Hall.'

The reply was terse, which suited Conrad. The last thing he wanted was prolonged discussion. He hurried on.

'Everything under control?'

'Nothing's changed. Handover still planned for noon and I'm not anticipating problems. You can never be sure, but it feels as right as it ever does. They want something, we want something. All I have to do is make sure the trade goes smoothly. Tom will be home today.'

James sounded relaxed, confident – which might mean nothing, because calming the anxious parents of kidnap victims was presumably routine. Conrad issued his final order.

'Let me know the moment he's safe. I'll be at the office. You're not screwing around with these people? I know you. If the opportunity to get back at them arises, you'll be tempted. Don't be. There's Elizabeth to consider and I won't have her put at risk because you get carried away with your own cleverness. Give them Trojan Horse. Once they've got what they want, they'll have no reason to hold her and she'll surely be released.'

'I have done this sort of thing before. If you don't trust me, get someone else.'

With that contemptuous dismissal, James hung up. Conrad smiled. He didn't put down the car phone, instead keying the office number. The Russia Telecom deal was reaching fruition, but doing business in Moscow was never straightforward. There would be no exchange of contracts until a Bahamas-based company was set up, and he wanted the paperwork waiting on his desk.

The new offshore front would enjoy a lucrative service contract, designed to skim off one percentage point of turnover on Conrad's new Russian business. He neither knew nor cared what mix of mafia, bent politicians and corrupt officials would benefit from this multi million-dollar arrangement. He'd always worked that way, and never begrudged the investment. Providing everyone got their cut, everything always went well. Especially when his share was the lion's.

Wiltshire

MacNAUGHTON'S FIRST LAW of human probability stated that if it was even remotely possible that two people could have, they had. And if John Tolley's buoyant demeanour was any guide, the law had been obeyed. The two men had met outside the Omega building, to await the helicopter's imminent arrival. The security chief clamped on a disapproving expression.

'I should've chaperoned you. You were supposed to be working last night, not engaging in sexual aerobics with my staff.'

Tolley grinned engagingly, sketching an invisible cross above his heart with a forefinger.

'We *did* work, Sandy. At least Louise did, while I provided moral support and fed the cats. And I do mean moral. Didn't lay so much as this trustworthy finger on her, honest.'

MacNaughton responded sourly. In the cold light of morning, his decision to back James Lancaster's quixotic rescue plan didn't seem like quite such a good idea. He sniffed disbelievingly.

'So where's the dedicated night worker, then – sleeping off intellectual exertions?'

'Nope. Still riding that computer of hers through cyberspace like an avenging angel. Claims to have unearthed solid leads on our kidnappers, but went all mysterious on me and refused to explain. Hoping to dazzle us all with that brilliant intellect you mentioned. Waste of time in my case. I'm already smitten, though I will admit I may be interested in more than her mind. She'll drive over to New Hall when she's through and reveal all.'

Tolley had raised his voice to compete with the incoming chopper, which brought the conversation to a temporary standstill. When the gold-and-black bird had landed, the MI5 man resumed, flippancy replaced by genuine concern.

'Are you quite sure you're up for this, Sandy? James Lancaster's got his own agenda. Me, I don't give a shit. But you've got a lot to lose. It's not too late to walk. We'll manage.'

The boy's heart was in the right place, his instincts sound. MacNaughton *had* been having second thoughts, but felt uncertainty falling away. The pilot swung open the door. Picking up the briefcase containing the doctored disk box, MacNaughton stepped forward.

'Sod the lot of them, John. Besides, you kids will fall on your arses if I'm not there to give you the benefit of my vast experience.'

Acting as a glorified security guard and spending leisure time growing the best damned chrysanthemums west of Lowestoft drove him mad, but circumstances rarely provided the chance to do much else. Now they had, and Alexander MacNaughton wouldn't – couldn't – let that opportunity go to waste. He'd once been good at this sort of thing, and there was no holding an old warhorse back when he smelled the blood of battle.

North Devon

T HIS WHOLE MESS must have something to do with Conrad's commercial activities. Kidnapping for money was un-British, but Liz Lancaster could easily imagine a slighted foreign business associate resorting to such unorthodoxy. She'd seen enough dubious characters around the dining table at New Hall to know that Conrad dealt with bad people from some of the world's least orderly places – Africa, Eastern Europe, the Middle East, South America. Most had calculating eyes, assessing her as a measure of their host's wealth and status.

With the benefit of hindsight, all seemed like bad people to cross. But that never bothered Conrad. Sometimes, he boasted about his ruthless approach to business. He'd dropped more than enough hints over the years to indicate that he'd double-cross the Devil if an opportunity arose, and take unholy pleasure in doing so.

Liz hoped they – whoever *they* were – wanted something other than revenge. If that was their objective, she'd hardly be sitting in this chill stone room, working things out by hissing gaslight. But she worried about Tom. Wondered where he was. Forced herself to believe the well-spoken leader spoke truthfully when he said Tom would go free. Prayed her husband would swallow pride and pay his debt in cash or kind, without trying to outsmart an aggrieved enemy.

The worst part was not knowing. And thinking about Jamie. James Lancaster. Somehow, he'd become involved. His American business dealt with kidnap negotiations. Perhaps Conrad had called him in, to deal with the exchange and make sure she and Tom came out of this ordeal safely. She recalled for the thousandth time the last moment she'd seen her lover. He was a soldier then, recovering from arm and leg injuries caused by a military training accident – an explanation she never believed. They'd just spent the night in her tatty little flat in Camden Town, with the intensity of lovers who know they're about to part. Over breakfast, with pain and rare uncertainty etched on his strong face, he'd reiterated his decision to leave for the States – retreating from the war with his father, leaving contacts and places that might remind him of his dead brother, abandoning the past to seek a future he could live with.

As he spoke, Liz had understood. James wanted her to

go with him to America, and desperately hoped she'd offer. But because he couldn't ask, she wouldn't volunteer. Like the crutch that compensated for his wounded leg, she'd be of no use once he was whole again – a too-painful reminder of whatever he was trying to forget. So she'd wished him luck. Ruffled his fair hair. Kissed him hard on the lips. And gone to work, blinking back tears that were begging her to change her mind.

Liz Lancaster often wondered if her naïve, unmarried self made the right choice. And whether it had been a mistake to stick by that decision through all that had followed. At least Tom would grow up without the burden of a family legacy too heavy to bear, because she'd devoted her life to ensuring that he was properly protected from the corrosive Conrad factor.

If Tom grew up at all. She was sitting in one of the plastic patio chairs, wrapped in a sleeping bag. Yet Liz shivered, enduring a panic attack she couldn't fight off. Her son was so courageous in adversity. The sharpened nail he'd given her was in her right hand, clutched so tightly the metal was hurting her flesh. Tom was her flesh, too, and the possibility he might become a sacrifice on the altar of Conrad's business was unbearable.

Liz made a fervent promise, even though she had no power to make it come true, ceaselessly repeating the mantra to block out everything else. She would survive, because she had to know.

Gloucestershire

HE COULDN'T STOP thinking about her. Imagining the confining walls of some dank cellar or airless room. Devastated as her son was taken away. Terrified that Tom was in danger, might not survive. Fearing for her own life. Despairing. Not even knowing that a man who once ran out on her had returned, and would do everything possible to set the record straight.

The best he could do for Liz right now was to recover her boy, and worry about the rest later. But there were a few quiet moments before the helicopter arrived, and

James Lancaster couldn't switch to detached professionalism. His eyes strayed to the life-sized oil painting that dominated one wall of New Hall's panelled library. Conrad's masterful figure stared down sternly, imposingly arrayed in the purple gown and black mortarboard of an honorary Cambridge graduate. The picture must date from the time when his father was still investing heavily in pursuit of a peerage, before damning Board of Trade enquiries made such a purchase impossible.

James sighed, depressed by melancholy insight. His father had read him more easily than he would any of the stodgy leather-bound volumes in this tranquil room. Conrad never bothered with books, but opening up people and looking inside was another matter. Though when it came to finer feelings, he lost the plot. Conrad's perception began and ended with all that was dark in the human psyche – exploitable flaws and weaknesses, insecurities and desires. The old manipulator had unerringly spotted the gap in his defences – targeting complex feelings for a woman who had once been a son's lover, and was now the father's wife. He'd known James would be unable to resist a Sir Galahad gallop to the rescue of a damsel belonging to another, in a sad attempt to right an earlier distress.

James went over to the picture. Malevolent dark eyes followed, held his as he looked up at the man who had blighted his life and was interfering still. But Conrad had a surprise coming. He might think his rebellious son was meekly following the master's agenda because it pandered to some deep-seated emotional frailty. Assume whatever game he was playing would end in victory.

But sharp perception could cut two ways. James knew Conrad Lancaster, BA, and didn't trust him or his agenda. Outside, he heard the throbbing beat of a helicopter engine – distant, but closing fast. He raised a hand in salute to his father, and turned to leave the library.

Moscow

FOR ONCE, Gregor Gorski would not be there, grandstanding the spectacular rocket strike designed to create a vacancy in the Kremlin. His rightful place at such an historic moment was at the side of General Sergei Sobchak, the man willing and able to become President of Russia. But first the ex-KGB colonel had to be sure the Sons of Dudayev were also willing and able to complete their mission. To murder hundreds of innocents in the name of Russian regeneration was hard. That they had done. Yet assassinating President Mikhail Yelkin would be more demanding still.

His team were professional soldiers fighting for a cause close to their hearts, and Gregor Gorski understood the military mentality. He was confident they would not flinch from their awesome duty. But as his plan came to its thundering climax, there was no room for complacency. He arrived at the door of the Pushkin Square apartment and knocked softly. Major Filatov admitted him. Looking haggard, the one-eyed Afghanistan veteran was alone.

'The others have already left for the airport, travelling separately. I thought it best to allow ample time.'

It was a sensible decision. The streets of Moscow were seething with security forces, and Gorski himself had been stopped and made to show his identity papers on three occasions during the journey from home. He nodded approvingly.

'Good. Everything is in place?'

The bulky equipment required to despatch President Yelkin into the afterlife had been moved to the top-floor apartment near Sheremetevo days before, in anticipation of increased vigilance by the guardians of law and order. It would not have been possible to spirit the murder weapons past them today. Filatov responded with a strained counter-question.

'Is today's action essential? We have surely done enough to discredit the government, and last night . . .'

His voice trailed into forlorn silence. Gregor Gorski spoke sternly.

'Last night was distasteful but necessary, Major, and I commend your courage. But we cannot weaken, or all those lives will have been sacrificed in vain. You must do your duty, for the sake of Russia.'

'Yes, Comrade Colonel.'

The soldier automatically stiffened to attention. Gorski smiled.

'Excellent. You are a true patriot, and may be sure your dedication will be properly recognized.'

An expression of distaste flickered across Filatov's world-weary face.

'This is not about personal aggrandizement, Colonel Gorski.'

'Of course not. But nonetheless, all of Russia will be grateful for what you are about to do.'

Gorski clapped Filatov's upper arm. He had been right to make this visit. But now resolve was stiffened, the Sons of Dudayev would do what was necessary, before vanishing for ever.

'Carry on, Major Filatov. General Sobchak is expecting me, and we will await developments together. The *Rodina*'s future is in your hands.'

As Gregor Gorski turned to leave, the poor fool saluted.

London

DAVID ABRAHAMS was one of Britain's best-known and most highly paid lawyers. The society solicitor presided over a long-established firm numbering the rich, famous and notorious by the score amongst its clients. Created a life peer for services to the Labour Party, he saw no contradiction in serving the wealthy, who were not only entitled to the best legal advice money could buy, but also capable of paying for it – thus supporting the firm's less lucrative activities. Conrad Lancaster didn't understand this Robin Hood mentality, but if Abrahams & Partners chose to waste time on *pro bono publico* activities to boost the firm's image, that was their problem.

Conrad used the place like a Tycoons' Advice Bureau, expecting the sixty-nine-year-old Lord Abrahams to be on personal call at all times. Their professional relationship was of long standing, and he'd contributed several million pounds to partnership profits over the years. For that, Conrad expected – and got – instant attention. His call shot through to the great man, who managed not to sound displeased at the intrusion. The lawyer wrongly assumed this was yet more arm-twisting on a personal matter that had been obsessing his demanding client of late.

'Hello, Conrad. If you're chasing that assessment on likely settlement ramifications, you must wait. Our family law team are on it, but these things take time, especially when the asset picture is so complex and there are no real grounds against the mother for seeking custody of your boy.'

Secret discussions had been going on for months, but Conrad had more important things on his mind than defending himself if his wife brought divorce proceedings.

'Screw Elizabeth. I've got a small problem that requires the urgent attention of your litigation people.'

'So soon? I seem to recall we've only just secured final resolution of your last excursion into the legal arena. Or have you forgotten Lancaster *versus* Pressdram Limited? Our computer's still printing the bill.'

The lawyer's precise voice contained dry humour. Conrad wasn't amused by the reminder of his encounter with the sharp-penned satirists of *Private Eye* magazine. He continued sourly.

'I hear rumours of a libellous television programme, David, containing serious allegations that could damage my business. They had the nerve to ask for a comment, and my comment is that I want it stopped.'

'None of these allegations are justified, of course?'

'Nothing can be proved. It's Jenny Symes and her damned *Guardian Angel* rubbish, out to smear me. You know what she's like. Chip on her shoulder the size of the Grand Canyon and pathological hatred of anyone who makes a success of life. Especially men.'

Abrahams cleared his throat.

'Jenny Symes is a well-respected investigative journalist, Conrad, and the BBC will fund the defence. We would put in the A team ourselves, naturally, but I must strongly advise you to consider this carefully. Were you to lose in court, the publicity could double the impact of any adverse revelations in the television programme.'

Conrad felt his blood pressure rising, knew his face

was reddening. Bloody lawyers. Always advising caution, when all he wanted to do was kill the bitch. He controlled anger.

'Don't give me that losing crap. Get into the High Court immediately and seek an injunction against Symes, the production company she works for and the sodding BBC. I've got a big deal going down and need time. Keep the damned thing off air for two weeks and you'll have earned your massive fee. *Capisce?*'

'I'll send someone round to take a statement, and I myself will find and instruct the best barrister who's not in court today. Don't worry, Conrad, I'm sure this matter can be resolved.'

The legal eagle had been there often enough to know when he had to fly. If feathers were ruffled, his soothing response gave no indication of the fact. Though Conrad did detect a familiar note of resignation – the plaintive tone of someone agreeing to do what he wanted, despite considering his demands totally unreasonable. He decided to be magnanimous.

'I do hope so. Thank you, David. As always, you're a life-saver.'

Conrad put the phone down, and immediately lifted it. His duty PA was there in an instant.

'Yes, Mr Lancaster?'

'Doreen, get the Acquisitions Department to run an ownership check on a television programme-maker called Pandora's Box Productions, and crunch the numbers to find out what the company's worth. I'm considering an offer. Make sure the information's on my desk within the hour.'

'Yes, Mr Lancaster.'

Conrad replaced the phone and reached for the humidor. His blood pressure was easing. Insurance never hurt anyone. He would offer twice the upper limit value of Pandora's Box Productions. In cash. They'd understand he was buying silence, and wouldn't allow one lousy programme to screw the deal of a lifetime. And if the offer was withdrawn – say in a month's time, when the black hole in the pension fund's accounts had been refilled – that was their tough titty.

Gloucestershire

AFTER TAKING the illegally imported consignment, which came in three innocent-looking black nylon tote bags from LA via Gatwick and Cambridge airports, he sent the helicopter away to refuel. The ex-navy pilot seemed happy to inject excitement into his bus-driver existence, but James Lancaster was mindful of who paid the wages.

He remembered a cautionary tale from his youth. Conrad had been chasing some deal, involving a difficult choice between overseas partners. In those primitive times before advanced electronic eavesdropping, his father had generously laid on Rolls-Royces to fetch and carry the foreigners throughout their London stay. Unbeknown to them, each driver spoke the appropriate language, and was on a handsome bonus to report back indiscreet business conversation, or dubious behaviour which might be exploitable. There were things about today's activities Conrad didn't need to know, and James wasn't taking chances.

As the chopper lifted off, Tolley and MacNaughton helped him to carry the heavy holdalls into New Hall, keeping their own counsel. James wondered if he could trust his silent companions. He hadn't picked up any suspicious vibrations, but these counter-intelligence types were devious. For all he knew, they'd spent the night at Thames House, conferring with once and current masters at MI5 – hatching some master plan of their own to trap would-be violators of national security, and to hell with the fate of an innocent woman and nine-year-old boy. But instinct told him they hadn't, and when instinct talked, he listened. He was also a pragmatist. If they'd betrayed him, there was nothing he could do.

When they reached the library, James looked at his father's portrait. Conrad's piercing eyes might watch, but at least his painted and varnished ears couldn't hear. Sandy MacNaughton produced a square plastic disk box from the poacher's pocket of his tweed shooting jacket. As a neat finishing touch, it carried a red *TOP SECRET* sticker on the laminated white outer cover.

'Homework. One modified disk box, with a direction-finding transmitter rather neatly buried in the protective lining. Access codes are on a slip of paper inside.'

The grizzled Scot had apparently overcome reservations James had seen the previous day, and seemed to be enjoying himself. John Tolley chimed in, holding out an optical disk between finger and thumb.

'One deeply flawed copy of the oh-so-desirable Trojan Horse programme to go in Sandy's box, courtesy of our digital wizard. Worked all night and still going strong when I left, bless her, starting to look for that proverbial kidnapper in the haystack. If anyone can narrow down the location, it's Louise. I fancy she's getting somewhere, but wants to surprise us. So, are we ready to go to war, gentlemen?'

Two security pros looked at him expectantly. James didn't disappoint them. He removed three Browning Hi Power automatics from a holdall, together with spare extended clips and two hundred-round boxes of nine-millimetre ammunition, placing them on the table.

'A present from Hollywood. No doubt you're familiar with the beast. I suggest we each carry one. I've also laid on some armed protection here at the house as a routine precaution.'

He delved again, coming up with an expensive-looking leather briefcase.

'Here's our very own Trojan Horse, complete with in-built Sat-Nav capability. These cases cost nearly a thousand bucks apiece without the electronics, and it's extraordinary how tempting they prove. I've nailed more than one guy who kept the damn thing when he should've known better. My office in LA will monitor progress and keep us informed on a dedicated mobile.'

'So how do we play things? We're short-handed for an op like this.'

The Omega security chief was stating the obvious. James said so.

'Of course we are, Sandy. But they're hustling us, and we have to do the best we can in the time available. Besides, I believe the kidnappers will exchange Tom for the disk, and don't want to jeopardize that by going in mob-handed. I may be wrong, but you get a feel for these things when you've been there as often as me. When the boy's safe we can send for reinforcements, but not before. There's the woman to worry about, and we must also consider what's best for her.'

Tolley and MacNaughton exchanged glances. The younger man delivered an unspoken affirmative, though his serious expression reflected shared anxiety.

'So who does what?'

'I handle the exchange. You back me up from a safe distance and take the Sat-Nav reports from LA. Sandy's aloft. Watching brief. Hold the chopper well back to avoid being spotted, but be ready to follow up any instructions from the ground. I've got secure two-way radios here so we can all keep in touch. Don't tell the fly-boy more than you need to. He's my father's man and Conrad mustn't know we're trying to scam these bastards, or he'll probably do something stupid that'll put Liz and Tom at even greater risk.'

MacNaughton came in.

'Your assumptions on the exchange?'

'They'll call with rendezvous details. Could be a place-to-place chase to let them check I'm alone, but I reckon they'll go for a quick handover somewhere close by. They believe they're safe, because they still have Liz. The threat of a bomb on Tom may be a bluff, but we can't take chances and they know it. They're very confident, Sandy.'

The Scot was unhappy.

'So are you. Perhaps over-confident. I can see a million and one things going wrong here, with the lad's life on the line.'

James was painfully aware of that, but hid concern beneath the show of confidence they expected.

'Look, there are no guarantees, but we'll get the boy. I'm damn good at what I do. As soon as he's safe you whisk him away while John and I go after them. I know it's loose, but it's the best we can do under the circumstances. Okay?'

Somewhere along the line, simulated confidence turned to genuine aggression. MacNaughton shrugged defensively.

'Okay.'

'John?'

James turned to Tolley, who had been watching the exchange, absent-mindedly disassembling one of the Brownings by touch. The MI5 man understood what was going on. Steady grey eyes weighed him up, then Tolley came through.

'Okay. But I reckon we've got half an hour before we have to leave for Bristol, so let's run through the whole thing from the top. Any chance of a hot cup? My brain runs better on coffee.'

He smiled an engaging smile and snapped the slide of the Browning, which had somehow reassembled itself. James found himself smiling back. John Tolley seemed like a good man to have on the team.

North Devon

HE NEEDED fresh air after too many hours inside the claustrophobic building. In defiance of his own order to reveal minimal evidence of human occupation, Andrew Rosson was standing with his back to the weathered warehouse door, drinking a last mug of instant coffee and looking at the empty harbour so recently occupied by *Lara's Song*.

The big powerboat might come in useful. When the operation was concluded, the four Russians intended to slip out of the country aboard the brand-new Squadron 65 – heading for the South of France with their mafia master's new plaything, so he could match the ostentation of all but the richest of neighbours during the regular summer month spent in Monaco with his family. Rosson wasn't supposed to know this, but had overheard Paul and Ringo talking in the language they didn't know he understood.

Should the old quayside warehouse be compromised before they were through, the boat offered the best chance of escape, allowing them all to sprint out of territorial waters before being intercepted. For that reason, he had been more than happy to build *Lara's Song* into his plans. But Rosson didn't want her berthed alongside their supposedly deserted hiding place for a moment longer than necessary, attracting the attention of any hardy walkers on the coast path. So he'd sent the boat to Bristol with Tom Lancaster on board. The opposition wouldn't be expecting a water-borne dimension, and the boy's smooth handover would be facilitated.

Of course there was danger. Should the authorities be involved, *Lara's Song* would never get out of Bristol Docks and down to Avonmouth, even if the tide was right. But Rosson had every reason to believe there would be no official interest in what was about to happen. Besides, the risk wasn't his. Should the unexpected occur, the losers would be John and George, the Russian crewmen. And their master in Moscow, who would be short of one million pounds, a flashy cruiser and the opportunity to show off to fellow fair-weather Monagesques.

Rosson wondered what agreement Gregor Gorski had reached to secure secondment of the mafia boss's best stormtroops. He'd been away for too long to speculate – but despite the total collapse of the regime he'd known, the masses would still be toiling to survive, whilst new political and moneyed élites conspired to thrive and prosper. The loan of four tough men and an expensive boat would return a handsome dividend in cash or kind, because that was how the system worked.

Then, in a moment of brutal honesty during which he sought courage to go on, Rosson put such thoughts from his mind. He didn't care about any of that – Gorski's devious objectives, corrupt alliances in Moscow, even money received for doing what was required of him. That was Dmitry Travkin's world, in which he no longer felt comfortable. All that mattered was coming through unscathed, so he could get back to the provincial life antiquarian book dealer Andrew Rosson had never really wanted to leave.

But there was no escaping a Russian past that had spilled into an increasingly stressful British present. He took a long look around the peaceful cove. Water lapped against the stone jetty. Above, the sky was blue. The giver of warmth and life was not yet high enough to reach to the bottom of the rocky well where he stood, but bright sunlight – already slanting half way down the opposite cliff-face – would soon arrive.

When it did, he would be gone. Rosson tipped coffee dregs on to cobblestones and turned back towards the warehouse. Before leaving for Bristol, he'd give final instructions to Bill Hellis and Paul, the sole remaining Russian. Ringo had left an hour ago on a mission of his own, authorized but not explained by Colonel Gorski.

Wiltshire

WHILE THE BOYS were off playing scouts, she'd been earning her IT badge. Louise Boss was happy to be involved. She'd taken to James Lancaster, who radiated authority and quiet confidence. Trusted his assurance that this was the way to proceed. Empathized with the ordeal of kidnapped Liz Lancaster and her child. Liked the men needing her contribution. Welcomed the break from Omega and Gordon Holland's incessant demands. Wanted to punish those who'd threatened her baby. Was not even displeased by the opportunity to examine John Tolley more closely, despite the sudden turbulence he'd brought to her self-contained life.

But most of all professional passion was engaged. This was Trojan Horse's first real deployment, and Louise was fascinated by the opportunity to test lethal capabilities against genuine opposition. She'd soon know, because the results of a sortie into the covert heartland of US Government intelligence-gathering would soon flow on to the big colour screen.

During the night, she'd penetrated the command and control programme of Cyclops – a military spy satellite that could legibly photograph a car number plate from low earth orbit. Thanks to her Cray's massive computing power and the devious nature of Trojan Horse, the crew-cut minders in the Pentagon's top-secret National Reconnaissance Office would never know she'd come calling, or that their sharp-eyed charge had been told to do some unauthorized snooping. All they would log was a rogue course correction and slight irregularity in the satellite's automatic instrument-testing routine – an aberration that would remain a mystery however often they checked the system, eventually leaving the frustrated engineers to conclude it must be one of those glitches that never get fathomed.

As everything returned to apparent normality, Trojan Horse would invisibly receive and transmit the data she had requested, with nobody but Louise any the wiser. She'd fine-tuned the satellite's orbit to take it over the area that interested her, and requested high-definition visual images of a strip of land five miles wide and ten miles long. She'd also ordered up an infrared scan.

Cyclops would make its next pass over Britain within fifteen minutes, and she'd soon know if Trojan Horse had strutted its stuff. While she waited, she was doing some electronic breaking and entering to pass the time. The electoral roll for the target area was freely available, and provided some two hundred names, reflecting sparse population. Their criminal records had taken a little longer, but now she had them the result was disappointing. The worst crime any of them had been convicted of was causing death by dangerous driving. No obvious suspects there. Undeterred, she moved on to council tax records and the Land Registry databank, which might throw up something interesting on commercial properties.

The Three Musketeers might be dashing to the rescue of young Tom Lancaster, but wouldn't have a clue where to go. D'Artagnan already knew she could narrow their search for Liz Lancaster right down. But an address would be much more impressive.

Who dares wins. Gordon Holland shamelessly expropriated the SAS's famous motto, because in his case it couldn't be truer. Omega's Managing Director was euphoric. He'd turned a no-win situation around, and yesterday's angst was a fading memory. Soon, Omega Dynamic Systems would slot into the same category.

By using native wit and keeping his nerve, he'd neatly managed to give Conrad Lancaster what he wanted, whilst avoiding unfortunate personal repercussions.

Nobody could prove he was responsible for compromising Trojan Horse. All he'd done was zealously check Omega's security procedures and expose a serious flaw. They should thank him for shaking out the rotten apple.

He didn't feel guilty about the summary fate of Peter Clough. Omega's former Data Manager had himself to blame. If he'd stuck by the rules, Holland wouldn't have been able to touch the poor fool, much less accuse him and point to the door. But the weakling had caved in to pressure, offered up Trojan Horse and paid the price. The world was unforgiving, and only the fittest could expect to survive and prosper.

Gordon Holland liked reminding himself that he was not only a survivor, but would also prosper – someone who was about to secure well-deserved reward for decisive action on Conrad Lancaster's behalf. The great man had telephoned him at the office to express fulsome appreciation for the sort of loyalty that's a rare commodity. Holland was no fool. He hadn't believed the cock-and-bull story about the Americans wanting a sneak preview of Trojan Horse, but the real reason didn't concern him. That was Conrad Lancaster's business, and the value of his contribution to that business was about to be recognized.

Gordon Holland looked around the lofty drawing room, seeking a misaligned ornament or rogue speck of dust. Following an acrimonious divorce, he lived alone in the small Georgian country house near Marlborough, but kept his home immaculate. You could entertain the Queen here without a qualm, so Conrad Lancaster would hardly find fault. He should arrive at any minute, and Holland felt quickening anticipation. They'd be discussing a vacancy at the top of Lancaster Trust's management structure. A move to London. A salary with lots of noughts on the end. Share options. Proper appreciation of talent and ability. A job so important and confidential that Conrad was coming to *him*, in his own house, to explain the ramifications.

The waiting was over. He heard the sound of an advancing engine and crunching gravel. Gordon Holland straightened his tie in a Regency gilt mirror over the marble fireplace and hurried to the front door. He who dares wins. But it was a false alarm. The caller who waited at the bottom of shallow entrance steps was not Conrad Lancaster, but a short man with lank brown hair, pallid complexion and ludicrous Mexican moustache, who had arrived not by peacock-blue Bentley but red Ford van.

He looked at his unwanted visitor with exasperation. The last thing he needed was a doorstep confrontation with some cowboy determined to lop his trees, sell cut-price horse shit or tarmac his drive. How would *that* look when Conrad appeared? He glanced over the man's wide shoulder, but thankfully there was no sign of the limousine. Gordon Holland swerved his attention back to the intruder, intending to send him packing.

Decisive words died, strangled by incomprehension. This must be some terrible mistake, an insane prank. A gun had appeared by the man's side, dangling in his right hand. A pistol, with long silencer tube hanging from the muzzle. When his eyes reluctantly returned to the sallow face, he found his reaction being studied with interest. Gordon Holland decided to jump back inside, slam the heavy door in the face of this terrible threat. But couldn't move.

He looked helplessly towards the hidden road, this time praying that Conrad Lancaster's car *would* appear, an angel of mercy to rescue him from the nightmare. But apart from a blackbird that darted from one dense conifer to another with a shrill alarm call, the driveway remained devoid of life. Without saying a word, the man smiled and stepped forward.

London

COMPONENTS were meshing beautifully, apart from one stray fragment that threatened the mechanism's smooth functioning. No matter – a brilliant engineer was about to fix the problem. Conrad Lancaster studied the detailed report on Pandora's Box Productions, finalizing his attack. Carrot first, then stick. But the latter should be unnecessary. People were greedier than donkeys, and if the carrot was juicy enough they could rarely resist the temptation.

The witch Symes owned one-quarter of the company – probably her price for bringing a high-profile presenter and associated business opportunities into the company. But the majority shareholder – and no doubt the brains – was Wendy Lang. Her pen profile described a tough fifty-year-old TV pro who'd been around for ever, a respected producer and hard-nosed businesswoman. Pandora's Box Productions had few concrete assets, but did own a thriving television commercial production facility, together with a strong backlist and title to current programmes on various channels, including the irritating consumer show that was about to libel him.

Results for the last financial year, filed at Companies House, showed pre-tax profit of only £195,000 on turnover of £5.5 million – but that would be after the principals had extracted generous remuneration packages as salary rather than dividends – with glitzy celebrity Jenny Symes surely the anonymous director who took out £2.25 million. Wendy Lang might resent the younger, more attractive woman getting all the glory, and a more than fair share of the money.

On paper, the outfit was barely worth two million quid, but Conrad was prepared to do better. He picked up the phone, gave his PA Lang's number and told her to get hold of the majority shareholder and MD of Pandora's Box Productions. Fast. The sooner that vindictive *Guardian Angel* programme was swatted, the better for everyone. Except the bitch Symes. He'd take the greatest pleasure in smearing her reputation. He was still smiling when the telephone buzzed.

'Wendy Lang for you.'

'Put her through. Ms Lang? Conrad Lancaster.'

Conrad waited, used to the effect his name had on the recipients of his calls. Silence. He frowned, and was forced to continue – dripping assumed charm.

'Ms Lang, I *must* apologize for calling you out of the blue, but we've had our eye on your company for some time. An extremely well-run and successful business, by all accounts, for which they tell me the credit is entirely yours. I have a most interesting proposition . . .'

He let the bait lie, and this time was rewarded with a bite. A gravelly voice – the sort that smoked sixty cigarettes on a good day – expressed cautious interest.

'Which is?'

'You've heard on the grapevine that Lancaster Trust is planning a major expansion into terrestrial television. Please treat this in absolute confidence, Ms Lang, but we're on the point of announcing an agreed takeover of one of the larger ITV companies. I need a top professional to run my entire TV operation. I've tasked two of London's top head hunters, and their final lists have only one name in common. Yours. Of course, I could have let them make a preliminary approach in the normal way, but decided to handle this personally. I have a strong feeling we'll soon be forming a mutually beneficial working relationship.'

'And my company?'

Definitely interested. Conrad laughed.

'Oh, it's nothing compared to what you'll pick up in salary and share options from your package with Lancaster Trust, but I'm prepared to offer five million cash for your majority shareholding, paid offshore if you wish. I'm the sort of man in a hurry who'll settle for nothing but the best and is prepared to pay whatever it takes. As part of your enlarged brief you'll naturally continue to run Pandora's Box Productions, which will receive substantial investment and become a serious player in the production world, and I do mean serious. I want to make you the most powerful and influential woman in television, Ms Lang. As well as the richest.'

The deep voice didn't hesitate.

'Sounds . . . tempting. You do know we're about to do a programme on you, Mr Lancaster? A not-altogether-complimentary programme.'

'Really? Sticks and stones spring to mind. Besides, I don't suppose it's the sort of thing new friends will fall out over. Perhaps we should meet. There's a great deal to discuss and I very much want to action this immediately. Could you make dinner tonight – at the Ivy, say eight o'clock?'

'I'll clear my diary.'

'Excellent, Ms Lang. I can promise you won't regret this.'

'I'm sure I won't. This sounds like a most wonderful opportunity. Until this evening, then.'

Conrad Lancaster felt the thrill of the kill. Despite her well-controlled reaction to the biggest carrot she'd ever see, Lang's greed buds were popping. He replaced the phone, lifted it again.

'Doreen, get hold of David Abrahams and tell him to hold off on that Pandora's Box injunction. Something tells me recourse to law won't be necessary, after all.'

Problem solved for the price of a good dinner, without so much as a public murmur. Money and power really were an irresistible combination. It shouldn't be difficult to dizzy and disorientate Wendy Lang for long enough. The point about carrots was that they weren't meant to be eaten, but used to encourage obedient movement in the desired direction.

His agent-in-place was in a hurry, and the controller listened intently as Beasley's low voice updated him on developments.

'The Omega leak was down to Gordon Holland, the MD, but Trojan Horse is secure. The boy should be exchanged for a useless disk around noon. Assuming he's recovered, everything goes fluid. The plan's to track the kidnappers electronically in the hope of locating the mother. The MI5 man Tolley is keen to find out who's been after Trojan Horse, which has been agreed as a secondary objective.'

'Will you need support?'

'When the time comes. I don't suppose there's a cat in hell's of releasing Liz Lancaster without it, even if the hideout's found. And you'll want a quiet word with the kidnappers, to be sure of getting the full picture on their paymaster. But that waits until after the exchange.'

Beasley paused, perhaps for thought. The controller understood his agent's anxiety. This thing could so easily spin wildly out of control. He supportively filled the silence.

'I've got a team at instant readiness. Just say the word. Any progress on Conrad?'

'Not really. I don't understand why he sold out Trojan

Horse. Conrad wants his wife and kid back, but the best way to achieve that was to involve the authorities. Even if he's arrogant enough to assume his duplicity won't be discovered, why take the risk? He'd lose his business if this came out, and come out it will. Holland will finger him in a flash if the pressure goes on. Something stinks, but I don't know what.'

Catching Beasley's thought train, the controller asked a supplementary.

'If he was after cash or other advantage, there'd be no need to go through an elaborate kidnap charade, which definitely wouldn't be regarded as an acceptable excuse for betraying Trojan Horse. The kidnap must be genuine, so what's he playing at?'

'I wish I knew. There might be something on the surveillance tapes, but I'm stuck with the action down here in the West Country. Could you get them checked?'

'Details?'

'I obviously haven't been able to follow him, but car, home and office are all covered. One receiver under the Bentley, another in the boot of a blue Volkswagen Golf with a scratched driver's door. It's in the multistorey at Grosvenor Gate, across from Conrad's place. Spare key in a magnetic box under the offside rear wheel arch. The last's at Lancaster House, in the boiler room at the bottom of a box of refuse sacks. I got through a fire door, the one far left of the service area at the back of the building. Leads on to a staircase. Boiler room's third door on the right at the bottom. Nobody about after the maintenance crew pack up at six. Must go, it's all starting to happen.'

Beasley went, the urgency of his developing situation underlined by the absence of their ritual closing exchange. The controller wondered how the operation would work out. If this one blew apart, his professional reputation would be ruined.

Moscow

L IVING THERE must be living hell. Double glazing fashioned from recycled polythene sheeting and sticky tape did little to protect the occupants from the impact of percussive sound as big jets took off in howling procession, engines on full thrust, passing barely one hundred metres above the crumbling concrete residential block, built in the 1960s to house airport workers. There had been seven flight departures since he arrived, each as shattering as the last.

But the top-floor apartment had no occupants – at least no permanent ones – and Valery Filatov wondered again at the pervasive influence of Gregor Gorski. With living space rarer than hen's teeth in Moscow, the ex-KGB colonel had contrived to empty the very place needed to create an ideal – and secure – firing point. For now, ragged curtains were drawn, and the living room was lit by an unshaded bulb hanging from the sagging ceiling on two plaited, fabric-covered wires. It cast sickly illumination over tired furniture and carpeting made up of irregular pieces with varying colours and patterns, fitted together like a shoddy piece of modern art.

Three of his men were readying American Stinger ground-to-air missiles – one each – talking softly as they compared technical details. They were trained on the super-efficient foreign weapon, would make no mistakes. All wore surgical gloves, because there would be no opportunity to cleanse the apartment afterwards. The back-blast from three Stingers might do the job, but he couldn't take chances. Once this afternoon's deadly work was done, the Sons of Dudayev would vanish, and must never be linked to serving officers of the Russian Army.

Gregor Gorski had organized their escape. Within moments of the strike, an ambulance would arrive below to pick them up. As it sped back towards the city, siren shrieking, shock and confusion would blind security forces to the fact that it had reached and was already departing the crash site, almost before the last blazing debris of President Yelkin's personal Aeroflot jetliner hit the ground. Then they would disperse to their units, never to meet – or talk about – this terrible experience. To anyone.

Major Filatov rubbed his good eye, which watered with

tiredness and the effect of acrid cigarette smoke that hung in the air like fog on a winter afternoon. He tried not to think about the consequences of what they were about to do. Failed. The memory of those innocent victims – mangled and slaughtered on the Metro by his own hand – refused to fade. Probably never would. And soon there would be more.

However drastic, the political impact did not unduly trouble him. Reluctantly, as a patriot, he accepted that Mikhail Yelkin was no longer serving the nation's true interests, and had to be forcibly removed in favour of a more able leader. In that respect, he would do his soldier's duty. But the physical impact as the stricken plane descended from the skies like a devastating bomb was something else. That conflagration might make the subterranean carnage at Okhotny Ryad seem like a peaceful riverside picnic. The major had no close relatives, no nearest and dearest, but still believed in the greater family that was Russia. Yet now . . .

The portable radio in his overcoat pocket crackled, relaying indistinct speech. The coat was over a chair beside the door. Relieved by distraction from painful thought, he walked over and extracted the handset, pushing the transmit button.

'Falcon Leader, receiving. Over.'

Released it.

'Falcon Four. Special forces everywhere, but I've found a secure position with good eyeball. Refuelling is being completed. I won't make contact again, until confirming target's presence aboard the aircraft and reporting take-off. Out.'

'Message received. Out.'

Major Valery Filatov lowered the radio and looked at his men. Falcons One through Three were watching – aware of the gravity of their lethal undertaking, but willing to follow his lead without question. He spoke sharply.

'What are you waiting for? We have less than three hours and only get one chance. I want those Stingers checked and double-checked.'

Right or wrong, they'd come this far. There could be no turning back.

Bristol

TO BE SURE, James Lancaster had parked in the long approach to castle-like Templemeads Station twenty minutes early, driving Liz Lancaster's powerful black BMW convertible. The car should have made him feel closer to her, but didn't. Now the business had started in earnest, there was no room for sentiment. He waited patiently, always the hardest part, surrounded by his hidden armoury. Apart from a Browning automatic in a snug shoulder holster, concealed by his bulky red ski jacket, the weaponry was mostly electronic.

The hide briefcase that was talking to the GPS network sat beside him, hard at work. He knew, because he'd switched on the wafer-thin built-in nicad battery pack back at New Hall, given it five minutes and phoned the office. A cheerful Operations Director back in LA had informed him he was receiving a positional signal loud and clear from Sticksville – like right in the middle of Glewcesstershire, England. The case would transmit for around ninety-six hours until the power failed, and LA would relay the result via mobile phone.

Inside the briefcase, a short-range direction finder built into the Trojan Horse disk box was also transmitting. That signal was being monitored by the back-up team consisting of Tolley and gamekeeper Don Sykes. Using the New Hall Range Rover, they would be close by. James had weakened the home guard, to reassure young Tom with a familiar face when he was released. If he was released. For the same reason, Duncan Bernadelli was accompanying Omega security chief Sandy MacNaughton in the JetRanger, which should be sliding into a holding pattern, ready to be called in fast should the need arise.

The stage was set; he could do no more. But so far the last piece of equipment had failed to do its job. The mobile phone on James Lancaster's lap remained stubbornly silent.

He had reservations, but there was only one way out of this, and that was forward. Indeed, now the engagement had begun, Andrew Rosson was relieved to find that fear had fallen away. The professional poise needed to see him through this final phase had emerged from his past, as the ghost of Dmitry Travkin effortlessly took control.

He neither had the resources nor felt the need to check on James Lancaster. Nothing would go wrong, because Gregor Gorski had promised that the British authorities would be kept in ignorance. Lancaster should come alone, at worst followed by one or two private operatives. The opposition could risk nothing while Liz Lancaster remained in his hands. They might travel hopefully, but wouldn't find the woman through him.

Everything was set. From the Astra estate car, parked beyond the Industrial Museum on Princes Wharf, he could see the mafioso John with the boy, sitting on a bench across the harbour, in front of a modernistic circular office building. The bespectacled Russian's arm was around the lad's shoulder, fingers close to that fragile young neck. They looked for all the world like a devoted father and son. Tom was intelligent enough to support the illusion. It was in everyone's interest for him to co-operate. After all, he was about to be freed – and more significantly, his mother was not. Rosson had observed the bond between them, and didn't doubt that Tom would do everything possible to protect her from harm.

This wouldn't extend to concealing the fact that he'd arrived in Bristol by boat. Wasn't meant to. Despite Rosson's assurances to crew members George and John, there *was* a remote possibility that the operation was compromised. If so, the two Russians and their master's luxury cruiser were expendable. Should *Lara's Song* fail to escape downriver on the floodtide in the fading light of evening, he'd know the operation had been betrayed.

Of course, aware authorities might let the boat run free, in the hope of tracking her. In which case he wouldn't know. But Rosson was confident George could hug the coastline to avoid radar and use the boat's blistering speed to maximum advantage. The mafioso was an experienced ex-officer of naval special forces, who possessed the skill and experience to lose hunters in the night.

Time to stop speculating. He'd already entered James Lancaster's number into his phone, and depressed the send key. Digits scuttled off an illuminated display, and the connection was made. Rosson attacked even before Lancaster could speak, trying to throw him.

'You were told to come alone, Mr Lancaster. Why didn't you?'

The man was good, deciding to tell the truth – or part of the truth to conceal a bigger lie – without missing a beat.

'One back-up car containing two people who know the boy, that's all. I've never met Tom and we don't want to panic him. They won't interfere until the exchange is over and you're long gone.'

'Make sure they don't. Remember that explosive device around your half-brother's waist. It's in one of those tourist money belts with zipped pouch, and may be disarmed by disconnecting the battery. But by then, as you so rightly say, my entire team will be gone, including the watcher with his finger on the button. You have the merchandise?'

'Inside an unlocked tan leather briefcase. Rather a nice one, actually, but my old man can afford it. The material's on one optical disk in a protective box that also contains access codes.'

Rosson laughed, none too pleasantly.

'I very much hope you're offering the genuine article, Mr Lancaster. Should you try to trick me with substandard goods, I'm afraid your stepmother will suffer an extremely painful and lingering death. I'll see to it personally, after my men have exhausted her entertainment value.'

Lancaster didn't dignify that with an answer.

'Instructions?'

'You know Bristol well?'

'I have a map.'

'Open it. To the west of your present location at Templemeads you'll see Chatham Wharf on the Floating Harbour. Make your way to SS *Great Britain*, to the right of the marina above the area marked Albion Docks Boatyard. You can drive there in a few moments. Take the case and stand by the big ship's anchor outside the Maritime Heritage Centre. You'll be contacted. Got that?'

'Yes.'

'You're wearing a red coat?'

'Yes.'

'Then get moving, Mr Lancaster. Let's do this properly. We're professionals, and I'm sure we both want everything to go smoothly.'

Andrew Rosson hit the cut-off key. Adrenalin was pumping. This battle of wits and nerve was rather stimulating.

He'd briefed John Tolley on his conversation with the negotiator as Liz's BMW stopped and started on slow-moving streets. James Lancaster intended to do precisely what he was told, and confine countermeasures to a discreet advance by the Range Rover, which was somewhere close behind. He accelerated over the Prince Street swing-bridge, finally free of dense traffic, and spun the car round a mini-roundabout on to Cumberland Road with a frustration-venting screech of rubber. According to his map, the next right turn should bring him to a public carpark close to his destination. If it was his destination. The kidnappers might possibly send him on a telephone chase.

James proceeded along the river embankment and turned into Gasferry Road at a more sedate pace, drove down to the carpark and reversed into a space near the road, ready for rapid getaway. He didn't pay and display – something told him he wouldn't be there for long, and if the sky fell in Conrad could probably afford a fixed penalty. He slipped his phone into the red ski jacket's zipped side pocket, lifted out the briefcase and locked the car.

He walked over, stopped by the canted anchor and looked around. It wasn't hard to spot SS *Great Britain* – recovered from the Falklands and housed in the very dock where she was constructed in 1843. Towering masts and spars rising above a new red-brick heritage centre confirmed that the ship dated from a time when marine steam engines were too revolutionary to be trusted. But James couldn't identify any opposition, because the few strollers looked like tourists. But someone was out there. Two minutes later, his mobile sounded. The middle-class voice issued succinct orders, and James realized this was no halfway house.

'Walk beside the railway tracks, back towards the city. After four hundred yards there's an open-air café called Brunel's Buttery. Sit at one of the tables and wait until you're contacted.'

The line went dead. James picked up his case and hurried along the harbour. To his left, an assortment of craft were moored against the high wharf. To the right, defying *PARKING PROHIBITED IN THIS AREA* signs, vehicles were scattered around an open area that looked like a former rail yard. Most were vans, with a black cab and sprinkling of cars, and many were occupied – it was obviously a popular place to eat lunch overlooking the water. He reached the café, which was doing steady business with users of the unofficial carpark. Behind iron railings and beneath three scruffy trees, there were bench-seat tables. He bought a coffee and sat down. Immediately, his phone rang.

'So far, so good, Mr Lancaster. Look across the water. To the left of the round building, two people are sitting on a bench under a tree, to one side of a red lifebelt on a pole. A man and a boy, who's your half-brother. Wave to them. When my man sees your signal he'll have Tom wave back. I trust you can identify him at that distance, but understand two things. We have no desire to cheat you, and the exchange happens my way or not at all. Keep this line open.'

James looked past the mast of a moored yacht. Saw the two seated figures. Put down his briefcase, stood up and waved. The small one waved back. The tiny figure looked like Tom, though he'd only seen photographs. Instinct said yes. He lifted the phone.

'I see them.'

'Leave the case and return to your car. Don't look back. Drive round the harbour and pick Tom up. He'll be told to wait for you. My man will be gone, but won't be far away. If anything goes wrong, the boy's history, and the city council will be facing a very messy clean-up job.'

'The woman?'

'Released when the merchandise is authenticated, not before.'

'As you said, we're professionals, and can only operate

successfully if we play by certain rules. I hope for your sake you're not about to break them . . .'

'Don't use your phone in the next ten minutes. We're watching. Goodbye, Mr Lancaster.'

James pushed the briefcase under the table with his foot, looking around to make sure no helpful soul would rush after him to return the damn thing. Nobody was paying any attention. He started to walk, then broke into a run.

He'd been told what to watch for, what he must do. So when the man in a red coat had stood up and waved, Tom Lancaster waved back. Wildly, excitement pounded through him. Soon, he would be free. Could get help for his mother. Hard fingers had tightened on his shoulder.

'Enough.'

He'd stopped waving. His thin companion didn't frighten him, despite menacing round steel-framed glasses that flashed when they caught the light, and the sort of broken foreign accent baddies often had in action films. But he was someone to be obeyed. Over the water, the man in red turned and walked away, then started to run. Tom had seen him put down a small case, and kept watching. To his chagrin, he felt the bottom of the woollen bobble hat being rolled down to cover his eyes.

'I go now. You stay. Don't look, don't follow, don't move. They come, you go home.'

The heavy arm lifted from his shoulder and he sensed Igor standing up. At least, it might be Igor. When they'd fetched him from the tiny cabin, Tom caught the name in a mutter of conversation in a language he didn't understand. Was Igor walking away? Tom waited, then tore off the hat, expecting angry words or a blow. Nothing. He blinked in sunlight that danced on water. Glanced around. No Igor. Looked across in time to see a man stooping to retrieve the abandoned case. He recognized him. It was the leader, the one whose face he'd seen in a dimly lit corridor when they tried to escape.

The man hurried to a white estate car and drove away. Tom thought about what he could tell, what useful information he possessed. He'd arrived in a big cruiser, which had to be moored close by. He didn't know where, because they'd put the Manchester United bobble hat on his head and pulled it down to act as a blindfold. How did they know the Reds were his team? Then they'd lifted him through the cabin hatch and walked him along the deck – he counted fifteen short paces – before guiding him up a ladder. One in front, one behind.

Then a car, followed by a short drive. Hands had helped him out, fastened something round his waist beneath his quilted dark blue school anorak. The car went and Igor rolled up the hat with a short instruction to do as he was told – which was make the short walk to this bench, sit quietly and watch for a man in red across the water. They'd waited for perhaps twenty minutes before Tom spotted the red-jacketed figure jogging along the far wharfside, but hadn't been bored, or frightened. Taking in the busy harbour scene was too interesting.

There was more, but that would have to wait. Two people were running towards him, the man in red and someone he knew – Don Sykes, the gamekeeper from New Hall. Relief jolted through his body. Tom stood up, turned to face them. They stopped, breathing heavily. Don Sykes was smiling broadly, but the man in red looked down at him seriously. He had a nice face with kind eyes that crinkled at the corners. He extended a formal hand.

'I believe we're related. My name is James Lancaster.'

Tom took and shook shook the offered hand, replying with equal formality.

'Pleased to meet you. I'm Tom Lancaster. How d'you do? You must be my half-brother, sir. My mother's often spoken about you.'

'Nothing bad, I hope?'

'Oh no, nothing like that. Will she be all right?'

'Of course, but we'll need your help. Before that, can I ask a silly question – are you wearing some sort of special belt, by any chance?'

His new brother raised comical eyebrows, to show this wasn't important. Tom lifted his anorak to reveal a heavy denim belt around his waist, the sort he'd seen holiday-makers wearing in France to keep money safe.

'They put this on me.'

His new brother nodded, as though the revelation was not unexpected. He produced a knife and folded open the blade, which clicked into place.

'Okay, here's what we do. You stand still, I'll get rid of it.'

James grasped the belt with his left hand, then cut it free with an upward stroke of the knife, which must have been sharp, slicing cleanly. He stepped back, closed the knife and walked away. Don Sykes moved in close and put an arm around Tom's shoulders. James stopped at the water's edge, turned his back and fumbled with both hands. A moment later, he strode back – the severed belt in one hand, two large bars of chocolate in the other. He laughed.

'Parting gift for a brave young man. Come on, Tom Lancaster, let's get you home. Your dad's sent a helicopter. *Our* dad's sent a helicopter. He's been worried sick. I'll give him a call and tell him you're safe.'

Tom looked up. He didn't care about that.

'Can we start looking for my mum now? I can tell you things.'

'I'm relying on it. We'll go back to the car. You tell me what you know and I'll let you in on our plans.'

The statement bore no trace of the condescension adults so often used to brush him aside as though he didn't exist. His father would have handed over the chocolate and told him not to worry about things that didn't concern him. But James was different. Tom nodded agreement, resisting temptation to reach for his big brother's hand.

London

HE CRASHED down the phone with a violence that matched his mood. These goddam Americans would not be told. Lancaster Trust owned a major New York publishing house, and Conrad had just finished shouting violent obscenities at the CEO. The man was earning a massive salary, plus stratospheric stock options, yet had the bloody penny-pinching nerve to argue with Conrad's specific orders.

The Pope's autobiography was up for auction and Conrad meant to have world rights to the puerile pontifications at any price. But his cautious executive was claiming they'd lose money if the advance went over $30 million. Didn't the bloody fool understand such a coup would be cheap at any price, carrying the Lancaster name to exploitable corners of the world that hadn't even heard of Coca-Cola? Some people were too stupid for words, and the CEO was one of them.

Monica Cogswell buzzed through. As he lifted the phone, which miraculously still worked, Conrad eagerly anticipated the Yank's grovelling climb-down. The man had worked out how much he stood to drop personally and become rather less concerned about how much the publishing company would lose, which was neither here nor there in terms of Conrad's global strategy. But his PA had someone else on the line. At last.

'James Lancaster. Will you take the call?'

'Put him through. James, have you got Tom?'

'Safe and sound, standing right here beside me. Want a word?'

The voice was cool, but what the hell? James had done the business. Conrad never doubted the happy outcome, but there was always a chance things might go wrong.

'Yes.'

He heard James say 'It's your dad', then Tom's clear treble voice came on.

'Father?'

'Thank God you're safe. I've been so worried. Are you all right?'

'I'm fine, but what about my mum? They didn't let her go and she's still in that horrid place. They made me leave her.'

Conrad detected an edge of panic, and smoothly soothed.

'Don't you worry, Tom, your brother will deal with that. Just get home and try to forget this nightmare. I'll get there as soon as I can, and we'll talk about a new school. Somewhere safe. I'll never let this happen again, Tom, I promise. I've got a present for you. A radio-controlled Lancaster bomber with four engines and a six-foot wingspan. How about that? I had it specially made. You'll like that – a plane named after us. We'll have fun flying it together. I'll take the whole day off work tomorrow.'

He listened to silence, as Tom absorbed exciting news.

'Thank you, Father. James wants another word.'

A good boy, Tom. The phone changed hands again. Conrad started issuing orders before the awkward one could turn nasty.

'Get him back to New Hall. I'll get down there as soon as possible, but it won't be until late tonight. Important dinner date I can't skip. Let the boy stay up. He probably won't be able to sleep anyway. I've just told him there's a rather special present on the way.'

'And Liz?'

Conrad sighed.

'Those bastards have got what they wanted. It goes against the grain to roll over, but Tom's back, and Elizabeth will doubtless be released in due course. Trojan Horse has been a high price to pay, but I don't care what happens now. Let them throw the book at me. And you still think I don't care! Those two mean everything to me.'

'Really? We'd best hope you're right about Liz, then.'

The line went dead. He contemplated the telephone sorrowfully. Same old James. Conrad got up and walked out to Monica's work station. Ever alert, the immaculately groomed lady of a certain age looked up from her keyboard. He leaned over and planted a smacking kiss on the top of her bottle-brown head.

'I've just had some really wonderful news, and you're a darling. Now, get back to Cyrus in New York. That naughty man really must learn to do as he's told or we'll have to smack his bum.'

'Yes, Mr Lancaster.'

Monica reached for the phone. Conrad watched, with inordinate pleasure, as a slow flush climbed her wrinkled neck.

When he returned to his office, Wes Remington checked the highly figured cherry-wood cabinet that stood below a high window. His spare hand was carrying a sealed signal from Langley marked *EYES: HEAD OF STATION ONLY*. There'd been no need to fetch it himself, but even the most mundane activity meant temporary relief. Sitting on his butt waiting for the world to explode was a pain. Inside the cabinet, a steady red eye meant the recorder still awaited its call to duty. Until the tiny light started winking knowingly, Beasley hadn't touched base.

The CIA's London bureau chief wasn't stressed out by this sin of omission – his agent-for-hire worked alone, and had to spread his time thinly. On the last assignment, he'd feared Beasley might be dead, but the man had surfaced after three weeks of silence with a tough job convincingly completed. As he tore open the signal, Remington idly wondered what he could buy his wife for the upcoming wedding anniversary – their twentieth. Helen already had everything she wanted, except a good marriage and respectful kids, and it was too late to do much about any of that. Maybe she'd like nothing better than a divorce, but he honestly didn't know.

The signal was an extract from Langley's in-progress weekly digest of economic intelligence, coming ahead of time because anything to do with Conrad Lancaster carried his flag. Marital problems forgotten, he absorbed the brief print-out.

FLASH . . . STANDING INFORMATION REQUEST [CODE – REMINGTON/LS000948.CL] – LANCASTER, CONRAD [CHAIRMAN AND MD, LANCASTER TRUST, LONDON, ENGLAND]. UNCONFIRMED REPORT [COUNTRY SOURCE – MOSCOW, CIS] INDICATES LANCASTER TRUST ABOUT TO COMPLETE PREFERENTIAL PURCHASE OF LARGE STOCKHOLDING IN RUSSIA TELECOM AT FIRE-SALE PRICE [COMMERCIAL ESTIMATE – PURCHASE PRICE 50 PERCENT BELOW TRUE MARKET VALUE ON DEAL SAID TO BE WORTH IN EXCESS OF ONE BILLION DOLLARS US]. FULLY DETAILED EVALUATION AND RISK ANALYSIS TO FOLLOW INSIDE 48 HOURS.

Remington whistled. Bingo. Nothing proven, and it would be interesting to see Langley's final conclusions. But something slimy was crawling up the back of his neck, and that particular worm knew its stuff. Conrad Lancaster had made millions from Russian deals over the years. Nothing proven there, either, but strong suspicion the Ruskies always got plenty in return. So what might be worth a billion-dollar giveaway this time around?

He rubbed his chin thoughtfully, then reached for the phone. Good old Gus Churchill of MI5 was about to find out the Special Relationship was alive and kicking. Hard.

Bristol

JAMES LANCASTER liked the half-brother he'd just found, and temporarily lost. A lot. There were strong echoes of Liz in the finely drawn bone structure and proud head carriage. He was gutsy, too, though when asking after his mother a trembling bottom lip and pleading brown eyes had defied the effort to be brave. But Tom's face had set and he'd gone very quiet after speaking to Conrad. Good for him.

The Lancaster Trust JetRanger was winding up for take-off, engine note deepening to hammering intensity. The chopper would skip to the safety of New Hall, where it would remain on stand-by. Sandy MacNaughton and Duncan Bernadelli were aboard with Tom, and the Omega security chief was tasked with debriefing the boy, who was observant and could certainly provide invaluable information.

As they drove up from town, Tom hadn't stopped talking, words cascading out as he outlined the kidnap story. Said they'd been held in an old building by the sea. Told of their abortive escape attempt. Proudly explained the freeing of his mother's chain, showing blistered palms to prove it. Mentioned the big powerboat. Estimated sailing time to Bristol as five hours at 20 knots. Described the man who picked up the briefcase, and his white car. Pressed for details of the rescue plan. James had eventually stopped him, promising to catch up for a proper question-and-answer session soon. He wanted the boy out of harm's way, freeing him to concentrate on Liz.

The helicopter lifted, slowly at first. Tom waved from the window. James raised an arm as down-draught washed over him, tugging clothes and ruffling his hair.

Then suddenly the gold-and-black machine was rising fast, before tilting into forward flight. The pilot had set down on Durdham Down – a flat expanse of greensward out beyond Clifton. The landing was probably illegal, but the few pedestrians and dog-walkers who'd stopped to watch didn't seem to mind. Show over, they were already dispersing.

Phase One complete. Now for the difficult bit. As he walked back to the car, James called up John Tolley on the two-way radio, to say he was on his way. The MI5 man had good news and bad. He'd followed the bugged disk box, and was in Tyndall Avenue, close to a strong but static direction-finder signal. But according to Lancaster Security's LA office, the briefcase had gone out like a snuffed candle five minutes after the exchange – probably dumped in water. Their opponent was neither greedy, nor a fool.

Don Sykes had the BMW parked on a yellow line, beside an ugly concrete water tower that was only half concealed by a ring of dense conifers. James checked the map and gave directions. After linking up with John Tolley, the gamekeeper would drive back to New Hall to reinforce the garrison, while James led the raiding party.

This was embarrassingly easy. Inter-academic dialogue had been initiated by Moscow University, agreement had been cordially reached a week ago, and he was expected. Andrew Rosson stood in the reception area, waiting by a curved beech-wood reception desk for the unwitting traitor. And here he surely was, right on cue – youngish, shortish, broadish, unkempt beard, premature bald spot, brown cord jacket with leather elbow patches, twill trousers, scuffed suede slip-ons. Rosson extended his right hand.

'Dr Blanch? I'm Desmond Wild. I believe you've been expecting me?'

The computer scientist's grip was firm, but slightly moist. The visible portion of his face shone with innocent enthusiasm.

'Yes indeed, Mr Wild. Your son must be extremely gifted to have attracted the attention of Professor Shebarshin at Moscow University. A great man in my field, respected throughout the computer world, some say a genius. It'll be a privilege to be of assistance. You have the disk?'

'Indeed I do. Dominic was both surprised and flattered when the professor agreed to evaluate his work, but he certainly puts in enough effort. He's an only child, you know. Started reading at age two and could do complex mental arithmetic at three. But now he's a teenager his mother's always complaining she can hardly drag him away from that wretched machine for long enough to eat a square meal, and he has no interest whatsoever in pop music or girls. Though secretly I think she's as proud of him as I am. We're all most grateful for your help.'

Rosson was almost beginning to believe the Wild family existed. Dr Blanch obviously did, taking his arm and steering him towards the stairs.

'Let's go up. It really is no trouble, and ISDN is as safe a way as you'll find to get the data to Moscow. Perhaps as you're local, Dominic might think about pursuing his studies here at the university? Sounds like just the sort of chap we'd love to have in the department. I could certainly put in a good word.'

'Most kind. I'll tell him.'

They walked along a green-carpeted corridor, past a large room filled with dozens of terminals, all being used by students, and entered an office. Unlike the good doctor, the room was antiseptically tidy, an impressive array of desktop hardware occupying a work station along the window wall. The atmosphere was artificially chill. Blanch perched on a typist's chair and pulled himself close to a large screen. When he was settled, he held out his hand.

'This shouldn't take long. You can sit and watch me make the transfer.'

Rosson handed him the precious disk box. Blanch seemed impressed.

'Ah, a proper transit case. Most professional.'

He took it, frowned.

'Strange. They're usually heavier than this. Lead lining, to protect against accidental exposure to any unfriendly magnetic fields or other nasties that might damage the data. Still, let's see what we've got . . .'

Losing interest in the irrelevant digression, he opened

the box. An alarm bell rang in Rosson's mind, but he spoke calmly.

'Dominic said something about an access code you need to get into the disk.'

The paper was already in the computer scientist's hands. His response was positively ecstatic.

'This is *excellent*. A random six-number code. Not six-*digit*, six individual numbers between one and ninety-nine. Very sophisticated. Right, I'll just slip the disk into the appropriate drive. . .'

Rosson watched as Trojan Horse was readied to bolt from the stable. Dr Blanch clicked his mouse, and file names flowed on to the screen. From force of habit, he lectured as he went along.

'That's disk access completed. Note there are dozens of files making up the complete programme. Normally, each would have to be opened and prepared for ISDN transmission, but we've developed a block data transfer system. I simply batch these up and they're sent in one burst, sight unseen. No disrespect to your son, but I suspect Professor Shebarshin has an ulterior motive. I'm sure he's fascinated by Dominic's theoretical astronomical analysis software – in fact he said as much when he telephoned last week. But as we've recently published on our new system, I think he wants to see it in action. Killing two birds with one stone, eh? A real feather in the department's cap if the great professor *is* interested in our little innovation.'

'From one of the dead birds, presumably?'

Rosson was getting impatient. Anxious to be away. For Trojan Horse to be gone. The bearded academic peered up from his screen, puzzled.

'Sorry?'

'The feather in your cap. Never mind. Silly English teacher joke. As an arts man, I'm afraid I don't understand this technical stuff. Will Dominic's material take long to send?'

Blanch smiled, equanimity restored.

'There's well over a gigabyte of compressed data here. Our system provides for accelerated transfer, but we're still looking at the best part of five minutes. I'll just key the professor's ISDN number and I'm ready to send.'

Rosson took advantage of his host's preoccupation.

'In that case, if you wouldn't mind telling me where the nearest loo is . . .'

'Last door on the left before you get to the stairs. There, we have lift-off.'

He didn't look up. Didn't notice his new English teacher friend casually pick up the disk box before leaving. A minute later, safely locked behind the red door of a tiled cubicle, Rosson was staring at trouble. Once he knew where to look, it hadn't been so hard to find. With the help of his pocket knife, he'd prised off the outer cover of the disk box. No protective lead sheathing. Just a miniature transmitter, sitting in a custom-cut hole in a block of white polystyrene.

So much for Gregor Gorski's assurance that the fix had gone in, that there would be no interference with the operation. Rosson sat very still, aware that his heart was thumping uncomfortably. He took a deep breath. Exhaled slowly. Lifted the direction-finder from its bed and studied the tiny tracker thoughtfully. This changed everything.

John Tolley had followed the bugged disk box to a large, two-storey modern building at the top of humpbacked Tyndall Avenue. His was a watching brief. So he had parked opposite, in the private carpark of the university's H. H. Wills Physics Laboratory, and done what he spent so much of his life doing – sat impatiently in a bloody car waiting for something to happen.

Now something had. James Lancaster got out of the BMW convertible, slipped into the Range Rover's passenger seat and – before Tolley could do more than point out the redbrick target building – made a call to his office in LA, to thank them for their efforts in following the briefcase. It was interesting to note a slight American accent creeping into the hitherto very English voice. The chameleon turned to him with a boyish grin.

'Don't know why I bother. The place seems to run a hell of a lot better without me.'

Tolley doubted that, but it was good to see James Lancaster in more relaxed mood as he lounged back in the leather seat and started to review possibilities.

'I've been thinking about what the boy said, John. Brought to Bristol by boat. Doesn't make sense. A boat's too easy to identify, detain. They're either monumentally stupid or supremely confident, and nothing I've seen so far suggests the former.'

James Lancaster frowned, a study in pensive concentration. Tolley had information to impart, but decided to work this one through first.

'Suppose the boat's expendable? Could be hired or stolen, in which case it's probably been abandoned already. But why use it in the first place? Not ideal low-profile transport for a kidnap victim in this era of horseless carriages by the million. Okay, so maybe they want to see if anyone shows an unhealthy interest in the boat, as a way of establishing if we've gone official. As we'll have to, should we want to follow the boat. Then again . . .'

He stopped, his sensitive ear detecting the slightest pace and volume change in monotonous bleeping from the tracker unit concealed beneath a travel rug on the back seat. Tolley sat up, needlessly lowering his voice.

'Our disk's on the move, James.'

Two pairs of eyes focused on the redbrick building, which had a bookshop on the covered ground-floor walkway. James Lancaster relayed Tom's description of the kidnapper – quite tall, not old or young, short dark hair going grey, dimpled chin, brown eyes. Last seen wearing light-coloured trousers and dark jacket. Tolley started the engine. Signal strength picked up as half a dozen young people emerged from green doors, walking in a loose bunch. Four boys and two girls, one couple arm in arm. Students. No one remotely fitting the description. Turning towards St Michael's Hill. He got the Range Rover moving, in time to see the group split in the shadow of a tall incinerator chimney – loving couple turning right, the other four going left.

'Take the big bunch.'

James Lancaster, echoing his own thought. Wait for a break in traffic, then follow slowly along the narrow street. Signal strengthening. Right decision. Stopping and starting to avoid catching up. Past a church. Round a mini-roundabout. Across the crest of a hill and into Hampton Road, parking on the zig-zag lines of a pedestrian crossing to watch the kids. Dividing again, one – the black youngster with a sports bag over his shoulder – peeling off to the right. Start up and chase the threesome. Signal weakening. Wrong decision.

'It's the black kid.'

James Lancaster, echoing his own thought.

'I'll try to cut him off. It'll take too long to turn and go back.'

Hang a right. Waverley Road. Accelerate hard. Hang another right. St Ronan's Avenue. Stop at the junction with Ravenswood Road. A hissed observation from his left.

'There he is.'

And there he was, ambling past stone-built bow-fronted houses, lost in Walkman sound. Bleeping intensified. They'd got lucky, but something wasn't right.

'Looks like a kosher student to me. Our man must have sussed the bug, unloaded it. I say we take him. We need to know. Agreed?'

James Lancaster, echoing his own thought. Instant decision, with a wrong call jeopardizing the operation.

'Agreed.'

The two men came out of the Range Rover together, leaving it blocking the junction. Ran across Ravenswood Road. Confronted the target, who managed to look startled, frightened and angry in quick succession. Tolley produced his wallet and flapped ID, hoping the card wouldn't be scrutinized too closely. Spoke firmly but politely.

'Sorry to trouble you, sir, but we have reason to believe something may have been concealed in your bag, or about your person.'

Very Mr Plod. The black kid pulled off the headphones and pushed back his shoulders aggressively. Tolley heard the tinny pulse of abandoned music.

'What's this, man? You can't go hassling me on the street.'

James Lancaster stepped forward, made and held eye contact. After a moment, he reached for the tote bag and unzipped it, speaking authoritatively.

'Let me take a quick look and we'll be on our way.'

He didn't wait for permission, but the kid accepted the inevitable. James Lancaster had that effect on people. Nothing visible, so he ran a quick hand along the sides, pushing down beside packed sports kit. Came up with the tiny bug. Tolley almost laughed at the student's dismayed expression, but still managed to ask a straight question.

'You ever see this before?'

'No way, man!'

The denial was explosive, believable. Tolley nodded, asked a supplementary.

'Where have you just come from?'

'University computer centre, man. I got a crashed floppy and they helped me retrieve the data. Two weeks' work there.'

James Lancaster slipped the bug into his pocket and rezipped the bag, patting blue fabric apologetically.

'Thanks, you've been most helpful. Sincere apologies for bothering you.'

They returned to the car, leaving a face full of unasked questions behind. Tolley drove into Ravenswood Road and parked. He felt good. Professional instincts told him his primary goal – discovering the final destination of Trojan Horse – was within his grasp.

Beside him, James Lancaster was slumped in his seat – looking, for the first time since Tolley had met him, thoroughly depressed. Must be almost human, after all. He spoke wearily.

'There goes our last lead, John. God, I've really screwed this up.'

Tolley smiled, indecently enjoying the moment.

'Self-pity, in one so bold – or are we worrying about the lovely Mrs Lancaster? Panic you not. I didn't get the chance to tell you, but this should banish the blues. Louise Boss phoned. She's on her way to New Hall and has something for us. Told you she'd come good. Let's have a sniff round that computer centre, then belt back and see what the even lovelier Louise has uncovered.'

He turned the key, rammed into drive and jumped the Range Rover away from the kerb, causing a slow-moving Morris Minor to brake sharply.

Moscow

LIKE A HUNTER who has stalked a dangerous beast, Gregor Gorski was experiencing the thrill that comes in the instant before the trigger is pulled. If his arm held steady and his aim was true, the quarry was doomed, but didn't know it. That was true power.

His rightful place was not thirty kilometres away at Sheremetevo-2 Airport, where the Sons of Dudayev waited to perpetrate their final outrage, but at the House on the Embankment, beside the man who would be President – a man who'd caught the mood of the moment. General Sergei Sobchak stood at a window of the apartment's grand reception room and stared over the Moskva River, linked hands pushing downwards behind his back, squaring broad shoulders and ensuring that his head was held high. A word sprang to Gregor Gorski's mind, and that word was 'imperious'.

As a soldier, the general had fought many battles and knew men must sometimes die for the greater good of the greatest number. As Russia's best-loved politician, his painful duty was to ensure that President Mikhail Yelkin's reckless rape of Mother Russia was not only stopped, but also punished. And the next presidential election would be too late.

Gregor Gorski understood this zeal. The former paratroop commander was doing his duty, as he had been forced to do so many times before. Believed that he was a man of destiny in the right place at the right time. That he was doing this not for himself, but for the Russia he loved. That as for another general he greatly admired, Charles de Gaulle, suffering in the political wilderness was something to be endured until the call came to restore the fortunes of a great nation laid low by ill fortune and weak leaders. That the only correct way to deal with malignant cancer was to cut it out with clinical precision.

The ex-KGB colonel knew all this because Sobchak had told him often enough, and Gregor Gorski took no small pride in the fact he'd helped to shape and reinforce those messianic beliefs. He carried a cup of strong coffee across the high-ceilinged room and stood beside his general. The clouds were low and Moscow looked unclean in dull light. But the weather was not severe enough to prevent the imminent take-off of President Yelkin's aircraft from Sheremetevo-2. He spoke respectfully.

'All you have worked so hard to achieve will soon become possible.'

The man who would be President flashed him a sidelong glance, his expression one of distaste, like someone who has suddenly smelt something unpleasant on the bottom of his shoe.

'This gives me no pleasure, Colonel. None whatsoever. Your methods may perhaps be necessary in the interests of Russia, but they are not my methods.'

Gorski detected the beginnings of self-justification, the process of transferring dirt to another, more expendable pair of shoes.

'Your scruples do you credit, General. But it must be said that any sacrifice resulting in the removal of the traitor Yelkin and his replacement with a true man of destiny is both justified and a patriotic duty.'

For a moment, as unblinking pale blue eyes fastened on him, the manipulator feared he had gone too far. Then Sergei Sobchak nodded sharply and transferred his gaze back to the city that would soon be beneath his political heel. He agreed with every word.

They stood shoulder to shoulder in contemplative silence, eventually disturbed by the mobile telephone that never left Gregor Gorski's person. With a muttered apology, he stepped away before taking the call. He'd already heard from KGB sleeper Dmitry Travkin, who had become soft-living English bookseller Rosson. Trojan Horse was on the way. This would be his friend at Moscow University, the genius in matters of computer science, confirming its safe arrival.

Bristol

SOME THINGS were best left unsaid, especially to the man in Moscow. The fact that his operation had been compromised was one of them, so Andrew Rosson had reported only that Trojan Horse data had been secured and despatched according to plan. He felt tired, and apprehensive. He'd been too long away from the cutting edge to take this sort of pressure. Had too much to lose. Was beginning to feel like a man who has ignored warning signs and run boldly on to the beach, only to find himself sinking in quicksand.

However much he sought justification in the initial thrill of action or thoughts of how the money might be spent, neither explained why he was here. The truth was simpler – turning Gregor Gorski down had never been an option. Now, there was no easy way out. He would have to finish this, and use every fibre of his being to come out the other side with hope for the continuing future of an antiquarian book dealer from Hay-on-Wye and the family he loved.

As he trudged down Tyndall Avenue towards the Astra, parked at the bottom of the sloping street, Rosson reviewed shifting sand and tried to identify some firm ground. By planting the tracking device on the black student at the computer centre, he'd bought time to slip away unnoticed – hopefully breaking a trail that might otherwise have led to a quayside warehouse in North Devon.

Upon reflection, he decided James Lancaster was likely to be acting independently, using well-developed skills to try to find his stepmother's hiding place. If the authorities were involved, Rosson would have been taken by now. But he still saw a spectre. There would be little point trying to trace Liz Lancaster if genuine Trojan Horse data had been supplied. The deal was simple – when the software programme checked out, the woman would be released. Lancaster had the boy, and no reason to doubt their arrangement. So data obligingly fired off to Moscow by the gullible Dr Blanch probably wasn't worth the cost of an ISDN transfer.

He unlocked the Astra and got into the driving seat. Should Gregor Gorski be deprived of the cyberweapon he coveted so deeply and had planned so meticulously to acquire, Rosson's life wouldn't be worth living – assuming he was alive to try. If the British authorities identified him as a kidnapper and spy, his life wouldn't be worth living – assuming he was free to try. But then again, if everything went according to the original plan, he might yet return to his wife and children as though nothing more than a routine overseas book-buying trip had been occupying him.

Perhaps he was imagining difficulties and danger where none existed. Even now, Moscow could be rejoicing in the capture of a living, breathing Trojan Horse. In which case the tracking device might be no more than a prudent operator's fall-back position. Even if the Lancasters *were* cheating, there might be a straw of hope. At the very least, they must be sure a fraudulent Trojan Horse wouldn't be immediately identifiable, because without breathing space their chance of recovering the woman was nil. There was time – but how should he use it to best advantage?

After considering the options for what seemed like an age, but in reality was no more than five minutes, Andrew Rosson opened the Astra's glove compartment and took out the mobile phone reserved for one purpose alone – negotiating with James Lancaster.

They were ready for the off, each with his own prize. James Lancaster knew the face of his opponent, and MI5's John Tolley the source of the Trojan Horse attack. With the help of his security service card, it hadn't taken long to find the unworldly Dr Tristram Blanch. Elicit the touching story of a brilliant programming wizard from Bath and kind interest shown in his work by Russia's most eminent computer scientist. And discover the bearded academic's dark secret.

Despite promising to act only as a conduit, without prying into the material, he'd been unable to resist temptation. When the lad's father answered a lengthy call of nature, Dr Blanch had copied the entire contents of the disk, even as original data winged along the ISDN line to Moscow University. Nothing sinister – he hoped to attract the prodigy as a student, and wanted a sneak preview of his capabilities. Remembering Louise Boss's briefing on the prolonged frustration awaiting anyone trying to unscramble her defences, James Lancaster had assured Blanch that this was no more than a routine enquiry, clapped him on the shoulder and wished him the best of luck with the wonder boy's programme.

John Tolley had been less amenable, warning of severe consequences should the Russian professor be appraised of their visit, demanding a description of 'Mr Wild' and being loftily informed that the computer department could do better than that. There were hidden security videocams, and doubtless the likeness of Mr Wild had been captured for posterity. It had, and further threatening use of Tolley's ID had secured the tapes. At a quick glance, they felt little doubt that the proud father of non-existent junior genius Dominic Wild and the kidnapper described by Tom Lancaster were one and the same. As they returned to the Range Rover, Tolley decided his prize fell short of the jackpot, gloomily explaining his reasoning.

'The fact it's Russia isn't enough, James. This Professor Shebarshin might be working for the mafia, government, or any competing faction therein. The situation over there's in turmoil, with political rivalries bubbling dangerously, Yelkin clinging to power at any cost, terrorism on the streets, new or reformed agencies intriguing for influence, faction fighting inside the ruling élite, a strong right-wing challenge from General Sobchak gathering steam. I need to know more.'

'At least they haven't got Trojan Horse, whoever they are.'

James answered automatically, more concerned about his next move than Tolley's problems. He had plenty of his own. Perhaps Louise Boss really had come up with something to put them back on track. They reached the car. He stepped towards the passenger side, and his mobile sounded. Tolley stopped, watching interrogatively. James found the phone, leaned against the Range Rover and answered brusquely.

'Yes?'

'I'm disappointed. You've haven't been practising what you preach. I seem to remember a smug little lecture about professionals playing by the rules. That tracking device represented foul play, Mr Lancaster. Well, you know those rules. Give me one good reason why my next call shouldn't result in the immediate termination of your stepmother, with extreme prejudice.'

The voice was angry. James Lancaster's instincts kicked in, and he replied almost without conscious thought.

'The reason is that you're making this call. If you didn't want something, she'd be dead.'

The tone moderated.

'Very perceptive. Might I be right in assuming that you supplied damaged goods, Mr Lancaster?'

Fencing for advantage. After a cut, always thrust.

'That's for me to know and you to find out. But you should be aware that I have excellent video pictures of a certain Mr Wild.'

'Ah, you located the helpful Dr Blanch. I rather hoped you'd follow that student for a while without taking precipitate action, supposing him to be a member of my team and wishing to conceal your duplicity. You took a gamble that seems to have paid off. But you're no nearer to finding Mrs Lancaster. Nor can you expect me to leave the country through regular channels, so your pictures hardly represent a threat.'

A neat parry. But there was a way through his guard.

'But if we assume for the sake of argument that you fail to deliver certain merchandise, what might await you at journey's end?'

The voice laughed.

'That's for me to know and you to find out. I think it would be wise for you to refrain from notifying the authorities about our engagement, if you haven't already done so. I hope not. Keep your phone close to hand. I may wish to talk again. For now I'll be generous, and spare your stepmother's life. There may even be a mutually advantageous way for you to recover her in one piece.'

Before James Lancaster could reply, his mobile went dead.

North Devon

SHE WOULD SURVIVE, because she had to know. The second and final gas cylinder had expired, the lamp fading even as she willed it to last for a few moments more. The globe of light had died with a pop, leaving her lost in darkness musty with the decaying odour of this forsaken place. She strained until silence reverberated in her ears, but heard nothing but her own shallow breathing. The torch still worked, though its beam seemed weaker each time she flicked the switch to check, which she did with increasing frequency.

Liz Lancaster sat in a patio chair, sleeping bag wrapped around her in a vain attempt to banish icy chill that was stealthily invading her numb body. She was aware of the cold, but felt no pain. Her mind had floated free, through thick stone walls to the world outside. Perhaps the sun was shining, offering light and warmth. Or rain might be falling, so she could turn her face to the sky and feel stinging drops hitting her face, drenching hair and soaking clothes.

Somewhere, her son was waiting. She hoped he was free to experience the sun and rain of a life yet to be lived, and wanted to be there, helping him along the way. Liz remembered her plea, repeated endlessly in the night as Tom slept beside her – *Spare him and take me, spare him and take me, spare him and take me*. Now he was gone, and there was no way of knowing if he was alive or dead. Yet she was tempting fate by asking for more – *First spare him, then spare me*.

She had thought about James Lancaster a lot over the years, wondering what sort of person he'd become, whether his great escape had paid off, if he ever considered what might have been. Then, such mind games were no more than sentimental speculation. But now it mattered. After all this time, did he care enough to move heaven and earth to save her son? To try to save her? Or was he indifferent, consumed by her treacherous defection to the father he hated?

Liz wanted tears to come, to flow unchecked and ease the pain of uncertainty. But they wouldn't. Dry-eyed, she stared at the darkness, and a revised plea began drumming in her mind. *Spare Tom, and let me know he's safe. Spare Tom, and let me know he's safe. Spare Tom, and let me know he's safe*. Then do with me as you will.

London

THERE WOULD BE a ferocious inquest, but Conrad Lancaster would have nothing to be ashamed of, or hide – and be able to prove it. Before leaving Lancaster House for the afternoon, he had instructed his duty PA to prepare Gordon Holland's new contract. The Omega MD was to be rewarded with a substantial promotion, for exemplary performance in bringing in the vital Trojan Horse project on time and under budget. When it emerged that the odious little man had conspired with James Lancaster to steal the cyberweapon – and disappeared without trace – the worst accusation anyone could level against Conrad was trusting two individuals who turned out to be deeply flawed. Poor personnel management was hardly a criminal offence.

The blue Bentley turned into Upper Brook Street and stopped in front of his imposing house. The chauffeur made dignified progress to the rear door, ignoring impatient traffic backing up in the narrow street. With the sixth sense possessed by natural-born butlers, Aitken had divined his arrival, and as Conrad stepped to the pavement his front door opened. He swept up the steps, past the manservant and up the grand staircase.

Before he showered and shaved in anticipation of his dinner date with the soon-to-be-bamboozled majority shareholder of Pandora's Box Productions, there was business to be done – confidential business best transacted away from the office. Conrad walked into the big first-floor drawing room and subsided on to his favourite velvet sofa, which audibly protested before accommodating his ample shape. A tap at the double doors indicated Aitken's arrival. The butler knew the form, gliding in with a silver tray bearing a decanter and cut-glass snifter. He set the brandy on a low mahogany coffee table within easy reach, poured a large measure and withdrew silently.

With a grunt of effort, Conrad leaned forward and picked up the glass, swirling aromatic liquid. A toast was in order. He raised the brandy and addressed his oldest friend and constant drinking companion.

'To Konrad Lankovitz, and all who sail in him.'

The Lancaster was Anglo-Saxon packaging. In private, he occasionally liked to remember who he really was. It had been a close-run thing, but Conrad never doubted that he would sail through the storm and emerge into bright sunshine. As always. Besides, there was no excitement without risk, no stimulation without danger, no satisfaction in victory unless bloodied and defeated enemies were left strewn about the battlefield. And this would be his greatest triumph.

He drank deeply, set down the empty glass and took his mobile from the briefcase at his feet. He knew the number by heart – not that he had one. Conrad was pleased by the thought. Weakness and sentiment were for losers. Three thousand miles away, in Moscow, another phone with a ruthless owner was located. Answered.

'*Da?*'

Conrad recognized the expressionless voice. He talked elliptically, in case this innocent business conversation was being monitored. At either end.

'Your consignment has arrived?'

'Arrived, but not yet gone through quality control.'

The Russian switched to near-perfect English. None too subtly, Conrad charged towards the true purpose of his call.

'You need have no worries on the quality side, none at all. I've double-checked, and guarantee the goods are genuine. Which just leaves two small matters outstanding.'

Gregor Gorski refused to be hurried, or respond to Conrad's unseemly eagerness. Instead, he asked a pedantic question.

'You have received the package we released in turn?'

Conrad brushed that aside. Tom had never been at risk.

'Yes, yes, safely picked up. Now, what about the rest?'

Gorski relented.

'Your unwanted goods will be dealt with as agreed. Tonight. I too have surplus goods, so everything can be cleared up together and disposed of at sea. With regard to signature of our next business agreement, the arrival of today's consignment should make important people very grateful, so I foresee no problems, providing the commission arrangement we discussed is in place.'

Conrad had heard what he wanted to hear. Elizabeth was history, and the life-saving Russia Telecom deal was solid. He became indignant.

'No need to insult my integrity. Have I ever let you down in all the time we've done business together? No, and I'm not about to start now.'

He ended the call. Relieved in spite of instinctive bravado, Conrad refilled his brandy glass. There was always a chance those tricky Russian bastards would renege on the telecoms end once they had Trojan Horse. But their cut would be worth billions of untraceable dollars over time, and there was nothing people liked better than wolfing down their cake before returning for unlimited further helpings. Greed never failed him. The deal would stick.

He raised his glass, and drank deeply in salute of humankind's avaricious nature – another example of which would soon be turned to advantage, as he dazzled and disorientated Wendy Lang with the promise of the pay-day of a lifetime. So much for the irritating threat posed by self-important TV journalist Jenny Symes.

In this instance, neutral ground was the Serpentine Gallery in Kensington Gardens. Wes Remington wasn't big on modern art, but the newly refurbished building offered refuge from a sharp breeze. Considering the lecture he'd received last time they met, the CIA man was enjoying this encounter with MI5's Angus Churchill. Murmuring 'I told you so', albeit in more subtle words, was undeniably satisfying. As was the elegant Englishman's perceptible tension, evidenced in tiny signs like clipped speech and claw-like grip on the cane handle of his umbrella.

Teatime visitors were thin on the ground. The two intelligence chiefs paused, apparently lost in admiration of a canvas that looked to Remington's jaundiced eye like a tortured mass of multicoloured, regurgitated spaghetti. When a group of chattering Japanese tourists moved on, they resumed discussion of Trojan Horse. The MI5 man was in self-justification mode.

'We've had grave suspicions for years, of course. The

Conrad Lancaster file would be a foot thick if we still kept paper records. But despite our efforts, we were never able to secure conclusive proof that he ever dealt with Soviet intelligence agencies. Lancaster's a clever man with highly placed contacts in many countries. Then the Berlin Wall came down, our budgets were slashed and he was put on the back burner, along with dozens of other undesirables. Nobody seems to care any more, Wesley.'

There was a plaintive note in Churchill's upper-class voice. He'd read the flash signal from Langley and drawn his own conclusion, which mirrored Remington's. Conrad Lancaster had sold out Trojan Horse in return for a lucrative slice of the Russia Telecom sale, at a bargain basement price. The Englishman continued sourly.

'Had a call from Special Branch down in Wiltshire just before I came out. Apparently some chap called Gordon Holland's just been terminated. Professional hit. Single shot to the head. He was Managing Director of Omega Dynamic Systems, proprietor Conrad Lancaster, and by strange coincidence developer of Trojan Horse. You don't have to be a sodding genius to see there's a connection.'

The American needled a little.

'So what happened to all that sanctimonious crap you gave me on the phone? Phrases like "good old Wesley persuades MI5 to jump on one of our biggest businessmen" and "screwing a deal that could be worth billions in foreign earnings to this country" spring to mind.'

Though he couldn't bring himself to apologize, Churchill managed to look abashed.

'Bad day at the office. The Joint Intelligence Committee officially hauled Five off Trojan Horse, which got right up my nose. One of the other agencies must have an op running, probably based on an agent in place. Military Intelligence. So you can at least rest assured that Trojan Horse is secure and Lancaster's under the microscope. No doubt we'll all be put in the picture eventually, when it's all over. Anyway, thanks for sharing the Langley signal, which may help me to win back a few points somewhere along the line. Nobody could have blamed you for freezing me out.'

After bitterness, gratitude. And in gratitude, indiscretion.

Wes Remington clapped his dejected opposite number's shoulder, feeling almost guilty that he'd held back so much more. But to tell everything would have been to reveal the existence of Beasley, his own agent in place. And Angus Churchill would have forgotten self-pity and turned on his transatlantic cousin like a rabid pit bull terrier.

They parted outside the gallery. Churchill hurried off towards Rotten Row, furled umbrella jabbing the ground at every step. Remington watched him go, before turning to cross the lake and wander back across Hyde Park to the embassy in Grosvenor Square. So Military Intelligence had an agent in place, did they? Remington found that *very* interesting.

Gloucestershire

THEY HAD SPENT the drive from Bristol discussing options. John Tolley's counter-intelligence objective was partially achieved, with their discovery that the covert operation targeting Trojan Horse originated in Russia. Just *where* in that troubled country remained to be seen, but the MI5 man had refrained from speculation. Instead, he'd applied his lively mind to the problem of recovering Liz Lancaster, for which James was grateful.

Without back-up, they had reluctantly decided to let the kidnappers' boat go. Initiating proper surveillance would be a slow business and they didn't have time to define the problem to the authorities, let alone explain their unofficial actions to date. There was also the negotiator's enigmatic phone call, which might lead somewhere. But their best hope remained Louise Boss and the promised revelations awaiting them at New Hall – revelations that would not be long delayed.

The two men fell silent as James Lancaster drove round and parked the Range Rover in the stable yard. Almost before they were out of the car, Tom burst from the kitchen door and dashed across the cobbles. He stopped, chest heaving, face alive with excitement.

'James, James. Louise has found out where Mum is.

It's by the sea. I tried to give you a clue on the tape by touching the salt. Guess what. Louise used some satellite pictures! I've seen them. I was on that boat for five hours before Bristol. I counted. The distance is just right – we worked it out. Can you get Mum back now, or do we call the police?'

The outburst ended on an expectant note. Uninhibited enthusiasm was infectious. James smiled.

'We'll talk about that, Tom, decide what's best.'

He ruffled his half-brother's hair, which felt soft and smelled of shampoo. He'd changed out of school uniform, into jeans and T-shirt. James detected the hand of Rita Bernadelli. No doubt the housekeeper had disguised her profound relief at Tom's return in a flurry of practical mothering, including a hot bath and clean clothes, along with the mandatory massive meal – a procedure well remembered from James's own childhood.

'Come on, let's go in and let Louise tell us for herself.'

He dropped a hand on to the boy's shoulder, feeling real affection for the lively youngster. If nothing else good came of this, Tom was safe. He wished there was some way of telling Liz that. John Tolley fell in on the other side, and together the three men walked to the house.

Conrad Lancaster's life-sized portrait looked sternly down as five co-conspirators trooped into the library. After updating Sandy MacNaughton and Louise Boss over coffee in the kitchen, they'd moved upstairs for Louise's big moment. Tom accompanied them, stuck to James's side like a Siamese twin. John Tolley managed a similar impersonation with regard to Louise.

The animated programmer had the floor – or, more accurately, the long table that dominated the centre of the room. She fetched half a dozen heavy volumes from serried shelves and used them to weigh down two lengthy print-out sheets to stop them rerolling. Her audience crowded round as she explained their significance, sparkling with the enthusiasm of a job well done.

First, she'd tracked calls made from the negotiator's dedicated mobile phone, and he had indeed stayed away from home base. She had logged two different locations in Herefordshire, probably of little significance. But the ploy of persuading him to leave the phone on stand-by had paid a better dividend. The orientation signal had eventually come to rest on or near the North Devon coast. Signal strength within the transmission cell had been weak, allowing her to narrow the location to a strip some one mile wide and five miles long.

It wasn't enough. Despite sparse population, there were seventy-odd houses within the block, without counting farm and industrial buildings. So Louise had sought further information. Working through the night, she successfully deployed Trojan Horse on its first 'live' mission, covertly reprogramming the latest US spy satellite, Cyclops, to cover the target area. She waited until the bird made its first daylight pass, then extracted the revealing print-outs.

At that point, Louise couldn't resist a promotional puff for her baby, giving a droll description of the American controllers' puzzlement – then dismay and despair – as *their* high-tech baby malfunctioned. The mystery would never be solved, and they would have no idea what Cyclops had been up to whilst AWOL. She was a skilled mimic, and laughter broke the tension.

One print-out was a glossy topographical photograph of the relevant strip, of such high definition that it was possible to make out individual farm animals. The second made no sense at first glance – a mass of contrasting colours printed on a transparent sheet. Tom was in on the secret, and fidgeted with anticipation as Louise performed her magic trick, laying the second print-out on top of the first, carefully positioning them to correspond. She let him explain.

'The top one's an infrared scan, so the red bits show a heat source. It's a way of telling where there are people and things like hot engines or central heating.'

Louise resumed the story.

'Infrared couldn't help if Tom and his mother were being held in a private house, but there was a possibility the kidnappers might be using a barn or redundant building. I ran a cross-check and came up with seventeen non-residential locations that were giving an unexpected heat signature, which is about as far as these print-outs could take me . . .'

Tom could contain himself no longer, bouncing on the spot as he butted in.

'Could have been animals inside or anything, so that's where I helped out. When Louise got here I told her about the boat, and the stone building we were kept in and being by the sea and everything. So we worked it out, where Mum is.'

'True. You have a genius for a brother, James . . .'

Removing the infrared overlay, Louise reached for a magnifying glass and laid it on the photograph.

'Only one waterside location fitted. There were several possibilities, mostly in settlements like Hartland Quay. This place is an isolated warehouse beside a cove, see, right there against the cliff? The other building's a boat shed. According to local authority records, the warehouse hasn't been used for years, but gave off a heat signature. I'd say we have a ninety per cent certain target.'

Sandy MacNaughton was the first with congratulations.

'Good work, Louise. And Tom.'

John Tolley went one better, flinging an arm around her shoulders and squeezing hard. She didn't look displeased. James Lancaster leaned forward and studied the magnified image, automatically noting the warehouse's superb defensive position. Louise freed herself and addressed her young helper.

'Tom, go downstairs and ask Mrs Bernadelli to make some coffee. Wait in the kitchen until we come down.'

Tom Lancaster pulled a face. But she'd obviously made a big impression, and he reluctantly did as bid. When the boy had gone, her smile faded.

'I'm sorry, but there's more . . .'

Somehow, James Lancaster knew that – whatever it might be – Louise's announcement wouldn't come as a total surprise.

As they settled themselves on leather-seated library chairs around the big table, she watched James Lancaster closely. He was hard to read, but in the short time since they'd met he had indicated a certain antipathy towards his father. Louise Boss decided to continue. Before she could do so, Sandy MacNaughton's expressive Scottish voice broke into her thoughts.

'I'm glad you sent him away, Louise. I didn't want to say anything while he was around, but I had a call just before you lads got back. My office with bad news. Gordon Holland was murdered at his home this morning. All the hallmarks of a professional hit. One shot to the head. It was a chance discovery and the killer probably intended to remove the body. Holland was made to kneel on a rug in the hallway before he was shot. But his part-time gardener turned up, saw the killer's van and knocked on the front door out of curiosity. Nobody answered, so he went to get the ride-on mower. Later, he noticed the van had gone, looked through the letterbox and the rest, as they say, is history. When we're through here I'll dash over to try and calm things down at Omega. Official hell will break loose, but I'll do what I can to keep them off your backs for as long as possible, if that's what you want.'

Louise felt shocked. For all their differences, this was the last thing she would have wished on the pompous executive. Hers was a world of numbers in the head, not bullets. But the men had been there before. John Tolley came in crisply from her right.

'Do that, Sandy. See what you can find out and let us know. There's a connection, but we need more information. Meanwhile, I'll switch off my mobile. I'm surprised Gus Churchill hasn't already demanded to know why I let it happen, though of course he has been warned off. What were you going to say, Louise?'

She cleared her throat, startled by the professionals' apparently casual acceptance of brutal murder. But all three were looking at her, so she went on.

'Well, it doesn't seem like much after a show-stopper like that, but here goes. Tom helped confirm the warehouse was where they were held, but I'd actually more or less decided that anyway. After analysing the Cyclops material, I spent the rest of the morning peeking into various databases, obvious stuff like local records. Nothing on sixteen of my hot infrared prospects, but the seventeenth was different.'

Louise paused, still unsure of James's likely reaction. He prompted helpfully.

'Our quayside warehouse?'

She nodded gratefully.

'The local authority received a planning application five years ago. Conversion to holiday flats. Eventually turned down because the local building inspector's report was unfavourable. Apparently there's a damp problem, because the back of the building is set against a cliff, but more seriously it's solid rock down there, which prevents the installation of septic tanks for a sewage system. Planning application refused. But guess who was responsible for putting that application in?'

Moment of truth. James responded without surprise.

'Might the name Conrad Lancaster feature somewhere?'

So much for fears that he wouldn't want to hear what she had to say. Louise flashed him a smile and continued more confidently.

'Next best thing. Planning permission was sought by the quarry company that originally used the warehouse to grade and ship cut stone. The quarry shut down decades ago, but the company still exists. Owns the original quarry workings, now flooded and used for water sports, plus three rows of former workers' cottages that *have* been converted for holiday letting . . . and our abandoned warehouse. That company is a wholly owned subsidiary of Lancaster Trust. Coincidence, or what?'

Silence, as the others digested implications. She swept them with a glance. But they were pros all right, revealing nothing as suspicious minds calculated at lightning speed. Sandy MacNaughton reacted with an angry question.

'Hell's bells. You understand what this means?'

All four of them understood only too well. John Tolley answered, simultaneously convinced and disbelieving.

'The enemy within. So Conrad Lancaster organized the kidnap of his own wife and child. But *why*? If he just wanted to sell out Trojan Horse for money, there was no need to go through this elaborate rigmarole, or subject his family to a terrible ordeal.'

That had puzzled Louise, too. But not James Lancaster. He looked down at the polished table, then spoke softly, so she had to strain to hear.

'I'd started to wonder myself, and none of this shocks me. You good people probably think you know my father. Ruthless businessman, never beaten in a deal, not averse to cutting corners or bending rules. What you see is what he is, right? But he's worse than that. Conrad's more than capable of putting his wife and child through hell. The question we should be asking is what's in it for him.'

He paused, staring at his father's portrait as though seeking the answer there. Louise sensed this wasn't easy for James, but was fascinated by a glimpse of the man behind the mask. So, by the look of them, were Tolley and MacNaughton. James continued, his voice monotonous.

'Father's never forgiven me for walking away from him. I used to go out with Liz, a long time ago. He knew I'd come running if she was in danger, and could have done this for the simple pleasure of making me dance to his tune. Or to punish her, if they have a bad marriage. Sounds bizarre, but believe me when I say nothing's beyond that twisted mind.'

Louise found the proposition hard to accept.

'Surely not. Maybe the ownership of that warehouse is a coincidence, or someone chose it deliberately to implicate him. We can't even prove it was Conrad who persuaded Gordon Holland to steal Trojan Horse.'

MacNaughton added sceptical weight.

'Doesn't add up, James. Assuming your father *did* get Trojan Horse from Holland, he could easily have passed it on without anyone knowing. Later, we discover the opposition has acquired the weapon, but by then the leak could have come from various sources. Very hard to prove Conrad's complicity at that stage, especially with Holland conveniently eliminated. And this can hardly be a cover story. Trading Trojan Horse for a kidnapped wife and child wouldn't be any sort of defence in law.'

James Lancaster shrugged helplessly, for once uncertain of himself.

'I agree, this makes no sense. But I know Conrad. There *must* be an explanation, if only we could see it.'

They sat in silence, collectively willing a logical answer to appear out of apparent illogicality. Without success.

John Tolley eventually restarted the conversation.

'Sandy's right. Now Holland's not around to confirm or deny Conrad's involvement, what connects him to the theft of Trojan Horse? Nothing but supposition. So why this gratuitous kidnap nonsense?'

James Lancaster stood up, wandered across polished parquet and stood with his back to Conrad's portrait.

'Let's play Just Suppose. Suppose Conrad Lancaster's family are kidnapped. He's a high-profile tycoon who loves them dearly, with an estranged son called James who hates him because his girl once fell for lovable old Conrad and married him. But Conrad will do anything to get his family back. James has proven expertise in such matters, so Conrad begs for help. Despite the fact he hates both his father and fickle ex-girlfriend, James races six thousand miles to the rescue. The grateful if gullible parent entrusts negotiations to the expert, offering to pay as much cash money as it takes to secure the safe release of his loved ones. With me so far?'

They were. James Lancaster's expression communicated controlled anger, but his unhurried voice remained almost conversational.

'Okay, so the expert tells his father not to contact the authorities on pain of certain death for the victims, and takes it upon himself to deal with everything. To deflect those authorities should they wonder why such an expert had suddenly appeared, James suggests a cover story. Something believable, like a security check on one of dear old Daddy's high-tech companies. Crazed with anxiety, Conrad agrees without a second thought. James makes an apparently token visit to Omega, then tells Daddy he's done a deal with the kidnappers. The ransom is a painful two million, in cash, but the distraught father doesn't hesitate for an instant . . .'

He wandered to the window and looked out over New Hall's tranquil park, arranging his thoughts. Riveted by the unfolding narrative, nobody interrupted. James turned from the window and started pacing the room, developing the scenario as he walked.

'Joy upon joy! Rich tycoon's young son is released, followed by his adored wife, reuniting the happy family.

The expert has delivered, despite burning antipathy towards ex-moll and long-suffering father both. James is a hero, Conrad is happy, the authorities are informed. But wait. Joy turns to shock, horror. Trojan Horse is compromised, stolen from Omega. The amazing cyberweapon has gone, along with trusted employee Gordon Holland, who has extracted the highly classified files from yet another trusted employee and vanished, right under the nose of recommended-by-MI5 security chief Alexander MacNaughton and ace Five operative John Tolley. Hand on heart, the tycoon looks the world in the eye and sobs "Betrayed!". Now where do you suppose all that might leave the aforementioned embittered son?'

A rhetorical question but, to Louise's surprise, John Tolley answered anyway.

'In jail for fraud and stealing state secrets. But there could be an even worse ending. Suppose the tycoon is not only determined to humble and humiliate the estranged son, but has also fallen out of love with his wife. Suppose she's threatening to take him for millions and remove his young heir. Suppose there's a hit-man around who specializes in single bullets to the head. Now where do you suppose all that might leave the unwanted wife?'

Louise looked at his troubled face, and decided John Tolley was turning out to be full of surprises. As they all went quiet again, considering the startlingly ruthless twist, James Lancaster's mobile rang.

North Devon

DURING THE DRIVE from Bristol, fear had spurred Andrew Rosson. He'd sprinted down the motorway to Bridgwater, vainly trying to outrun chaos and uncertainty invading a hitherto orderly operation. His first instinct – to turn around and drive back to Hay-on-Wye, simply abandoning the whole mess to its fate – had to be suppressed. Retreat might buy precious days or weeks with his wife and children. But no more.

His video likeness had been captured at the computer centre. The woman and child had seen his face. He'd be traced and prosecuted for kidnap – with a few nasty extras under the Official Secrets Act thrown in to keep him in prison for ever. Should they somehow fail to find him, an angry man in Moscow would make sure they did. James Lancaster had virtually admitted to supplying false Trojan Horse data, which would enrage Gregor Gorski when he found out. The ex-KGB colonel was not the man to shrug off such failure.

By the time his white Astra estate left the M5 at Bridgwater and headed west along the coast road, Rosson had convinced himself he was trapped in a no-win situation. But then, like an antibiotic finding and attacking a virulent infection, the determination and resourcefulness that once marked him as a star KGB trainee had started to reassert. He'd slowed the car, reconsidering a gamble that involved leaping into the unknown. Perhaps it was the only way, the lone glimmer in gathering gloom.

After circumnavigating Barnstaple and setting course for Bideford, he'd pulled off the road. Decisively, Rosson opened the Astra's glove compartment and took out the phone reserved for one purpose alone – negotiating with James Lancaster. He hit redial, clearing doubt from his cluttered mind and deliberately relaxing his grip on the phone. For this great escape to stand any chance, he must show no weakness.

Gloucestershire

THE UNEXPECTED interruption stopped speculation in its tracks. James Lancaster reached for his phone, wondering if it was his errant father, somehow sensing suspicions being heaped on his head and instantly mounting a counter-attack. How typical that would be. He pushed the call pick-up button.

'Yes?'

'Mr Lancaster, remember me?'

Not Conrad, but a voice that had become familiar. The negotiator. James glanced at the others, who were watching intently. He offered them information in a neutral response that was neither aggressive nor welcoming.

'Ah, our friendly neighbourhood kidnapper. What d'you want this time?'

'I hope the boy is recovering from his ordeal. I'm sorry, I have children of my own.'

Even as the reply came, Louise Boss was snatching up her laptop and heading for the phone point in Conrad's study. Call-tracing. The negotiator had injected a human dimension, trying to build rapport. But James didn't reply. The man wanted something, and should be forced to declare himself. After the briefest of pauses, the caller continued.

'We're both professionals, Mr Lancaster, though chance has cast us as opponents. Professionals have standards, as we were saying earlier today. Please bear that in mind as you consider my proposition . . .'

'I'm listening.'

James was careful to sound neither curious nor eager. But the even voice continued confidently, as though some sort of unspoken agreement had been reached.

'I ask no more, Mr Lancaster. I've been considering our situation since last we spoke, and have formed the view that you supplied damaged goods. If this assumption is correct, you've placed me in an awkward position. My principals will not be pleased.'

'So?'

Neither encouraging nor discouraging. But a pitch was imminent.

'Should I report these suspicions, I will be ordered to dispose of your stepmother, as punishment for your disobedience. This will achieve nothing, but that's how it has to be. Perhaps your deception was designed to buy time, which you are using to discover Mrs Lancaster's location. This endeavour may even be successful. But you now know you'll be too late to find anything but a body. So agonizingly close to success, yet so tragically far from a happy outcome.'

Dark picture painted, the negotiator stopped. Moment of truth. James understood. The man was no longer negotiating for nameless principals, but on his own behalf. Time to nudge.

'We have your photograph. A witness in young Tom, who can both identify you and testify to your part in the kidnap. Why add a murder charge to the list? If you're trying to save your skin, spell out the terms.'

This one was cool, meeting James's attack humorously.

'Excellent technique. Pick your moment, then go for the jugular, at which point the trembling victim falls to his knees and begs for mercy. Unfortunately, life's not quite like that. But you're right, I *am* seeking an accommodation. I have something to give – the life of your stepmother, plus information regarding the attempt on Trojan Horse. How much might those things be worth?'

James considered the offer. Temporized.

'I'm in no position to make promises, but you can tell me what you're after.'

The negotiator had a shopping list.

'In return for the woman's life and information of great interest to your security services, I want immunity from prosecution on criminal and secrets charges, for myself and a colleague. Let me be honest. I have no wish to harm Elizabeth Lancaster, and will play no part in her murder. But there are complications. I have associates who are unpleasant people. If the Trojan Horse deception is discovered, they'll kill the woman without compunction. Me too, if they find out I've betrayed them.'

'Assuming such an arrangement can be agreed with the authorities, what guarantees will you require?'

Test question. If the answer was wrong, this conversation was pointless. James waited for the reply that would determine his response.

'Come on. We both know there can be no guarantees, Mr Lancaster. I doubt you've even informed the authorities of this situation. Even if you have, protracted discussion would be required to reach formal agreement. I'm in no position to bargain, so my offer of help is unconditional. As you said, I'm out to save my own skin, but my only insurance is what I alone know about this operation, which may or may not enable me to negotiate a satisfactory arrangement after the event. I'm in a tight corner, Mr Lancaster, and must take that chance. Well?'

Right answer. He looked at Tolley and MacNaughton,

who'd been following the one-sided conversation as best they could, waiting for the missing half with taut stillness.

'I must talk this through with my colleagues. I'll call you back.'

'Do that. There's very little time.'

'Give us five minutes.'

James Lancaster had not said 'me', but 'us'. As he put down the phone, the significance of his unconscious choice hit home. He'd always been a loner, learning early that trust leads only to the pain of disillusionment. Yet now he was feeling relief at the prospect of sharing this life-or-death decision with two men and a woman he barely knew. And trusting another he didn't know at all.

Moscow

HE HAD HEARD but not been able to see President Mikhail Yelkin's distant arrival. Sirens screaming, the presidential cavalcade had swept on to the tarmac at Sheremetevo-2 seven minutes ago and stopped beside the waiting Aeroflot jetliner. But Falcon Leader didn't need to see for himself, because Falcon Four was his eye on the ground. Unnoticed by swarming security police, the hidden observer had watched the unmistakable white-haired figure of President Yelkin emplane – followed by a sycophantic entourage of power-suckers and protected by an outward-facing fan of Presidential Guardsmen with raised rifles. Falcon Four had bravely lingered at his vantage point until the big plane started rolling along the taxiway – jumping the queue – in order to confirm that the next take-off would be the target.

And now, his last whispered report filed, Falcon Four would be breaking cover. Running. Hoping to avoid the attention of security forces who, with the President safely aboard his aircraft, would hopefully be relaxing. Trying to get as far away as possible before the doomed Ilyushin soared off the ground and into the sky . . . only to meet three fiery-tailed Stinger ground-to-air missiles coming the other way.

Major Valery Filatov set down the two-way radio, silently

wishing Falcon Four safe passage. He'd discharged his duty well, and the final act could be played without him. The one-eyed soldier looked around the gloomy top-floor apartment. Faces set, his men were ready to make their contribution to the future of Russia, the history of the world. Was this the determination that propelled Gavrilo Princip from the Sarajevo crowd in June 1914 to fire the shot that killed Archduke Franz Ferdinand? The tension felt by anonymous gunmen in November 1963 as they waited behind a picket fence above a grassy knoll in downtown Dallas? Did these and others like them ever think of turning and walking away, leaving deadly work undone?

For him, that possibility had passed in the blink of a tired eye, as he watched a mother with two youngsters, her arms attempting to shield them from the press of humanity in a crowded train halted at Okhotny Ryad. He could have reached out and touched their living warmth. Instead, he pressed the button that sentenced them to death. Filatov could see those faces still, and to allow them to have died in vain would be to insult their memory.

As he pulled ragged curtains aside and opened the crudely double-glazed window, stale cigarette smoke poured past him, sucked into the great outdoors and dissipated in an instant. They had all been smoking, but the last cigarettes had been extinguished, stamped out on jigsaw carpeting. The major felt a numbing sense of futility sweep through him, at the ephemeral nature of man and his sordid endeavours.

But this was no time to weaken. He draped a frayed rug over the sill to air, providing visual explanation for the open window, and checked below. There was no unusual activity around the decaying residential block. A dozen children were playing in the street, voices shrill as boys kicked a football and girls played tag. He knew the Ilyushin's forward momentum would carry blazing debris and the aircraft's falling body well clear, but still felt like leaning out of the window and shouting a warning. Instead, he signalled to his men, who lifted their Stingers.

They took up position with backs to the outside wall, lined up next to the window. The plan was simple. Major

Valery Filatov went to the back of the room, beside the door that led to kitchen and bedroom. There he would stand, watching the square of light that would soon be filled with the sound, then sight, of President Yelkin's plane. He would give the signal, then step through the door, closing it to protect himself from the back-blast of launching missiles.

As his men fired the three Stingers in quick succession – each stepping to the opposite side of the window after firing, clear of the next launch, he would go to the kitchen and pick up four AK-47 assault rifles, in case they had to fight their way out. It was unlikely. Security forces would be paralysed by the sheer scale of the disaster, and Gorski's promised ambulance would have whisked them away before order and discipline could be restored.

The major made eye contact with his men, one after the other. They were ready. Through the open window, the unmistakable sound of jet engines building to pre-take-off tempo carried clearly. The finest – and final – hour of the soon-to-vanish Sons of Dudayev was upon them.

As operations went, this should not be hard. According to his briefing, the last thing four traitors within the top-floor apartment should be thinking about was a sudden, savage attack from the rear. In consequence, the colonel of Spetsalnaya Naznacheniya chose only an élite ten-man anti-VIP squad, which had slipped unobtrusively into the building's rear entrance from a city maintenance truck, dressed like workmen and carrying their equipment in toolboxes and sacks.

An apartment on the ninth floor had been provided for their convenience, allowing the Spetsnaz unit to don their light body armour, helmets and black battle fatigues, unremarked by curious residents. Six of his men had sealed off the top floor. Three stood behind him, the Heckler & Koch MP5s beloved of special forces everywhere poised. Behind them was the last and most important member of his team – the cameraman. Modern battles were fought and won on the world's television screens.

The colonel slid open the cover of his digital watch. Since his graduation from higher airborne command school at Ryazan twenty years before, he'd seen action in many theatres, but none more important than this. They had wired charges to the flimsy door, in case it was bolted within, but either there was no bolt or the occupants were suffering from acute but misplaced over-confidence. The key he had been given turned in the lock, and he pushed the door fractionally ajar. No reaction from within.

Gripping his cocked MP5 lightly but firmly, he used the stubby barrel to push open the door, revealing a hallway. Empty. He recalled the floor plan. To the right, the open kitchen door assigned to one of his men. To the left, a closed bedroom door assigned to another. Ahead, the closed door of the main room, where the traitors would be. That had been reserved by the Spetsnaz colonel for himself, supported by one man and – incongruously – the videocam operator.

He stepped quietly forward across the hallway, a black shadow at his shoulder. The shadow depressed the door handle, and together they burst into the main room. Three men stood facing them, encumbered by bulky rocket launchers, lined up beside the open window like metal ducks at a shooting gallery. Almost before the traitors could react, a storm of controlled firing engulfed them, momentarily pinning them to the wall and filling the room with gunsmoke. Then they were falling in untidy unison, missile tubes thudding from dead hands to gaudy carpet. Three down.

The Colonel became aware of a presence to his left, shielded by the open door. He met the eye – just one – of a man who stood tall in shabby civilian clothes, arms dangling limply. His scarred face was calm, unfrightened – that of the soldier he was, who had seen enough violent death to last a lifetime and beyond. For a long moment, they stared at one another. Then Major Valery Filatov nodded sagely, as though to confirm that he understood and gave absolution. His nemesis understood too, raising the hot MP5 and shooting the traitor twice in the forehead.

Behind, in the doorway, the kneeling cameraman was capturing the action for posterity, watched by the two Spetsnaz troopers who had not been required to fire a shot. As the colonel spoke into his radio, the cameraman scuttled forward and rearranged the three corpses so the faces were visible, before resuming station. Through the open window, bellowing sound invaded the room, as a delayed take-off finally got under way.

The camera rolled, holding steady on the tangle of bloodied bodies and deadly rocket launchers. Then, as engine noise rose to a deafening crescendo, the cameraman panned to the window. Artistically framed in the last eddies of powder smoke, the presidential Ilyushin soared safely into the sky.

Gloucestershire

THEY KNEW where Liz was imprisoned, but couldn't be sure of reaching her in time. The negotiator's offer might keep her alive until the cavalry arrived, and was irresistible. After talking things through with the others, James Lancaster had called him back within the promised five minutes and reached agreement. The man wouldn't be talking to them if he wasn't desperate, so there was nothing to lose and everything to gain.

James had tested their new partner, demanding Liz's location as proof of good faith. Without hesitation, the remote quayside warehouse was described, confirming Louise Boss's inspired detective work. The deal was simple. To the best of his ability, he'd support a rescue attempt. Should the Trojan Horse deception be exposed before such an operation could be organized, he was the conduit through which a vengeful order to eliminate the hostage would be passed. He'd stall, not relaying the instruction to those who would kill Liz without hesitation. In return, John Tolley had promised to help the turncoat barter his sensitive information for freedom.

Tolley had reassuringly exaggerated his influence within MI5. But the negotiator must have understood that for him, too, there was nothing to lose and everything to gain. Having come so far, he could only hope the secrets in his head would prove sufficiently attractive to compel official interest. Apart from one co-conspirator he should be able to control, the negotiator had warned of four heavily armed hired guns who could not be influenced – one guarding the gate, one at the warehouse, two more due to arrive by boat from Bristol later. They were the watchful enemy, precluding any likelihood of being able to snatch Liz and run, though that remained an option.

Sandy MacNaughton had left for Omega in Louise's car to deal with complications arising from Gordon Holland's violent demise, and dampen acute anxiety that would be exploding in high places – on both sides of the Atlantic. The negotiator had pleaded ignorance when questioned about the executive's murder – but upon reflection, the man had admitted the hitherto unexplained absence of one gunman the previous day, which now started to make dangerous sense.

The task of initiating the official rescue operation had gone to John Tolley, who was taking off in the Lancaster Trust helicopter for London, where he would brief his people, liaising with James while the plan took shape. Tolley had earlier used Conrad's conference phone to speak with his superior, Angus Churchill, making them laugh with a gamut of insultingly comic expressions as he meekly answered a volley of impatient questions with the briefest possible explanations. Hopefully, security service wheels were already spinning faster than the chopper's accelerating rotor blades.

With Louise and Tom beside him, James watched as the JetRanger lifted off into gathering dusk. The pair had struck up an instant friendship, and Louise willingly agreed to stay at New Hall until the operation was concluded, providing Sandy MacNaughton fed her cats. She was listening with apparent interest to Tom's shouted explanation that the first primitive helicopter, called a gyroplane, had been built by a Frenchman whose name he couldn't remember back in 1921. Louise, suitably impressed, suggested they should go back to the library, hook up her laptop to the Internet and see what other fascinating aviation facts they could unearth.

Favourable first impressions of Tom were reinforced by his level-headed reaction to the latest developments. For someone whose first instinct was to ask a question, and his second to ask another, he had been remarkably restrained. James had decided to be as honest as possible. When he'd explained that Liz was in real danger, Tom merely nodded gravely – though a bitten bottom lip had betrayed the cost of this brave effort.

After the helicopter vanished, the three of them walked back to the house, as mechanical noise diminished and more gentle country sounds reasserted themselves. The calls of birds going to roost and distant tractors working until last light would soon be overwhelmed again, by the lusty bellow of a powerful motorcycle engine. James had nominated himself for the sharp end, and needed to race to North Devon for a covert rendezvous with the negotiator. He'd use the Honda Hornet abandoned by the kidnappers, the fastest available means of transport.

Louise and Tom went to fetch the satellite photograph and a large-scale map of the target area filched from the Ordnance Survey database. Duncan Bernadelli contributed a road atlas and leather gauntlets, plus the red ski jacket James had worn in Bristol. Its thermal insulation would provide welcome protection as he hurtled through chilly night air. Gamekeeper Don Sykes had provided lace-up calf boots that fitted well over two pairs of thick socks. James rummaged through the equipment flown in from LA, finding a lightweight black coverall that slipped neatly over his jeans and sweater. He selected several more items and finished packing the Hornet's twin pannier boxes. Last in were his mobile phone and a Browning pistol.

The big bike stood in the yard, muddied but unbowed by its ditch-bottom ordeal. A helmet had also been recovered and dried by Rita Bernadelli in her Aga's slow oven. A small crowd gathered in the stable yard. James Lancaster straddled the Honda and looked round anxious faces – Louise, Tom, two Bernadellis, Don Sykes – every one silently willing him to succeed. James pulled down the still-warm helmet's visor and started the bike.

London

BACK IN BUSINESS, and buzzing – that was the energizing reality that had transformed Angus

Churchill's day. John Tolley had delivered, spectacularly, and the head of MI5's K Branch was in his element. With Trojan Horse saved and valuable intelligence already gathered by his man Tolley, a satisfactory outcome was virtually guaranteed. So he could now afford to admit to constructive insubordination. Or to put it another way, brilliant initiative.

As of five minutes ago, John Tolley's sensitive mission had been officially sanctioned by him. He'd already informed the all-powerful Joint Intelligence Committee of developments, and an emergency session to discuss their collective response had been called. Churchill looked forward to discovering what Military Intelligence had been up to, and rubbing their brass noses in the fact that *his* agent not *theirs* had cracked this one.

Better still, he could point a firm finger of accusation at Moscow, and dangle the tempting prospect of a key opposition player who was ready to turn, revealing all about the operation to steal Trojan Horse. As if that weren't enough, he could also casually explain – thanks to Wes Remington's kind but indiscreet revelation about the Langley signal – the oft-suspected-but-never-brought-to-book Conrad Lancaster's motive for treachery. Churchill himself would never have revealed such a useful card to an opponent, even in the friendliest of games.

Cheerfully whistling 'Colonel Bogie' between his teeth, he reached for the phone. It seemed only fair to reassure dear old Wesley that everything was safely in hand, and remind him that the British security service still had teeth. No need to go over the top by displaying vulgar satisfaction. The message would speak for itself. All in all, this was turning into rather a good day for MI5 in general, and the prospective Sir Angus Churchill in particular.

His dinner date was late, but Conrad Lancaster didn't mind. He went to his table and ordered a large brandy for himself and a bottle of champagne for the MD and majority shareholder of Pandora's Box Productions. Wendy Lang was, after all, a woman of substance – a point she was making by keeping him waiting, even though he was promising to make her seriously rich.

Conrad sniffed his balloon glass appreciatively, but didn't drink. Deferred satisfaction only added to the pleasure. The woman could behave as she liked, but he'd have the last word. After stringing Wendy Lang along until her company's pathetic *Guardian Angel* exposé could no longer damage his interests, he would take exquisite pleasure in the moment of withdrawal. He'd invite her to another intimate meal, ostensibly to celebrate final completion of her deal of a lifetime, and break the bad news over dessert.

In the meantime, there were other good things to contemplate. With Trojan Horse safely delivered into Gregor Gorski's hands, Lancaster Trust's mouthwatering Russia Telecom deal was as good as in the bank. Another rabbit pulled from the hat, another triumph for the boy from Whitechapel who'd vowed to take on the neighbouring City of London and win. Would they never learn? As icing on the cake, he'd even settle a couple of old scores at the same time. Goodbye Elizabeth. Farewell James.

Then there was young Tom. Conrad promised himself he'd put in a real effort to get to know the boy, to mould and guide him. He'd made errors of judgment with Peter and James, and suffered for his mistakes. This time he'd get it right.

He was roused from his reverie by a stir that ran through the Ivy's knowledgeable patrons. It was early, but most of the fashionable restaurant's tables were occupied. The diners' attention had been captured by two new arrivals, who were undeniably striking. The taller one needed no introduction. In a dark red evening dress that left little to the imagination, Jenny Symes was surveying the room with the confidence of someone who is used to being the centre of attention. Beside her, in a black trouser suit, stood an immaculately presented older woman with a strong, square face beneath a glossy helmet of close-cut dark hair. Wendy Lang.

Conrad screwed up his eyes in disbelief, focusing on the unexpected manifestation. It didn't go away. What the hell was Symes doing here? That, at least, would soon be explained. The pair were making regal progress in his direction, and he quickly composed his face. They stopped beside his table, but made no attempt to sit down. Symes greeted him sweetly.

'Conrad, I don't think you've actually met my boss and senior partner, Wendy Lang?'

Before he could formulate a suitable reply, the older women chipped in, her deep voice containing melodious cadences of contempt.

'We're flattered by your more than generous offer to buy Pandora's Box Productions, of course. But on reflection we've decided not to accept.'

'We're very happy with things the way they are, Conrad.'

Symes again, with Lang following up almost before she'd finished speaking, producing a videocassette from her deep-cut jacket pocket.

'Rather flattering to know this tape is worth several million pounds to you, Mr Lancaster. But we've always prided ourselves on doing top-quality work. Even those notoriously difficult BBC lawyers were impressed, so this particular edition of *Guardian Angel* will be going out next Wednesday at seven. I know they do say all publicity's good publicity, but this will be the exception that disproves the rule. By all means run this past the eagle-eyed Lord Abrahams, though I'm afraid he won't be able to help this time. You'll find Jenny's not only got all the facts straight, but also evidence to prove them in any court you care to nominate.'

Wendy Lang laid the tape on the white tablecloth and stepped back. Conrad stared up venomously at the deadly double act, making no attempt to lower his voice.

'Bloody dykes. You just wait. When my tabloids have finished with your sordid sex life, you'll be sorry you were born.'

Unruffled by startled glances from neighbouring diners, Wendy Lang smiled pleasantly. Jenny Symes placed a slim hand on Wendy's well-tailored shoulder and leaned forward.

'What tabloids, Mr Lancaster? I have a friend in the City, a banker. I owe him a small favour, so I invited him to run his professional eye over that tape before we came here. I rather got the impression his bank will be selling every last Lancaster Trust share it holds first thing in the morning, and I don't suppose the rest will be far behind. Hugo's a dear boy, but so *indiscreet*, and you know how those bitchy bankers love to gossip. I'm afraid the only newspapers you'll control in future are the sort people use at night to keep warm on park benches. Sleep well.'

The two self-possessed women turned as one and strode from the restaurant, followed by every eye in the place. Conrad Lancaster drained his brandy in one gulp, dabbed his lips and savagely screwed up the napkin. As he threw it on to the table, he was already calculating new odds. This represented a serious setback, but every silver lining must have a cloud. Those slimy City slickers could dump every share they owned – the only pity was that he couldn't raise any more capital to buy, buy, buy. When news of his big Russian deal broke, they'd stampede back into Lancaster Trust like demented lemmings, and his offshore holdings would be a gold mine.

He breathed deeply, rage spent and equanimity restored. Never let the bastards grind you down. Conrad Lancaster waved an imperious hand, and a waiter materialized. He would dine alone, and dine in style.

Thinking fast, he finished noting down the co-ordinates supplied by the agent-for-hire known as Beasley, who was waiting patiently for his reaction. The Trojan Horse operation had gone critical, and there were difficult decisions to be made. The controller explained.

'We've just received an urgent summons from the Joint Intelligence Committee. Emergency meeting in one hour's time. Now the word's got back to Five they're not wasting a moment, but it'll still take time to agree on a rescue package and even longer to organize an effective response on the ground. Sounds like a job for SAS, but first the Committee has to grant authorization, and then proper surveillance has to be put in place ahead of any action. I very much doubt that they'll be ready to go in before tomorrow night.'

'Too long. The lid's ready to blow, I feel it. I'll get in as close as possible and do what I can, but without back-up things could get tricky. If we lose Liz Lancaster I'll never forgive myself, let alone you, you old bastard.'

For once, there was no trace of customary flippancy in his agent's taut response. The controller pondered his options, thinking aloud.

'Officially, my hands are tied until JIC makes a decision. Unofficially, I might be able to call in a favour or two. Leave it with me and I'll see what I can do.'

It was as good as a promise, and his agent-in-place was satisfied.

'Good. Remington?'

'CIA's the least of our worries right now. Beasley may have come to the end of his useful shelf life as far as the Americans are concerned. Whatever, we'll look after dear old Wes Remington.'

'Steady on. What about my money? I've only had advance expenses thus far, and I've bloody well earned the full fee on this job.'

The reply indicated restoration of Beasley's usual good humour. The controller fired back.

'Scrabbling around for small change, are we? Don't tell me you haven't paid the gas bill again. Shame on you. Look, keep Five posted on developments through John Tolley, and he'll let you know what JIC decide. Where are you now?'

'Sitting on a bloody Japanese motorcycle somewhere in darkest Somerset, freezing my bollocks off and trying to read a map by torchlight. Call me back inside the next thirty minutes if you've got anything helpful to say. After that I'll be going in and my phone will be off, so I'll just have to manage without you.'

The controller laughed.

'What's new? Be lucky, and be careful.'

'Not this time. We're talking caution to the winds here, old buddy, and I do mean all four of them.'

Ex-Captain James Lancaster ended the call before the controller could remonstrate. Colonel Robin Wesley of Military Intelligence looked at the phone with reluctant admiration, before using the keypad to punch a Hereford number.

Thank God there were still some people in the world who refused to accept that discretion was usually safer than valour.

Moscow

THE TIME had come, and gone. Long gone. General Sergei Sobchak was tense, pacing the high-ceilinged room anxiously. News of the atrocity at Sheremetevo should have broken by now, but the television set in one corner of the room stubbornly refused to relay good news. Every so often, he glanced across at his companion, as though tempted to seek reassurance. But for once Russia's most popular politician could find no words, prowling on in restless silence.

Ex-KGB colonel Gregor Gorski watched serenely from his customary post beside the coffee table, savouring the moment. Everything would go according to plan. Deferral merely added to the satisfaction of a job well done, to warming knowledge that *he* was responsible for removing every credible challenger for the presidency. He lit a French cigarette, noting that only two of next week's allocation remained in the blue packet. The wicked self-indulgence seemed justified.

Gorski looked at his mobile phone, which lay mute on the table-top. He'd been hoping for good news from Moscow University, but perhaps the professor of computer science who was also a genius had been carried away by excitement, as the arcane achievements of the West's cleverest military programmers unravelled before his very eyes. Or perhaps his tired work station had temporarily collapsed under the strain of unscrambling Trojan Horse. No matter. The professor would get there in the end, and the stolen cyberweapon would surely allow the *Rodina*'s ordained place in the family of nations to be fully restored.

He mashed the filtered Gitane in a saucer that already contained four white butts, but not before lighting his penultimate cigarette from the expiring stub and inhaling deeply. The nicotine overdose made him feel light-headed, but the feeling was appropriate. Not every day did one man managed to manipulate the future of a great nation.

The temptation to use his phone to check out events at Central Airport was almost irresistible, but Gorski resisted. Neither did he telephone the professor. Instead, there were loose ends to tie. He keyed a number and hit the call button. After a long moment, the phone beeped to confirm contact with a distant recipient, and the radiophone on the bridge of *Lara's Song* was answered. He had reached the senior operative of the four-man team generously loaned by his new partner from the Moscow underworld.

Gorski spoke in English, which the General did not understand – a move designed both to impress Sobchak and deny him awareness of the matter discussed. He did not expect problems at the British end, but still asked.

'You are safely out of Bristol, without interference from the authorities?'

'No sign boat is watched or followed. We get back to pick up others in two hours.'

The accented voice echoed around the ether. So Conrad Lancaster had delivered on his end of the bargain, and could be rewarded. Gorski imagined the cruiser slicing through sea – thrusting into ozone-fresh air and flying spray, imposing powerful will on turbulent wind and water. It was a heroic image of freedom he found rather attractive, though such pleasures were not for him. But he was not allowed to dwell. The spell was broken by a gruff question.

'Final orders are confirmed?'

Gregor Gorski moistened dry lips, and murmured into the mouthpiece.

'Yes. Kill Rosson and Hellis as soon as you arrive. And the woman. Then your mission is complete.'

The ex-KGB colonel ended the call. Glanced across at the man who would be President, who stopped his aimless perambulation and stared back. For a moment, General Sobchak looked uneasy, as though sensing some nameless horror. If only he knew.

As a man of destiny, he was sometimes forced to work with dubious material and make difficult decisions. General Sergei Sobchak might be a politician now, but never forgot he was a soldier first. Soldiers liked meeting and beating enemies in open combat through sheer determination and force of arms. There was something distasteful about Gregor Gorski, whose devious methodology left much to be desired. In truth, the man who would be President couldn't bring himself to like the man at all.

But such people were necessary and, in their own ways, he and Gorski were patriots, motivated only by Russia's best interests. To be fair, the fixer had delivered on his promises, pushing him to within a heartbeat of the presidency. Sobchak had little doubt that an election would be called following the death of President Yelkin, and with the government's two most powerful contenders preceding their leader to the grave, victory should be a formality.

Yet still, as he watched the spare figure at the coffee table, one hand playing with the mobile phone he'd just finished using for the umpteenth time – the man meeting his gaze with an expression bordering arrogance – Sergei Sobchak felt disturbed. As he soothed away this negative emotion with the thought that there would be no place for Gorski in his new administration, the room's double doors opened.

A man entered. The general's experienced eye identified the uniform, even before the awful implications struck home. He was a lieutenant-colonel in the feared Kremlin Regiment, formerly the KGB's Ninth Directorate. Their morale and loyalty to the President never faltered. Behind the officer stood six uniformed men, weapons in the ready position. There was no sign of the bodyguards who were sworn to protect Russia's most popular politician with their lives.

The interloper's eyes swept across to Gregor Gorski, who had risen abruptly to his feet. Returned to Sergei Sobchak, who stood as though paralysed, shocked into immobility. The officer spoke politely, his voice firm but unhurried.

'I must ask you both to accompany me. It will be better for everyone if this can be accomplished with dignity. I have no wish to humiliate either of you, but must insist.'

Sobchak heard his voice ask a blustering question.

'What is the meaning of this . . . this *outrage*?'

The lieutenant-colonel watched silently as Gregor Gorski walked over, stopped beside his master. Sobchak looked up at the taller man appealingly, as though the supreme manipulator could miraculously end this hallucination. Gorski shook his head, the lined face resigned.

'It's over, General. We have tried, but . . .'

The sad-faced ex-KGB colonel turned away from him and addressed their tormentor.

'Mikhail Yelkin?'

The officer smiled, irony ill concealing satisfaction.

'You will be pleased to hear that President Yelkin has survived a cowardly attack, out at Sheremetevo. The terrorists known as the Sons of Dudayev were responsible, but they are no more. Now, please, if you don't come willingly I must order my men to take you.'

The man who would not be President felt his shoulders slump, and shuffled forward obediently, walking like a tired old man. Gregor Gorski was right. It was over, and there could be no dignity in defeat.

North Devon

EVERYTHING WAS THE SAME, but seemed different. Despite driving at a snail's pace, Andrew Rosson eventually arrived at the track leading down to the quayside warehouse. He stopped the Astra and went to open the padlocked gate, leaving the headlamps on and the car door open. An irritating buzzer sounded, telling him about the lights, as if he didn't know. There was no one to hear – except Ringo, who drifted out of the darkness and watched silently, hand on a dangling machine-pistol.

Was it imagination, or did the squat Russian's attitude seem threatening? Since being told by James Lancaster of an Omega executive's murder, Rosson had entertained little doubt that cold-eyed Ringo was the killer. This awareness was unwelcome, with implications Rosson didn't like at all. Contrary to Gregor Gorski's assurances that he was in absolute command, the four mafiosi from Moscow must be operating to some hidden agenda. He even felt uncertain about Bill Hellis – who had, after all, casually suggested killing the woman and child merely to eliminate them as witnesses.

WITHIN THE WALLS

Ringo waved the Astra through and closed the gate. As the car bumped down the steep track, Rosson began to revise his plans. He'd said nothing to James Lancaster, but secretly hoped to smuggle the woman out while the others ate, slept or watched television. Now, he doubted that quietly vanishing into the night would be possible, especially as George and John would soon arrive back from Bristol on *Lara's Song*, adding more suspicious eyes to his difficulties.

He drove along the cobbled quay and turned into the boat shed. James Lancaster wouldn't be far behind, because they'd scheduled a meeting by the shed in half an hour. Rosson had warned him about the track-top sentry, and promised to check out the situation inside the warehouse before they met. If he should be delayed, Lancaster would wait.

Rosson stood on the quayside, listening to the slop and gurgle of water against the jetty. Further away, he could hear the ceaseless rumble of rolling Atlantic breakers crashing against unyielding cliffs, but here in this peaceful haven the sea had no power. On impulse, Rosson took out his phone and pressed the memory key that would connect him with his home, letting anticipation build as the connection was made. The lilting female voice that answered was Welsh, and unfamiliar, but like a fool he asked anyway.

'Cheryl?'

'Mrs Rosson's out. I'm the baby-sitter, but I can take a message.'

He was disappointed. Tried not to reveal the fact. Felt it necessary to explain.

'Oh. Well, just say her husband called. I'm away in Europe, on business. Are the kids still up?'

'I just put them down, ten minutes ago. I suppose I could always wake them.'

The unknown minder wasn't keen.

'No, don't do that. Tell my wife I should be home by the weekend, with any luck.'

With any luck was probably the understatement of the decade.

'Right you are. Goodbye, then.'

The girl hung up, doubtless hastening back to some TV show or spotty youth she resented being parted from. Andrew Rosson put the phone in his pocket, sucked a few more breaths of clean salt air and walked briskly towards the warehouse, the thin beam of a pencil torch lighting his way.

The sentry was good, but not good enough to hide for long from the penetrating gaze of night vision goggles – one of five items James Lancaster had taken from the Honda's pannier boxes after hiding the big bike in a stand of wind-bent trees a mile back. The other four were the Browning Hi Power automatic pistol plus spare ammunition clip, a sheathed heavy-bladed knife with one serrated edge, medium-sized Maglite focusing torch and mobile phone.

After locating the locked gate, he'd retreated, then pushed under a rusty chain-link fence where badger or fox had excavated a convenient run in sandy soil. James had wriggled towards the gate, settling beside a scrubby gorse bush and studying the eerie green tableau of trees and rock presented by the image-intensifying goggles. Below, the distant sound of surf never ceased. Close by, more moving water – a stream hastening to the sea. There was no moon, and darkness was total – no reflected light to pollute a blank sky, or distant but welcoming glow from some homestead window.

The sentry betrayed himself the moment he moved, parting from the black trunk of a gnarled oak, flexing wide shoulders to combat stiffness. A short man. Armed and presumed dangerous. Without the goggles, James would never have spotted him. With them, avoidance was easy. He slid backwards, then crawled down a grassy slope, angling towards the stony track at a point where it zigzagged round a rocky outcrop, out of the sentry's eye-line – even had he, too, been able to see in the dark. Ahead, startled rabbits fled his coming.

When he reached the outcrop, James stood up. Thanks to satellite photography, the terrain was familiar. He walked downhill, rubber-soled boots silent on springy trackside grass, stopping when the ground levelled and unmade track turned into uneven cobblestones. To the left, the warehouse loomed tall beneath the sheer rock face, sightless windows staring at him and faint strips of light leaking round the edges of large entrance doors. To his right, the enclosed harbour, a bottomless lake asserting its presence with a murmur of restless water. No motor cruiser. Ahead, iron quayside bollards leading towards the boat shed.

Nothing moved. James Lancaster took the Browning from the zipped thigh pocket of his black coveralls and stepped forward. There was time for a quick look round before his scheduled meeting with the negotiator.

Perhaps the impossible might be possible, after all. Everything seemed reassuringly normal. The generator still chugged monotonously, making sickly yellow light for the stone staircase and passageway. In the room they'd made their own, Paul was asleep, buried beneath blankets on a bottom bunk bed. Bill Hellis, can of beer in hand, was watching television.

The East Ender had shown little interest in Andrew Rosson's report of a successful exchange in Bristol, grunting 'Good, hope that means we soon get out of this bloody miserable dump' before returning to the evening news, which was throbbing with the excitement of a failed assassination attempt on Russia's President Mikhail Yelkin. Renegade right-wing soldier-politician General Sergei Sobchak had been taken into custody, and Rosson wondered if there was any connection between Moscow power struggles and his own unsuccessful attempt to steal Trojan Horse. Either way, Sobchak's predictable appointment with a firing squad was a stern reminder that failure could have terminal consequences.

Rosson briefly considered taking the initiative – simply going to the woman and trying to smuggle her out. But she might not be up to it, or if James Lancaster had not yet arrived, they might hit trouble, even should they get out of the building unseen. The features that gave the warehouse good defensive qualities also made it a trap, and Ringo was somewhere in the night, blocking the only escape route. Holding Bill Hellis and Paul at gunpoint wasn't a sound option, either. A gun might be all-powerful, but keeping two dangerous men at bay whilst trying to deal with a disorientated captive wasn't on. If there was time or opportunity to explain, Bill Hellis might be persuaded to co-operate. But there wasn't, and Rosson was unsure of his old KGB classmate's loyalties.

So he slipped a half-empty bag of white sugar into his coat pocket and grabbed one of the sawn-off shotguns, loading the weapon with two long red BB goose cartridges from a cardboard box of twenty-five. Rosson lifted the dangling padlock key from its nail. He could get through the prisoner's door, but not unlock her restraining chain. Paul must have those keys in his pocket. Never mind, he'd find a way. To avoid suspicion, he went to the table and picked up his blue balaclava helmet.

'I'll check out the woman. Did she make any trouble today?'

'Nah, she's lost it. Never said a word or ate a thing. Scared shitless, I reckon. Her gas lamp ran out and she was just sitting in the dark, staring at nothing. I changed the cylinder. God knows why, considering she belted me over the head with the last one.'

Hellis replied without looking up from the portable television. Maybe he was on a nostalgia trip, reliving his lost Russian youth, as he watched a fur-hatted reporter standing in Red Square, jabbering about President Yelkin's unblemished record as the world's greatest survivor. Rosson left them to it. As he walked along the corridor, he stuffed the balaclava into his pocket. The time for hiding his face was past.

He hoped Hellis was wrong. Liz Lancaster would need both physical strength and mental courage if this was to work out.

The rattle at the door roused her from restless sleep. She instantly looked at the iron ring Tom had freed, fearing that it might have become dislodged while she dozed. But the chain around her waist still trailed to the wall, and an ignorant eye would assume she remained firmly tethered. Liz Lancaster had received two previous visits during the course of an endless day, the second soon after her precious gas lamp had expired.

Mercifully, after leaving her unappetizing pasta lunch on the patio table, the stocky kidnapper had fetched a new cylinder. For a moment, she'd stared at the open door, feeling an overpowering urge to tear the chain from the wall and run. But Liz felt painfully stiff, and remembered what had happened last time. Almost before her body slumped in defeat, he was back with a light-giving blue cylinder. When the lamp was burning again, bringing reality and definition to her dark prison, he'd taken away congealed spaghetti, leaving her to brood. If only she could be sure Tom was safe, none of this would matter.

Her third visitor was the leader, carrying a gun but wearing no mask. Those pleasant bank-manager features carried no threat, but did communicate tension. He pushed the door shut, crossed the room and set his shotgun down on the green patio table, before kneeling in front of her and resting a hand on the cocooning sleeping bag. She felt his padded touch on her thigh and a jolt in her chest. He was the bringer of bad news.

'Tom?'

Liz hardly dared ask, but the question uttered itself. He shook his head, and she almost laughed at his attempt to clamp on a reassuring expression.

'Tom's fine. Your stepson collected him as arranged. He's fine, I promise.'

She wanted to believe him. Didn't. Felt weakling's tears prickle her eyes. Made an inane remark.

'He's not my stepson, he's *James*.'

The grip on her thigh tightened.

'Please listen, Mrs Lancaster. This is important. Tom's okay, and I've spoken to James. No time to explain, but we're going to try and get you out of here. Soon. It won't be easy. There are people who will try to stop us. You must be strong. We can't manage without your help.'

She stared at him blankly, distracted from the terrible certainty that Tom was dead.

'You've spoken to James?'

His expression became intense, but the voice contained nothing but persuasive reason.

'Look, he gave me a message for you. Something only

the two of you could know about, so you'd be sure I'm on your side. He said, "I hope you've still got Peter's ashes." Make any sense?'

Liz's mind went back to a grey day in Suffolk. To that angular crematorium. A lover hurting in body and mind. Another life reduced to the still-warm contents of a black marble urn. Conrad had never taken any interest in his son's last remains, and the urn reposed in an old carved oak chest in her bedroom at New Hall. She looked up, met without fear eyes that had once frightened her.

'What d'you want me to do?'

Relieved, he patted her thigh.

'Good girl. Sit tight, but be ready to go at a moment's notice. I'm going to meet James now, and if he agrees we'll try to get you out. I must lock the door in case one of the others checks. Keep the gun. It's loaded and the safety's off, so you just have to point and pull the trigger. But for God's sake be careful. The next person back through that door should be me or James. Move around, get your circulation going. You'll see Tom again soon. He's a good kid. I like him.'

He stood, spun on his heel and went out. Liz spoke softly, addressing the closing door.

'So do I.'

This might be a cruel deception designed to break her spirit, but hope flared. Liz kicked off the sleeping bag and got to her feet. After overcoming momentary unsteadiness, she touched the shotgun, then held out her hands to reviving warmth that rose from the hissing gas lamp. If Tom was alive, he was owed a visit to the Imperial War Museum, where they had a Sopwith something fighter aircraft on display. She'd promised.

By the night vision goggles' green light, he saw a smaller aperture within the warehouse's main entrance doors open and a figure emerge. Alone. A small torch blazed on and the man strode purposefully along the quayside. James Lancaster waited, concealed behind the boat shed's weathered stone wall. He held the Browning automatic loosely, harmlessly pointing at cloudy sky, though the pistol was cocked and his forefinger rested alongside the trigger. When the negotiator was almost upon him, James jumped from his hiding place.

'Put out the torch.'

The torch snapped off. The man stopped. After a last look round, James removed his bulky goggles. They stepped into the boat shed, which contained a white Astra estate car and a red Ford van. James switched on his Maglite and set it on the Astra's roof, pointing at the cobwebbed wall. After weighing the Browning in his hand, he put pistol beside torch. The negotiator watched, a slight smile on the sort of forty-plus face seen in a hundred suburban golf clubhouses any weekend. He extended his hand – not as a meaningless ritual of greeting, but in a return to the gesture's primitive origins. He was acknowledging the fact that James had disarmed himself.

'Mr Lancaster, we meet at last. I'm Andrew Rosson. At least, that's what they call me now.'

James shook the offered hand. Something – that damned reliance on first impressions again – encouraged him to be honest.

'You know I can't make any promises, Mr Rosson, even if you help me get Liz back?'

'Andrew, please. We don't need to go over that ground again, James. I've made my bed and will lie on it, even if it turns out to be in a prison cell, though hopefully things won't come to that. Have you talked to your people?'

Decision time. To trust, or not to trust?

'I have. Some high-powered meeting in London has just decided this place will be hit by the SAS tomorrow night. As to your deal, they're interested, but that's between you and them.'

Decision made. Rosson nodded impatiently, dismissing an uncertain future and returning to a more urgent present.

'Fair enough. Listen, there's an alternative. If we move fast, I think we can get her out now, and I think we should. I've just talked to her. She's not in the best of shape, but circumstances are favourable. There are only two men here, with another up by the gate. But two more are due back any time on *Lara's Song*, the boat we used in Bristol. They're trigger-happy Russian mafiosi, ex-soldiers and policemen. Not the sort to put up their hands and come quietly. With automatic rifles inside there's bound to be a fire fight if we wait, and casualties would be inevitable.'

James considered the options, realizing as he did so that he was accepting Andrew Rosson as a trustworthy comrade-in-arms, for better or for worse.

'What's the plan?'

'I brief you on the internal layout, then we go straight in. Liz is in a locked room on the first floor, at the back. No window. I can give you the key, but she's chained up. You'll have to deal with that. We can't use the main staircase, which would involve passing our guardroom. But there's a ladder at the other end of the building. You use that, while I go up the stairs and keep an eye on my two guys. You spirit her out the back way. I give you five minutes and follow. We meet by the track. The three of us vanish into the night. We can get out without running into the sentry?'

James patted the discarded NVGs.

'Oh yes. These magic goggles would let me navigate to the stars and back on a moonless night. But when the boat turns up the others will jump aboard and do their own vanishing act, once they realize what's happened.'

He didn't give a damn about anything but Liz Lancaster, but appreciated that awkward questions would be asked if they pre-empted a major official strike-and-rescue mission. Confirming his credibility – and commitment – Rosson came up with the right response.

'I'm the only one with any useful intelligence on the Trojan Horse operation, James. What's more important – netting small fry or Liz's safety?'

They looked at one another in the Maglite's fractured illumination, sharing a moment's awareness of everything that could go wrong. Then James reached for the Browning.

'Let's do it.'

He eased the throttles back, and *Lara's Song* almost lost steerage way. But his judgment was precise, and idling

1,200-horsepower MAN diesels generated just enough momentum to keep the big cruiser's sharp bow moving in the right direction, cutting through a steady swell being driven by a following wind towards dark cliffs that towered less than half a kilometre ahead. Passage through that narrow harbour entrance was tricky enough in daylight. By night, impalement on needle-point rocks was a very real danger.

But the former officer of Soviet amphibious special forces in the helmsman's seat on the high fly-bridge felt no fear, confident he would berth *Lara's Song* successfully. In his time, he'd teased infinitely worse craft into much trickier places, without the help of aids such as remote-controlled searchlight and bow thrusters. Besides, he dared not put so much as a scratch on the brand-new Squadron 65. His master in Moscow had invested a million pounds in this little toy, and would not be appeased by pitiful excuses about vicious cross-currents and roaring riptides.

Behind him, sitting in the open-air dining area, Igor was dutifully ignoring the generously stocked bar. They would need clear heads. Instead, he was sitting at the round table – oiling, checking and reloading their handguns. This part of the assignment was nearly over. Within fifteen minutes, they would rendezvous with their waiting compatriots. Shortly thereafter, two soft Englishmen and the woman hostage would be deader than Vladimir Ilyich Lenin, though rather less well preserved – and a bargain struck between powerful men in Moscow would have been fulfilled.

Then the four mafia soldiers would sail on to the South of France, where they were to be rewarded with a stay at the boss's Monaco apartment, before flying home, business class, loaded with perfume and *haute couture* for waiting wives. But first, they were all anticipating a libidinous week of wine, Frenchwomen and song. Who said crime didn't pay? The helmsman smiled and glanced down at the impressive array of glowing dials before him.

The decision to abandon Russia's ramshackle armed forces in favour of a more lucrative career had been inspired. One day, if he pursued his new line of work assiduously, he too might own a magnificent boat like this.

The unobtrusive route to Liz's cell was via an iron ladder clamped to the stone wall, going right up the building through square apertures cut in each floor. They had got into the warehouse without challenge, and stood at the foot of the main staircase. Their plan was straightforward. Rosson pointed towards the opposite end of the cavernous ground floor. James Lancaster pulled down his night vision goggles and gave a thumbs-up sign, before drifting away towards the distant ladder.

Rosson went up the stone staircase and stopped by the industrious Honda generator on the first landing. He peered round the corner, but the corridor was empty. He unscrewed the generator's fuel cap and poured in sugar. Within minutes, the four-stroke engine would sputter and die, its choked cylinder head ruined beyond repair. Meanwhile, James Lancaster would be getting into position at the far end of the corridor, waiting for concealing darkness to fall.

The Honda missed a beat and the lights dimmed. For a moment, its sturdy pulse seemed to recover, but remission was short-lived. With a final choking shudder, the engine stopped. Rosson stood in sudden darkness, listening to intense silence. The smell of burned sugar mingled with exhaust fumes was strong. He put on his torch and walked to the guardroom. Along the corridor, James Lancaster would be moving. Inside, Bill Hellis had just lit a gas lamp, and Paul was sitting on the edge of his bunk scratching tousled hair. Light reflected off a blued revolver on the pillow beside him, validating Rosson's earlier decision not to make a precipitate move. He stated the obvious.

'Bloody generator's packed up. Come and give me a hand, Bill, see if we can get the damn thing going again.'

Rosson turned to Paul.

'Make some coffee, will you?'

Unsuspiciously, the long-haired gunman stood up, went to the portable stove and shook the kettle.

He raised the heavy goggles. A thin line of light at the

bottom of the door told James Lancaster she wasn't in darkness, and he didn't want to confront her with a frightening Martian apparition. Especially as Liz had a gun. Voices carried to him, including Rosson's. He stood very still. Two people emerged into the corridor, thirty feet away, backlit by dancing torchlight. Went in the opposite direction without even looking his way.

He quietly unlocked the door and stepped through, pushing it shut behind him to prevent telltale gaslight spilling into the corridor. The sawn-off shotgun's twin muzzles were rock steady, pointing at his chest, the eyes behind them equally steely.

'Hello, Lizzie. Long time no see.'

'Jamie.'

Liz Lancaster lowered the gun. She was wearing a crumpled cream sweater and black slacks. Her hairstyle was different, a shorter cut, and the copper hair was tangled. The pale oval face was thinner, and dirt-smudged, but otherwise Liz wasn't so very different. He unsheathed his knife.

'Let's see if we can get that chain off you.'

He knelt in front of her and hooked his left hand under the double-wrapped chain at her waist. The links were light, but made of high-tensile steel. The padlock was small, but a top-quality brass Yale. Big problem. Liz laid a hand on his shoulder.

'Tom dug the ring out from the wall. It just pulls out.'

James went to the wall and took hold of the iron tether-ring. Close up, it was possible to see grainy paste packed between two courses of stone, around the anchor point. He pulled gently. She was right. The ring came free almost without resistance. He carried it back, the chain chinking as he went.

'I thought he was kidding. We'll have to wrap this round your waist to get it out of the way. Careful, we don't want to make more noise than we have to.'

She smiled spontaneously, and his heart went out to her.

'They don't keep women chained up in the States, then?'

He smiled back.

'Only at weekends.'

Liz stood up. He wound the chain around her waist. Four turns were enough. He tucked the ring through the last loop to leave both her hands free.

'There. Can you walk all right?'

'I'm a bit stiff, but I'll manage.'

'Okay, we're going out the back way. There's a ladder down to the ground floor. We can't use my torch, but I've got these see-in-the-dark goggles, so stick close. Ready?'

'Any chance of you carrying me?'

'Only if you don't mind getting shot by a gang of bloodthirsty Russians.'

Liz giggled. Nerves. Or courage.

'Thanks for the offer, but I'd rather walk, if it's all the same to you.'

James Lancaster took out the Browning, turned off the lamp and pulled down his goggles. He put his spare arm round Liz's shoulders, led her into the deserted corridor and padlocked the door.

Andrew Rosson had spun things out, to buy the escapees time enough, but was eventually forced to admit that restarting the generator was a lost cause. As Bill Hellis straightened, wiping oily hands on stained blue jeans, the door banged below. Surely James Lancaster would not be so careless? He wasn't. The voice that shouted up was that of George, unofficial leader of the four Russians.

'Anyone here? We're back.'

Damn. James and the woman wouldn't be clear yet. The two mariners clattered upstairs behind bright torchlight that slashed across condensation-glazed walls. The four of them met up on the landing. Rosson managed to force normality into his voice.

'Bloody generator's out. Safe journey?'

The one he called George stared at him, a challenging look on his saturnine face.

'Why would the journey not be safe?'

Rosson picked up negative vibrations, but he smiled easily.

'No reason. Kettle's on. I expect you two could do with a nice hot coffee.'

They walked to the guardroom in a loose group, Rosson leading the way. The three mafiosi greeted one another boisterously, with much handshaking and shoulder-slapping. Bill Hellis went to the stove, where the kettle was emitting a busy plume of steam. The Russians started talking among themselves, using the native language they believed neither Rosson nor Hellis understood.

Rosson's mind translated automatically. They were chattering about forthcoming fun of the lewdest sort, to be enjoyed after delivering *Lara's Song* to the South of France. Then he heard George say, with no change of tone, 'But first we must earn our corn – let's kill the Englishmen and the woman now and have done with it'. He caught Rosson's eye and smiled, as if to emphasize the inconsequential nature of the conversation.

For a paralysed instant, nothing seemed to move. Even as he reassuringly smiled back, Rosson glanced at Bill Hellis. He was making coffee, pouring boiling water into a line of mugs. The kettle stopped, and Rosson knew that Hellis had heard and understood. They might be a long way down the road from KGB training school, but deeply inculcated survival instincts hadn't gone away.

Paralysis dissolved. As he dived for the sawn-off shotgun propped against the wall, Rosson saw Bill Hellis swing his arm, sending the kettle flying towards Paul, the nearest Russian. Reacting fast, Paul swayed aside, simultaneously drawing the blued revolver from his waistband. As the kettle hit the wall, Hellis charged. Paul fired once before the heavy-set man hit him, and the pair of them went down in an awkward tangle of limbs. The other two Russians were taken by surprise.

Rosson rolled into a crouching position, shotgun levelled. George and John froze. He stood up. Paul extracted himself from beneath Bill Hellis's inert body, and Rosson jerked the shotgun in his direction.

'Don't try and pick up your gun.'

They looked at him angrily. It was only a matter of time before they did their sums. Three potential attackers. Two barrels. The thought of the shortened shotgun's fearsome destructive power at short range might frighten them, but Rosson knew something they didn't. His gun wasn't loaded. He quickly backed towards the door.

'Don't move, gentlemen. The first person who puts his nose outside will get it blown off.'

He shut the door and ran. They didn't believe him. As he reached the end of the corridor, a torch beam stabbed the darkness and a bullet smacked the stone wall in front of him. The sound of the gunshot reverberated in the empty building. Rosson dropped the useless shotgun and spun round the corner on to the landing, out of the line of fire, but was unlucky. He stumbled over a petrol can belonging to the murdered generator, almost falling. He regained balance in an instant and fled down the stone staircase, but the delay was decisive.

As Andrew Rosson reached the bottom step, torchlight pinned him and a giant fist punched his back, flinging him towards the door that meant freedom.

When the first shot was fired, James Lancaster had almost reached bottom. They had descended at Liz's pace, which was laborious. He snapped a terse 'Stay there' and jumped down the ladder's last two rungs, turning in time to witness the result of the second shot – a body catapulting forward from the staircase to fall by the double doors. Hard to be certain by green goggle-light, but he felt sure it was Andrew Rosson. The clothing matched.

James dragged out the Browning, snapped the slide and raised the heavy pistol in a two-handed marksman's stance, advancing two paces. Light flared in the goggles, and a figure came down the stairs, shining a torch on the fallen body. Now, there could be no doubt. Rosson was down. The figure raised a pistol. Before the coup de grâce could be administered, James fired – three groups of two shots each, almost too fast to be separated by human ear.

The figure staggered, then crumpled. At ninety feet by image-enhanced light, it was good shooting. A burst of automatic fire erupted from the top of the staircase – random shooting designed to put him on the defensive. Two rifle-carrying dark shapes hurtled down the stairs, hurdled the fallen bodies in unison. He fired twice, but they were gone through the doors. James waited for a moment to be sure they wouldn't shoot from the doorway. But there was no sign of movement, and he called Liz.

He sat her down with her back to the protective base of a cast-iron support pillar, then moved forward slowly, pistol in the ready position. Instinct told him the enemy had fled, but he wasn't about to take chances.

The two Englishmen were dead, and so was Igor – shot by an unknown assailant as he went to finish off Rosson. In theory, they should complete their mission by executing the woman. But the former officer of Soviet amphibious special forces had weighed other factors against such a dutiful course of action, with not much time to decide.

The deal hadn't included anyone shooting back, and he'd put himself inside the mind of his master in Moscow. Which would be preferable – getting his million-pound boat back in one piece, or losing *Lara's Song* thanks to loyal soldiers who perished in a possibly unsuccessful attempt to kill an insignificant woman, now presumably protected by at least one skilled and dangerous shooter? And then there was the question of his own life, which still promised much.

Whilst crouching at the top of the staircase, pondering the matter, he'd poked the Armalite AR-15 brought from the guardroom through metal balustrading and hosed the ground floor with thirty waspish 5.56mm rounds. Beside him, Konstantin awaited his lead, second Armalite in hand. Below, the glow of Igor's fallen torch had illuminated two huddled bodies, obstructing their passage to the small door that opened outwards, and stood invitingly ajar.

Some decisions aren't so very hard. After changing the Armalite's box magazine, he'd touched Konstantin's forearm, pointed towards the door and held up three fingers to indicate timing. Konstantin had nodded understandingly. In sequence, he'd held up the same three fingers – one, two, three. At three, they'd hurtled down the wide stone staircase as one, leaping over still bodies and bursting into clean night air. Shots were fired, but neither of them was touched.

They'd scooted across slick cobblestones and reached

Lara's Song without incident. Now, with engines running and Konstantin waiting to cast off the stern mooring rope, the big cruiser's bow was lazily drifting away from the quay, turning towards the harbour's narrow exit. And freedom. The clouds had blown away, and a luminous half-moon rode high in a starry sky. Harsh ambient light revealed a deserted quay – no enemy darting from the warehouse, no friend hurrying down the track in response to the sound of gunfire.

Blipping twin throttles, he watched impatiently for the missing cliff-top sentry. If Yegor didn't show up in two minutes, he would have to fend for himself.

One dead, one still alive. James Lancaster pulled the door shut, put down the Browning and knelt beside Andrew Rosson. Gently, he turned him over. The dropped torch shone across a shirt front and jacket sodden with blood. Exit wound. But Rosson was still breathing – irregular, bubbling breath that indicated a lung shot. Eyes fluttered open in a waxen face, focusing with difficulty.

'James?'

'Andrew. Thanks for your help. We couldn't have made it without you.'

'She's safe?'

'She's safe.'

He didn't add 'thus far' – God alone knew what assorted weaponry might be trained on the protective double doors. Rosson's eyes closed, but after a moment he spoke again, the voice weaker.

'Gorski.'

James leant closer.

'Who?'

'Gregor Gorski. The one who organized all this. There's more, but that's the information your security service really wants. They'll work it out.'

'I'll tell them.'

Rosson went quiet for a moment, then his eyes opened again. This time they didn't focus. He tried to smile. The voice strengthened, almost sounding like that of the negotiator of old.

'Nothing's for nothing in this world, James. I need a

WITHIN THE WALLS

favour. Make sure my wife isn't told how I died. She knows nothing. She thinks I'm Andrew Rosson, but we're all Russians here, except you and Liz. I liked the boy, he has spirit. I've got kids of my own, two girls. Younger than him. Why do Russians always kill each other? I can trust you, James, we're both professionals. Promise she won't be told about any of this. Cheryl, my wife's name is Cheryl.'

His mind was drifting. James spoke urgently.

'I promise. Now stop talking, Andrew.'

'Dmitry.'

'Dmitry, then. Just hold on. You're not going to die.'

But he did, with James Lancaster holding his hand.

She'd done as she was told, and sat huddled against the cold iron pillar, hugging her knees to try to conserve the precious warmth that remained in her body. Tom was safe. James had come, and now *she* was safe. So why was she shivering uncontrollably, and why were wanton tears streaming down her face? Liz tightened the fist that was her right hand, until the point of the nail that her son had sharpened dug deeply into her flesh.

Kneeling beside the dying man, he'd been aware of faint engine noise beyond the double doors – the throb of marine diesels ticking over. The kidnappers' boat. He wondered if the three surviving Russians meant to finish the job before leaving, and were regrouping for an attack, or waiting for him to show himself. But as he reached down and closed Rosson's lifeless eyes, the engine note quickened.

James Lancaster turned off the torch, picked up his Browning and pushed open the small access door. Eerily moonlit, the long white cruiser was turning slowly in mid-harbour, angling towards the narrow passage that led to the sea. He could make out only two people, high on the rakish superstructure – one seated, the other standing with a rifle aimed at the quay. The range was extreme for a handgun, but still within killing distance. He considered emptying the Browning's clip at them, but decided there'd been more than enough killing for one night. Besides, his gun flashes would attract return fire, delivered with interest by that lethal automatic rifle.

The trail of disturbed water behind the boat's stern lengthened, and she started picking up speed. Within a minute, she would be through the exit, gone for ever. Without understanding, James saw a scorching fire trail streak across the water. The white cruiser exploded like a giant flashgun, searing the instant into his consciousness even as it temporarily blinded him. A microsecond later, sound and shock waves slammed him, accompanied by a blast of intense heat. He was jolted against the door frame, and felt sharp pain in his side. Vision cleared in time to see a spectacular fireball roll up and disappear into the night, leaving a mushroom cloud of oily smoke behind. Debris pattered on the quayside and splashed into the harbour. Then there was silence.

James shook his head to clear disorientation. After a moment, still disbelieving the evidence of his own eyes, he stepped through the door and stared at burning water, holding the useless Browning. A cheerful Geordie voice addressed him from the side.

'Don't shoot. I've promised faithfully to take the missus to bingo tomorrow night.'

The unofficial back-up promised by his controller, Colonel Robin Wesley, would seem to have arrived. The imposing black combat-suited figure stepped forward, lowering a launcher tube and raising his helmet visor.

'Staff Sergeant Norman Pape of Her Majesty's Special Air Service Brigade. My envious admirers call me Bilko. You don't know me, sir, but I know you. Saw you being carried out of an Irish farmhouse with a busted arm and drilled knee-cap about ten years ago. I was on obbo, up on the hill, buried under a pile of bracken lousy with sheep ticks and eating my last Mars bar. The things we do for Queen and country.'

James massaged his side. Hopefully, the painful injury was nothing more serious than cracked ribs.

'And if you hadn't been there, I wouldn't be here? I was told, but never got the chance to thank you. Just for once, though, it would be nice if you could manage to turn up before I get damaged.'

'We'll try harder next time, sir.'

Bilko Pape's dry response did not contain excessive sympathy. James waved his Browning in the general direction of the track.

'There's another man up top somewhere. He was watching the gate.'

'Trussed and stuffed like a Christmas turkey. Lucky he didn't finish up in the oven with the others. Mrs Lancaster?'

'Alive.'

'The boss said you'd sort it. There's just a few of us here, unofficial like, in case you needed a hand. Very low profile.'

James remembered the boat.

'You certainly did an excellent job in that respect.'

'As it happens, my finger slipped on the trigger. Accidents can happen to anyone.'

Bilko didn't sound remotely remorseful. James raised his eyebrows.

'Like fleeing kidnappers, to name but two?'

'Aye, but not to me. I'm a hundred miles away.'

For the first time, Staff Sergeant Pape's leathery face smiled. James slipped his peashooter Browning into the thigh pocket of his coveralls, turned and walked slowly towards the old warehouse.

After what seemed like eternity, he came to her in the darkness. Shivering had stopped and tears had dried. There had been an explosion, a massive concussion that shook the building and left her ears singing in silence that followed. But she hadn't moved. She thought about the four Lancaster men who had dominated her adult life – Peter, Conrad, Tom and James. One long dead. One she hated. One she would die for. And now the one that got away had found her, alive, in the darkness. Strong hands helped her to stand. She swayed. His arms enfolded her, and Liz clung to him with all the strength in her body.

Legs dangling towards water, which reflected the fiery twinkle of floating wreckage that still guttered fitfully, James Lancaster sat at the quay's edge and phoned a sitrep to John Tolley in London. Liz knelt beside him, an arm slung round his neck. The warehouse's guardroom had yielded one more corpse and – more usefully – bolt cutters. He'd thrown snipped chain into the harbour.

When he finished the call, she reached over and squeezed his hand. Her grimy face was pale, and she said nothing – numbed by her prolonged ordeal, and the delayed shock of its spectacular ending. James keyed his father's mobile number. After a few seconds, the phone was answered.

'Lancaster.'

No first name, as though there were only one. James asked a weary question.

'Where are you?'

'New Hall, of course, with Tom. What the hell have you been up to? Your phone's been switched off all night.'

'I want to talk about Liz.'

The nasal voice was dismissive.

'Relax. Elizabeth will be fine. We played ball, so they'll release her in a few days, bound to. Tom's back, that's the main thing.'

'Wait there for me.'

As he broke the connection, cutting off the possibility of further discussion, vehicle lights swept across them. Two black Range Rovers, called by radio from some nearby hiding place to collect the four-man SAS squad. Staff Sergeant Bilko Pape had been watching from a discreet distance. As the transport pulled up, he marched briskly to their side.

'We must be off. Hell to pay if we're caught here. We're supposed to be on a night march in the Brecon Beacons.'

Behind him, two SAS men were carrying the handcuffed track-top sentry into the warehouse. The lucky one, who'd survived to face MI5 interrogators before being quietly deported to experience the tender mercy of his mafia boss in Moscow. There would be no sensational court case to flag this messy business to the world. James looked up into Pape's solid, sun-seamed face.

'So how am I going to explain this bloody carnage?'

'All in a day's work for someone of your abilities, surely? Credit where credit's due. They'll be impressed.'

Sergeant Pape looked studiously impassive, staring at the starry heavens. James decided against letting him off too lightly.

'Was it really necessary to blow that boat out of the water?'

'Not strictly necessary, no, sir. But we didn't want those nasty men to get away, now did we? Besides, I couldn't resist seeing how a Milan would work on a plastic boat. After a while, you get bored with vapourizing rusty old decommissioned tanks on the range. Now, can we drop you off anywhere?'

Helicopters were on the way and the powers that be would expect him to be waiting when they arrived, for a full debriefing. But James answered to no man, and had other priorities. Tomorrow would be time enough for the inquest. He looked at Liz, who nodded almost imperceptibly, then accepted the offer gratefully.

'Let's get the hell out of here before the cavalry arrives.'

With surprising tenderness, the big soldier helped Liz Lancaster to her feet. As they walked to the lead Range Rover, he muttered a final comment to James, cultivated cynicism slipping for a gratifying instant.

'Not bad work, sir, not bad at all.'

When they were settled in the comfortable back seat, Bilko Pape scrambled in beside the driver and half turned.

'Where to?'

'New Hall. I want to go home. Jamie knows the way.'

Liz answered. As the Range Rover made a three-point turn, she leaned against James. He could barely hear her murmured words.

'Thanks for coming.'

He smiled at the back of Sergeant Pape's silhouetted head.

'Glad I did. You certainly haven't lost the uncanny knack of getting into bloody awkward situations.'

She didn't misunderstand.

'Conrad, you mean? Yes, well . . .'

James badly needed to know why, but didn't press her. There would have been no answers if he had. Despite the bumpy ride, she was deeply asleep before they reached the top of the track.

Gloucestershire

THE KEY Rita Bernadelli had given him turned sweetly in the lock, and he swung open the door. A single wall lamp burned in the big kitchen. Liz Lancaster took a long look round, as though she'd never expected to see Rita's immaculate domain again. After a moment, he put an arm round her shoulders and guided her along the passage and through the swinging green-baize door that led to the main hall. They had to face this tonight, and he steered her towards the sweeping staircase.

James Lancaster had guessed where his father would be, and light spilling from a half-open door was confirmation enough. He dropped his arm from Liz's shoulder, and they went quietly into the vast library, stopping on the threshold to absorb the scene that greeted them.

Tom was sitting in a high-backed chair, feet swinging. Though watching his father dutifully, his body language was not that which might have been expected from someone who loved aircraft. Conrad was kneeling beside a huge model of a World War II Lancaster bomber. He pressed a button on the hand-held control box and the bomber's top turret spun, four tiny replica Browning .303 machineguns swivelling to menace the book-lined room. His father's nasal voice was high with triumph.

'See, you can even make the gun turrets work. You wait until we get this beauty into the air tomorrow morning.'

Tom was the first to see them, some instinct causing him to glance up from the demonstration. Apart from a sudden widening of the eyes, his expression didn't change. But he was up in a flash, hurling himself across the room before Conrad realized what was happening, taking off two paces before he arrived and crashing into Liz's open arms. As they clung together, making frantic little mewing sounds, James clinically observed the dawning of comprehension on his father's upturned face. Blood drained as he watched, leaving fleshy features fish-belly white, frozen by shock.

In that instant, James Lancaster knew for sure.

Beside him, Liz put her son down. Spoke clearly, the Australian inflexion more pronounced than usual.

'We'll be going in the morning, Tom and me. We won't be back. Come on, you, it's well past your bedtime. You can sleep with me tonight, as a special treat. For me, little man, not you. Goodbye, Conrad.'

She took her son's hand and led him from the room. James took two paces forward.

'Surprised to see her?'

Conrad recovered sufficiently to scramble to his feet. He collapsed on a leather library chair, tore his blue polka-dot silk tie loose and undid the top button of his voluminous white shirt. His breathing was shallow, and no colour had returned to his face.

'What . . ?'

James advanced two more paces.

'What's your wife doing here? I know it's a shock, but remember that phrase you threw at me not two days ago? Why employ a dog and piss on a lamppost, or words to that effect. Well, this particular dog has done the dirty work all right, but not yours. Liz was never meant to come home, was she?'

Two more paces. Conrad's face took on a hunted look, piggy eyes darting from side to side, refusing to meet his son's relentless stare. The instantly delivered denial was unconvincing.

'I . . . of course I'm pleased Elizabeth's back. She's my wife, for God's sake. No. No, I'm delighted. You've done a first-rate job, son, as I knew you would.'

Already, defences decimated by surprise attack were being reorganized. Pathetic. Two more silent paces. Conrad couldn't help himself, blurting out the question James had been waiting for.

'Trojan Horse?'

At last, those shifty eyes met his, pleading for any answer but the one James would give. He took the last two paces.

'I was able to resolve this without compromising Trojan Horse, despite your heroic determination to part with it whatever the consequences for you. Or me, as you actually intended. But that's a long story, which I'll be telling to my new friends at MI5 in the morning. I really hope you don't have too much riding on your failed betrayal, because if you do, it's gone, all gone.'

'Son, listen to me, please . . .'

The voice faltered. Conrad never knew when he was beaten, but must have understood there was nothing more to say. James looked down with contempt.

'Goodbye, Father.'

He turned and walked away, leaving a broken man staring blankly at the commanding oil painting of Conrad Lancaster, the great tycoon.

AFTERMATH

Moscow

THE CELL was luxurious, compared to most within the Russian prison system – three metres by three, with an iron bed bolted to the floor, flushing toilet and table. All for one person! Invisibly built into the light fitting that was never switched off, a fibre-optic eye relayed the occupant's every move to a screen two floors up, at ground level.

Not that General Sergei Sobchak moved much. Indeed, apart from times when he picked at meals, answered nature's call or lay on the horsehair mattress and slept, the man who would not now be President gave a good impersonation of the grand statue that – but for present ill fortune – might one day have been erected in his honour. The fallen soldier-politician sat on the bed for hours on end, stocky body motionless, staring at an unpainted concrete wall.

Perhaps he understood. With the violent deaths of the Duma's high-profile Speaker, Gennady Churkov, and Interior Minister Anton Mossberg, two of President Yelkin's most potent internal rivals were no more. With the arrest of General Sergei Sobchak for orchestrating those deaths, the President's only external challenger was neutralized, throwing his misguided army of supporters into disarray. Best of all, Sobchak's outrageous attempt to assassinate

Mikhail Yelkin had provided ample justification for a security clampdown that allowed a ragbag of dissidents and unpatriotic criminal rabble to be rounded up.

Resplendent in his new uniform as general commanding the Kremlin Regiment, Gregor Gorski had spent many hours at the screen, watching the unsubtle former paratroop commander who had been foolish enough to believe he could challenge the absolute authority of President Mikhail Yelkin, by fair means or foul.

Unfortunately, Sobchak was Gorski's only prize. The Trojan Horse operation had gone belly up. Only today, the computer genius at Moscow University finally admitted defeat. After four days' unremitting toil in his digital factory, Professor Shebarshin had failed to unscramble the data supplied from England, concluding that it must be a worthless fraud.

General Gregor Gorski shared the professor's angry frustration at Russia's loss of a decisive strategic weapon for the twenty-first century, though his own loss of face with Mikhail Yelkin was potentially more damaging. However, the President was not entirely familiar with the potential of cyberweaponry, seeming more than satisfied that his major political opponents had been crushed like the cockroaches they were. And, by way of consolation, all the idiots responsible for bungling the British operation were dead. Except the big, fat, greedy one.

He looked again at the screen. Sobchak had not moved. There would be a public trial, but the outcome was not in doubt. Russia's least popular politician should not have been so indiscreet as they walked and talked in Gorkiy Park, allowing direct orders to kill over 150 innocents on the Metro and assassinate the President to be captured on tape. Watching the broken prisoner on television was addictive, as the nation would discover, but confronting him in person would be even more satisfying. Gregor Gorski had spent many hours imagining the expression on General Sergei Sobchak's face when he finally realized how comprehensively he'd been duped, manipulated and gutted by a grand master of deception. Postponing that exquisite moment had been a pleasure, but now he could contain himself no longer.

Before he set his general's cap at a precise right angle and walked downstairs to confront his victim, there was one outstanding score to settle. Gregor Gorski had to telephone his old friend Conrad Lancaster in England, and inform him that the lucrative Russia Telecom deal would not after all be concluded with Lancaster Trust, but a more reliable partner.

Herefordshire

DESPITE a phone promise left with the sitter, her husband had not returned by the weekend, and now it was Monday. Andrew often made book-buying trips, but was rarely away for more than a few days. This visit to Eastern Europe had been his longest by far, stretching into a third week. Cheryl Rosson wasn't altogether sorry. A decision was required, which could thankfully be postponed until she actually had to face him.

Although Cheryl felt slightly drunk, she poured another glass of red wine, set a mournful Joan Armatrading CD wailing on three-quarter volume, and slumped in an armchair. Once, in the carefree early days of their seven-year marriage, she and Andrew used to talk about everything. But the man she wed had changed. Despite her efforts to elicit information about the exciting discovery of a nobleman's hidden library, occasional phone calls from the Czech Republic had been brief, symbolizing their growing inability to communicate. Three brief postcards along 'wish I was there' lines hadn't helped.

To a degree, Cheryl blamed herself for the deterioration of their relationship, because her expectations were high. Before Andrew, she had found stimulus in a wide circle of friends. But these had faded away – to marriages and new families of their own, job opportunities away from Hay-on-Wye, or simply because she no longer seemed to have time to give them. Easy enough to cite the demands of two young children in mitigation, but this was no more than a self-deluding excuse. The frustrating truth was more destructive. And for that, Cheryl blamed her husband.

She sometimes thought he would have been happiest of

all on a desert island – an island unto themselves, like an introverted Swiss Family Rosson freed of any requirement to interface with the outside world. Andrew was convivial enough with business contacts, but positively disliked the idea that they, as a couple, should have an active social life. She and the kids were all he wanted.

Cheryl coped with increasing isolation, but not well. Andrew's need was too great, too demanding, too claustrophobic. Idly following her desert island theme, she decided he was like a shipwrecked mariner clinging to a floating spar. Any spar would do, but his happened to be her. At the same time, she was aware that her husband's emotions had a self-contained core she was never allowed to see, let alone touch.

Cheryl upended the wine bottle, shaking the last few drops into her refilled glass. At least sex was still good. The flame that ignited on their first date still burned, spontaneous recombustion briefly consuming doubts and unhappiness. But sex with Nat was also good, or better. And now the thrill of that illicit passion had become complicated, because he'd asked her to leave Andrew, bring the girls to the old farmhouse where he plied his scriptwriter's trade. That was where she'd been when her husband had last phoned – with her lover, receiving a proposal that could change her life. If that was what she wanted.

She liked Nat, who knew lots of interesting people and introduced her with pride. He had a wicked sense of humour. They laughed a lot, argued about putting the universe to rights, ate expensively at discreet restaurants, and had a thoroughly entertaining time together. Over two years, during many opportunities provided by her husband's trips, they had become intimate friends.

But she *loved* Andrew, who was making her miserable. It was an impossible choice.

Cheryl Rosson finished the wine – no more, she was driving – and looked at her watch. Nearly time to fetch Kate from playgroup, then Emma from nursery school. As she went out through the front door and walked towards the battered Volvo estate, somewhat unsteadily, a police car turned into the drive.

London

SHE NEVER TIRED of watching herself on screen. It was like observing a stranger – a performer whose professionalism never ceased to amaze, because *that* Jenny Symes was not the Jenny Symes she knew and lived with. Perhaps artists experienced similar feelings when they stepped back from a finished canvas – seeing realization of what they'd set out to achieve, yet still slightly awed by a result that transcended its creator.

As the end credits of *Guardian Angel* scrolled up the large flat screen opposite their bed, Jenny giggled, aware that these strange thoughts probably owed something to an almost-empty magnum on the bedside table. But they were entitled to celebrate. The Lancaster exposé was the best programme Pandora's Box Productions had ever made. As the closing credit – *PRODUCED & DIRECTED BY WENDY LANG* – faded, they looked at one another. Wendy reached for the remote and killed a trailer for the BBC's latest fly-on-the-wall documentary series, featuring the angst-ridden life of a Liverpool Citizens Advice Bureau. She, too, was euphoric, raising her champagne flute.

'Congratulations, Jen. We make a great team.'

Jenny Symes modestly lowered her head.

'I couldn't have done it without you, Wendy. When everyone else thought I was a brainless bimbo with big tits who was only good for fronting the lottery show, you had faith. I'll never forget that.'

Alcohol might have made Jenny maudlin, but she meant every word. Wendy Lang slid a strong arm round her bare shoulders.

'Come off it, kid, you make it sound as though there was nothing in this for me. Quite apart from anything else, I could've banked a fortune last week, as a direct result of your determined activities. It's not every day an old gal like me gets a multimillion-pound proposition.'

They drained their glasses, then Jenny asked a question that had been nagging for a while.

'Did you seriously consider selling out to Lancaster, taking all that money for killing my programme? He would have wanted my scalp as part of the deal.'

Her partner reflected, then answered quietly.

'I was tempted. Business is business, Jen, and I'll never get another offer like that. Principles are fine and noble, but hardly provide a secure financial future. Plus he was offering me a once-in-a-lifetime queen of TV job. Besides, you'd've made megabucks, too, even if it meant picking up your career elsewhere . . .'

She paused, and Jenny felt a prickle at the back of her eyes. So even the great Wendy Lang had her price. Before she could react, the culprit continued.

'But then again, the world's best investigative reporter was telling me the bastard was broke, and who'd trust *any* man further than they could spit on him?'

Wendy's gravelly laugh exploded, filling the bedroom, and Jenny Symes felt herself being swept into a fierce but loving embrace.

Gloucestershire

FOR ONCE, he was running late, through no fault of his own. First – horn blaring – he'd forced his red Post Office van through a media encampment which had sprung up around the entrance to New Hall, following that sensational *Guardian Angel* programme two nights ago. Then he'd had to wait patiently until a harassed retainer emerged from the Hansel and Gretel lodge cottage to admit him through wrought-iron gates that normally stood open, but today were closed.

Norman Webley really didn't mind the delay. As he sped through open parkland, foot flat to the floor in an effort to make up lost time, he took pleasure in the fact that his God-given gift – the ability to read mail without opening it – had reached new heights of achievement. For the first time ever, he'd read an entire sackful of letters as he sorted them. Hate mail, the lot of it, apart from one circular telling the lucky Conrad Lancaster that his property had been selected as a show house, enabling him to purchase replacement uPV doors and windows of the highest quality at a give-away price.

The postman was in heaven. He hadn't needed to buy a

drink for over a week, such was the interest in goings-on at New Hall. What with the kidnap, rescue and now the master's precipitous fall from grace, he wouldn't have to buy another for the foreseeable future. There was a downside, of course – his daily round was taking an extra hour, as he paused to communicate developments free of charge to his regulars. But that, too, was a pleasure.

As he turned on to the open area fronting the house, where the driveway split around an old stone fountain to form a large turning circle, roving countryman's eyes caught something that wasn't quite right. Instead of driving around to the back for his cup of tea, he stopped the van and got out. The something was a small black box, incongruously sitting in the middle of a long sweep of close-cropped grass running down to the ornamental lake. Puzzled, he went over for a closer look. It was a control box of some sort, with an extended metal aerial and various knobs and switches. The curious mailman looked around, and spotted another unusual sight.

In the middle of the lake, at the end of a rainbow trail of leaking fuel indicating how far it had drifted, was a huge model aircraft. Weird. Norman Webley wandered down to the waterside, and made his third discovery. Concealed from above, the body of a corpulent man in a sodden blue dressing gown floated face down against an encroaching stand of bullrushes, bobbing gently in the pool of surface scum and driftwood pushed into this quiet corner by the prevailing breeze.

London

WES REMINGTON of the CIA had decided to let his opposite number at MI5 rebuild bridges, though the price was another lunch at Angus Churchill's fossilized club in St James's. The American arrived early, and was ushered to a room full of tired furniture and elderly men. Green-shaded table lamps were dotted around and a coal fire burned brightly in the Victorian grate, smokeless fuel a grudging concession to modernity. Beside the fireplace stood a brass toasting fork for those who'd once singed muffins at public school and never kicked the habit.

He suspected that fewer members than usual were dozing in leather armchairs. Instead, there was a mutter of conversation, and most were reading newspapers with macabre interest. Occasional snorts of disapproval could be heard. The morning papers made sharks in feeding frenzy look like comatose goldfish. The blood in the water was Conrad Lancaster's. Less than twenty-four hours after the tycoon's mysterious death, his business empire was unravelling faster than a toilet roll tugged by a Labrador puppy.

Remington's favourite was the *Globe*'s front page. A colour portrait of the late great Lancaster, bloated and arrogant, was surrounded by a thick black border decorated with repeating white £ signs. A massive *R.I.P.-OFF!* headline – doubtless concocted by the paper's legendary editor, Sir Dennis Wilkes – screamed the message. If old Conrad was up there somewhere, looking for a morsel of comfort, striking exception to near-universal condemnation was provided by his own tabloid – which carried an eight-page tribute to 'a commercial Titan of our time' and made no mention of alleged impropriety by the tragically deceased proprietor. But the knee-jerk loyalty of cowed hacks wouldn't last. By tomorrow morning they, too, would be caterwauling from the same requiem sheet.

Still, Conrad Lancaster was beyond punishment for his unsuccessful attempt to betray Trojan Horse, and a lifetime's dubious dealings with the Russians. Perhaps this was the best outcome. Trading on the innate unwillingness of governments to have dirty intelligence linen washed in public, Conrad might even have cut a deal that let him survive unprosecuted. Shameful, but Remington understood how the system operated.

He sighed. Maybe he was getting too old for hands-on involvement in the shitty espionage business. His wife thought so. Helen was pushing him – hard – to accept a regular-hours desk-jockey posting to Langley. It would be a significant advance up the totem, but end his freedom to ride the range. The dilemma was insoluble – advance his career to please Helen . . . or kick her in the teeth again by selfishly sticking with what he liked doing best?

No-win deliberation was interrupted by the belated arrival of Angus Churchill, who made a grand entrance, standing straight-backed as he swept the room with haughty eyes. The effort was wasted. Few grizzled heads turned. Undaunted, the head of MI5's K Branch strode jauntily across the room. He pulled an armchair close and sat down. After checking that they couldn't be overheard, he leaned conspiratorially towards Remington.

'Today's special is Cumberland pie. I took the liberty of ordering for both of us. You'll love it, and I promise not to reveal your dark gastronomic secret to the lovely Helen.'

What the hell was Cumberland pie? Wondering if Churchill was doing this deliberately, he replied weakly.

'Sounds delicious, Gus.'

His tormentor continued smoothly.

'Bread and butter pudding for afters. So, we've all ended up smelling of roses, Wesley. Trojan Horse was never in danger, because Military Intelligence did have an agent in place. James Lancaster, would you believe? The old man's son. Did undercover work for them years ago, before he left the army. I'd guess they reactivated him on the grounds that he was particularly well qualified for this one. And of course Langley was proved right about Conrad Lancaster's duplicity.'

The CIA's London Head of Station allowed himself to look surprised, but it was an effort. Two different agents-in-place so close to Trojan Horse was much too much of a coincidence for any pro to swallow. He was pretty sure that – as Beasley – James Lancaster had never stopped working for Military Intelligence. But Churchill didn't need to know anything about Beasley, or the agent-for-hire's US-financed covert operation in friendly Britain. Like the man said, they'd all come out smelling of roses. Remington prompted gently. With Gus in such an upbeat mood, it shouldn't be hard to tease out all he knew.

'So what about this strange kidnap thing? Made no sense to me.'

Churchill beamed, delighted to demonstrate superior knowledge.

'Private business. Conrad's wife was about to take him for millions in a divorce settlement, so the cunning old devil dreamed the whole thing up as a right-and-left. Right barrel, he gets a lucrative business deal from Moscow in return for Trojan Horse, blaming an employee who was supposed to disappear without trace. Left barrel, the Russians blow away the troublesome gold-digger after a staged kidnap, and he gets to keep his son and heir. He was some operator. Pity he's gone, really. We had all the taped evidence we needed and were seriously considering turning him, using him as a double against the Russians.'

So, he hadn't been wrong about crime not necessarily being followed by punishment. Remington nudged again.

'What about the Russian end?'

'Set up by an unpleasant piece of work called Gregor Gorski. Ex-KGB. I'll send a full report over in due course, but it seems he was working for President Yelkin all along. Gorski's been a busy boy lately. Apart from chasing Trojan Horse, he had a hand in the spectacular fall of General Sobchak, right-wing populist and major Yelkin rival. There's even a suggestion he organized the terrorist group that slaughtered politicians and populace alike. Devious bastards, the Russians. Of course, we can't react officially on Trojan Horse. Yelkin may be a founding father of the Megalomaniac Tendency, but our Foreign Office and your State Department are in accord. Much as I hate to turn the other cheek, we must not upset the man, because the alternatives look even worse. I can't even retaliate by expelling a few of those so-called Russian diplomats who're busy spying their arses off.'

'So how come you're so goddam cheerful, Gus?'

Churchill's face lit up.

'Thought you'd never ask. Well, James Lancaster couldn't have coped on his own, as things turned out. Despite being warned off by the Joint Intelligence Committee, I sent my best operative in anyway. None of this fascinating Russian stuff would have come out without his help. Now, the JIC may have been annoyed by my initiative, but those who matter in Five were rather impressed. Holding up our end, and all that. I've been given a hint that I'm first in line for the deputy directorship when it falls vacant later this year. I'm not a political animal, as you know, but it will certainly be good to occupy a senior position where one can really make a difference, as I hope you may eventually find out for yourself.'

In that instant, Remington decided to turn down the Langley posting. He reached over and patted his companion's pin-striped arm.

'Congratulations, Sir Gus. If anyone deserves blasting into the stratosphere, you do. I'm sure you'll go all the way.'

Remington wasn't a fan of deferred dissatisfaction. Best get this over with. He stood up.

'Shall we eat? So what exactly *is* Cumberland pie?'

Side by side, looking for all the world like two normal middle-aged men, the fellow intelligence professionals strolled towards the dining room.

Wiltshire

DUST had settled, and fates been determined. Three weeks after Conrad Lancaster's death, an army of receivers had invaded the collapsed Lancaster Trust, attempting to understand complex architecture and recover something – *anything* – of value from the rubble. Omega Dynamic Systems would be shut down when a buyer was found for the company's proven software products and development work in progress.

Not for sale was Trojan Horse, which was transferring for final commissioning to the US Government's lead command and control research facility, the Rome Laboratory at Griffiss airbase in New York State. Louise Boss would be going, to oversee her baby's coming of age. And when that project was completed, she intended to stay there. Louise had been offered top-level entry to America's sophisticated military computing programme, the most exciting place in the world for someone with her ambitions and ability.

Beggar's Roost had been rented to two young teachers who'd agreed to take on the cats along with the furniture, fixtures and fittings. Louise's powerful Cray work station had been crated and air-freighted to the States, and she would be following tomorrow. To his surprise, John Tolley was happy for her. After the Trojan Horse debriefing, an expansive Angus Churchill – delighted by a final outcome that left his professional prospects undamaged or even enhanced – had given him time off. He and Louise had hardly been apart since. Far from fretting at enforced inactivity, the workaholic Louise's uninhibited aptitude for leisure had been impressive.

Such intensity came as a revelation to Tolley, who had never before abandoned himself, or realized how joyous commitment could be. And now he'd discovered something else. This novel experience not only brought personal fulfilment, but also unexpected ability to find satisfaction in putting another human being's needs above his own. However badly he wanted Louise, he couldn't burden her future with his acute sense of impending loss.

Tolley raised his empty mug in silent salute to selfless nobility, ironically acknowledging that the truth might be less uplifting. Louise Boss had openly admitted to dumping lovers who demanded too much, and another had just dropped her for not being able to give enough. So maybe he hadn't said anything for fear of spoiling what they had.

A purring cat rubbed around his feet, broad grey head butting his leg in a determined attempt to win attention. He hardened his heart and got up to fill the kettle. They'd slept until mid-morning, exhausted by the night's exertions, but Louise was out of the shower and would soon be down. After coffee and conversation, they planned to visit the skeleton-staffed Omega building for a last set of tennis. He'd managed to take a few games off her in the past couple of weeks, suppressing suspicion that she'd let him win. Then Louise wanted to say *au revoir* to Sandy MacNaughton, who'd be at home planning the autumn chrysanthemum campaign with the meticulous attention he once devoted to counter-intelligence work.

Louise Boss bustled into the kitchen, radiating life and energy. She gave him a violent hug and kissed the end of his nose. The cat ran for cover. He fetched her a cup of coffee and they sat at the pine table. She sipped hot liquid.

'Mmmm, I needed that. So, are you finally going to overcome my awesome service game today?'

'Nope, I'll settle for thrashing you on a tie-break, Boss.'

She grinned.

'In your dreams, Tolley, in your wet dreams.'

He looked at her animated face, and the decision he'd been mulling over for nearly a week made itself. Daunting though fear of rejection might be, part of the package he'd opened with such pleasure was the ability to expose himself to emotional damage.

'If you can bear to be serious for a moment, there's something I want to ask you . . .'

He watched as Louise's expression changed. Sparkling *joie de vivre* vanished in an instant, replaced by the intense focus he'd observed when she was working at her computer. He'd come to understand how intuitive she could be. Had Louise guessed what he was about to say, even now thinking she didn't want to hear it? But finding the answer rather than never knowing was the point. John Tolley made a determined effort to sound casual, but suspected he wasn't very convincing.

'Lancaster Security is setting up an office in New York, and James has offered me a job. Only the number-two slot, but quite a challenge for a burned-out spook like me. Money's not bad, either. What d'you think?'

Louise understood the implications all right, arching her eyebrows and meeting his anxious eyes. It was impossible to read the enigmatic expression, but if her next words were 'That's up to you', he'd scream.

Moscow

HE WAS NOT one to act in haste and repent at leisure. But more than three weeks had passed, and – far from diminishing with time – the insult to his honour loomed larger than ever. And now, he had decided something must be done to set the record straight for all who mattered to see. This wasn't the reaction of a hot-blooded man bent on revenge, but cold commercial logic.

The mafia boss stared at the unfortunate creature who stood rigidly before him, fearing for a life that was rightly forfeit. Yegor had arrived back in Moscow only that morning, deported by the British authorities. To his credit, the sole survivor of a disastrous deal with Gregor Gorski had reported in immediately, rather than bolting for some seedy rat-hole and waiting to be found. Yegor shifted uneasily, fingering his drooping moustache as he tried to hide behind his hand. You wouldn't think it to look at him, but the little polecat was a natural-born killer. There might yet be a way for him to regain favour, respect and status within the warmth of the family's bosom.

The patriarch's criminal empire depended on fear, and any hint that he could be defied was bad for business. As was any suggestion that he failed to look after his own. Three of his best men were dead and unavenged. This might have been bearable, had Gorski come through. But far from delivering influence in high places, the two-faced ex-KGB colonel had gone to the opposite extreme. Since the failed assassination attempt on President Yelkin, there had been a ferocious law-and-order crackdown, as his government sought to reassert authority and give faceless masses the stability they craved. Ferocious law-and-order crackdowns were *very* bad for business.

With a slender forefinger, he absent-mindedly stroked one of two things that lay on his leather-cornered ink blotter – a glossy wire-bound colour brochure issued by the Fairline boat company of Sussex, England. That fiasco was irritating, to say the least – an outlay of one million pounds, gone without trace, and he'd never even seen the luxury Squadron 65 cruiser that so excited him. He'd ordered another, but the replacement would not be ready in time for his summer break in Monte Carlo.

The mafia boss picked up the second object – an equally glossy black-and-white picture of ex-KGB colonel and new presidential favourite General Gregor Gorski.

He studied the dour features for a moment, staring at lifeless eyes, then walked round the desk and handed the photograph to Yegor.

London

AFTER a desk-clearing week in Los Angeles and a mind-clearing week in the Oregon mountains, James Lancaster had hopped back to LA in his Cessna and been flown on to London in the corporate Gulfstream V. Ostensibly, the purpose of his flying visit was to brief John Tolley personally on his responsibilities at the New York office, though that hardly justified flying all those miles. And, much as he was looking forward to seeing the sardonic MI5 operative again, his first call hadn't been on Lancaster Security's newest employee.

James could have used his own key, but rang the doorbell. He'd lent Beasley's apartment in Dolphin Square to Liz and Tom, for as long as they needed a breathing place. Not that she knew anything about Beasley. Wes Remington must have guessed rather too much about the agent-for-hire, who had therefore ceased to exist – no doubt confirming the CIA man's suspicions. There was no reply, and James rang the bell a second time, though sensing that no one was home. He could have phoned, but liked the idea of a surprise visit. Disappointment was dissipated by the high, excited voice of his stepbrother.

'James!'

Tom came bounding along the carpeted corridor from the lift, with Liz following along behind more sedately. He skidded to a halt beside James.

'Guess what. We've just come back from the Imperial War Museum. It was brilliant.'

'The boy's besotted with ancient fighter aircraft.'

Liz had caught up. Unabashed, the boy in question chipped in from his mother's side.

'They've got a Sopwith Camel, James, a real one. Very manoeuvrable, but the rotary engine threw out castor oil which soaked the pilot's shoulder.'

'Is that a fact? Well, I've got something for you, as it happens.'

James held out his gift as Liz unlocked the door. Tom peered into the carrier bag, elfin face alive with curiosity. The computer game met with enthusiastic approval.

'Prince of Persia – great! Can I load it down now?'

'Why not? I want a quick word with your mother, but we could all go out for a pizza later.'

He was talking to empty air. Tom had flown. Liz shrugged helplessly, and led James to the spacious sitting room and indicated the sofa. She took off her coat, poured two drinks at a side table, handed him a tumbler and perched on the arm of a matching chair.

'This is a nice surprise. I'm glad you caught us. I was going to give you a call. We're taking a trip. Australia. Tom's always wanted to see where I grew up, so we're going to look up my family. Seems like a good time. It's been twelve years since I saw them.'

James made a casual suggestion.

'If you ever come back, maybe you'll both visit me in the States some time. I'd like that.'

She smiled.

'Maybe we will. If he's curious about down under, he's crazy about America, and I'll bet you could show us a great time. It's good to see you, James.'

They leaned across and clinked glasses, then retreated into companionable silence. His mind went back ten years, to the last toast they had shared, before their last night together. Liz caught his eye, and James wondered if she was also remembering. She was at ease in faded blue jeans and loose yellow-and-black rugby shirt, showing none of the tension etched into her face after the kidnap ordeal. He changed the unspoken subject.

'Tom all right?'

'He regards the kidnap as a huge adventure, with you as the caped crusader who rode to the rescue. You've made quite an impression. He went a bit quiet at the funeral, but soon got over that. I wouldn't say he and Conrad were close.'

James edged closer to things that needed to be said.

'Why the West Suffolk crematorium?'

The widow reflected, but had an answer of sorts.

'You know how fond of your brother I was. I can't really explain properly, but going back there just seemed right, like closing a loop.'

'I went back, too, after Conrad first summoned me. I never told anyone, but he left a note. Peter, I mean. The woman who found his body gave it to me after the funeral. "I'm so lonely", that's what he wrote.'

Liz said nothing. She knew how to listen. James continued slowly, rubbing his temples with stiff fingers.

'Why did Conrad hate us so much, Liz? He was an evil

old sod, but you weren't supposed to come out of that warehouse alive, with me getting blamed for the whole rotten mess. That's over the top, even by his standards.'

After a moment's thought, Liz answered. She also knew when to contribute.

'I can't begin to explain why you two always fought, but can tell you I was planning to divorce Conrad. He wanted to keep Tom for himself and couldn't bear the thought I'd get custody. As another minor irritation, he put New Hall in trust for Tom years ago, and would have lost control of the estate. Hardly a major disaster, but your father couldn't even bear to come second in a wooden spoon race. I'll tell you another thing. Conrad never really came to terms with losing you and Peter. It wasn't Peter's weakness or your stubborn defiance that really hurt him, Jamie, but the fact you'd both *gone*. In his own way and on his own terms, he desperately wanted someone to hand his precious empire on to.'

James was genuinely surprised.

'You're kidding.'

'No, I'm not. He lost two sons, for different reasons, and that ate away at him. Conrad was a very bad loser, and wasn't going to lose Tom.'

She got up and fetched the Scotch bottle, refreshing their glasses before settling beside him on the sofa. Silence lengthened. James stared at the dematerialized Beasley's tasteful wallpaper for a while, then asked the question that had obsessed him for far too long.

'Why, Lizzie?'

There, it was out. She didn't need him to expand.

'Why did I marry Conrad? I could say he caught me on the rebound, and I suppose there's some truth in that. You left me, James, which was hard to deal with. But I won't pretend that I found Conrad unattractive. I'd just become his PA, remember, and the world of big business was glamorous and exciting for a naïve young Aussie. Sounds lame now, but back then your father could seem very charming, sexy even. I didn't want to think about you, or Peter, and he tried very hard to help me forget.'

It made a sort of sense, but James hadn't heard anything that properly answered the question. Liz knew that, turning towards him. Her expression was sad.

'Wait. While you were away wherever you were, getting smashed up, I got careless with the pill. That last night at my flat in Camden Town . . .'

James looked at her in disbelief.

'You didn't get pregnant?'

Liz bowed her head, and a curtain of red hair fell across her eyes.

'Try to understand, Jamie. I had no real friends in London. I couldn't go home to Australia. I'd just watched you walk away because you weren't ready to let one person into your life, let alone two. Abortion was unthinkable. Your father could hardly be expected to hold my job open, so I couldn't have kept a roof over our heads. Conrad knew, before we were married. In some twisted way, it only made him more determined to have me. But if you wanted to know why he hated you, that's the reason. Conrad was terrified you'd discover the truth.'

'Lizzie . . .'

Her hand tightened on his thigh, strangling his response. Before he could find the right words, she went on urgently, her voice low.

'I promised Conrad that Tom would never find out, and now I'm asking you to promise you'll never say anything, either. Please . . .'

The door crashed open and Tom hurtled into the room.

'Prince of Persia is absolutely brilliant, James. I've already reached level two. Persia used to be ruled by a shah, but now it's called Iran and mullahs are in charge. I think they're sort of high priests. Is it time for that pizza yet? I'm really hungry.'

Unselfconsciously, he wriggled on to the sofa, pushing between them. Liz's pleading eyes found James above the boy's blond head. He turned to Tom.

'Okay, my clever little brother, let's eat. Pizza with all the trimmings, on me, but I bet you a double milk-shake you don't make level three before tomorrow night.'

'It's a deal, but I'll win!'

James Lancaster hoped he didn't hear an echo of Conrad in the enthusiastic response. He put an arm around his son's shoulders, and suddenly they were all laughing.